RED DENARII

RED DENARII

L. EDWARD PEACOCK

PRIMIX PUBLISHING
THE WRITE CHOICE

Primix Publishing
485c US Highway 1 South
Suite 100
Iselin, NJ 08830
www.primixpublishing.com
Phone: 1-800-538-5788

Published by Primix Publishing: 08/20/2024

ISBN: 979-8-89194-232-5(sc)
ISBN: 979-8-89194-233-2(hc)
ISBN: 979-8-89194-234-9(e)

Library of Congress Control Number: 2024912110

To

Sandra Jean Peacock,
my mother and my best friend.

You are free from the troubles caused by this world.
May you be in peace for eternity.

1943 - 2024

CONTENTS

PROLOGUE

Evil is more than just a thought. How does evil even enter a moral mind? Could it be a carefully placed whisper, to make the mind think it manifested the thought itself.

L. E. Peacock

CHAPTER 1

FROM THE GRAVE

The Sanhedrin has buried one of the followers and is content with the arrest of the of the leader, while Pontius the hand of Rome sips wine from a goblet as the sun goes down. Outside the walled city of Jerusalem, a figure stands at the foot of an unmarked grave. "Rise, I command the dust to give up your body. Rise and breathe the air of the living again." Says the figure. The figure steps back from the unmarked grave as two hands push their way out of the sand, struggling to pull the rest of the body free of the grave. The once dead with the rope still around his neck, stands at the side of his own grave with a confused look on his face.

The once dead man, ask the figure before him," How Is this possible? Are you one of God's angels sent to take me to heaven?" The figure answered, "I am not here to take you to heaven." The dead man said," How is this possible that I have cheated death by such an unforgiveable crime that I committed." The figure said," I am not here to pass judgment on you. You only pointed out the rabbi and his fate will fall upon the hands of Rome. I am here to empower you. As of now, you are immortal. You must hurry to leave this place and you are not to try and enter the gates of the city. The city dwellers consider you mixed with the dust of the earth. So, I am telling you do not attempt to return to the city."

As the apostle wiped the desert dust from his eyes the mysterious figure had disappeared into dust. A confused apostle looked all around him for the figure that brought him from the ground. He did not see him, and the urge of thirst drove him toward the city's fortified wall that surrounded it. As he made his way closer to the walled city, he saw a Roman sentry patrolling the wall perimeter. The apostle walked closer to the sentry and the sentry turned to him with glowing red eyes and said," I told you not to attempt to enter the city. It is evident that you question my powers. I told you that you would not taste death but now, you will be the bringer of death on every full moon. Now go into the desert, you will not return here until I tell you that you can. The next moment, the apostle looked around and saw that he was no longer outside the walled city of Jerusalem. He is in unfamiliar land. A land of rocks and endless sand. He looks to the sky, and sees the moon was only three quarters full. Behind him all traces of what he was familiar with is gone, just like yesterday's sunlight. The apostle realizes then that his teacher had warned him of such an adversary. He is alone except for the sounds of the jackal yelping in the night. He doesn't know what immortality is. He knows only that he is thirsty and hungry. He is driven to continue because he has to. He does notice that his senses are different.

The desert wind blew the smell of food in his direction. Guided by smell, he walked toward a group of rocks. A scent of something that could be food. With no means of making a fire, his stomach doesn't care. As he got closer to the cluster of boulders, the scent grew stronger. He stopped to see and watched for movement at edge of the boulder, there was no movement, but he could smell it. A meal. As he crouched down, he could hear a hissing sound. It is a serpent. It's the deadly cobra or the adder, he did not care. One of them is going to die tonight. He reached for the serpent, and he was bitten. Though its fangs buried deep into his hand, he reached and grabbed the animal. He pulled it from its place of hiding place by its tail, the serpent struck him again until he bashed the serpent's head against the boulder.

He threw the defeated animal out onto the sand to get a better look at it, it is a desert cobra. The serpent was wiggling around, its head unable to strike anymore. he bit into the serpent's body it was still moving. He severed the head from the rest of the body and began to squeeze the blood from its now headless body. With his teeth and fingers, he was able to skin the animal. He began to eat of its flesh, the serpent's muscles still moved about as he devoured it. Remembering the words, the fallen one had said to him. That he will not to taste death. Not only has he been struck a couple of times but now he is eating the desert cobra.

He is putting Satan's words to the test. He will either be dead from the desert cobra's bite or will not. After he had eaten what he could stomach from the serpent. He continued walking further into the unknown landscape. The sun will be arriving in a few hours and he will need to seek out some shelter from the scorching desert heat. As he continued to make his way to the foothills of a mountain range, and waited to see if the serpent's venom had any effect. As time went by and had trekked a good distance, He felt no effect from the bites. Even the areas that the serpent struck; there were no traces of pain anymore. Something unusual is going on and he does not understand it. He does understand a need to seek shelter from the relentless desert sun that will be arriving.

There was an overhanging ledge several cubits up on the slope. He began climbing upward and the jagged rocks were unrelenting against his bare feet going up the rocky slope. Scorpions were scurrying to get out of his way as he continued to climb. He is almost there at the ledge, and heard a familiar voice say, "Come on up Judas, the view is beautiful from up here." Judas said," Haven't you done enough to me for one night? All I want is somewhere to lay my head and rest. You probably deprived me the chance of redemption." Lucifer held out his hand to help him up, Judas refused his hand and pulled himself up on the ledge.

Lucifer said," I saved you from ridicule and from being treated like a mongrel dog in Heaven. Do you think your God would just forget about what you did to his son? If you were allowed in Heaven, and I do mean if? Judas said," What else is there that you can take from me that you do not already have?" Satan laughs and says, "I already own you. I plucked you from the grave and so far, you have not shown me any gratitude for it." Judas said, "I have walked through the desert barefooted, I have been struck by the desert cobra, I ate the raw flesh from the desert cobra and climbed up on this rock face just to pay homage to my deliverer from death." Satan said," Show me where you were struck."

Judas held out his hand. Satan said" Hold on for one minute while I put some light on the subject." Suddenly Satan's hand became a blaze. He held it over Judas's hand, the fang marks were gone. He looked at the other arm the fang marks are no longer there. Satan said," You don't get it do you? You are immortal, you can't be killed like an ordinary man. You have crossed the threshold of ordinary. You are thirty-eight years old and will look and remain thirty-eight years old if you kill and eat human flesh. Otherwise, you will age but at a different rate." Judas said," What if I do not want this existence if it means having to kill people and eat them." Lucifer said," It is too late to back out now, the wheels have been put into motion. Tomorrow night you will feel different about killing, you will not want serpents and desert creatures to eat. Before I leave you, I offer up this bit of advice.

You must keep on moving and do not get involved with anyone or they will just turn into dinner." With his flaming hand he started a fire and from the fire he withdrew gold coins and gave them to Judas. He said," you will need the coins tomorrow to barter with and oh yes, stay away from silver. The silver denarii given to you by the Sanhedrin has imbued a curse from the upper management. Tomorrow you will find that you have a new skill, and you will see what immortality really means." The deceiver disappears. Leaving the mind of the former apostle spinning. Though his body is immortal, his brain is requesting sleep. He is thinking all this is just a bad dream.

He just lays down on the dirt floor of the cave. He hopes that after waking up, none of this really happened. He finally succumbs to sleep only to find himself standing in a desert oasis. The shadow of a date palm shades him from the sun. A familiar voice calls him to enter the large tent. He pulls back the flap of the tent and walks in. The smells of spices and incense fills his nose. He began to feel as if he had been drinking too much wine. The tent was filled with people in strange looking clothing. They were not dressed in tunics. He has never seen the likes of such a manner of clothing. As he walks by these people, they point him toward a person sitting on a throne.

He walks closer to the person on the throne, there are two huge, armored guards. One of the guards, pushes him down on the ground and says, "Kneel before the king, desert dust." He stood back up and the guard came at him again. Before the guard put his huge hands on me, a voice tells the guard to let him be. As he drew closer to the throne, he did not recognize the face, but the voice was familiar. "Welcome to my tent Judas. Don't you recognize me? He said, "I do not recognize your face but, your voice I do recognize. You are the one that set me up by giving up the lamb for slaughter. You are the one that placed the thought in my head. You are the fallen one that has damned me."

The figure on the throne said," Judas, I placed only one thought in your head. That thought was greed and the rest you did on your own free will. I did not tell you to strike a bargain with the Sanhedrin. You created that scheme in your head before it happened. But let us not squabble over who is to blame for what. You did me a favor Judas, by getting rid of an enemy of mine. I can make your life here a lot easier if you pledge your allegiance to me." He said, "Don't you mean, to worship you?" "Allegiance, worship… they mean the same." Remarks Lucifer. He said, "What can you do for me? Put an extra batch of serpents to feast upon in the desert. A softer rock for me to rest my head upon. You have made me an abomination and you want me to worship you. Your arrogance is why you were cast out of heaven." He turned and was walking out of the tent. Lucifer said," You will ask for my help, Judas. You just think that this is the lowest point in your life." As he was walking out, a sharp pain woke him. A black scorpion had struck him in his left ankle. He threw it against the cave wall and ate its remains.

He realized that his existence was no dream. He placed the gold coins in his pocket and left the safety of the shallow cave. He started climbing higher, taking advantage of the early morning, before the sun gets too high. He was not far from the summit. His feet were bleeding from being scraped against the rock faces. He continued with purpose until he reached the top. He sees a body of water to the right and open desert to his left. He is standing on a mere foothill in comparison with the attached mountain range before him. There wasn't any sign of civilization on the righthand side of the peak, but could see in the distance in the open desert, a small encampment. He began climbing downward and began thinking to himself. To use the coins to buy some sandals and some provisions. After that, he'll have to follow the mountain range to Egypt…maybe.

He says to himself, "I am a man that does not exist anyway. I need a new name. The old me is dead." The morning sun is continuing to rise higher in the sky. He knows it will not be long before he will be feeling the full fury of the sun. He trudged forward, the camp is farther away than it appeared from the mountain. His stomach now, cries for food and water, the sun is reminding him of its presence by its hot breath The sand grows warmer to his bare feet, he pushes forward towards the camp. Though it takes every bit of his strength, he has made it to the edge of the camp. There are camels tethered to the tent pole and as he grew closer, they became restless.

A desert nomad came out from the tent to see what startled the camels. The nomad pulled a sword from his sash and said," Are you here to steal my camels?" He told the man with the sword," I would like to buy some sandals, some food and water. The nomad said," How did you make it across the desert without sandals stranger?" He said, "I had been living in a cave on the other side of the mountain and had worn out my other sandals." The nomad told me before he allowed me inside of his tent, to show him the coins. I reached into my pocket and took out one gold coin. He then welcomed me into the tent. As I entered, there were other nomads inside and they were all looking at me. The nomad that invited me in said to the members of his group, "Look my brothers, a man from the mountain has come down to visit us and he has money."

I suddenly got a bad feeling about this. One of the other nomads said," How do you know he has money?" The nomad replied by saying he has shown me and said, "The mountain man wants to buy some food, water and even sandals." The other nomads laugh. A couple of nomads had begun moving to get behind me, it appears that I have entered a tent of thieves and killers. As I explained to them, I only want food and water. One of the nomads had thrust his sword into my back and I looked down only to see the tip, sticking out of my stomach. The attacker withdrew his sword and to his as well the others amazement, I was still standing. I turned to face the attacker and He came at me with his sword. I side stepped his thrusting attack and grabbed his sword hand. As I was wrestling the sword from his hand, I felt the cold steel of another sword penetrating my body.

I took his sword and his head off. One by one the nomads fell by my sword. After all the nomads were dead or dying, strewn about the tent. I felt on my body where their swords had penetrated, there were no wounds. Only my blood stained the tunic I am wearing. Those men that were not yet dead, I finished them off by beheading them. I did not know if there would be others on their way here so, I gorged myself on the food that they had. I removed a pair of sandals from one of the dead and got an extra pair

from another. I looked around for some clean clothes to wear and stripped away the useable clothing that wasn't bloodied. I gathered their swords, their valuables, and found that these band of thieves had amassed a lot of stolen articles. Valuables that had been taken from some weary traveler that had been killed and left in the desert for the vultures.

I bagged up food. The valuables and swords and rolled it up in a rug, tied it up and drug it outside. The camels were very uneasy for some reason around me. They tugged at their ropes trying to get away. I grabbed the bridle of the lead camel and told the camel that no harm would come to him, or the others and the camels calmed down. I do not understand what just happened but, these animals understood what I told them. I tied the rug with the valuables on to one of the camels and I went back into the tent to find a container of water. I found several containers of water and before I set out on the journey. I found a bowl and gave each camel some water before I set out for the desert. I thought for a moment, I will need some shelter from the heat. The tent would take me too long to dismantle. I had left out one of the swords for myself and began to cut a large section of the tent with it. I could use it as a lean to shelter with the poles from the tent.

I gathered rope and the staking poles of the tent and fastened it to one of the camels. I tied the second camel to the lead camel, the third camel to the second and took the bridle from the lead camel and pulled. They followed me across the desert, carrying my newly acquired wealth. As I was walking across the desert, I began thinking about things. Only a few days ago, I was an apostle of Jesus and had seen him cast out demons. Now because of what I had done, I have become property of the king of demons. Resurrected from the grave, wearing only the tunic that I was wearing before I hung myself, without sandals or anything of value. I was a man without anything and now have a caravan of camels, food, water, and valuables. The desert sun is in the center of the sky. I can see the heat vapors as the sun pulls the moisture from the ground.

For several hours the camels and I slogged across the desert sand but, I could see some type of structure in the distance. My nose caught the smell of food being cooked and I quickened the pace of the camels. I was compelled by some unknown reason. My body started to ache; it was not from the stab wounds of the sword wielding thieves. I kept pulling the animals forward and realized that they were slowing me down. I released the bridle and I ran toward the small desert village. My camels had stopped following me, as if they know something. As I get closer to the village, the pain had such intensity I could no longer run. It was so bad I stopped and lay on the ground writhing with pain throughout my whole body. I felt as if my body was being stretched and pulled by unseen hands. My head felt like it was about to split, my very being was going through some type of change. The pain stopped and I opened my eyes.

Desert looked different, smelled, and even sounded different. I looked at what used to be my hands now look more like the talons of a falcon. My body was rippling with new muscles. I ran my hand across my face and found my mouth having teeth like a lion. My new senses took over, the sounds of people and the presence of food were drawing me closer. I looked behind me for my camels. I could see them creating more distance from me. I am now something that they fear. So, this is what the great deceiver was talking about. I was no longer in control anymore. I was hungry or this thing that I have become is hungry. I was no longer in need of sandals. An animal does not need sandals. The beast started to remove the clothing but decided to keep it on. The clothing will allow the beast to get closer to its prey without alarming it.

A man was at the well drawing up water just up ahead. The beast wanted to rush in on the man but withheld its urges and chose to walk in closer to check out the surroundings. I could hear voices coming from inside the earth and straw constructed dwellings. The air was thick with smells, everything from animals to humans and food being prepared. The man with the water bucket starts toward the structure. He did not notice me but the beast noticed him. The man walked into his home and the beast walked behind the structure to see what else was around or should I say vulnerable. He made a scan of the area and there was another earthen structure only a short distance away. The beast listened for the sounds in the structures, It was not dark yet.

The beast decided to make his move, there is an open window on the rear side of the structure. He stops beside the window's opening and listens. He hears a man and a woman speaking, they are in the front part of the dwelling. The beast jumps into the opening and rolls to his feet. In the moment of positioning to standing, the beast knocks over a chair. The beast presses himself against the wall and waits for the victim to walk in. The man walks in, and the beast grabs him by the throat and breaks his neck before he could get a sound out. The beast pulls the body out of sight of the doorway and waits. The woman starts calling her husband's name and there is no answer. The woman walks into the room and beast grabs her head and twisted it off from the body. The beast began to feast on the fresh kills, eating to slake his appetite for flesh.... human flesh.

The beast ate his fill and was energized. The beast has never felt such strength coursing through his body. He dove back out of the window from which, he had entered and this time with more agility. He then clung to the wall, listening and pondering his next move. The beast peeped around the corner of the dwelling to see if there was no movement. The beast did not see any movement, but he heard movement into the dwelling, that he just left from. A neighbor or a family member, had walked into the house and would find the slaughtered couple. The beast knew what was coming next. He decided to move to the next dwelling and use a different tactic. The beast decided to climb up the side of the second dwelling, to be able to observe and listen from a higher vantage point. The beast heard the person scream in horror from finding those people. The beast heard the person running from the dwelling and into the dwelling that the beast is on top of. The beast listened.

He heard the man tell his family to close the windows and the doors, that he is going to warn the rest of the settlement. The beast moved across the top of the dwelling and leaped on top of the man, and slashed his throat as he dragged him behind the next dwelling. This is all a game to the beast, to kill for the sake of killing. The beast returned to the second dwelling, he stops at the window to listen to the sounds inside. He crashes through the flimsy window and finds a small boy staring at him. He removes the boys head with one swipe of his razor like claws. He hears movement in another room and finds a pregnant woman whimpering in a corner. He lunges on her before she could scream and bites down on her tender neck, ripping her windpipe and main arteries …she is dead.

He hesitates for a moment and rips the newborn baby from its mother womb. He exits the window with the newborn, climbs on top of the next dwelling. He eats the newborn like it was a lamb's leg. I am powerless to control the beast and it sickens me to what lengths the beast will go. The beast it seems, has an insatiable hunger for killing and human flesh. The moon is high in the desert sky and the beast can see all around him. The beast managed to wipe out the whole village though he did meet some resistance from a man with the sword…… it was a futile resistance. As the night began to turn to day, the beast appetite had been fulfilled. All the inhabitants of the small village were dead.

The pains returned, the beast howls in pain as his body transforms from beast to man. I look at my hands and they are no longer instruments of death and destruction. My clothes are bloody and tattered. I was repulsed by what happened and I vomited up last night's dinner of human flesh. I stood up and yelled out, "Is this what you want Lucifer? Does this please you Lucifer? Are you getting your enjoyment from all of this?" Then behind me I hear a familiar voice say, "You have turned into the perfect killer. You killed the assassins before the change. I told you that you would be the bringer of death. Didn't I? If you offer up, the night's killings and piled them up and burn as an offering to me. I might help you get to another region much faster than by camel. It is up to you.

I said," I am already damned in the eyes of the Lord, and I cannot undo that what has already been done." He gathered up all the wood and lamp oil that he could find. He placed a pile of wood in the center of the village, placed the bodies on the wood and poured lamp oil on the wood and the bodies. Lucifer pointed at the pile, and it burst into flames. I said," Are you happy now, can we leave this place?" Lucifer said," Aren't you going to say something for this offering?" I said," I dedicate this burnt offering to the prince of lies." Lucifer said," Now that doesn't sound like a proper dedication. You can't go back to Judea because you belong to me. Now! Tell me something I want to hear before I get angry." I am not going to do your bidding. I killed and ate a baby from its mother womb. How am I supposed to feel good about myself after that?" Yelled Judas.

The dark one grasp Judas by the neck and said, "The rabbi only told you and your apostle friends that Hell existed. I am going to send you there. Let's see how long you last until you ask for me to stop the torment." Lucifer laughs as he snaps his fingers and Judas is chained in complete darkness. The only sensation he feels is that he isn't in his human form, but in the body of the beast. The beast fights against the chains and the chains hold firm. He hears sounds that are unrecognizable. His nose catches a smell that he does find familiar. The smell of blood and flesh. He sees movement in the distance that walked in front of a roaring flame. He hears something getting closer to him and a torch suddenly lights in front of him.

A large creature, a demon laughs and holds a human arm out to the beast. The demon laughs as the beast lunges out at the flesh. The demon says," You can have some if you beg for our master's mercy." The beast withdraws and says, "I'm not that hungry Go back to your cage vermin!" The demon takes a bite out of the flesh and walks back into the darkness. The beast had no way of keeping track of time. Just the constant harassment by Lucifer's demons. The continued taunting and the beast's hunger only increased. Even though the beast can see in the darkness, this darkness can be felt like something weighing him down. The beast yells out," I deserve this." Do you hear me you bastard creation of God. I deserve this. Do you hear me?" As the beast sits down on the ground.

He hears a female voice saying," You'll only anger him more is that what you want?" The beast says show yourself to me. Come out of the darkness. Suddenly a torch lights up and reveals a beautiful naked woman. Are you here to torture me with your seductive looks? There is no use in trying. You are down here working for him. I just as soon kill and eat your body than to make love to it. Just leave me." yelled the beast. The beautiful female form changed to a grotesque demon and said in a gravelly voice," You want to continue playing the hard way. It is your choice. It has always been your choice, Judas." The light went out and the beast was alone again in the darkness. The beast laid down and went to sleep.

He began to dream of a peaceful place. Sitting on the shore of a serene lake and suddenly the lake catches on fire, and he feels the heat off the flames as a hot breeze blew toward him. From the flames walk a man dressed in a gleaming hooded cloak. he walks up to Judas and says, "There are no such things as good dreams in hell Judas." The hooded figure reveals himself and it is the great deceiver. The beast wakes up and sees that the deceiver is standing next to him. "How do you like it here so far Judas? Do you still think you deserve this?" Asked the deceiver. "You are the reason I am here. You planted the thought in my head. I am responsible for the rabbi's death. No! You are responsible for his death." Exclaimed the beast.

"Yes! I planted the idea. You simply put things in motion, but it was the Jews that condemned your rabbi. I was there and saw it happen. Pilate asked the crowd. Who do they want to be crucified. Is it the

Nazarene or Barabbas? The crowd called out for the release of Barabbas and to crucify the so-called king of the Jews. It was your peoples fault Judas. Not yours." exclaimed the deceiver. "How can I believe you? I wasn't there. This could be another of your fabricated lies.' Yelled the beast. "Let me show you. "Said the deceiver.

Instantly, Judas is standing in the back of the crowd with the deceiver as the scene plays out in front of him. Judas screams out at the tops of his lungs. "The rabbi is innocent! The rabbi is innocent!" They can't hear you. This is a replay of past events. I merely wanted you to see for yourself what happened." Said the deceiver. Judas drops to his knees and says," I am doomed. Take me back to hell, where I belong." The deceiver says, "I am willing to give you another chance to redeem yourself with me. A ruler in Egypt needs to feel the pain of lose for not paying his pledges to me. I can return your camels and the spoils you took from the assassin nomads. You sent them to me. They are paying for their deeds now."

The deceiver snaps his fingers and Judas is wearing the clothing he had taken from the dead nomads and he sees the blood stains on his arms from the battle. He has the rope in his hand and the camels are there. The camels and I were at an oasis in the desert. I said, "I thought we were going to Egypt?" Lucifer said," We are standing on the works, that were created by the fallen." The dark one waved one hand as in one motion, pushed away centuries of sand. The sand began to reveal huge objects that I have no words to describe. My mind could not grasp the sheer scale of these structures. I said, "It was the flood, wasn't it?" The dark master covered the monuments of old with the desert sand. The dark one said, "The Egyptians could not have conceived such an undertaking.

There will be two more nights of the full moon. It would be best if you leave your camp here and go into the city before the pains begin. Remember. Make the ruler feel the pain of loss. Kill someone close to him and leave a mark. I will show you the mark when it is time." Before I could ask a question, The king of lies was gone. I pulled the camels to a nearby date palm laden oasis, only to find that I was not the only person there. I said to myself, it looks like I may have to kill for spot to camp again.

As I pulled my camels toward a tent that was already set up in the middle of the oasis, a voice says, "Welcome weary traveler to my tent." As I drew closer, the older man that welcomed me and saw my bloodied clothes. The older man said," sir, what has happened to you? Why are you so bloody are you injured?" I told the older man that I had ran into some blood thirsty thieves and I had to fight me way out and it is their blood that is on me. The older man said," You must be a skilled man with a sword to have escaped with the three camels and your belongings plus your life intact?"

I told him that I only require some water to get cleaned up and change my clothes. I said," I am tired and weary from walking the desert all night." The older man said, "One of my daughters will bring you water and cloth to clean yourself. Then if you wish, you are welcome to some food and water to drink. I know that you are tired and are welcomed to take a nap in my tent until you have rested to put up your own tent." I told the older man that I appreciate his hospitality and would take him up on some food and water but, did not want to impose any more on him and would set up a makeshift camp. I said," I do not need a big tent like yours since I have been traveling light and it is just me."

The older man turned inward of his tent and told his daughter to get water and a bowl for the stranger to clean up. The older man turns to me and says, "What is your name stranger?" I said, "My name is Jeremiah." The older man said that his name is Salaam and he said," Once you get cleaned up, come into my tent and let's talk." I told him that I would be there as soon as I got cleaned up and presentable. I pulled the bridle, and my camels followed me to a spot at the edge of the oasis. I tied the camels to a date palm and began to unpack some of the confiscated clothes. As I was doing this, I could hear movement behind me. I turned around and a young girl approached me with a bag of water and a bowl to wash in. She walked up to me and said," Here you go sir. My father told me to bring you this."

She sat the articles on the ground and as I turned around to face her, I could see the shock in her face. I told her not to be alarmed and I said," I am not injured it is the blood of the robbers that tried to kill me." I could see in her face, that this intrigued her quite a bit. I said, "What is your name?" She said that her name is Kara. I said, before you go back I may have something for you. I took down the bag form the camel, which held the spoils from yesterday's escapade.

I felt inside until I found something that I could give to her in a gesture for her hospitality. I pulled it from the bag, and it was a golden bracelet. I told her that I do not have any money to give her so, I offered her the bracelet. Her eyes lit up and said," I should not take this, I only brought you water and a bowl to get yourself cleaned up. You do not owe me this." I told her to take it any way as a gift of gratitude." I thanked her for the water and told her tell her father that I would be there shortly after I make myself presentable.

Kara thanked me for the bracelet and walked back towards her father's tent. Kara did not go back to her father's tent, I could sense that she was watching, hidden behind some palmetto bushes. I peeled down the bloodied clothing to my waist. I took a tattered cloth and dipped it in the water and washed my face and scrubbed the dried blood from my arms. I bathed my chest and bathed the areas of my back that I could reach. I unrolled the bag that held the clothes that I had taken from the thieves. I found a tunic and I could smell the remnants of its earlier owner in the fabric. The tunic was of strong body odor, I could not enter the man's tent smelling like a camel. I untied the carpet from one of my camels and unrolled it on the ground. I found a container that held scented oil in it. I sprinkled some of it onto the tunic and I undressed completely.

I slid the tunic on and from the valuables taken from the thieves, I took a sword from the pile. I rolled the collection back up, tied up the ends and anchored it back onto the camel. I washed away the blood from my hair with the limited amount of water and was able to rinse a lot of it out. With quick moments of my head, I was able to sling away some of the excess water. I was still being watched from palmetto palms and wild ferns. The water I had left, I gave each camel an equal share. I grabbed the empty water bag and the bowl and walked toward

Salaam's tent. Kara had beaten me to the tent. I stood at the entrance of the tent until I am invited in.

I hear Kara says, "Father, we have a visitor." Salaam invites me in and tells me to come and sit on the rug and eat with him. I sat down and thanked him for the water and the bowl and said that they came in handy. I told him that I had brought him a gift for his hospitality and presented the jewel encrusted scabbard and sword. Salaam told me that I did not have to do that, and I told him it was a sword that I had taken from one of the thieves that tried to kill me. I said, "The man that it belonged to does not need it anymore." Kara and her father laughed at my comment. Kara held out her arm that had the bracelet on it and said," Look father, Jeremiah gave me this. Isn't it beautiful?" Salaam said," My goodness Jeremiah, we thank you for these gifts. Now. let us have something to eat.

As we began eating another woman comes into the tent. Salaam says, "Jeremiah, this is my wife Kateri. She has been to gather dates for the trip to Jerusalem." Kateri says, "Where is your home, Jeremiah?" I told her that I came from Jerusalem." She said," I do not mean to pry but are you heading to Egypt. If you are? Be careful about mentioning your beliefs. That is why we are going to Jerusalem; we seek to hear of the one called Jesus." I told them that Jesus had been arrested, likely to be crucified. His flock of apostles have been scattered in fear of they and could meet the same fate.

The Romans have a very heavy presence there and it would not be wise for you to seek the one called Jesus." Salaam said," This is indeed a most fortunate circumstance running into Jeremiah. Where do you think we can seek safe haven, Jeremiah?" I said, "If I had to guess, the remaining disciples will go to Jordan and go into hiding for a while." Salaam asked me what I believed in. I told him that no matter how pure a man is in his heart; he will be pursued by the fallen one. Waiting for the chance to catch the man at his weakest and makes his move." Kara said," Have you met the fallen one?" I said, "I met up with a band of his followers last night and they thought I would be an easy victim. Let us eat and not glorify the fallen one and his followers."

Salaam said," You are right. Let us not waste another minute talking about such things. Salaam said a prayer over the food, and we ate. Kara could not keep her eyes from me. I ate and focused on what I had to do. I knew I had to get away from these people before the pains started or they too would fall victim to the beast. I noticed yesterday, that the pains started hours before the sun went down. I gulped down the food and told the family that I had to get a few things to carry with me into Cairo" Before I could speak Salaam said," You are a half a day's walk to Cairo from here. He said," Why do you want to go to Cairo, knowing that it's dangerous there."

I said, "I seek a man that I can sell the thieves' collection to, so that I can buy passage on a ship." Kara asked me where I would go on the ship. I replied to Kara that I did not really have a set destination." I asked them to keep an eye on my belongings for me while I was gone. They agreed that they would, and I thanked them for the generosity and I made my way toward my campsite. I heard Kara ask her father could she talk to me? Her father said yes but do not be a hindrance to Jeremiah.

I could hear her running to catch up to me. She got beside me and said," Do you have a wife, Jeremiah?" I told her that I once had a wife until she was killed by some Romans that were attacking those that were following Jesus. Kara said," I could be your wife." I asked Kara how old she is, and she told me that she is sixteen seasons. Kara said," I have not laid with a man before and I am drawn to you." I said," Kara, you do not even know me and now you want to lie with me. Let us keep what we have now as a friendship." Kara said," Do you not find me pleasing to look at?" I told her that she is more beautiful that any Egyptian princess. She said," Why then, won't you lie with me?" I told her that if I make it back from Cairo, we will discuss it okay.

I turned my focus on getting some items to sell and take two swords with me. I could smell her womanhood; she was as ripe as a pomegranate ready to burst. I turned to look at her and she had pulled up her sarong, exposing her genitalia to me. I said, "Kara, please. What if your father or mother were to see this?" She said," My body tells me that it wants you inside it." I was already with an erection and trying to get out of there. She walked over to me, and she said," Jeremiah, if you don't pleasure me. I will scream that you raped me." I said," Kara, you deserve better than me.

I am afraid that you were to lie with me and become pregnant. You would bring shame on yourself and your family, for we are not husband and wife. Besides, I could get killed in Cairo and the child would not have a father or a husband for you." Kara said," You will be back tomorrow, and I will be aching for your return." I told her to take care of my camels and my belongings while I was gone. I said," If by some twist of fate, I do not return, all these items and camels are yours okay." She hugged me and as I pulled away from her, she had tears streaming down her face. She said," You better not get killed Jeremiah, it would rip my heart into." I grabbed my bag of trinkets and stuck one of the swords in my sash, headed toward Cairo.

I left the protection from the sun's rays as I walked out from the oasis. The sun was in the middle of the sky and I had to get far enough away from Kara and her family, before the pains began. I did not want the beast to slaughter them like a butcher cutting up meat. I already bear a heavy burden on my conscious for what I did to the village. I continued walking and suddenly Judas isn't alone. "Judas forget about trying to sack Cairo of its jewels. Do as I ask and you'll never be lacking. If you simply obey my wishes? You would not need riches." A voice said.

CHAPTER 2

DEATH COMES TO CAIRO

"Tonight, I will kill as many Romans that get in my way as well as the Egyptians. I 'll will get your revenge upon the Pharoah." Lucifer said," Sounds like a night of mayhem and blood lust. Speaking of lust, why didn't you go ahead and have your way with that beautiful desert flower. She was willing to give herself to you."

I said," It is not me; I think it has something to do with this curse that you cast upon me." Lucifer said," You are right. The human female is drawn to the primal urge senses of that part your animal counterpart has." I said, "I do not want to bring a child into this world that bears this curse." Lucifer said," You are thirty-eight years old and if you fathered a child; it too would change at thirty-eight. The mark you will leave is a five-pointed star. I am the morning star and leave the mark on the pharaoh's offspring. I was about to say something else and Lucifer was gone.

I could see smoke in the distance coming from the city. As I walked toward the city, the pains started. I noticed a pile of boulders and I headed for them. The pain was becoming more intense. I must make it to the rocks. I do not need to be seen by the sentries, caught out in the open during the change. I made it to the rocks and placed the sack on the ground next to me. All that was human is about to change into a creature that has only two things on its mind; killing and eating. After the pain of the change has subsided, it will be a while before the sun goes down. The creature grows impatient, and I try to reason with the thoughts the creature was having.

The creature wants to run right through the city gates and start killing and eating. I tell him that if he does that, he will have to fight the whole legion of Roman guards. I told him that if he can control himself; he could walk in through the gates without drawing attention. I told him to pull the hood down, keep his head down and walk slowly through the gates. Then once in the gates, find somewhere secluded until I can help him figure out the next move.

The creature got up, pulled the hood down and walked toward the city. As he got closer to the city gates, he lowered his head so that the wall sentries could not see his face. I forgot to tell him not to make eye contact with anyone; even if someone spoke to him. A beggar walked up and asked for money, I told the creature to keep walking. The beggar made eye contact with the beast and before the beggar could screaming with terror. With one swipe of the creature's right hand, the beggar lost his head. A sentry yelled out, "You, stop right there!" I told the creature to run for cover it was time to hide. The creature ran between two structures, it was full of beggars and squatters. The creature just plowed through and managed to climb to the top of a structure.

Through the creature's ears, I could hear people screaming in terror saying words like a demon is among us, or the destroyer is back. They were not too far off with their description. I told the creature that we need to get away from the turmoil. The creature leaped over onto the roof another dwelling, then another. The creature did it so effortlessly, such power and skill. The creature has stopped listening to me, he is hungry. The creature is hunting, listening, and sniffing the air for the next victim. He hears someone walking just below the edge of the dwelling. The creature leans over the edge to size up the prey. It is a man dressed in a sack cloth tunic. The creature lunges and snaps the man's neck, in one swift movement and throws the limp body on the roof. The creature will be able to feast unhindered. The creature leaps onto the ledge of the earthen dwelling.

He tears away the clothing to get at the flesh and begins to fill his empty stomach. The skies have darkened over Cairo as the clouds move across the face of the full moon. The creature continues to feast on the once breathing body of a man, reduced to bone fragments and a puddle of blood and entrails. Now that the beast is full, I'll try and inject a thought. I told the beast that he needs to scout out where the pharaohs sleep. Like an animal after the kill, he is reluctant to leave it. I assured him that another chance to make a kill will present itself, the night is still young.

The beast crept over to the edge of the dwelling and looked out over the sprawling city of Cairo. He saw a structure that stood higher than rest of the earthen dwellings of the slaves. That must be the house of the pharaohs, there is where the riches of the Nile rest. The beast jumped down from the dwelling, staying close to the shadows and out of the view of the palace guards. The ideal entry point would be the rear of the palace, though it will be guarded and hopefully less torch lights. The full moon already provides enough light to give us away, between the occasional cloud passing in front of it. The creature arrived at a point where he will have to risk being seen. There's another dwelling across a wide gap used for cart paths and people.

He hears movement from around the corner, he waits and listens. He hears the sounds of one person's footfalls in the sand. The person is coming right to the beast and as he turns the corner; the beast shoves him out of the way. The beast runs across the pathway and leaps on top of the dwelling. The man starts yelling," Guards, I have been attacked by a demon of the night." The beast lays flat against the roof of the dwelling and listens. He hears a couple of guards go to the man. One the guards said," Have you been drinking too much wine again, Omar?" The other guard said," A couple of nights ago Omar saw a golden elephant." the guards laugh at the man and went about their duties. The beast got up and headed for the opposite end of the building. He gets to the edge of the building and surveys the area for guards and the location of the palace. The beast grows hungry again.

I guess it is from the spent energy that he's used up. I urge the beast onward toward the palace perhaps, an easy kill will be waiting for him. The beast leaped across to the next dwelling and saw that the palace has a second level being patrolled by guards. We are in a bad position; we could be seen by the palace guards from their upper level. A different approach will have to be taken the beast had to lay low to avoid detection, until he could jump down from the roof of the dwelling. The timing of the jump had to be when the guard turned to walk in the opposite direction. The guard arrived at his point and turned, the beast lunged for the ground and headed for the security of the darkness. He cautiously walked between the city wall and earthen dwelling. Moving through the darkness with eyes accustomed to the darkness, he listens and sniffs the air. He hears two men talking and they are coming down the same alley. I told the beast just to pull the hood over his head and lay down with his back next to the wall and pull his knees close to his chest. The guards will think that you are some beggar sleeping and probably won't do anything. In the case that they provoke you to move on, go ahead and kill them both quickly and silently.

The beast laid down, pulled the hood over his face, pulled his knees to his chest and waited. The guards with their torches walked up to the beast. One of the guards said, "Did your wife kick you out of the house because you had too much wine?" The beast lay there unresponsive and the other guard kicked the beast. The beast sprang upwards and killed both guards and extinguished the torches in the sand. Neither of the guards were able to yell out a warning. Before the beast began to feast on the kill, he listened for the possibility of more guards coming his way. The smell of a fresh kill was intoxicating. The beast couldn't wait any longer and began feeding on the dead guards. The beast gorged himself on human flesh and was satisfied to the point where I could interject my thoughts on moving on to the palace. The beast left the mangled bodies by the city wall and walked to the end of the alley. The alley opened to a large area that contained statues and a manicured garden of plant varieties.

Hiding places were cut down to a minimum, going in through the back is going to be difficult. I got an idea, I suggested to the creature to get as close as possible to the palace, and if any guards get in the way just kill them; then return to easier hunting grounds until the morning breaks. The creature moved cat like, utilizing what cover he could use to conceal his presence. There was a large reflecting pool of water at the of the creature. A guard on the second level outpost saw the creature's reflection in the pool and alerted the palace guards. Two guards came rushing toward the creature and the creature killed both guards and retreated into the network of the common slave dwellings.

Several palace guards tried to catch up to the creature but were outpaced by a more superior being. The creature found a place to hide in the darkness until the chaos calmed down. He could hear the guards going from house to house looking for him. The tunic that the creature is wearing, now blood soaked and tattered needed to be replaced. The need for fresh clothing would be important, after changing back to my human appearance. Moving through the dark corridors between dwellings, the beast moving silently and scanning his surroundings and taking in all the sounds and smells of the night in Cairo. Morning will be coming soon, and the search has turned into desperation. He continues and hears voices coming from an open window. He moves closer and listens. A man and a woman are arguing. He positions himself to look into the window.

The couple are in another room, the creature jumps in through the open window. He rushes into the next room, grabs the woman, and holds his mighty hand over her mouth. The beast sees he is in the presence of someone in power, a Pharoah. The man began pleading for this girl's life. The beast says," You have forgotten about the pledge and you have brought me here. This girl will pay for your mistake." The beast rips the young girls head off and throws it at the Pharoah. The beast carves the star on the back of the dead girls back and jumps out the window into the night. Now it is important that he leaves the city before morning. That means, going over the city wall and back to the pile of rocks, which he has hidden the items for trading.

I told the creature that it would be easier to cross over the wall if a dwelling is closer to the wall and jumping would be made easier. The creature took my hint and jumped on top of a dwelling to have a look at a possible escape route. From the top of the dwelling, the creature scanned the area and sees a way out. Leaping from roof top to roof top, stopping occasionally to avoid being seen by the guards posted on the wall. Time is growing short, and the morning is approaching. The beast hastens the pace because he knows the pains are coming. He leaps on the last dwelling that is next to the city wall. Just as he makes his landing, a guard on the wall saw movement on the roof. The beast saw that the guard made eye contact in his direction. He crawled to the edge of the building and sprang toward the wall, taking the guard with him over the city wall. As they both hit the ground, the creature ripped the windpipe from the guard's neck and ran into the desert.

I told the beast to run like he has never run before. It is imperative that he achieve as much distance from the city that he can before he reverts to human form. Getting to the pile of rocks isn't important now, it's about distance from the site of the guards on the wall. The pains had started, it began with a dull ache in my body. The beast turns his head to look back to see, how much distance he has covered.as he stands on the top of a sand dune. The pain strikes and the creature rolls down the back side of the dune. At the bottom of the dune, the transformation from beast to man takes place. After the excruciating pain of the change had stopped, I lay at bottom of the dune exhausted. I rested there for a moment, long enough to get myself together.

I wondered how far off course I was from the pile of rocks that I had hidden the items that I am to use for trade. I climbed back up the dune to look for the pile of rocks. I could see the city of Cairo off in the distance and to the right of me I could see the pile of rocks. Judging the distance, I am not far away. As I made my way towards the rocks, I hear a voice from behind me say," It doesn't have to be this way Judas?" I turn to see where the voice was coming from and it was a light brighter than the sun, I could not look directly at it. I turned away from it and continued to walk towards the rocks. The voice, I didn't recognize it at first but now it is clear whom it belongs to. I continued walking and the voice was closer behind me saying, "Judas, it doesn't have to continue this way. "I didn't turn to look in the direction the voice was coming from and I said, "If I hadn't followed you? I wouldn't be in this mess that I am now. Before you say anything else, you've beaten death. Just as you predicted, you have been raised from the dead. I too was raised from the dead but, not by the God of Abraham like you. Teacher."

The teacher said," Judas, it wasn't your fault." I said, "It was my fault. I could've disobeyed my greed but, free will chose a different course. So, depart from me because there is no saving me now. At the end of days, my heart will no longer be hardened like the stone figures of the Egyptian gods. Then, I'll ask for your forgiveness." I stopped walking and turned around; the bright light was no longer there. I remembered what the teacher had told us," Woe to the man who betrays the son of man. For it would have been better if he had never been born." My fate has been sealed and I might as well accept it and I can't blame anyone but myself. I made it to the pile of rocks and pulled the sack cloth bag; that held the collection that I had hidden among the rocks. A scorpion was disturbed from his hiding place and he raised his stinger in defense. Lucky for him that I wasn't hungry.

I took off the remnants of the tunic I was wearing during my night of carnage. I put on the clothes that I had taken from the assassins, reached into the bag and felt around for a pair of sandals. I put on the sandals. I pulled out the water bag and washed off the dried blood from the areas that I could see rinsed my face and had a drink of water. I've got a good hour of walking before I get to the city of Cairo. As I was walking an idea came to me. I could extort gold from the pharaohs by telling them to pay me or the creature will come back and kill more of his family. I guess before I can do that, I'll have to ask around to see if anything exciting went on last night. I saw in the distance an indication of death. A group of vultures were circling in the air; the scent of death has drawn them to Cairo.

The desert sand is beginning to warm as the sun continues to climb. My mind began to think about things before I made some bad choices. Suddenly, I wasn't alone." Stop thinking about the past Judas, I mean Jeremiah. There is no changing it now." I said, "If you had arrived at little sooner Lucifer, you could've met your emissary?" Lucifer replied," I saw how you handled yourself and you have taken responsibility. That's a quality unlike other humankind. They would cast the responsibility on anyone but themselves. I applaud you." Lucifer clapped his hands together and said, "You like the way that power feels, don't you? You know you don't have to back into Cairo. You have done what I asked. "I want to kill some more Romans. They killed many of my people." Replied Jeremiah.

"Don't stay in Cairo too long. Follow the Nile and remember to pay homage or you'll go back to hell." Answered the dark one. As I turned to ask a question, I was alone again, and I could see the city gates just ahead. I walked closer to the opened gates and two spear wielding guards were at their post. As I walked closer, the two guards were now facing me. One of the guards asked me to state my business in the city? I told him that I only wanted to barter some of my goods for some food and some fresh clothing. They let me pass and as I walked forward, I asked them where the market was? I went in the direction that they told me. I could smell the location of the market but, it would've seemed odd to the guards and brought attention.

As I drew closer to the market, my sense of smell was being overwhelmed with different scents. I could smell different aromas of spices, cooked animal flesh and even musky scent of people that haven't bathed in a while. I hope I don't smell that bad, as I come in contact with other people. Both sides of the market corridor were filled with everything from salted fish to clothing. As I was walking and looking at different things, I could hear people talking in hushed overtones about last night's murders. I walked up to a spice merchant and asked him where I could get a bath and a change of clothes. The spice merchant told me if I had something to trade, I could get all that I need on the other side of the market row, the last stand on the end. I noticed that he was staring at the sword at my waist as he was talking to me. I thanked him for his information and walked across to the other side of market row. I got the impression that the spice merchant had recognized something about the sword.

I walked down the row of vendors and I could hear someone following me. I turned around and two men were stalking me. They were wearing the same type of sword and had a red sash around their waist. One of them asked me," Where did you get that sword?" I told him that I won it in a battle." The man tells me that I'm a liar and that I had stolen it. I told him that I have no quarrels with him but if he insisted on insulting me. I will have another sword to trade with. The man and his accomplice drew their swords and came towards me. I had just enough time, to take a second sword from my bag. I have a sword in each hand now. The two men came in closer and began to circle me. Like a top, I spun around lobbing off the head of the attacker behind me.

By this time a crowd had formed, it is just me and the man that accused me of stealing. I said, "Are you ready to join your friend? "The man yelled," You just killed my brother and now I'm going to kill you." The man lunged at me swinging wildly with his sword. I blocked his attack with one sword and slashed him deep into his side. People in the crowd were telling me to finish him because he belongs to a clan of thieves and murderers. I told the man as he was holding his bloody side, "These two swords, are from the men that tried to kill me and they also died in the process." I was about to finish the guy off and two Roman guards came up and stopped the fight. One of the guards asked, "What is going on here and who started this? Before I could speak for myself, a merchant stepped forward and told the guard what had happened.

The merchant told the guard that the attackers were both wearing a red waist sash, meaning that they belong to a gang of murders and thieves and prey upon people as they cross the desert. He said," My brother and his new wife was on their way to Jordan and was killed by this band of thieves. Only one person survived to tell me the story and he lost some fingers in a sword fight with them. "I said," I merely came to Cairo to trade the items for food and some clothing." I opened up the bag and took out two more swords. The Roman guards were intrigued and asked did the swords belong to dead men as well? I told them yes and I asked them to let me pass and they did not listen. I told them that I was trained to use the sword as a young boy. My father was a gladiator that had won his freedom, unfortunately my father is now dead. One of the palace guards said," What of the two dead men? are you going to just leave them there on the ground?

I said, "I will help load them on a cart to get them out from in front of the merchant's place of business. Do either of you know where we can get a cart? And where do you want the bodies taken?" The two guards looked at each other and one guard said, "We don't care what you do with the bodies. They just must be removed from the market place. "The guards walked away and I asked the merchant; if he had a suggestion to remedy the problem? The merchant told me that he would send his son to the end of the market row. He said," My friend has a cart that we could use but, he will require payment." I said," Would he accept a sword in payment? "The merchant said, "The sword would be more than enough for the job. I'll barter with my friend on services rendered. How about you and I do some bartering You said that you need food and the bodies taken out of here. For one of the swords, if you are willing to part with it?

I told him that I would agree to such a trade. The merchant asked me to help him move the dead men from front of his business. I helped the merchant drag the dead men off to the side of the building and covered them with sack cloth. I said, "What if the guards come back and see the bodies placed at the end of the building?" The merchant said, "The bodies will be gone before the guards circle back through." The merchant called for his son and a young boy, about 10 or so years old comes from out from the merchant's place of business. The merchant gives his son some coins and gives him instructions of what to do. The merchant turns to me and said, "While my son goes on his way, we can do our trading." I asked the merchant to choose which sword he wanted? We chose the one that I had in my right hand. He then asked me did I like roasted goat and rice? I told him that it would be perfect, and I just need to get cleaned up.

The merchant then told me that he would get me what I needed so that I could go on my way because, people saw what happened on market row and there could be some of the dead men's kinsmen in the crowd. The merchant then hurriedly got me a pan of water. I rinsed the splattered blood from my hands and my face and dried them on my tunic. The merchant then brought me a container of food and gave me a wineskin of wine and bid me goodbye. I thanked the merchant and made my way to the end of market row. I looked upward and the sun is in the center of the sky as well as a group of vultures were circling. The scent of death was in the air. The bringer of death is in Cairo. I thought to myself, I have unknowingly brought extra attention to myself. Especially in this part of the city.

I need to unload the rest of the spoils and get myself a clean tunic, that isn't blood stained. As I made my way through the maze of people, I would feel the stares and hear the murmuring of voices as I passed. I continued my way and looking for a place to just sit down and eat some food. I'm starving and my stomach feels like it is eating on itself. I heard a voice from behind me talking to me. I turned around and a dog was following me. I stopped and looked around to see if there was anyone else around? The crowd was too far away, and the voice sounded much closer. I kept on walking; the heat of the sun is playing tricks on my mind.

Then I noticed beside me was the dog. The dog said," You're not going crazy and you are the only one that can hear me. Just keep walking until we get to the edge of the palace gardens. There you'll be able to sit down and eat and we can have a talk. I kept on walking until the area opened to the edge of a pristine garden with statues and exotic plants. I sat down underneath a palm tree and the dog sat down next to me. I said," Are you one of the devil's spawns come to torment my mind?" The dog said," No, I'm not one of Satan's creations like yourself. I continue to stay as a dog until I die. Because of your condition you're able to hear me and from what I've heard from some of my canine friends; you really shook up the city last night."

I said," Aren't you afraid of what I am?" The dog said, "I wouldn't be talking to you, if I was afraid of you. Besides, If someone saw you talking to me? They would think that you had been kicked in the head by a camel. How about sharing some of your food with me? I know you have some food because I can smell it." I took the small clay pot from my bag and removed the lid. I put a portion of the mixture of rice and meat in the lid, placed it on the ground. The dog quickly inhaled the food like he hadn't eaten in a while. The dog sat on his haunches and said," Do humans taste like pork? That's what I've heard from other dogs. I've never tried myself because I rely on them for handouts." I said, "I'd rather not talk about it. It's a part of me that I have no control over." The dog told me that the full moon will occur again tonight, and I have a few hours before the change begins. The dog then says, "I'll be going on my way, there are some men coming and I feel that they aren't going to be very friendly."

The dog walked away and I put a handful of food in my mouth. I put the clay pot on the ground and as I looked up three men were walking towards me. I was still in a crouching position, and I felt for the handle of a sword that was in my bag and my left hand had a palm full of sand in it. The men walked up, and one said," If you draw your sword you will die, if you give us your belongings; we may let you live." The man that was talking was the only one that had drawn his sword. I sprang upwards, throwing the sand into the man's eyes. At the same time, I had drawn my sword and lobbed off the robber's hand that held a sword. The two other men ran away, leaving their bleeding friend scrambling for his sword with his only hand. The man was in agony and saying that he is going to have to kill me. The man began swinging his sword wildly at me, I blocked his advances and finished him off by running my sword through his body.

I picked up my bag and left the area, looking for somewhere to hide away from the crowd that had witnessed the sword fight. I made some twist and turns around the earthen dwellings and found myself in another part of the city. After tonight, I 've concluded that I must leave Cairo tomorrow. Too many people have seen what I look like and witnessed me kill men in two sword fights. My idea of coming into the city and ran sacking what I could, has not turned out so well. Though I did find out that I could communicate with dogs, I guess the visit to Cairo wasn't a total loss. The dog was right about one thing in particular; there will be another full moon tonight. I can feel the muscles in my jaw begin to tighten and the slight aching in the rest of my body.

I must find a place out of the public eye to transform and I must do it soon. I made it down this alley until it opened up in front of a temple, built to honor one of Egypt's many gods. I walked up the stairs and entered a quiet sanctum, filled with the aroma of burning spices. I looked for a side room to slip into; the change is coming. I managed to find a small room tucked away and no one was in there. The change hit with ferocity, my body was being stretched from the inside out. Someone is going to hear my moans of agony and they will be the first victim of the night. The transformation was complete and I could hear foot falls against the tiled floor of the temple. There is only a cloth curtain that covers the entrance to the small room that the beast now resides in. The beast now against the wall next to the entry point, waits for someone to make a mistake and walk in.

A voice says," Come out of there beggar, this is a house of worship not sleeping quarters." The beast waits in silence, ready to pounce. The unaware man walks through the curtain and becomes a meal for the beast. The beast made quick work of shredding the flesh from the dead man's body with his razor- sharp claws and canine-like teeth. The beast ate just enough to temporarily slake his appetite. He knows that he can't stay in that room. He stops eating and listens for anymore movement in the adjacent room. He doesn't hear any movement and leaves the room and heads to the rear of the temple. It is still daylight, and it wouldn't be wise to go out the front entrance, the city doesn't need to know that a monster is on the loose. The beast found a rear exit and was able to find a place to hide and think about the next move. The sun still has the sky, time to wait for darkness so that I can move about, the beast does not handle patience very well.

The beast sniffs the air and sorts through a myriad of assorted aromas from human waste, spices being cooked, to the scent of rotting corpses from last night's kill. Listening to the sounds from people bickering over trivial matters to the sounds of chickens clucking and the occasional rush of the wind from the desert, bringing in the end of the day. The mind of the beast begins to wonder and ask questions that I can't answer. I tell the beast that he is in control at the moment, and I am only along for the ride until the sun rises tomorrow. The beast was getting agitated because I didn't answer his question, which he asked me what should he do now? Before I could suggest, a familiar voice from the corner of an earthen structure says, "come over here. There are food scraps back here to eat." The stray dog that I had met earlier stuck out his head for the beast to see and the beast made a dash for the corner of the structure.

The stray dog said," You're not going to eat me, are you?" The beast replied in a guttural voice," No, where is food?" The stray dog said, "The meat scraps are under the mixture of soured smelling vegetables and rice, with a blend of insect larvae. I wish I had fingers like you to pick out the bad stuff." I started rummaging through the trash seeking out morsels of meat when, a familiar voice said, "I didn't resurrect you so that, you could be foraging for food in the refuse pile with a dog." Standing in the shadows was my new master. He said," I want you to kill in the house of pharaoh again tonight and write in blood this symbol upon the pharaoh's wall." Lucifer pointed at the ground and an image of an upside-down star appeared in the sand.

Lucifer said," You are property of the morning star. Now go and pay homage to your master. Remember you are immortal. The men's sword or spears means nothing to you, you are superior to them. Do as I asked, and your treasure will be waiting for you outside the city's wall in the morning." Just as mysteriously appeared, he disappeared the same way. I looked for the dog and he had gone; I didn't blame him. The shadows of the night will make it easier for me to get about even though, the full moon is casting a considerable amount light by itself. I've grown hungry again and I've been given a task to complete. I needed to get an idea of where the location of the palace to where I am now so, I dug my claws into the wall of the earthen structure next to me. I cautiously climbed up the wall, being mindful of sentries posted on the city wall. I pulled myself high enough to peer out over the roof tops and I could see the location of the palace. I am not that far from my objective and I pushed away from the structure, landing without any noise. I made use of the shadows cast by the structures as I made my way to the palace grounds.

According to Lucifer, he wants me to just storm in and commence to killing. My animal instinct tells me to use the layout of the surroundings as a means of a calculated surprise attack on my intended victims. As I move in the shadows, stopping momentarily to listen, sniff the air and watch for opportunity to present itself. I had gotten to end of the last structure and there is a considerable wide-open area, that leads to the front of the palace grounds in front of me. I see palace sentries moving about and the palace grounds are illuminated by torches. I see a few areas that are not illuminated by the torches and have some blind spots for the palace guards.

I'll be able to conceal myself until I can get close enough to do a full assault. I watched the guards and as they reached the end of their appointed areas, they would turn and start the task again. I made my move to an obelisk that is situated among the plant life and assorted statues of past pharaohs. The anticipation of a kill has made my hunger pangs intensify. I saw the moment to move, and I did. One guard saw me enter the palace and followed. I dispatched him quickly by tearing his head off and made my way into the palace of pharaoh. I should say, a puppet of Roman because Egypt is no longer a dominant force and has been overtaken by Rome. I killed another palace guard as I made my way up the stairs. The scent of incense and aromatic oils were wafting through the air, as I listened to female voices chattering from a room.

I could hear palace guards flowing into the downstairs level. I followed the sounds of the female voices. I rushed into the room and took the women by surprise. One by one they fell lifeless on the floor, I ate parts of one young female and thought about the symbol, that was shown to me by my new master. I looked over the dead bodies strewn about the room and one of the females, appears to be of royalty. I rolled her body over on her stomach and with my talon like index finger, I made the symbol of an upside- down star into her tender flesh. I tore one the servant girl's arms from her lifeless body and made my escape. I was still hungry and the arm should slake my hunger while on the move. I jumped from a window that was a considerable height. The landing would've broken a normal person's legs but, I'm not a normal person anymore.

I scrambled off to a dark place to eat the tattooed arm of the servant girl. I could hear the chaos left in my wake. I heard someone said that the princess is dead among the screams coming from the palace. The beast doesn't feel remorse or have a conscience. He only wants something in his stomach, to slake his appetite. The beast stripped the meat from the arm bone and was on the move again. My body feels the coming of the new day. The beast must find somewhere out of view of someone seeing the transformation. The city wall, we must get over it. The beast leaped on top of an earthen building, to get a perspective of where to better escape from the city. He crouches low because there are sentries posted about the perimeter of the city wall. He sees a building that is close enough to the wall that he'll be able to leap from the building and onto the wall. Now the task to plot a course to that building which, means going through a maze of earthen structures and crossing an unsecure area.

The element of concealment will be thrown out of the window once, the beast gets there. My thoughts to beast were, "It is the only option other than exiting through the city's main gate." The beast leaped from the building and ran full force through the maze of buildings toward the goal. A few hapless people were knocked down, as if they were only a child's toy knocked aside. The individuals didn't see what hit them. They are the lucky ones that lived to tell about bumping into death and surviving, in the wee moments before sun rise. Pure determination and not hunger was in control now. The body begins to ache; it's a race with time itself. The beast crossed the open gap and was seen by a young boy that was standing in the doorway of his family home. The boy wiped his eyes and wonders if what he had seen was real? Wondering if somehow, that it was only a remnant of a dream that he had just woken up from.

The beast didn't slow up; he didn't have time to be stealthy. He reaches the building and leaps onto the roof and makes a mad dash for the wall. His movements didn't go unnoticed, a sentry sees something leap from a building, onto the wall and leaps from the wall. The sentry does not believe what he has just witnessed. In his mind, it isn't humanly possible to do such a feat. The sentry disregards what he thought he saw to being a figment of a mind that has been sleep deprived. The beast had made it out of the city and now in open dessert except for scattered stonework that had been quarried by the pharaohs workers. The beast heads towards the stonework, the pains are increasing as the sun's rays breach the horizon. The beast collapses among the huge stones, writhing in agony as the transformation from beast to man commences. After a matter of seconds that seemed like an eternity; I had returned to my human self.

I was tired and could use some sleep after last night's activities as the beast. Just as I was about to close my eyes, I realized that I wasn't alone. Standing at my feet, a man dressed in unfamiliar clothing." Hello, my loyal subject; here is not a place to take a nap. The city will be looking for a killer and since you've done my bidding, I have some fresh clothing and payment in the bag. You need to get dressed and own your way. "I knew who the figure was as he spoke, though his face and appearance were different. I said," Where am I to go now or are you going to just place me somewhere?" My new master pointed and said," Follow the Nile. Take the bag of gold coins and remember to pay homage to me. Also, you'll be wise to stay out of Rome, Athens, Malta, and the island of Crete for a while because some of your previous cohorts; "the apostles "will be in those areas. You would be recognized by them. It would be an awkward situation since they saw your body dangling from the tree."

He then disappeared and I hurriedly changed my bloody clothes and put on a fresh tunic, slipped on the sandals and grabbed the bag of coins. I began to walk in a hurried fashion away from Cairo to follow the Nile. Though it is morning, the sand is still warm from the previous day. I climbed up onto the sand dune in front of me and at its summit, I looked across the open space towards the Nile. As I was going down the backside of the dune, I hear a familiar voice say, "It's not too late Judas to repent, I know that you were coerced into betraying me." I turned to look and there was my former master floating above the sand dune. I said," Rabbi, please stop tormenting me. I am responsible for what I did. At that time I was a weak and vulnerable human being and now I am not. So, go and console the other apostles. Remember you said that we would be hated because of you. The remaining apostles are under human influences that no longer apply to me."

I looked behind me, expecting a response and the rabbi was gone. I picked up the pace and kept going. In the back of my mind, I thought about where I was before meeting up with Jesus. I thought of the possibilities that could have been different if; I had never met him. I suppose I had that question to ponder for a long time; since I'm immortal. I continued forward until the terrain changed and I caught the smell of water. Judas followed the mighty Nile River, living on the fringe of settlements. While in contact with people, he would always wear a covering to help hide his face. The cycles of the moon were ever present just as the presence of the dark one watching him. He killed many along the Nile and made dedications to his dark master. This life continued and Judas learned the Egyptian language and writings.

He changed his name many times as he moved about and learned different trades. Roman outpost dotted its way throughout Egypt and they were one of the despised things he had to deal with. He did manage to kill many Roman soldiers as the beast, but it also drew some unwanted attention not only from the Roman army, but the dark master also wasn't too happy. After a night of killing and the change back to human was complete, he found refuse and went to sleep. Judas hears a voice and sees a familiar face. He says," Stop tormenting me this way Satan by appearing as Jesus." "Look upon my hands and feet. Do you not see the mark of the nails? Judas it is never too late to ask for forgiveness." Said the Rabbi. Judas said, "You are wasting your time my rabbi. How can the great Creator forgive me, when I cannot forgive myself for what I've done to you? It's too late and for what it's worth my rabbi, I am sorry for being selfish."

Then I woke up and was alone, so I thought. Another figure was standing at my feet and said," Good morning, Judas. you've really embraced this new life, haven't you?" Judas said, "I knew that it wasn't Jesus, it was you." Satan replied by saying," Nope, he came by to see if you are committed to this new lifestyle. You surprised me and I warned you once before about the Romans. Do you think you can single-handedly take on the whole Roman empire? Leave Rome to me. Rome will be a footnote in history because they have forgotten my price. Now, "Do as your told and follow the Nile." Judas continued to follow the Nile and began thinking about how he can rebel against his new master. He took on the trade of a stone cutter. He was a natural with the hammer and chisel and was quickly moved to do more ornate and precision types of work.

He was placed in the temple to make carvings and Egyptian writings on the walls. He began asking questions about a reoccurring character on the temple walls. The Egyptians called the character Anpu (Anubis) a creature of the underworld and bringer of death. Judas knew he could use this in a unique way. He continued working and gaining the acceptance of the Egyptian scribes. One day, he drew the figure of Anubis in an area out of plain view. He did this purposely to avoid detection. He wrote that Anubis is Ra's biggest disappointment. Judas wasn't talking about the Egyptian's gods at all. He is hoping that this message will be understood in a much later time. As he moved to various locations, he would repeat the same message again. It didn't go unnoticed and there would be wrath. As the time grew close for the next full moon, Judas would distance himself from the main population. He began to seek those travelling to sell their goods. He found such a target and hid before the change took place.

A group of men dressed in Arabic tunics are sitting around a fire talking to each other. This is the last night that they will see. The beast lunges from the brush and grabs one of the men and drags him into the jungle. The man screams briefly until the beast rips out his throat with his powerful jaws. He doesn't begin to feed on the man because, he knows the others are waiting for him to strike again. The men scramble to get their swords and clubs to do battle with an unknown killer. The beast rushes the men and takes another, killing the man as he drops him at the edge of the camp. The beast felt the tip of a sword pierce his flesh but, it only made him angry. One by one the men are killed, and the beast can eat without being interrupted. He gorges himself until his hunger is satiated and has become drunk from the blood of the men. The beast said in a gravelly," Is this what you want master? While the beast aligns the corpses in the five points of morning star, he stops and yells, "Is this what you want? The defiant beast then drew the star while urinating. The beast laughs

CHAPTER 3

1187 JERUSALEM FALLS

And howls. The howl was short lived, something unseen hit the beast so hard that the beast is knocked unconscious.

He is not aware that centuries have flown right by him, as his body is hurled through a rip in time. The beast awakens as the abrupt stop occurs and finds himself at edge of a war-torn camp of warriors, of a stranger dress of clothing. The beast found refuge and hid until daylight. As the change from beast to human takes its course; the smell of death is in the air. I am naked, cold and must find some clothing. I am back in civilization again; the surroundings look vaguely familiar. A distant memory flashes in my mind, and I now recognize where I am. I am back outside the walls of Jerusalem. I smell the stench of death that waifs with the desert wind. I manage to find some clothing, a dead man wearing a white tunic with a red cross emblazoned on it.

The dead man was also wearing a strange metal like cloth under the white tunic. I quickly disrobed the rotting corpse and retrieved the sword from the clutches of the hand of a corpse. I had to find a way into the city gate, as I surveyed my surroundings, an arrow pierced my side. The dark master had thrown me into the midst of a battle. I continued to make my way to where the city gate is, a volley of arrows continued to riddle my body with holes. A voice from the walled city speaks in an unknown language, and a volley of arrows from the city wall fly through the air towards those that look to kill me. I managed to make it to the entrance of the gate, and the gate was opened to me, men wearing the same white tunics quickly drag me inside and close the gate. I had lost a lot of blood, and my body was carrying many arrows.

I didn't understand the men's language as they hurriedly carried me to a structure. I could hear the moans of dying men around me before I lost consciousness. While I was sleeping or in some state half awake, the dark master came to me. He said, Well Judas or Ramses whatever name you want to use, by now you've found yourself back in your beloved walls of Jerusalem. You didn't think I would notice what you were drawing on the walls in Egypt. Again, the walls of Jerusalem are against a warring army but it's not the Roman empire. The faction waiting to storm the city is led by Saladin, the leader of the horde that commands the Ottoman Empire.

You're amid a holy war that Jerusalem cannot win. So, if you continue to defy me? Let's see how these crusaders accept a monster in their midst." Before I could voice words of defiance, I was awakened by the pain as arrows were being pulled from my body. My ears began to soak in the strange language being spoken. Men were gathering around me and saying," Does anyone recognize this man as one of our own? "I could hear other voices saying, "He does look familiar but I'm not certain. We need to question this man; he could be a spy. Another voice said," If he's a spy, why did the enemy try to kill him? From the looks of his wounds, he may not make it anyway."

I began speaking to the men in the language that I had not spoken, since I was in Jerusalem last. I heard one of the men say, "He's speaking in Aramaic, and saying death to the unbelievers." I'm very weak yet, I can sense my body repairing itself from within. I began to pretend to go in and out of consciousness. It would be very unnerving to the men around me, if I got up from my presumed death bed as if nothing happened. One of the men brought me a dipper of water and I drank it down as if it would be my last drink. I lay there listening to the men, trying to form the words in my mind before attempting to mimic their way of speech. Then from somewhere deep in my mind I blurt out,"

Don't they know that the Quran is the writings of some mad man that had fallen prey to the dependency to opium far too long?"

The men began to laugh and one man said," He must be one of us. No follower of Allah would speak such a blasphemous phrase." Another man; someone of upper rank said," Place this man under guard until we can determine his identity. Right know we must deal will the horde of Saladin and hold Jerusalem if we have breath to fight my fellow crusaders of the Holy cross." A man with a sword pointed at me and told me to walk into another room. I sat down on a small chair and the man with sword ask me where I am from. I told him that I am from Jerusalem and that was stripped of my clothes by Saladin's men and was told to run. I said," I must have been used for target practice, a few arrows went in me and that's when I saw the body of one your fallen men.

I played dead until I was able to remove the clothes from one your dead. I was struck a few more times trying to get to the city gate. I could be a lot more useful to you if you get me some food and dressing for my wounds." I instinctively knew that their leader was listening from the doorway. He walked in and said, "I'll send for the physician and as for food, we are rationing provisions because Saladin is trying to starve us out so that we'll be weaken for the invasion." I said, "Saladin has us at a disadvantage, he has many men with archers and swordsmen to spare. Jerusalem has but one advantage, it has a wall. The enemy will have to breach the gate and the wall to defeat us. As I was talking to the crusader, I felt the indications in my jaw that a full moon would be occurring tonight. I didn't want these men to face another monster inside the city walls, while the evil empire of a false god is on the outside of the Holy city.

An idea came to me… I asked the leader to call for the high priest and the leader of the crusaders, he asked me why? I told him that it involves the redemption of their very souls. I looked at him directly, eye to eye and the leader told another of his sentry's to fetch the rabbi and to be quick about it. I was served some bread and water and by now my wounds had all but disappeared by now. A physician came in to tend to me and told the leader that my wounds weren't life threatening. The leader called the sentry that had brought me in and said, "Where are the arrow marks that were on this man's legs? The sentry's face was that of shock and he pulled his sword. The sentry said, "What manner of sorcery is this? Who or what are you? I said, "Do you believe in the God of Abraham and the story of Lot? Now thrust your sword through me as you would one of Saladin's men." The sentry thrust his sword deep into my ribs and quickly withdrew it. The priest and another sentry came into the room. I raised my tunic as the men watched my wound heal before their eyes.

I told them that I have a short amount of time before the horde of the false god is upon the city. I asked that you send for a priest to witness this and you all need to ask the Lord for forgiveness. You'll need to release me from the city because I intend on sending as many of Saladin's men and Saladin himself to hell. You must hurry and get me to the gate and quickly close it behind me. The angel of death is about to descend upon the land, The leader asked me my name and I told him, "I'm the spiller of blood and the thing that nightmares are made of. So, hurry and get me to the gate." The men grabbed me and hastened me to the city gate and as the large door opened, I ran as far as I could straight into the oncoming armed men of Saladin. I was changing into the beast as arrows was piercing into my body. The beast didn't slow down, tearing riders from their horses backs, shredding flesh from men's bones and eating of it, as the beast cut a wide path of death deep into Saladin's attacking force.

Several hundred or so of Saladin's men died at clawed hands of the beast that night. Despite my effort to try spare Jerusalem, it fell at the hands of Saladin's horde. The next thing I remember was waking up and hearing a familiar voice. "Well Judas or whatever you call yourself no did you think you could save Jerusalem by taking on the whole advancing forces of Saladin, in hopes that God would somehow forgive you. As I lay on the desert sand, trying to focus my eyes on the figure that was talking to me, I stood up and looked around me before I made a reply. I could see the results of what the beast had done the night before as well as the futile efforts of the crusaders. There were dead bodies scattered about as far as I could see. I know who the figure is, the bringer of my torment. For now, I won't acknowledge his name. The figure dressed in attire of the heathen empire said," I see you are surveying some your handy work from last night."

I replied by saying, "I see you are dressed like the heathens that worship a false god." I could see the expression on the figure's face change into absolute rage. The figure said," I am your god! I brought you back from the grave. "The figure hesitated for a moment and said, "So, I did put you in a no-win situation and instead of killing the crusaders, you killed Saladin's men. Did you know that the crusaders themselves killed people because they didn't believe in God. Instead of trying to convert them, they killed them." I said, "I bet that Saladin and his men are just as guilty of killing Christians." The figure said, "An idea is like a plant, as the plant grows the roots spread. In the case of the ottoman empire or Islamic faith, it is an ideology. It is deeply rooted in the Arabic race." I asked the figure, "Who do you believe in?" The figure grabbed me by my throat and replied, "I believe in myself of course and until you start realizing whom you are dealing with, you will continue finding yourself in precarious situations. I think it is time for the beast to evolve, to blend into his next killing environs."

As my tormentor disappeared, I was hurdling through to what appears to be some sort of tunnel. I could hear my tormentor laughing and saying, "When you pay homage to me? Be respectful or you'll find your way back in hell." The tunnel ends and he is in a strange land, a lush green land, not the familiar smell of the desert conditions that he's accustomed to. This time he didn't land here naked as a newborn. He's dressed in a different manner of clothing, not a tunic or sandals. He has on clothing that covers his legs separately and his feet are completely cover in some type of animal skin. One thing is for sure, he's extremely hungry. H has got to find some food. he began walking, sniffing the wind, listening and scanning the unfamiliar land that is alien to him. As He crossed this open field, and could see there was movement a great distance away.

He followed his instincts toward the movement in hopes of finding food. The wind changed direction and was blowing towards him, it had a familiar smell to death. He quickly became aware to what he was walking into, I could see men and horses engaging in battle. He decided to use a much less obvious approach, he took to the forest edges. He didn't want to draw attention to himself because, he had no way of knowing the difference between friend or foe. All he knew was that he was starving and thirsty. he continued forward and his keen sense of smell caught the smell of water nearby. He followed his nose cautiously he could feel he was being stalked from a distance. He continued slowly until he made his way to the edge of a river and bent down to cup water with his hand. During this time, I could hear movement behind me.

A man's voice said, "Bonjour monsieur." My mind was reeling and somehow, I understood what this person was saying. I slowly turned and saw a lone archer pointing a drawn bow at me. I replied, "Bonjour, are we losing or winning against our enemies?" The archer then said, "Where did you come from?" I told the archer that I'm a mere traveler and lost everything I owned after I was robbed during the night. I stood up and turned around, facing the archer. I'm letting him see that I was completely unarmed. The archer lowered his arrow and un-drew his bow.

CHAPTER 4

1430 DAVID LE STONE

The archer then said," My name is Andre St. Claire, what is your name traveler?" Without hesitation I replied," You may call me David Le Stone." The archer chuckles and said, "David you need a sling to help me slay the English." I told him a sword would be better but considering the circumstances, I would have to hurl a stone by hand. The archer said, "Come with me David Le Stone, you must be hungry from your journey. I am out on a scouting expedition and seeking men to help fight back the English that are trying to take Orleans." I followed Andre and hoping that we would happen upon a meal. My stomach is empty, and body is like a fire in need of wood to burn. Andre leads me cautiously through a forest and I'm worried if there will be a full moon tonight. I haven't felt the usual signs yet…. the jaw pain, body aches and heightened senses. I'm only feeling extremely hungry. I caught a whiff of something burning. Andre turned to me and said, "We could be in enemy territory, be on the lookout.

We made our way to the edge of a clearing, to what appears to be some resemblance to a small farming village. By the looks of it, we're too late. The primitive homes were now just smoldering heaps of charred remnants of someone's home. We decided to stay in the safety of the forest and slowly circle the village to see the enemy is present. I don't know what the enemy looks like and I'm watching Andre's actions as well as my surroundings. We don't need anyone trying to pull a sneak attack from behind. Andre stops and motions for me to crouch down. I can see movement by men and I figured out who the enemy was. The enemy was wearing some type of metal clothing that had a red square with some gold images on it. I saw the enemy run his sword through a defenseless villager. I slowly made my way closer to Andre and in a muffled voice, "I need a sword if I'm to help you fight the enemy." Andre said," Hold on David, let's wait and see how many English are left. If there are just a few of them, we can get close enough, find some extra weapons and take out the few English before they can join up with the forces in Orleans."

My sensitive hearing caught sounds of horses coming our way. I told Andre to lay down and pretend that he is dead. Andre asked me, "Why! David?" I told him to trust me and lie perfectly still and wait. I lay there waiting as the horses drew closer, thinking about what I'm going to do once they get here. I heard one of the men on the horse say, "Be on the watch out for villagers hiding in the forest edges." Another voice in the group announced, "There are two laying on the ground over there." I could her the horses stop walking and the sound of two men dismounting from their horses. I could hear the sound of steel as it was being drawn.

I wait for the right moment until they get closer, with every foot fall sound my muscles tense up. Just as the English warrior is about to thrust his sword into my back, I turn on my side as his sword thrust into the dirt. I grabbed his sword and kicked him in the chest. I thrust the sword into the English warrior and spun around to counter the attack of the other. He too fell from my newly acquired sword. Andre had fired an arrow into one of the men on horseback and dropped him to the ground. Only the lone rider remained, he made a fatal mistake. He charged at me with sword in hand in means to run me over by horse I stood still and waited for him. Just as the horse was about to run through me, I quickly leaped to the side and as the rider turned to come at me again, Andre's arrow found its mark into the skull of the now dead English warrior.

Andre said," Where did you learn to fight like that?" I simply told him that I was going on instinct. Andre replied," Instinct my French ass, you just don't wake up one morning and suddenly have those type of fighting skills." I told him that my grandfather was a expert swordsman and taught me those skills as I was growing up. I began to spin a yarn that my grandfather had gone into hiding because there were men who put a price on his head. Andre asked me what my grandfather do, to have a bounty put on his head. I simply told him that my grandfather never told me what he did after all the badgering. I changed the subject by coming up with a plan. I told Andre that we could put the English armor on, put the bodies of the dead men on the horses and ride down to the village.

Andre said, "Are you insane? What do you think will happen once the other English fighters find out we're not English?" I told him, "We kill them of course and if there is any Frenchmen left in the village, we recruit them into this ruse and make our way to Orleans." Andre says, "That sounds so crazy, that it just might work if we're not killed by our own countrymen." I told him that there is that risk of course but the element of surprise just worked for us, didn't it?" Andre said, "Now there is something wrong here. You told me that you were robbed of all your possessions correct, but you were able to best those men with your skills?"

I told him that by not carrying a sword, the robbers didn't feel I was threat to them, so I just gave up what I had to them. Andre asked me what did they take, and I told him a few gold coins and some dried meat. I said, "Speaking of food, I won't be in prime fighting condition until I can get some food in me." We then proceeded to change clothing with the dead English warriors, tied the two dead warriors to their horses and we headed towards the village. The horses were frightened of me, so I gave them a reassuring rub on their necks while looking them in the eye. They knew that they could be food for the beast. My stomach was screaming for something to eat and could smell faint remnants of cooked food.

We rode slowly towards the English warriors, and I was looking all around me, making sure, that we wouldn't be attacked by some hidden

French villager. As we grew closer to the English, one of the English on horseback was saying something. I didn't understand him at first until my mind unraveled the language. I understood what the English warrior was saying, he was saying that we should hurry to join them. I told Andre to follow my lead, there was only five of the English and we can take them. Before I could dig my heels into the sides of the horse, the horse went into a full gallop. The reins in one hand and the other clasp around the sword waiting to get closer to my first target. Just as I was within striking distance to draw my sword, everything just stopped. It was like all motion was frozen in time. Out of the corner of my eye, I could see a figure walking up to my right.

Suddenly my body was unlocked from this frozen motion while all else around remained frozen still. I knew who the figure was it was not by recognition but by the figure's actions. The figure dressed in that of an English warrior said, "Well hello Judas, I mean David Le Stone. It appears you and your new- found friend are about to do the English warriors some bodily damage? Am I right?" I said," Well, I was about to send this man to his maker until, you showed up. What have I done this time to piss you off; dark lord?" The dark one said," First, this visit isn't because I'm pissed off, I've dropped in to see how you like your new surroundings? You've adapted well and I am willing to let you stay for a while. It depends if you do as I asked in the very beginning? Remember who brought you from the desert sand, gave you immortality and powers no mortal man possesses." I replied," Yes, you're the one that turned me into an animal during every full moon. I am grateful for that gift."

The dark one's face changed into a different face of pure evil and unbridled rage. A force pushed me from the back the horse and onto the ground. The dark one said," You are to stay clear of the warrior maiden. Do you understand?" I climbed back on the horse to deliver my retort and the dark one was gone. Everything was back in motion, I drew my sword and thrust it deep into the throat of the surprised Englishman. Andre was battling with another and two more on foot were rushing towards me. I jumped from the horse and met them head on. Only one of them was able to stab me with his sword, he and his comrade didn't live too long. Andre rode his horse over to me and by this time, some of the villagers had figured out what was going on.

Andre called out to the villagers in French saying, "To every abled bodied man, to come out and listen to US." Some leery village men approached us and began to ask questions. Andre began telling the men that I had hatched this plan in order to get close to the English to kill them. I told them that we needed weapons and I explained to them that we wouldn't have to wear the English garments until we can use them to get inside the city walls of Orleans. I said, "The English has caused you much hardship and brought death to your homes. We are weary and hungry from battle could you spare some food and drink for us?"

An injured man came forward and said, "We will give you food and water but, we cannot spare any men to help you in your fight. What men we have left are farmers, not warriors. We just want to be left alone. Our king doesn't care about his people so, why should we care about him. We are aware that more English will come, and we would rather die here at our homes than to fight to defend the king's fortress. It is a noble thing that you and your friend are doing, you have nothing to lose but your lives. Me and my kinsmen have everything to lose. We have toiled our whole lives here and this is all that we know. We have each other to count and no one else."

I said," Take the swords that we acquired from the English to defend yourselves in payment and we have two extra horses that we do not need. "A young boy stepped forward and took the reins of the horses while an older man came forth and took the swords. The leader of the villager's said, "You can come with us to eat and break bread with us under one condition, you must change your clothing. Those that lost their loved ones to the English today, doesn't need to look upon you dressed as you are." We agreed to abide by his wishes, we gathered our clothes that were tied to saddles. The leader motioned for us to follow him, he took us to a home and told us the woman inside will show you where you can change.

I knocked on the wooden door and woman came to the door. I could see the anguish on her face and could tell that she had lost someone today. The villager leader pulled her to the side and explained to her what our purpose of this visit. After he finished, she quickly ran over to us and thanked us for killing English marauders that had slain her husband and her son. She pointed to a room for us to change and she would fix us some food. Andre and I went into the room and while changing, I told Andre in muffled voice, that we can't just eat and leave these people. I said, "We need to at least offer our services to help bury the dead."

Andre said, "I wished I could agree with you, I fear there will be more English coming this way. We need to get the food, the water and go. We are just strangers that happen to be passing through. Even though we took out the English, we're not wanted here." I had to turn my injured side away from Andre, I didn't need for him to see the injury slowly heal itself before his eyes, he wouldn't understand. As I pulled on my clothing I said, "I suppose you are right. I do agree with what their leader said that their land is all they have beside their families and we have nothing to give up but our lives. So yes, we don't need to impose upon these people no more than we must."

After we had tied our belts back on, thrust our swords back into their scabbards then, walked back into the room where the woman and village leader were waiting. We could see that food and a bottle of wine was on the table before us. Andre said, "We are indeed grateful for the food and drink, but we should be going. If you can spare a days' worth of food for us, we'll be on our way?" The woman said, "Please sit and eat. You've bought us more time than we would've had by killing the English murderers. My son is probably dead because he left our village to fight the English. You've met my husband and heard his view about decisions. After witnessing today's carnage, there's no running away from death."

In my mind I was back at the table with my teacher. I picked up a piece of bread from the table and broke it and said, "May the one who died on the cross keep you all safe, amen." Andre said," I didn't know you were a religious man as well as a skilled swordsman David le Stone?" I said, "How could you know? We met today for the first time." We ate bread, cheese, dried meat and drank some wine. We also talked about how they could set up a sentry to signal the village before it's attacked again. The village leader simply told us that they didn't have the manpower to have such. He said," We'll put the swords to effective use when they come."

The leader's wife had given us bag with food in it and a bottle wine. I told them that we were grateful as we got up from the table. The leader walked with us to our newly acquired horses. As I was about to tie our English clothes onto the horse, the village leader said," Leave that with me, it will only make you a target. Besides with your skills, there are other English out there you can kill and take their garments." I got on my horse and as Andre and I rode off, the village leader yelled, "Viva le France!" We answered back Viva le France. Neither of us struck up any conversation as we rode back into the forest. Sitting at that table struck a chord deep into what's left of my soul.

If Andre really knew who or what was riding with him, he would lose his mind. I find it hard sometimes to keep it all together myself. To Andre I'm David le Stone, the killer of the giant… After we had been riding a good distance, Andre turned to me and said he had to relieve himself. I stopped and got off to stretch my legs and took a leak myself. Andre climbed back onto his horse and said, "David, the village leader's words really made me think about what I'm doing. The king doesn't give a damn about me as a person. If wasn't for the sake of revenge, I'm just a tool to him." I said, "What would you be doing if this messed up situation wasn't happening?"

Andre said," I would probably be out hunting food for my family if they were still alive. The English came through my village and killed everyone while, I was out looking for food. I've been following their movements and I know where the English are going. I know I can't be a one-man crusader against the English and I didn't mean to drag you into this." I said, "When you happened upon me, I was a man without anything. I now have a horse, a sword, food in my stomach and a new friend. Now stop trying to figure out the workings of life and take it as it comes. That means we must take it head on. You weren't born feet first, were you?"

Andre began laughing and said," You are a sage as well, monsieur le Stone. You speak as someone much older than your appearance. "I told him that I grew up around adults and wasn't exposed to children. "You could say I was forced to grow up fast. My childhood got bypassed. Let's change the subject and focus on the future. For instance, how far is it to this place called Orleans anyway?" Andre told me that was about a two-day ride, to his best guess. I said," Judging by where the sun is in the sky we better find somewhere to camp and not draw attention. I don't want some English soldier running me through in my sleep.

Let's pick a spot and scout a wide circle around us. We have about two hours before sun goes down." Andre said," Monsieur le Stone, you have put a lot of thought into this haven't you?" I replied by saying, "We could be the hunted instead of the hunters and try our best to stay several steps ahead of the hunters. You pick us out a spot and I will scout it out. Just remember, no ravines and we must have an escape route." As I watched Andre go deeper into the forest on my left, I began to focus on my surroundings and use my senses as I make a large circle, in relation to where Andre would be. As I continued to circle around, my ears caught the sound of voices and it wasn't French.

I worked my way back to find Andre and he was piling up sticks for a fire. I got up close to him and said, "We have company, and they don't speak French." I pointed to the direction to where I heard the men talking and told Andre that we need to find another camp site. Andre got back on his horse, and we went in the opposite direction of the enemy camp. Andre said, "It's a good thing you scouted out the area. We could be victims of a surprise attack. What is puzzling me is, how could you hear them and not risk them hearing your horse. "I told him that I heard something, I got off my horse and slowly made my way closer to the noise. I didn't need to get any closer to see them, it was voices of many men.

I said," I'm too tired to fight off more than ten men at a time right now. Let's go and find somewhere to catch some much-needed rest." The sun was sinking lower in the sky and the shadows of the forest were growing larger. I could see in the dark with no trouble but, I didn't need to show my new friend this ability. It is going to be a cloudy night; I could see the stars as they peep through the passing clouds overhead. I'm reluctant to be a friend with Andre because, he'll usually wind up dead simply by association. Andre said, "David, how do you know where we're going?" I told him to be quiet and just follow close behind me. As I was drowning out the noises of the horse's footsteps, I was listening, sampling smells as the gentle wind of the night is passing through. My sensitive nose caught a whiff of something being cooked the same time my finely tuned hearing could hear voices traveling with the wind.

The wind was coming from my right and I can't make out the voices whether it's French or English. All I know it's extremely risky in thinking it's friendlies plus my body needs rest and it needs food. I stopped walking and Andre ran into my horse. Andre said, "Why did you stop so sudden? I almost stuck my head in your horse's ass." I giggled a little and told him that let's stop for a moment, eat something and rest for a little while. We just can't build a fire because it would draw attention. Andre drew from his horse the bread, dried meat, and a bottle of wine that we got from the kind people at the village. Andre handed me some bread and a piece of dried meat as he pulled the cork from the wine bottle. Andre took a drink from the wine bottle and said, "Eat, drink and be merry because tomorrow we may die." I asked him where did he get that quote from? He said that it's somewhere in the Bible.

He then said," You've read the Bible, haven't you? I replied, "Maybe a few pages." Actually, I don't know what he is talking about. I told him that we must eat and have a few slogs of wine, we must be on our way. I said, "We are not safe here." Andre took one last swallow of wine and put it back in the pack on his horse. I took a piece of dried meat and chewed on it; my stomach was still hungry. I gently tug on the horse's bridle and we continued walking in the forest. I had no idea of where I was in this strange land. It had no semblance to the desert; the smells and the sounds of night are different here. My vision has fully adjusted to the limited light by the crescent moon as clouds pass in front of the sky light.

Andre breaks my concentration by saying," How much more shall we travel? I'm getting tired." I told him to be quiet and just trust me. We continued walking and I began to sniff the change as a light breeze pushed through the forest. I caught the scent of an open pasture and we do not want to be caught in the open. I stopped walking and tied my horse to the nearest tree, and I told Andre to do the same. Andre speaking in a muffled voice said," David is this our resting spot?" I told Andre to stay here while I scout around, sit here quietly, and don't build a fire. I headed to my right in a straight line, carefully listening and watching all around me. I saw some movement up ahead and walked towards it. The movement became clear to me, it is a large canine.

I continued to walk forward towards it until the canine stopped and sat down on its haunches. As a drew ever closer to the animal, I could see that it was much larger than a dog and longer hair than a hyena. I'd gotten within an arm's length from the animal and I crouched down to be at the same eye level with the canine. I whispered in a faint voice, "Do you have something that you wish to say?" The large canine said," I'm glad that you aren't hunting me and there's no need to whisper, there aren't any humans around close enough to hear us speak." I asked the canine, "What type of canine, are you? You are larger than a dog and have more hair than a hyena."

The large canine replied by saying," I am a wolf, and I was the top predator in the forest until you showed up. You are the first of your kind and you take on the traits of my kind when the moon is full." I asked the wolf; did he have a name? The wolf replied, "I been called a sheep, cow, horse killer but, to my pack I'm known as King." I said, "My human friend isn't in any danger from your pack, is he?" King lets out a yelp and tells me they are on their way here to me and no, your friend and the horses will not be harmed." I sat down on the ground and began asking King about locations of the English. All the while I could hear that moment as other wolves were approaching from all directions. It wasn't but for a moment, until I was surrounded by the whole pack. As King finished telling me what he about the English, King asked his pack members about any new developments with the English locations?

Then all at once, here came a flood of questions about me. Their main question was their pack on my menu? I assured them that they are my allies and would share with them my kills. King told the pack that my human friend and horses are off limits. I told them to be in my shadow, when the moon is full and my friend has no idea of what I truly am. I told them that I would must steer away from my human friend while the moon is full because the beast looks upon humans as food, any human. I asked King did he know when the next full moon will be because, I just arrived in their time as of today. King tilted his head and said that the next full moon would be in 2 nights and asked what did I mean in his time? I told him that I would explain to him later but now I need to get back to camp because my new friend is afraid and wondering where I am.

I told them all that If I had enough food with me back at the camp, I would gladly share. I then told them if I happen upon a deer and kill it, I would leave their share for them for their loyalty. I also promise them a lion's share in 2 nights. I got up and told King and his pack that I wish them luck on tonight's hunt. I began walking back towards where Andre is and once, I got close enough to see him, he was a bundle of nerves. He has his bow with an arrow loaded. I got within talking distance and told him to relax. Andre said," I was beginning to think that you had either gotten lost or met up with our friends the English." I told him that I did some scouting, know where the English is, and it is safe to sleep here tonight. Andre said, "Can I build a fire?" I told him that it's too risky, but we need to get some rest because I'm tired.

I double checked to see if the horse is securely tied and patted them on the neck to give them some assurance of their safety. I took a rolled packed from the horse, placed it on the ground and laid my tired body down. Before I went to sleep, I thought about the meeting I had with King and his pack of wolves. Animals especially the canines, automatically understand me and I can relate to them on their level. I don't think humanity is ready to accept that I am in their midst.

I drifted off to sleep and found myself face to face with my tormentor.

My dark master said," Well, I see you've made new allies with the wolves I see. Are you planning to use their information and slaughter the English in two nights from now?" I said, "I know what I would like to do but, since I'm your property, what do you have in mind?" The dark master said," Now that's what I like to hear. It's good that you are coming around to my way of doing things, you are progressing

Judas, I mean David Le Stone. So, let's say you tell your friend to go ahead of you and you'll see him in two days. If he resists leaving tell him that you intend of blending with the English and looking for their weakness. Tell him that your intentions are to kill their leader and to break up their ranks from the inside. And if Andre doesn't buy it, use your power of suggestion." I asked the dark master what he's talking about? The dark master told me to make direct eye contact and force your will upon him, tell him what he is to do and that's that. Oh yes, I almost forgot, don't forget to pay homage to me in a way that the English will notice and terrify them. You know, use your imagination and it will show itself."

He disappeared and my mind drifted back to my fleeting time with Kara. Time slips away and I'm awakened by Andre. I sit up and my body is covered by the morning mist. A fog drifts through the forest, and I tell Andre that we need to move and use the fog as a cover to hide us. Andre said," Hold on for a minute. Let's have something to eat and some wine before we head out. My stomach is empty." I agreed and told him that let's get some food and drink some wine but we need not tarry here too long. There is an English encampment to the right of us, that I saw as I went scouting. Andre asked, "How many men do you suppose there are camped?" I told him by judging the size of the camp, there could be at least 75 to 100 men. Andre then asked me what my plan is. I took this opportunity to try and force my will upon him.

I said, "Andre, look at me and I'll tell you what the plan is." Andre was staring blankly at me and I proceeded to layout the plan. I told him to go ahead of me and that I am going to go amongst the English, dressed as they are and kill their leader and break up their ranks. I told Andre that once he gets in company of the French, tell them what I'm doing. "I know I can count on you because you are my friend, and you can make things happen." I smacked Andre on the shoulder and broke eye contact with him. Andre said, "So, you are going to take on the whole English camp by yourself, somehow, I know you can do it. I just don't understand how. I guess I'll be seeing you in two days old friend." I said "How can we be old friends since we only met yesterday?" We laughed, shook hands and I gave Andre the extra horse to take with him, since I'll be travelling light.

I aimed Andre in the direction he should go, and I headed towards the English camp. As the horse neared a clearing, I stopped and changed into my English garb, make sure, that I use an English sword at my side. I bundled up the peasant sword with my peasant clothes, jumped on the horse and was riding right into the enemy's territory. As the horse was making steady strides, an idea came to me. I'll wait for one of them to start a conversation and make small talk, may even get the chance to practice forcing my will upon someone. As my horse got closer to a group of English fighters, three English swordsmen approached me and one of them ask me. "Who is your King, answer incorrectly and we'll kill you right here." A voice in my head said," King Henry the sixth." I told the men in their dialect, "king Henry the sixth of course."

CHAPTER 5

1430 JONAS CAIN

The men removed their hands from their swords and welcomed me to join them. I got down from my horse and one of the men asked me, what happened to the other men that were with me? I told them I went out on a hunt for food, and I got lost, I've been riding for two nights. One of the men stops walking and turns to me and said," I think you're a lying spy for the French." I let go of my horse's bridle, drew my sword and lobed off the head of the Englishman. The other two men were astonished at the rate of speed that it happened before they could blink. One of the men with his hand on his sword said, "Why did you kill one of your own? "I replied by saying, "the next one that calls me a liar shall meet the same fate."

One of the two remaining men asked me my name. Without a thought I said, my name is Jonas... Jonas Cain. One of the Englishmen said, "Well Jonas Cain, you are a very skilled swordsman, and a man of your skills needs to meet our commander. "I followed the men through the English encampment, tugging my horse behind me. I could feel my steed's breath upon my hand, he was giving me a signal. I stopped walking and looked back at my horse. Another Englishman was trying to tug at my belongings. I said," There are two things I hate, a liar and a thief." One of the men that were walking beside me told the would-be thief to leave me be or meet the fate of a man that called Jonas Cain a liar. The thief drew his sword and said, "You killed my friend in cold blood and I say you're a spy," as he snatched my belongings from the horse. All that I owned unfurled on the ground, the peasant sword, a bottle of wine, dried meat and cheese.

By this time, a crowd of men had encircled me and I had to think quick. The Englishman with his drawn sword said, "Explain yourself spy." I told them I had kept the peasant sword as a trophy from the first Frenchman that I killed while in France. Does that make me a spy, how many of you have kept such trophies of war? All the while, I was slowly turning to keep a watchful eye at my back to avoid someone's sword finding its mark in my body. At the same time a commanding voice rang out, "What in the bloody hell is going on here?" I could hear behind me another sword being pulled from its scabbard. The would-be thief was in front of me and closing in, I quickly drew my sword. Without turning to face my advancing emissary, the point of my sword was aimed at my emissary to the rear.

I said, "How many will die at my sword before you realize I am, whom I say I am? The would-be thief lunged; I side stepped him as his sword wound in my emissary behind me. I picked up the peasant sword and I have a sword in each hand now. I guess the leader of the English had seen enough of his men getting bested by me. The commander yelled, "I demand that this to stop instantly, everyone put your swords away." The crowd of men had put away their swords as the would-be thief had expired, and the other Englishman was gravely wounded and probably won't see tomorrow's light judging the amount of blood loss. The commander walked up to me and asked my name and why did I kill his men? I said, "I'm Jonas Cain and I killed only two of your men, the would-be thief laying there mortally wounded the third man.

They brought it upon themselves by asserting that I was a liar and a spy, there are two things I despise, being called a liar and someone trying to steal from me." The commander said, "Relax Jonas Cain, judging by your fighting skills you weren't taught these skills by the king's army. Where did you learn the skills?" I told the commander that my grandfather was an excellent swordsman before he was forced to retire from the Spanish Armada." The commander said, "Come, let's get something to eat and I want to hear more of this. "I picked up my things, rolled them up and placed on my horse, grabbed the reins and followed the commander to his tent. Two English soldiers accompanied us to the commander's tent.

The commander told one of the soldiers to take my horse to get him water and food. The soldier pulled on the reins and the horse wouldn't move, he yanked again, and the horse refused to move. The soldier said, "Jonas Cain, your horse refuses to move, he will be well taken care of." I walked back to my horse and rubbed him on the nose and told him that water and food awaits him. The horse snorted and swished his tail and followed obediently behind the English soldier. The commander looked astonished by what he saw. The commander said, "Your horse has unwavering loyalty to you and understands you. So, if your horse trusts your actions and your words then, be it far from me not to trust one of God's creatures." As we walked into the commander's tent, I told the commander that I had saved the horse's life. I had the commander hanging on every word. I had gotten so good at spinning tales, I almost believed them myself.

The commander pointed to a chair for me to sit. The commander said, "Don't stop now, continue with this amazing story. "The commander handed me a goblet of wine and I thanked him for the hospitality. I began by telling him that a group of men that I was with were attacked by the French on horseback. We were a small detachment sent on a scouting mission and got caught in the open with the river to our backs and the riders to our front. Though I am good with a sword, the riders were using their horses as a battering ram pushing us closer to the river. A good many of my fellow men died that day and I sent a few Frenchmen to hell myself. I kept fighting and a rider kept pushing towards the edge of a considerable drop to the water. The rider got too close to the edge and we fell into the river. I was able to push myself clear of the horse or he would've fallen on me. The horse's rider didn't make it and I could see that the horse was struggling to keep his head above water. I took a risk and swam out to him, picked up his head so that he could breathe and led him to solid footing.

He no longer takes his commands in French. The commander said, "Before you tell me of your Spanish grandfather let's get something to eat and I'll tell you the plans I have for you and your rescued horse. My keen sense of hearing is pick up voices of discord against me, thinking to myself I did make a forced introduction. The commander went over to the corner of the tent and retrieved wooden bowl with dried meat, cheese and bread. I said, "It is I that should be getting you food because you saved me from having to take on the whole legion of men." The commander said, "I was watching you fight; I couldn't afford to lose any more men. It is evident that your grandfather was a fierce swordsman and has taught you well.

I only wish I had more time that you could train my men to fight as well as you Jonas Cain. In two days, we shall be at the gates of Orleans. There we will do battle with the French and their warrior maiden D 'Arc. Have you heard of this warrior maiden? "I told him that I've only heard stories but discarded them as campfire tales. The commander informed that his scouts have returned and told of such encounters. He then said," I am tasking you to bring down this warrior maiden to break the spirit of French in and around the stronghold of Orleans." I told the commander after today's performance you men would rather run me through with a sword than this warrior maiden.

The commander chuckled and said, "From what I witnessed, the men are more afraid of you than dying at the hands of the French soldiers and their warrior maiden. After we've eaten, there is still enough of daylight left to show some of my men some of your refined fighting skills except, you'll be demonstrating using wooden swords. I don't want to have to bury anymore of my men. I agreed that I would show them some basic defensive moves. I drank my fill of wine and ate heartily because my body craved fuel to burn on. My body knows what is coming in two nights from now. All my senses always begin to heighten days before the full moon. I wiped the remnants of food and wine from my mouth with my hand and waited for the commander to finish. The commander finished with his meal and wiped his mouth with a linen cloth, I guess it is an English custom

The commander said," Come now Jonas Cain, follow me to the

training area." As we left the tent the commander told one of his subordinates to gather five of the best swordsmen in the regiment and have them meet in the center of the camp. I walked along with the commander towards the center of the camp, I could hear murmurings of angry men as we passed them by. In front of us I could already see a crowd has gathered as well as I could hear many footfalls closing in behind us. We had reached the center of the camp and the commander's subordinate walked forward to us. The commander asked the subordinate," Are the five best swordsmen here? "The subordinate replied," Yes, commander!"

The commander then said, "Will the five skilled swordsmen step forward?" The five men stepped away from the circling crowd and all had their hands ready to draw their swords. The commander pointed to the swordsman on his left and told the other four to return to the surrounding circle. The commander announced to all the men watching to pay attention the skills that are going to be demonstrated and to apply the skills in battle with the French. The commander told me and my opponent to leave the swords in their scabbards, secure the scabbard the sword hilt to prevent anyone from dying during this training. I secured my sword to the scabbard with its own leather strapping, my opponent did the same. The commander as he was exiting the training area, he told us to fight each other as if we were fighting the French. The instant the commander was clear my opponent came at me full force. Each time my opponent attempted to land a deadly blow, I countered his move and stopped my advance once my opponent yielded.

The commander told the defeated opponent to return to the circle and told the next man to advance to the inner circle. I bested the first four men even as the fourth man threw dirt into my eyes, he yielded. The last man appeared older than the other four and said that the weight of the scabbard may have been a disadvantage to the other men. He went on to say that the French won't be fighting with their swords sheathed in their scabbards. The commander said," No! I cannot afford to lose one of my best soldiers." The fifth aggressor said, "You won't be losing me, you'll be losing Jonas Cain." The fifth swordsman is bigger man than I as he came at me with an unsheathed sword, I countered his attempt, and the blow shattered my scabbard, revealing the sword. I cannot allow myself to just easily defeat him as I did the four. I'll have to end this small battle with finesse. I must show these men that I'm human.

We fought hard; I wasn't going to make things easy for him either. The fifth aggressor is beginning to get winded I wasn't tired, just hungry. I slowed my advance to give the appearance that I too was tiring, and I must make it look genuine. I said to the fifth aggressor, "I don't want to have to kill you to make you stop, besides, I don't see the pleasure in killing someone's grandfather." The men in the circle were heckling the fifth aggressor saying, "Go ahead and put him down, grand papa." This made the aggressor mad and he fell right into my trap. The fifth aggressor came at me with a two handed, overhead swing. I countered his attack and as he was trying to push me in I merely relaxed my body and fell backwards, pulling my knees into my chest I was able to flip him over my head and, at the same instance I sprang up and placed the tip of my sword into my aggressor's ass before he could stand up. I asked the aggressor does he yield? The winded aggressor said," Yes, I yield Jonas Cain."

I placed my sword back on the ground and offered my hand to help the fifth aggressor to his feet. The aggressor grabbed my hand and I pulled him to his feet. The fifth aggressor said, "You are one crafty bastard Jonas Cain and I'm afraid I'm too old to learn the fancy swordsman's skills." I placed my hand on his shoulder and addressed the men by saying that my skills aren't better than theirs. I explained to them that I anticipate my moves by reading my opponent's body movements. I then told them to make their opponent angry because their raw emotions cloud their thinking and causes them to make mistakes. I said, "Commander, with all due respect can the men and I have some food and drink now?" The commander said," Yes, Jonas! You and the men have earned food and drink." The commander turned towards his tent and went on his way. The fifth aggressor approached me and stuck out his hand and said," No hard feelings Jonas, I'm Peter Swain. Follow me and we'll get something to fill our bellies." I followed Peter Swain along with a group of men to where a campfire was licking the side of a big black kettle, I could smell something that could quiet my hunger pangs. I thought to myself that these men have no idea of whom they have allowed to be amongst them. I was distracted from the thought when I got a swift slap on the back. I turned to my left and it was aggressor number two. He said," You had better watch your back, Jonas Cain.

There are a few men that would still like nothing better than to run you through with a sword for killing two of our own." I said," They better be worried about being run through by the French." Peter Swain said, "Don't pay him no mind, he's a sore loser." I told Peter that I would be sleeping with one eye open tonight. "I don't think anyone will try to sneak up on you tonight, especially with your catlike reflexes," replied Peter Swain. I said, "Even a tired cat needs to sleep." Peter assured me that no harm would come to me and told me that I'm the only man that bested him. I followed Peter to where I guess he would be resting for the night. The smell of scattered campfires is all around me and I realize that I cannot befriend Peter Swain because, in two nights the animal I become has no friends, they're just food.

I sat down on the ground within a legs length from the fire and laid down upon the cold earth. I could feel the cold sword as it pressed against my leg since it no longer had a scabbard to cradle it. I lay there with my eyes closed and listened to my surroundings. I could hear Peter to the right of me, settling down with grunts and groans along with the sounds of men talking until I succumb to sleep. I found myself in a different place wearing different clothes and hearing a different language. Just as I was getting used to my surroundings, the dark master made an appearance. "So, Judas, I mean Jonas Cain. Do you think you can obliterate the English by yourself? exclaimed the dark master. The monster you created will kill without any remorse in two nights from now plus the alliance you've made with wolf pack leader named king." The dark master laughed and said, "Your French friend knows you as David Le Stone and the English know you as Jonas Cain, aren't you making your identity difficult?"

David is the good and Jonas is the bad man. I replied. The dark master said, "I don't care what you call yourself, pay homage to me and obey me. Do you hear me Judas Iscariot?" My keen sense of hearing awakened me, I opened my eyes just in time to react. I rolled to one side with sword in hand to avoid being stabbed by one of my aggressors. The aggressor's sword plunged into the soil and I was ready for his next move. With the commotion going on, Peter Swain had walked out from his slumber. Peter asked, "What in the bloody hell is going on here?" I said, "I was almost run through in my sleep by this gentleman here. Since I'm a light sleeper, I've cheated him out of an easy kill." Peter looked at my aggressor and said, "Is that true?" The aggressor said that I had killed two of his friends and he was intending on seeking revenge. Peter then went on to say that his two friends brought their deaths upon themselves.

The rest of the camp had awakened by now and came to see what was unfolding. The commander had walked up and demanded an explanation. Before I could give an account, Peter Swain told the commander about what had happened. The commander told the aggressor that since he had awakened the whole camp, that he is to finish what he started so that the camp can go back to sleep. The aggressor came at me with a full attack as our blades met in combat. The aggressor did manage to nick my arm, I continued with this battle of wills. I had worn the aggressor down to the ground, my will is far more superior. I asked my aggressor does he yield? The aggressor replied, "You'll have to go to sleep sometime Jonas Cain?" The commander said, "Finish this Jonas, so that I can go back to sleep." I stuck the sword through the aggressor's throat and he expired. The men in the camp walked back to their respective spots to sleep.

Peter said," I'll help you take the man's body to the edge of the camp. I grabbed the man's legs as Peter took hold of the arms of the lifeless body and we made our way to the edge of the camp. I thought to myself, King, and his pack will make use of the aggressor's body. I was tired and my body needed sleep and I made it back to where I was lying and found sleep but, my mind was still at work. I found myself back among the disciples when I first met my first master. I was eating with the disciples at a table inside someone's home that had invited us to eat and have a place to lay our heads. My master had blessed the food, eaten and walked outside. I asked Peter where had our master gone? Peter replied by saying that our master goes and talks to the father in private sometimes. I eat a few more bites to get my fill, I had questions in my mind that needed answers. I slipped out the door of the home, walked around until I found my master kneeling and praying. My teacher finished the prayer and told me to approach him. The teacher said," You have questions don't you Judas? You don't know why you follow me do you?"

I answered by saying, "Rabbi, I don't know if it is my heart telling me to follow you or this voice in my head that urges me on?" The master said," It is free will my disciple. It is something that man is born with, that is imparted to you by the creator of the known and the unknown things of this world. Free will is a choice that you make to do what is right or to do wrong. Right now my disciple, there is an ongoing war that is unseen." I said, "I do not understand what you speak of this ongoing war that is hidden." The great deceiver is at work every day and every night plotting to undermine all that is good by planting deceit in impressionable minds. Currently, we are his biggest targets to overtake in his conquest."

I was awakened from the dream by the commander's subordinate yelling to get up, that French troops had sprung a surprise attack. I got up and shaken off the slumber from last night. My mind recalls that conversation with the rabbi, but now a new day has dawn, and my clothes are damp from the morning mist. Men are gathering their things and I grabbed my sword and followed my nose to where the horses are. An English soldier was trying to get my horse. My horse wasn't going anywhere, regardless of the tugging and lashing with the reins. I approached to ask the soldier why is he trying to take my horse? The English soldier said, "You can have this worthless animal, he lacks proper training." I told the soldier that the horse only has one master and that is me. I patted the horse and told him that all is well, I jumped upon his back and we headed for battle. I looked back at the soldier, and he was taking another horse.

The air was thick with dust kicked up by the advancing horde of men and horses. I craned my neck to see as far in front of me as I could, my line of sight was blocked. I and my horse tried to nudge our way to the outer edge of the wave of men and horses, our efforts are useless. We are wedged in the middle of this mass, going the same direction, at the same pace… forward. I could hear up front, the clash of the blades against shields and flesh, moving closer to that sound now as the English horseman spread out to meet the second wave of French soldiers. I got down from my horse and told my horse to run to safety, that I would find him. The horse turned and ran like his life depended on it. I sliced my way through many Frenchmen, I hope Andre isn't with this group of men. I was constantly turning and twisting my body to keep from being impaled from the back and the side, my reflexes were being tested.

I looked to the right and saw one of the English soldiers that I sparred with, wasn't lending a hand to keep the French from closing in on me. I became more aggressive and relentless, pushing my way forward with my blade. Then someone got lucky and thrust a blade into my back, I spun around and lobbed off a few heads…. two were English. I was bleeding but I had no choice but to keep on fighting, I could feel the blood flowing down the back of my leg. This just angered me more to the point, that I didn't care who was in front of me, they were going to die. I heard a bugle blow and someone yelling in French "battre en retraite", the French were withdrawing from the battle field and into the woods. A squad of English soldiers continued their pursuit of them but stopped at the woods edge.

The commander rallied the remaining men that were still in fighting condition, to pick up the men that were wounded and carry them to a hedge row of trees opposite of the woods that now hides the French. I reached to feel where the blade entered my body, it is gone like this morning's meal. My clothing is still soaked with my blood and my strength is waning. I need food and drink for today, I am still a human until the full moon controls the beast tomorrow night. I stuck two fingers in my mouth and whistled a high pitched "turreeeeet." I waited for a few minutes and watched patiently. I was looking to see from which direction my trusted horse would be coming from then, I knew where. I could hear the French yelling kill the Englishman's horse, kill him.

My horse came out from the forest with arrows sticking out from him, my friend was gravely wounded and yet he made it to the center of the battle ground before he collapsed. I ran out to him as the commander was yelling for me to come back, I did not listen. The French archers were sending volleys of arrows my way, I picked up a shield as I walked to my horse. I squatted down and told my horse that he has served me well and that I will not let him suffer on the battle ground. I gave him a hug and told him to close his eyes. The arrows had stopped for a moment, I guess the French were waiting to see what is to transpire. I raised my sword and cleaved the horse's head from its body. I retrieved my pack, stood up and yelled screamed in anger," You will all die in those woods tonight." Arrows began to fly around me but none found its mark.

One of the English soldiers said, "I suppose you are going to take on the whole French army because they shot your horse?" I said. "Take me to the commander, I have an idea." I followed behind the English soldier passing by the wounded and dying troops laid out on the ground. The English soldier took me to the commander, he too was wounded by an arrow in his leg. While the field physician was tending his wounds. I said, "Forgive me commander for this impromptu visit, but if I can borrow a moment of your time? The commander said, "If myself and my men stay in this hedgerow without proper cover, we'll all be dead before sunrise." I explained to the commander that there is no doubt that the French plan to attack us once it gets dark. I said, "We need to create a diversion. At the moment of dusk, have a couple of men to set fire to the hedge row ahead of us, to give the illusion that we are moving in that direction.

I take a few men, head in the opposite and go into the woods to flank the enemy. And in the process set some fires within the forest, currently the wind is blowing towards us. I know that it is a great gamble but, we might as well dig our graves here, commander." The commander was wincing with pain as the field physician was bandaging his leg. The commander said, "What is the plan for those that are stuck here, wounded and the dying, Jonas? I said, I've entertained such a thought but we must hurry before dark, the sun will be falling in two hours."

The commander called the sergeant at arms and told him to follow my plans to the letter. The sergeant wasn't too pleased by the plans from a subordinate, but he didn't want to die in this hedgerow. We got the men to prop up the dead as if they were waiting for an attack and covered the wounded with branches and small trees. The wounded with swords in their hand lying hidden had a better chance of surviving, than being left out in the open. Once that was accomplished, the sergeant asked what is my next strategy?

I asked the sergeant how many fighting men do we have at our disposal? The sergeant said, "About fifty or so men left that is able to fight." We need to build a bid fire away from the hedge row, and three quarters of the men will move away from the fire into the darkness so the light of the fire doesn't affect their vision. The French will storm the camp only to find no men here, except the dead and the well-hidden wounded. Theirs eyes will be affected by the glare of the fire, then the men can make their surprise entrance while a few soldiers light the hedgerows up ahead, I and a few men will flank the French under the cover of darkness. To make this work, you must tell your men to trust me and we'll live to see tomorrow. The sergeant began barking orders for the men to gather around and gave the men explicit orders and we were on the move. In the distance I could already see that the French had campfires going and men carrying torches.

Things were set into motion. Luckily, the clouds had hidden a partially full moon and my body is in preparation for tomorrow night's change. A group of men hurriedly followed me as we ran down the hedgerow that ran parallel to the forest, only to be separated by an open span of ancient farmland. My eyes are designed to this and as I was running, I was estimating what depth of the forest would the French occupy and how far back from that should we cross the open, to enter the forest. A man behind me asked, "Where are we going?" I told him no more talking and we ran across the open field into the forest. Once we got into the forest, I gathered the men close to me and told them to follow closely behind me and once we get close to the French, one group of men will go to the left of me and the other group to the right.

We moved quickly through the forest, the men behind me were

making more noise than I but, I'm not a normal man anymore. My keen sense of hearing was telling me that we are getting closer to the French and the smell of my wolf companions are in the area. The wind has changed direction, it's blowing directly in our face. I told the men to cancel the fire and split as we rushed into the French camp. It was blade against blade and many Frenchmen fell by my sword as well as my English Marauders. We dealt a crippling blow to the French and then we rushed to the aid of the remaining English soldiers at the hedge row. We met some resistance crossing the open field but, their loss was greater than mine. The English hedgerow camp was strewn with the dead and dying of English and French. My men and I joined the fray beating down the French into submission or death.

The fighting was over, captives were taken, and the commander sent a group of soldiers to scavenge what was left of the French camp. As I was wiping the blood from my blade on the clothing of a dead Frenchman, the commander called to me. I walked over to him and said," Yes, my commander of what service may I do for you?" The commander said, "Jonas, you aren't new to this art of battle, are you?"" What do you mean, my commander? I replied. The commander said, "The average soldier wouldn't know how to dream up a plan in such short notice unless he isn't a mere soldier. Just who are you, Jonas Cain?" I said, "I've always had this gift to think on my feet or I could have been someone before, such as a Roman general."

The commander laughed and said," Jonas Cain, since you've brought us victory tonight. You shall eat and drink with me once my men have returned with the spoils of war that we've taken from the French." I told him that it would be an honor. I walked around checking the dead to find a replacement for my sword. An English soldier saw me and said, "Just take his sword and scabbard. His fighting days are over." I merely nodded my head to his suggestion and relieved the dead man of his weapon. My keen hearing overheard someone saying, "What shall we do with the prisoners? Shall me make sport of them?" An idea came to mind and it would keep my dark master off my back. I walked over to where the men had gathered and stepped forward.

I said, "Do you think that the French keep prisoners? They are mere soldiers such as we and have no royal status. They crossed the field to kill us and since I'm not about to share any of my food or drink with them, I think they should be sent to Hell. How do my brothers in arms feel about that?" The English soldiers were encircled around me and the prisoners, their feelings of anger had been fueled by my rousing. A voice from the crowd said, "They follow the warrior witch, chop off their heads and send them to their master." The prisoners were already on the knees, hands bound behind their backs, at least a dozen men. I stopped in front of the first prisoner and said," Any last words before I send you to your master?" The Frenchman spat upon my shoe and I severed his head from his body. I picked up the Frenchman's head and said, "I guess he wasn't one for talking." I tossed his head into the fire.

The English soldiers were under my spell and captivated by my actions. Many of the Frenchmen were insulting me in French before I delivered sentence until I got to the last man. The French soldier declared that the warrior maiden is not a witch, but gets instruction from God. I said, Only the king and the priest at the king's church have conversations with God, so what you are saying is blasphemy." I raised my hands and asked the crowd of English soldiers," What do we do with blasphemers?" The crowd answers, "Chop off his head." I lobbed off the French soldier's head, stuck my sword into the Frenchman's eye socket and tossed his head into the fire.

Since I already had the crowd fired up, I said, Let's make a bigger fire for these blasphemers, toss on their worthless bodies, and send them to their master Satan, for whom they serve." The English were in a fervor, throwing dead bodies, wood and about anything that wasn't worth using into a now growing blaze in the night. The commander walked up to me and said, "It appears you have gained favor from the very men that wanted to kill you. Don't keep my soldiers up too late celebrating, tomorrow we make our way to Orleans and to do battle with the French warrior witch. You have done well Jonas Cain." The commander walks away as an English soldier brings me a wineskin. I uncorked it and had a long drink and thanked the soldier. The English soldier then went into conversation, saying that he was following close behind me in the forest.

The soldier said, "Jonas, I heard the men fighting their way through the forest, but you moved like you had the hand of providence leading you." I followed that gut feeling or if it makes you feel any better… providence. I replied. The English soldier chuckled at my comment, took a swig from the wineskin, told me that he's had enough for tonight and was going to take a nap. I can feel the influence of tomorrow nights change, I'm not tired and I noticed how effortlessly, that I could slice through those men without using brute force. I won't need a blade tomorrow night and I'll have to figure out a way to separate myself before the change. I walked around looking for a stone to sharpen my blade and work off some nervous energy. I saw an English soldier using a stone on his blade and I asked him could I using it. The English soldier said, "Of course you can use it, just don't walk off with it. This stone has been my good luck charm since I came to this heathen country. "

I sat down beside him, he gave me the stone and I began to run the length of the cutting edge with the stone. The blade has battle damage and I sprinkled some sand on the blade as it lay on my lap. I rubbed the blade with the stone and I could feel the sand cutting down the jagged areas. The English soldier was watching me as I went through the process until I finished the blade by using the stone only. I felt of the blades edge, and it was restored except for a couple of notches taken out during battle. I thanked the English soldier, got up and found a place off to myself to go to sleep for the night. I lay there on the bare earth beneath me, and I could catch moments of a crescent moon as to what appears as rain clouds pass above. My mind wanders back to thoughts of a former life, away from this new experience.

Man hasn't changed from the time of Jesus, always at war with each other. I drift off to sleep to find myself in the company of the dark master. I see how you dedicated those Frenchmen to me with the help of the English…. nice touch and the English did it without knowing it. exclaimed the dark master. I said, "You wanted me to pay tribute to you and I saw an opportunity." The dark master said," So! How do you like France so far, Jonas Cain?" I replied by saying," It isn't any different than any other battle-stricken place that you have put me in." Now Jonas, you put yourself here by rebelling, replied the dark master. He then said," It's entirely up to you whether or not to abide by the rules, Jonas Cain? "The dark master disappeared, and I found myself in a mighty fortress, a vision that I could only compare to the palace in Egypt.

There were tapestries adorned on the walls with all kinds of markings on them from the cross to lions and dragons. This is truly a place of a king with such adornments. A familiar voice said, "You can go from a mere soldier to king Jonas Cain. King Jonas Cain has a nice ring to it, those three words just roll off the tongue like a destined combination of words. I turned to see where the words emanate from, and out steps a beautiful woman from behind a wall. I said, "Let me guess, you work for the dark master and he's using you as bait." The woman said, "Now Jonas, wouldn't you like to have a beautiful queen to lie in your bed." I drew my sword and it turned into a serpent at my feet.

The woman's face began to change into a fanged monster, she picked up the snake and threw it at me. I was startled awake the same instance as an English soldier kicked my foot. The English soldier said, "Wake up Jonas Cain, lets fill our bellies before we make our way to kill the French in Orleans." I shook off the vivid dream and made my way over to where the men were gathering. I got there in time, just when there were no more wooden bowls to hold the gruel. I was starving, my body needed substance. I picked up the corner of my outer garment and the cook ladled the hot gruel into it. The other men saw me and followed suit. I found a place to sit, eased myself down without pouring on the ground. The gruel was hot but I didn't care. I began scooping it up with my dirty fingers and placing it in my mouth. I had more running down my chin than in my mouth, no matter…. my body yearned for it.

Just I was scooping in the last morsel, the sergeant said, "Break camp, we've got a battle to attend to. I put sand on the outer garment to soak up the gruel. It's just a matter of time when I won't be needing this outer garment, the beast comes tonight. I found where a horse was tied up and he seemed nervous around me. I untied his reins and walked up to him and looked at him face to face; I told him that he need not worry and told him that I would give him plenty of warning ahead of time. The horse nodded his head and snorted, I jumped on his back and followed the men on horses, while the foot soldiers columned in ranks behind us. We were waiting for the commander and the sergeant to lead. A brief time went by, and they arrived with their banner bearers with spear tipped poles. The commander told the sergeant to send out the scouts and four horseback riders split into two groups as they galloped off ahead.

I could hear the foot soldiers behind me say, here comes the march to battle speech. The commander brought his horse in closer to us and began his oration. He begins by saying," Men we've fought long and hard to get to this point, many of our brothers have died in the process and many Frenchmen have fallen to our blades. Today, we march upon Orleans and our objective is to kill as many French that stand in our way and lay siege to Orleans. May God protect us on this quest, long live the King." The commander turned his horse forward and pointed forward. As I looked around me and saw the spectacle unfold. I was surprised at the number of men and horses, there has to be at least a 100 or so men and horses in this gathering. I could feel the early morning sun warm my back and smell the dust being kicked up by the line of riders in front of me.

I could already feel the muscles on my bones preparing for what is to come. I have a couple of hours to go before I have to separate myself from this gathering of the English army. The wind was carrying the smell of smoke to my keen nose as it blew into my face. My horse becomes agitated, he doesn't like being in the middle of the line of horseback riders. The horse to the left and right of him are bumping into us. My horse would quicken his gallop, only to be matched by the riders on either side. I sensed that the horse had picked on my intentions, and he slowed down to the point, that allowed the other riders to pull ahead. The horse made a quick turn to the right to avoid being trampled by the line of riders, that were just a mere five blinks of an eye from being on top of us. Now we were on the end of the line of riders, hugging the edge of the forest line, on our way to Orleans.

I patted my trusty steed on the neck as we galloped in unison with the other riders. I can only guess that the horse knows my true intentions and is aware that I mustn't be seen changing in front of the eyes of the

English, plus the fact he knows that horse flesh isn't on the mind of the beast. We didn't have to ride far until the English ran into resistance by a wave of arrows being launched by French archers from behind the line of French soldiers on horseback, waiting with their lances to do damage. I looked to the left from whence we came from, the men and horse were riddled with arrows. Now, the full charge has been given and the French horseback riders are coming straight at the front line.

I hear a command for the English archers to release arrows and saw them hit their targets into men and horse alike. I stopped my horse, got both of my swords, and told my horse to go from this place. An English horseback rider saw me and asked why did I do that? I simply told him that I didn't need him anymore and I suggested that he is bigger target on that horse for the French to aim at. The English soldier saw what was happening around him and took my advice. It is going to be sword against sword from here on the ground. My nose had already picked up the scent of spilled blood and now

CHAPTER 6

EATING ENGLISH AND FRENCH

I am in the thick of this madness, sword against sword until the vanquished fall under my blade, yet to move on to the next. Though I did receive some wounds which due to close quarter fighting, it happens even from your own men. My wounds didn't slow me down, it only angered me, forced me to push on. This fighting went on for hours untilI could feel the signs of the change beginning to take place. My jaw began to hurt as well as the body started to ache, the powers of the full moon are calling to me. An idea came to me in a flash of brilliance. As I was fighting with the French soldier, slashing at each other, matching swing for swing, I left myself open for a moment. The French soldier saw the opportunity and thrust the blade into my stomach. I lay there for a moment appearing to be dying, as the fighting around me continued me. I began to slowly crawl towards the edge of the forest. I had almost made it to the edge when I French soldier stabbed me in the back.

The average person would've died right there, since I'm no longer an average man, I am compelled to keep going and find somewhere out of view to change. I crawled into the treetops of a long dead tree that had toppled onto the forest floor. Nighttime has not arrived yet, still the changes take place. I could hear the moans of the dying men on the battlefield as I began screaming in pain myself. The beast is coming and in a moment the French and the English will suffer from his viciousness. The pains have stopped and now I see through the eyes of a predator. The beast tore off the English uniform top, the shoes are no longer needed and the beast craves flesh. The beast could hear all the sounds, taking in all the smells and now makes his way to the edge of the forest, to take in the view of the battlefield. He sees the field strewn with bodies of the dead and the dying and as he looks towards to where the battle has moved forward towards Orleans, the urge to kill is stronger than to just feast on the dead or the dying. The beast uses the edge of the forest as he makes his way forward towards the fighting.

The beast doesn't have to go far before opportunity reveals itself. An English and a French soldier are at the forest edge, fighting sword against sword. The beast looks around to see if there are others near to see him as he springs the trap. The beast stalks his prey, waiting for the perfect moment to strike. He watches as the Frenchman lands a fatal blow to the English soldier; the Frenchman's back is to the forest. The beast grabs the French soldier, pulling him to the ground and rips the throat out of the Frenchmen with a single swipe of his mighty claws. The beast tears away the soft flesh of the Frenchman's body and consumes it. The beast eats only enough to slake his urgent need to kill and eat, for he knows that as soon as the sun goes down, he will be able to strike without needing the forest as cover.

The beast realized his pact with his friend king and howled, signaling the arrival of the top predator and the willingness to share in his spoils as the results of his killing. The beast listened for a distant response and the response wasn't so distance. The beast could hear yelping not too far away, his wolf companions were already in the area. The beast left his fresh kills behind and decided to move forward towards more intense fighting. The beast could hear men fighting in the forest not too far up ahead. He cautiously made his movements through the forest as an animal slowly stalking, staying hidden, listening, and testing scents of the forest. The falling sun cast shadows in the forest that allow the beast to use it to his advantage. As he draws closer to his intended prey, he hears more than just two men fighting. The beast now moves slower to gain a closer view, in order to plan his attack. He sees there are more than just a few men fighting and the smell of blood has sent his animal mind into a sensory overload.

The beast can't resist the urge to wait, he moves in closer to the nearest victims. The moment comes as he lunges, knocking both men to the ground as the beast rips off the head of one man, with one swipe of his clawed hand. The other victim dies due to a lethal bite to the neck, ripping flesh by the jaws of the beast. The sneak attack by the beast did not go unnoticed, the French and English saw him and fled from the woods. The beast knows in a little while that any sunlight left will be gone and the night will be his. He shreds flesh from his last kill and waits for the sun to disappear. He could hear men screaming that there is a demon in the forest in two languages, to stay out of the forest. The sun slowly takes its time to give into the coming of the night. The beast hears the French and English splitting up into their own factions.

The beast could hear a Frenchmen yelling to his troops, to stop the English reinforcements from going into Orleans. The beast looks up at the sky through the trees, it appears to be a cloudless night. To the beast means that he would not be able to move freely in the open without being seen. His presence has already been noticed but, not to the extent that the beast intends onbringing tonight. There's an open field in front that leads to Orleans, to the right is a patch of forest, there the English make their refuge. To the left is but a narrow hedge row of trees and bushes and the beast made a decision. The beast would run parallel to the patch of forest where the English are, using the forest cover he's in now until he has no choice but to make the crossing. The beast runs down the edge of the forest, every muscle finely tuned like that of a jungle cat in hot pursuit of its next kill. It only took a matter of moments before the beast had reached the end of the forest line.

He peers out from the forest at the battlefield between him and the forest where the English fled. Then something happened, a thought came into the beast mind… his friend Andre. The beast doesn't have friends, the beast knows only killing and eating of flesh and to continue killing until the sunrise. For the sake of chance, the English are much closer and instead of just running out in the open, he stays close to the ground using the sparse cover of the dead on the battlefield. He did not like crawling like animal and his body demanded more food plus, the moon has no clouds to hide itself either. At the forest edge, an English soldier sees something moving among the dead on the battlefield. The soldier yells out, "Ready your swords men! Something is moving among the dead and is coming our way, move out from the forest and hurry, it's coming." The beast surprise attack is of little use now so, he makes a full run towards the English. The beast enhanced leg muscles propel him faster than a normal man can think, pure instinct, the instinct of a top apex killer.

The beast runs through the English soldiers ripping through their flesh, though some English swords pierced the beast body, the beast continued undeterred with an unrelenting attack. A group of English soldiers with their commander, decided to risk losing their life to the French than lose it to some unknown demon of the night. The beast detects the smell of water in the air, a lot of it and he hears explosions off in the distance. Far ahead of the beast's location a battle ensues at the entry of Orleans. A siege of the region by the English had been going on for quite some time. The beast has no way of knowing what is causing the explosions and his curiosity has taken over. The beast stops the attack and goes back into the forest. His lust for human flesh has been satiated and his mind is wondering about the explosions, he must see with his own eyes. His mind harkens back to when Saladin attacks the city of Jerusalem with cannons and wonders if man has progressed past the cannon as a means of killing each other.

The beast pushes his way into the thick underbrush and manages to flush out soldiers that have hidden themselves cowardly from the fighting, the beast dispatches quickly with one swipe of his lethal clawed hand. The continues towards the edge and his view is still limited. As he peers around the massively tall oak, he looks upward, jumps up on the side of the tree and climbs higher until, he can see what lies up ahead. He sees that there is a fortress being fired upon by cannons and the fortress is returning fire into the battlefield. The night air carries the smells of cannon smoke, spilled blood and a river that is unseen from this vantage point. The smell of water only makes the beast want it more, the instinct to crave water takes precedence over the power to kill…. for the moment. The beast climbs down from the ancient oak and realizes he has nowhere to hide beyond the forest, to reach the river.

He needed water even if it meant killing a hundred or two hundred men to get it. A plan was hatched in the mind of this calculating apex predator. The beast began looking around for a dead Frenchman's body. It didn't take long before he lucked upon one very dead Frenchmen. The beast removed his clothing and put them on, took the Frenchman's sword and looked around for another sword. The beast now has a sword in each of his mighty hands, he runs full speed into the battle, killing indiscriminately both English and French soldiers. He doesn't care, he's fighting his way to the river for a much need drink. The beast moved with precision, turning, slashing, cutting men in half as if they were twigs, cutting a swath towards the river. Some soldiers managed to strike the beast, but there blows did nothing except to anger the beast, the soldiers that made any contact, didn't survive it. The smell of water is becoming stronger and so has the thirst for it, he continues killing a foe that is by far outclassed.

A familiar voice behind the beast said," You are thinking of just jumping into the river and escaping this, are you?" The beast doesn't turn around to see, he maintains his focus on making it to the river. The beast says, "I thirst, must have water." The voice says," I can take you from this and give you water, you do remember what I asked from you?" The beast becomes agitated and turns, baring his teeth and says, "I pledge to you and offer all that I had laid waste to you, master." "That wasn't so hard now, was it?" replied the dark one. The next instant, the beast is in a forest and the pains return as the moon gives way to the rising sun. The change is completed, and I am a man again, still I thirst. I stand up and see that the forest is littered with the dead, I look among them for a wineskin. There are dead English and French soldiers scattered here and after a while of searching, I found a nearly full wineskin.

I pulled the wineskin from a dead English soldier and drank all of the wine. I looked around and tried to get a sense of where I am. I began asking myself, is this the forest I started from? I began testing the air with my nose to see if I could detect the river. The smell of death is too heavy and the wind carries with it a scent of the long dead rotted flesh of men. I picked up two swords, took the belts from the dead and fashioned a way to hold one sword on my back, the other sword at my waist. I began walking forward to see where the forest stops. I continue testing the air and it is more of the same, death. After I had travelled a great distance, my ears could hear something familiar, cannon fire. My stomach begins to rumble; it hungers for food. My ears pick up the sounds of wild pigs and I make my way towards them.

I start looking for a dead archer because I'll need the proper tools. My search was successful, a dead archer and a quill with arrows. I've never tried my skills as an archer but, my stomach desires food. The beast spent all that he ate last night fighting his way to the river, yet never got a drink. The master pulled me, the beast from the chaos but, the sounds of war in the distance tells me that time to myself is short lived. I continue to focus at hand on getting my next meal, as I carefully got closer to the sounds of the pigs. I could see what they were doing. A sow and her pigs were eating the flesh from the dead. I crouched down to get closer so, that my chances of making a good shot count, since I've never used a bow before. I edged my way ever closer without being detected, now is the decisive moment. I slowly rose up behind a tree, drawing an arrow and aiming at the pig that is closest to me.

My arrow skipped across its back, the pig squealed a little and continued to eat. I'm too anxious, that's why I missed. I gently pulled an arrow from the quill and drew it. This time, I pulled the arrow to my right cheek, remembering what I saw the archers do in battle, now I could see down the arrow and its intended mark. I released the arrow, and it went into the side of the pig. The pig was still trying to get away but, it was mortally wounded. I walked forward to collect my prize and the sow charged at me. I had just enough time to drop the bow, retrieve my sword and land what I thought would be a decisive blow to the sow's head. She was only dazed and came at me again with her jaws snapping, I side stepped her and lunged my sword to the hilt into the large sow's back. The sow was dead, and the rest of the pigs scattered to the safety of the forest. I finished dispatching the pig to end its suffering and began cutting the pig into manageable pieces to cook.

I realize that I can't just have a banquet and lay down with a full stomach afterwards, I don't know where I am or where my enemies are. So, I hurried made a small fire and skewered the meat on green limbs, stuck the ends into the soil, leaning the meat over the fire. As the meat began to cook a thought came to me, I am exposed, and the smoke could give me away. I decided to remove myself from close proximity to the fire. I took several paces back into the forest with my newly acquired bow and quill, I need a vantage point. I saw the perfect place in front of me, a large oak. I tied on the quill, placed my arm between the bow and the draw chord and proceeded to climb upwards. I got high enough to see around me but, not too high in case I need a quick exit down. I straddled two limbs with my back against the tree and relaxed for a moment, closed my eyes, and listened.

I could hear cannon fire and men yelling off to my left, my ears tell me that for now, I am alone. I smell water again, the wind blows from behind me that, tells me that I'm across the river. I could go to sleep but, my stomach yearns for substance. I crawled back down the tree and I could feel something was watching me. I drew my sword and out walks two wolves then three wolves, I put away my sword and they walked towards me. Four of the wolves lay down as their leader sat on his haunches. I wait in anticipation and then the leader speaks, he says," Members of my father's pack have alerted us that you are here among us, and we honor the pact you made with my father.

I am Star, my father's oldest son." I told Star that I would share my kill with his pack and to leave me just enough to fill my belly for now. Star then says, "Members of my father's pack have seen the beast on two legs in action and I was taught by my father that we are top predators except for man yet, you are more than a man." I said, "Before we get into a lengthy conversation, my food is burning over the fire." I walked over to the fire and turned the meat over. One side did get a little overly done but, I'll still eat it. I asked Star was he or his pack members hungry? "We have been eating the dead and the dying soldiers that are in the forest and for now there is no need for us to hunt for food. I am anxious to see this man-beast in action for myself so, when I'm old I can tell the young pups that I was in his presence." I said," Before you start glorifying me, I've done the most unforgiveable and I deserve this curse."

Star says," You have a good heart but it was your mind that was corrupted by the great deceiver. Wolves and other animals do not plot, we do what it takes to survive, the old give way to the young, the weak die and the strong continue. The cycle continues until the great creator decides for all of this to stop." I almost let my food burn while listening to Star, I got up and removed the food from the fire. I said, "You are wise like your father and you are right about the difference between man and animal.it is choice or freewill that gets man in situations whereas, you and other animals rely purely on instinct. Tonight, there will be another full moon and you just might get your chance to see the beast on two legs. The wolf kills to feed its family (the pack), the beast on two legs kills for three reasons, one to satisfy its hunger for human flesh and the other is for the sport of killing and offering sacrifice to the dark master."

Star asked, "What happens if you stop offering sacrifices?" I told Star that I stop being here in his time and then I had to explain to him what I was talking about, while I finished eating what I could of the cooked pig. I asked Star what lies in that direction, as I pointed left. He told me that it is a large stone house that the men are fighting over with lots of open area surrounding it and said behind him is forest and to my right is forest. As he was talking to me, my ears caught to sound of movement from behind me. Star's four subordinates stood up gave a yelp and ran into the forest behind me. I asked Star what is going on and he told me that some of his pack members could be out there.

Star said," y scouts are going to check it out, we'll know in a little while." We waited until the sounds of yelps could be heard. Sounds like we are about to have company, I spoke. Star said, "Soldiers are coming this way, we'll find out if they are French or not." It wasn't long before I was surrounded by the whole pack, they all laid down and one walked up to Star and began whispering in his ear. Star said, "A group of English soldiers are moving this way, but they are staying close to the outer edge of the forest." I asked the scout, "How many men? Is it a small group or large group?" The scout laid down and said," At least four times as many as there are of us here."

I made a quick count of the wolf pack, there are ten wolves and that means forty to fifty men. Star told me that if I had a plan that I had better hurry up and think of something. I put out the fire by throwing sand on it and cut up the large sow into manageable parts for the pack with my sword, as the pack patiently watched. Star bowed down to me and said," You do have an honorable heart." As he turned to leave Star asked, "Why do you want to go to Orleans?" I told him that I would like to see this female warrior with my own eyes. "The warrior maiden is supposedly getting help from the creator." Replied Star. As I was gathering my things I replied back," Maybe she can help me with my situation and thanks for your friendship." Just before Star and his four guards disappeared, Star laughingly said, "Don't eat any of my pack tonight."

I laughed to myself and thought back to my friend in Cairo, many lifetimes ago. Since I've eaten and gave some thought on where I'm going from here. I could do a repeat of last night, leave on this bloody French garb, find somewhere and take a nap. It will be a couple of hours before the beast awakens. Sleep…. that's what I need, time to shut my eyes to the world. I walked around and found some brush and dead tree limbs and built a temporary shelter to conceal myself. I untied the quill and laid down the bow, I crawled under the makeshift shelter, laid on my side and thought about today's events before I closed my eyes. I had finally calmed down enough to drift off to sleep and found myself on the bank of a tranquil river.

I was just sitting there watching the water flow by and a voice from behind me says, "Do you mind if I join you?" I turn to see, and it is a young woman with short hair, an attractive one at that. I told her to have a seat and enjoy the view. The young women sat down beside me and takes my hand and places it on her face. She pulls me forward and kisses me on the lips as I close my eyes, then withdraws back, I open my eyes to see the vilest creature. The creature starts laughing and says," Do you think you can get help from the warrior maiden?

The master sent you here to make sacrifices to him, look at the river, this is what he wants." I look at once was a tranquil river which now flows with dead bodies in a river stained with blood. I pushed the vile creature into the river, the creature grabbed me and I awoke suddenly, to see my arm was stuck in a branch.

I look up through the branches to see the flickering of sunlight as a light wind blows. I feel a slight pain in my jaw, the beast comes soon. There's no need for me to go anywhere, I won't be in charge until the moon releases her grip upon me. I remain on the ground, the pain comes, and it wreaks havoc all over my body until the change is almost complete. My vision is blurred until I am seeing through a distinct set of eyes now. The beast takes in a few long breaths as he stretches his new muscles, turning his head looking, listening, and testing the air with his nose. It isn't dark yet, and the beast must use the element of surprise. The hunger for a fresh kill pushes him towards the outer fringe of the forest where the soldiers are. He makes use of the forest shadows to get closer so, that he'll be able to gauge his next move.

He sees a lone straggler, an English soldier at the end of the line of men. The beast begins to stalk his prey. He wants to run and make a quick kill but, that would draw the attention of the others. The beast slowly makes his way closer, closer, and closer until the beast attacks the straggler from behind, snapping his neck pulls him into the woods to begin feasting on him. The beast doesn't get his fill on the first victim, he hears a soldier calling for the missing man. The beast moves away from the first kill and watches as other soldiers enter the forest. There is at least 10 or so men looking for their missing comrade, the beast waits for the next target to get close. One of the men has found their dead comrade and as a target gets closer, the beast using the distraction to kill another. This went on until the beast had decimated the search party and gorged himself on the last kill.

The sun's rays are no more, the moon seems to be hidden by the clouds. It will be the perfect night for the beast, for he will have the cover of night to mask his movements. It appears that the English will feel the beast wrath tonight, last night the beast killed both French and English, just to make it to the river. He thought about that and realized he never got that drink of water that was promised instead, he was placed at a different point on the chess board by the dark master. The beast stopped thinking and let the rage, that is and has been pent up inside take hold. He had to take it out on someone or something. He remembered what his daytime counterpart did with the bow and arrow.

He started searching the dead bodies for weapons of any kind, knives, swords and of course a bow and quills. With the ability to see in the dark, the beast wouldn't have to get up close to kill, the stomach is filled for now. The beast is anxious to test this way of killing without having to exert himself. He tears the garment from a dead English soldier and wraps his wares of tools for killing. He slides the bow over his head, his many quills with arrows and starts moving towards the English. Cannon fire then erupts in the direction that he is moving towards. He could see the torches flickering up ahead through the forest, the English are camped out in the open at the edge of the forest. The beast hastily moves towards his intended targets, he needs to find a vantage point. The beast walks the perimeter of the woods near the English camp.

He takes notice of posted guards at each corner of the camp, each having their own torch at their side. The center of the camp had a scattering of smaller campfires going. The cannon fire has gone silent, I guess the French can't visibly aim the cannon at a specific target in the dark. The beast has chosen his first target, he gently places his tools of death on the ground and pulls out a dagger. The soldier is facing the forest and before using the dagger, the beast does a test. He finds a fair-sized rock on the ground and lobs it to the center of the camp. He watches as the rock strikes an unsuspecting soldier on the head sitting by the fire. The beast wanted to laugh but, continued to watch as the men scrambled around trying to figure out where the attack came from. The guard nearest to the forest edge has turned towards the commotion in the center of the camp.

The beast is still hidden and makes an animal noise. This draws the attention of the lone guard and he walks to the edge of the forest to investigate. The beast makes another sound like that of a young pig and the soldier walks deeper into the worlds. The beast has sprung the trap and the soldier lives no more. The beast shredded muscle and skin from the soldier with his talon like claws and feasted, while he planned his next move. The beast took the dagger and threw it into a crowd of men, without aiming just as hard as he could throw it. He waited to see if the dagger had made its target, it managed to stick into a soldier's head. The beast wanted to laugh out, a loud evil laugh at the game he initiated. He decided to move to another position and attack from a different angle. By now the guard's attention is at the center of the camp and the beast was ready to something different. He had a few swords and lot of arrows, he took a sword, grabbed the hand grip with an overhead swing and let it fly. The beast watched as a man was skewered, took another sword and lobbed it in another direction. The sword found a target but didn't kill instantly.

It had struck a man in the back but, he saw the man crawling on the ground a little way. The beast moved again a bit farther from the second position, the beast was enjoying this type of killing, this has turned into game to him. He sees the men pointing towards the forest and the beast decides to do something bold. Since the moon is hidden by the clouds and the beast senses the smell of rain coming, he takes his wares of killing and moves to the open field. He far enough away from the camp that the men cannot see him. The men don't have the same ability as the beast, the ability to see in absolute darkness and the beast will use this to his advantage.

The beast places his killing tools on the ground and assesses what he has left. He counts six swords, three daggers and four quills of arrows that hold eight to ten arrows. The beast takes the quills, leaves the sword and daggers behind. He's going to make a frontal attack on the far end and work his way back to the daggers and the swords, to use last. He sprints to the location, puts the quills on the ground, pulls out an arrow, draws the bow on a target and the arrow flies. The arrow finds its target and sticks a soldier in the chest. He hears the men saying, "Our enemy is all around us." The beast pulls another arrow and aims in the group of men. He hears the scream of a wounded man, and knows the arrow found its victim. He launches another and moves into another position and he continues this tactic until he has spent all of his arrows.

The beast drops the bow and circles around to the last of his remaining tools for killing. The clouds began to rumble and flashes of lightning kicked out from the sky. He picks up his tools and surveys the damage that he's done to the English, many are dead and dying. Though the men were being attacked from all around, they chose to go into the forest because of the rain. The beast takes his wares and goes into the forest, the rain doesn't bother the beast, his anxiousness to make another kill excites him. Peels of lightning strike the ground and lights of the whole area, the lightning hit near the area where the beast came from, lighting up the surrounding area. An English soldier happens to catch a glimpse of the uniform that the beast is wearing. The soldier says, "It's a single Frenchman that's killing us off, keep your wits about you men, he's followed us into the forest.

Get those torches lit and move in close." The group of men of fifty or more and been cut down dramatically. The rain is now here and the forest only slows the downpour. The beast has spent some of his energy while playing his newly found killing game. The hunger for flesh from his stomach demands its needs are followed. The beast decides to use the same tactic, he takes his tools and starts systematically killing men as he circles around them, unseen. Now, there are only six English soldiers left, the beast takes the two remaining swords and charges headlong into the six men. The English didn't have a chance, the beast is relentless in his attack until they are no longer among the living. The beast shreds flesh from one his victims and eats until he feels something familiar. The pains of the change from apex predator to man have started and he moves away from the dead English soldiers to find somewhere out of the pouring rain, he manages to find a clump of twisted vines to get under.

He lays down as his body is racked with pain until the change is complete. The man returns and succumbs to sleep. I found myself in an open field littered with dead bodies, the carrion hunters circle up above and I'm not alone. I said, "I had a feeling you would be showing." The dark master said, "The beast really enjoyed himself last night, using the tools made by man to bring death upon them. I must say these past two nights, the beast has brought down many men. So, why do choose to defy me Judas? I told you not to help the warrior maiden, and you are determined to meet with this woman." I said, "The English claim she is a witch and gets her messages from beyond. If she is a witch, she must be in league with you."

The dark master moves within inches of my face and said, "You have been helping her indirectly by killing off many English soldiers. She will rally the people of Orleans and break the siege of Orleans by the English. She is indeed considered a witch by her own people and the English, do you know why Judas? It's because she is getting help from the other side of the fence. If you went up and told her that you killed over two hundred men in two nights? She would believe you and has probably been told that are near Orleans. She is an oddity like you and neither of you could fit into the current society now. Humans are a fickle animal, today you could be the hero that slayed the might of the English and next week you could be burned at the stake for being different. I know I'm stretching it a bit between you and her as far as being alike but you will understand. Don't forget your promise to me once you awaken or I'll progress you forward into another time so, I bid you an adieu, Judas."

The next moment I wake up and the rays of the sun are cutting through the forest canopy. I stood up and my clothes are soaked with blood. I picked up a sword and headed to the edge of the forest and it opened to a vast clearing. The field was scattered about with the dead, the land was pock marked from cannon ball damage. A head of me was the huge fortress of masonry and the reduced amount of English was trying to guard the castle gate. I grabbed another sword and ran into the fight. I was taking out the English from their flank, my sensitive hearing caught a voice from the fortress parapet yell, "There's a lone Frenchman taking out our enemy by himself. Re-aim the cannon to give him some assistance." The cannon fire was all around me as I continue closer, to where the archers on the wall began to cut the small English army down from above. I was crossing the bridge to get closer to the gate and an arrow struck me in the back. I fell on the ground because I knew that I was being watched.

I slowly got up, grabbed the arrow and attempted to pull it from my back, but it broke. I continued forward to the gate began slashing the English outside the fortress wall. I killed 20 or more men at the gate before I faked passing out. I lay there and listened as I heard a voice from the parapet say," The French army has breached the wall, the English are retreating. I waited and all clear was given and the gate was opened. I lay there and a voice says," There's the lone Frenchman that took on the English, someone help me pick him up, he may still be alive." I released the grip of the two swords that I held and they fell from my hands as men were carrying me into the fortress.

I could hear the chatter of voices as I am being moved into some inner room and placed on a table. One of the men pressed his head on my chest and says, "He has a heartbeat, go and bring the physician here and hurry." As I lie there, I began to retrace the battle to the gate in my mind, I did feel a couple of strikes to my body, possibly in my stomach and my back, I'm not rightly sure. I was in a moment of rage and the compelling drive to go forward pushed me to the point of numbness to pain. The room became busy with activity as I felt my clothing being removed. I hear the physician, I assume, giving orders to bring hot water and garment to clean me up, so that he can examine me. I feel the hot water being rubbed across my stomach and the physician saying he has a deep cut to the stomach and needs to roll me over on my side, to examine my back side.

I feel the hands of men pull me to my side, as the physician wipes dirt and dried blood. The physician tells the men to hold me there, so he can apply ointment and sew up the open wounds. I could fell the needle piercing my skin and the pull of the stitching, I lay there unflinching. The physician tells the men to roll me on to my back and he went to work stitching up the wounds on my stomach. I could feel the continued washing of my body, I was dried off and taken to another room, placed a much softer surface than the table I came from. I went to sleep and this time the dreams weren't plagued with bad memories, vile creatures or even the dark master. I was floating in nothingness, a place devoid of any reference.

I could compare it to floating in the night sky, that didn't have stars. In my sleep, I could hear someone praying at my side. I awaken and turn my head to see who was praying, there beside my bed was a young woman praying, as well as others kneeling with heads bowed until she finished. The young woman looked up and saw me looking at her, she grasped my hand and said," Brave soldier what is your name?" I coughed and said, "I'm David Le Stone and who might you be fair maiden? The young woman answered, "I'm the Maiden D' Arc, but you may call me Jean and it seems that divine providence has sent a mighty warrior to Orleans to vanquish the English. I'm sorry that I have disturbed your sleep monsieur Stone, but I felt compelled to come and pray at your side after hearing what you did by yourself.

It is indeed a miracle that you're alive despite your severe injuries. I will have a hand maiden sent to take care of you while you rest, you deserve it." The maiden D Arc rose up to walk across the room, turned and said, "We shall talk later monsieur Stone." I bid her thanks for her prayers and bid her adieu. I began thinking, was it her praying that stopped my tormentors in my sleep? I only pondered for a moment, and I went to sleep. My human form was weak, tired and required rest. I thought back to the moment when the dark master told me not to help the warrior maiden and he told me that she knows who I am, yet she prayed at my bedside.

The dark master has lied to me from the start and by telling me not to help or seek out the warrior, causes me to reverse his gestures for some twisted plan of his. I was fighting to keep my eyes open and heard movement in the room. A young woman was carrying something that smelled like food. I raised my head to look and the young woman said," Relax monsieur Le Stone until I get set up, so that I can feed you some le bouillon." The hand maiden raised me up in the bed and stuffed blankets behind my back and my head. I moaned to show signs of severe pain, even though I did ache while my body was repairing itself from the inside out. It has been such a long time since I had looked into the face of innocence. I say that she is innocent because she is but a child, she doesn't look at me as some wayward woman.

I asked the young girl her name? "It is Marie, monsieur le Stone," she replied. I asked Marie, why am I placed here in a room by myself and not with the other injured or dying soldiers? Marie said," Maiden Jean d arc witnessed what you did along with others and they say that it's a miracle, that you alone killed all those men and yet, you live." I told Marie to serve me some bouillon, so that I would have the strength to spin the tale about pure survival. I was starving and Marie couldn't spoon the bouillon fast enough, so I took the bowl and drank the warm liquid from the wooden bowl.

Marie said," You're moving too fast monsieur. Let me lay you back down, you need to rest. I want to make sure you keep that down before I feed you anymore." Marie placed her arm around my neck, removed the blankets from behind me, then gingerly laid me down on a pillow. I told her that she is strong for a young woman, and she told me that she lived on a farm with her parents, until the English murdered her family and was saved by maiden d Arc on her way to break the siege of Orleans. Maiden D Arc was on the battlefield with you, monsieur le Stone." I was shocked to find that out because I had killed French and English alike. I was about to ask her a question about the warrior maiden when I heard someone else enter the room.

Marie turned to see and greeted the warrior maiden. The warrior maiden asked Marie had I been fed and Marie answered with a yes. The warrior maiden said," Now You may go Marie and thank you for looking after Monsieur le stone for me." The warrior maiden's attire had changed from warrior to a cloak still adorned with the French king's seal. She pulled up a chair and sat by my bed. She said," I'm not quite sure how to open this conversation, so I'm going to be forward with this. You may have heard rumors about me and some claim that I am a witch. I can promise you that I'm no witch and the information that drives me comes from the divine. The divine or messengers that they call themselves, visit me in my dreams and give me guidance. They told me that a man that is caught between two worlds, would cross paths with me."

I said, "Every man is caught between two worlds, that of good and evil. Two worlds or states of mine could be determined to accept the way that things are or to bring about change, every person struggles with that." She then tells me, "I know that David le Stone isn't your real name, the messengers told me that you've been betrayed. You were told not to help me yet you sought me out. The messengers can be very vague about the things they reveal to me, even though I pressed for answers; they would simply tell me that things are already predestined to happen." The maiden asked me could she hold my hand for a moment? I asked why is that necessary and she told me to just trust her. I held out my left hand and she gently grasped it. She closed her eyes, and I could feel her hand beginning to slightly tremble.

Her body movements became so erratic that I released from her and she fell to the floor and was convulsing. I got up from the bed, picked her up and shook her free of this malady. She woke up, gasping for air and grabbed my arm. Holy Jesus! She exclaimed. "You were in Jerusalem fighting against Saladin, how is this possible? That means you are several hundred years old but yet, you look like a man in his thirties." I was astounded by her ability and wondered how far back did she go back in my life. I said," You got all of that by merely grabbing my hand?" I helped her up from the floor and sat her in the chair. She took notice that I had strength enough to get out of bed and help her up. I laid back down on the bed as I watched her face, I could almost hear her questions that were about to be asked. She said," By all laws of nature you shouldn't exist." I asked her how old she was. She told me that she is eighteen.

I said," What do you know about the laws of nature when you've been alive for only eighteen years. My shoes are older than you because I took them off a dead English soldier, at least he smelled older than eighteen." She began to laugh at my comment and by her demeanor, she was more relaxed and less frightened of me. In a relaxed quiet voice, she leaned towards me and said, "You can't die, can you?" I told her that we need to be somewhere that we cannot be heard by prying ears. She said, "The moon will not be full tonight and I plan on feeding you and taking care of you myself."

I told her that it wouldn't be viewed as proper by hanging around some old man like me and to send in the hand maiden. I told her the hand maiden wouldn't be prodding me for questions like she is. She leaned over and gave me a kiss on the mouth and said," I'm not afraid of you, your heart is pure. It is the circumstance that controls you that is evil." As she was walking to the door, I asked her where can I relieve myself? She giggled and said, "I'll help you to the window and I won't look at your private parts." I said, "I'm supposed to be lying in bed and unable to stand up and you are going to help me to the window? What if I lose my balance and fall out of the window, you'll be able to see holding my private parts as I fall to the ground."

She was pulling on my arm and helping me up and laughing about what I said. She told me to stop speaking and stand up. I placed my arm around her shoulder, and she walked me over to the window. I could tell by the stains on the masonry, that someone had already been using the window. I looked out the window and we are a good distance off the ground. I pretended to get off balance and she straightened me right up. I told her to turn her head and spoke that I can handle it from here. As I was urinating, I said, "Oh my, the water is really cold in the moat." She said, "As old as you are, you probably invented that joke.

Let's get you back to bed." I thought to myself when she grabbed my hand, the weight of the world seemed to lift from my shoulders. I sat down on the edge of the bed before I laid down and said," These are dangerous times and speculation can cause a panic. Do you understand what I'm talking about?" She said, "I think so but, since you are older and wiser, I'm all ears." I told her to go and check outside the door and come back. She went to the door, opened it, peered left and right, and returned to the chair next to my bed. I said," I was there with crusaders and Templars. I witnessed the fall of Jerusalem for a second time. Those men could be labelled as heretics. It was Saladin's men or even his faith that took Jerusalem. They could have been called even witches because of their belief whatever it was. A rogue rumor can spread like some evil disease that has no boundaries."

The young maiden was intrigued and was snared by every word. I then said, "That's enough for today, you need to go about your business as usual and be mindful of what I've said. I need to eat more and rest, send in your hand maiden." She helped me to lean back on the bed and told me she would see me later. I watched her leave the room and wondered how long I would get to stay in this time before I made my master mad again. I stared at the ceiling for a while until I heard the faint footfalls outside the door, the door opens, and Marie has a tray. I said, "I hope you brought me something a little heavier than le bouillon?" Oui monsieur le Stone, she answered. "I have brought some bread, cheese, and wine, so don't try and gobble it up at once. You are still in my care. To think about it I should stay and feed you, to make sure you go slowly."

I told her to stop talking and start slicing something. She giggled at my anxiousness to eat and began slicing up the bread and cheese. Marie began toying with me by giving me smaller portions and I growled at her barring teeth. She laughed and said, "Does the bad dog want a bigger slice?" Just as I was about to play along, I heard a different sound of footfalls… someone heavier and the faint sound chain mail against armor. I held up my finger to wait and there was a knock at the door. I whispered to Marie to place the food in the chair, and I laid back against the cold fortress wall. Marie said," Entrez vous." In walked a man and Marie bowed to him and said," I shall leave I come back to feed you monsieur le Stone." The man of royalty spoke and said," You may stay young Marie. I'm about to pay homage to a great warrior from what I hear and to offer him a job in the French Royal guard."

I slowly placed my feet on the floor to stand and bow but, the royal wouldn't allow it. The royal said, "Monsieur le Stone, I want you to be my royal personal bodyguard, your swordsmanship is no longer needed on the battlefield. From what I've heard you single handedly took out a regiment of English soldiers by yourself. For such a feat as that, you are favored in the Lord God's eyes just as Maiden d Arc I sat there for a moment letting all of what the royal said sink in. I said, "My king." The royal stopped me before I said another syllable by saying, "For now, I am the Dauphin Charles Vll until my coronation but, we have to rid the English from our lands you and my messenger from God, Maiden d Arc are the tools to make it happen.

Are you up for the job, monsieur le Stone?" I said, "How can I turn down such an offer from the future king of France? Monsieur Dauphin, currently I'm kind of laid up so to speak." The Dauphin chuckles and tells me to get well as he leaves the room. Marie tells me to lay back before my wounds open back up. She grabbed my legs and placed them back onto the bed, as I leaned back against the cold fortress wall. Marie picks up a knife and begins to slice up more bread and cheese. I asked her could I have a drink of wine? She picks up a goblet and raises it to my lips, the wine is good, far better than I had a few days ago. I pushed on her hand to pour more and told me to take it a little at a time. I have to keep reminding myself that I'm supposed to be recovering from near death to not raise suspicion. I know my cover is blown with the maiden d Arc, I wonder just how much she really knows, who I am and what I've done?

Marie continued to feed me more food than the first time and my stomach is somewhat satisfied for now. Marie asked me did I want some more wine? Oui, my sweet Marie, I replied. She poured wine into the goblet and I held out my hands. She said, "I'll give it to you only if you promise to drink it slowly." I told her that I promise, and she gave me the goblet. I drank it all in one gulp. Marie said, "You promised." I told her that I drank it slowly in one gulp. Marie gathered up the food implements and told me that she would she me later this afternoon. As she was walking out the door, she turned to me and said, "Get your rest monsieur le Stone," she walked out the door and closed it.

I thought to myself, at least it isn't wintertime, me laying here with just a blanket on me. I looked around the room and saw no clothing or the weapons that I had. I am completely defenseless for the moment. There is something about the French Dauphin Charles that I have a gut feeling of distrust. I know how nobility can use people for their own rise to power. I remember how the Pharoah's used up their own people as a shield. I lay there for a moment and nodded off to sleep. The next moment, I'm lying in the desert sand and the sun is blinding my vision. A shadow steps forward and blocks the sun and says, "Have you forgotten our agreement, monsieur?" I sat up and bowed my head and said," Forgive me master for not verbally paying homage but, for every life that I've taken on the battlefield and in the forest, I did for you.

You brought me back to spill blood for you and that's exactly what I've been doing." The dark master said," Who do you think you are trying to appease with that declaration? Is it for yourself or are you trying to be as crafty as I am? I asked you not to help the warrior maiden and now she knows something about you, that can be used against you. Do think she can offer you a safe haven from what you become every month when the moon is full?" The dark master puts his hands on my shoulders and said," Wake up" At that same instant, I'm awoken by the maiden d Arc. She said, "You were mumbling in your sleep, and I shook you.

Some bad memory is torturing you, isn't it?" I sat up in the bed and told her that it is more than a bad memory. I looked at the foot of the bed and there was a stack of clothing. She looked at my chest and stomach and said, "Your wounds are completely healed as if by some miracle. Perhaps my prayers were answered after all." She then, told me that she is going to step outside the room while I get dressed, then I'm to go to the door to notify her that I'm clothed. I did as she asked, got dressed, put on the boots and walked to the door. Maiden d Arc said, "You clean up nicely monsieur. I want to take you to meet some people, they are eager to meet you." I said," What kind of trap am I walking into, maiden d Arc?" She smiled and told me it isn't any sort of trap. I grabbed her arm, stopped in the hallway, and said, "Before I take another step; you'll have to tell me your plan or else." Maiden d Arc said," Or else what? You don't have anything to worry about, you're a hero in the eyes of the people of Orleans.

Your public is waiting to see this man who killed many English single handedly." I said," You are treading on dangerous ground, be mindful of what you do." She grabbed my hand and led me down a staircase until we reached the bottom. She glanced back at me, smiled, and led me through a door out into an open courtyard. In the courtyard, there was the French dauphin, a priest, French soldiers and ordinary French citizens. At this point she had released my hand and placed her arm around my arm and walked towards the French Dauphin Charles

Vll. The French Dauphin said, "How is this possible, earlier today when I visited you were a bloody mess? And you are arm and arm with the Maiden d Arc, am I witnessing a miracle?" Maiden d Arc said, "I prayed and asked God to heal this man before I left my room this morning. As you can see Monsieur David le Stone is standing here and even his wounds have healed.

The maiden asked me to lift my clothes to expose my chest and back. People began to circle around and look where the wounds had completely closed up. I could hear murmurings in the crowd, voices saying maiden d Arc is the hand of God. I really got nervous when the priest started walking towards me. As the priest got closer, he made the sign of the cross and I made a showing by dropping to my knees and bowing my head. The priest touched the top of my head and the palm of his hand blistered. The priest yelled in pain, and I got up and said, "He doubted God's work and got punished."

The French citizens started picking up rocks and began throwing them at the priest. I had to think of something fast and out of my mouth comes, "Whomever is without sin throw a stone at me." The stoning stopped and the priest came up to me and asked for forgiveness. I told the priest and the crowd of people that only God can forgive and that they all should go into the temple and ask for forgiveness. To my amazement, the priest led the people to the temple, leaving me standing with the Dauphin, his royal guards, and maiden d Arc. The Dauphin turned to me and said, "Monsieur le Stone, that took some fast thinking and at elevated risk upon your part. Maybe I should rethink your position instead of being one of my royal guards, you could be my royal advisor? You stopped a marauding crowd from killing a priest, a man of God and I couldn't have stopped." I said," The king of France can stop or start anything because he is king, and that king will be you Dauphin."

I got down on one knee and bowed my head to reverence. The Dauphin laughs and says, "Rise royal advisor to the king, let's go and get something to eat. All of this drama has made me hungry." Maiden d Arc came up to me and nodded her head, indicating the mistake and asked could she walk with me? I told her of course as we followed behind the Dauphin and his royal guards. We were led into the great hall, though it showed signs of its previous occupation by the English, it was a mastery of design. We then sat down at a large wooden table and my nose was picking up the smell of cooked meat.

The Dauphin said," You'll have to excuse the surroundings but it's only a matter of time before we erase the garnishment caused by the English. I brought you in here to express my utmost gratitude for the retaking of Orleans." A servant had brought a tray of goblets and placed them in front of everyone at the table. The Dauphin said, "I raise my goblet to you my warriors of France and may we soon rid our country of the English vermin that invaded us." We all followed by saying "santé! "We drank from our goblets as the servants were bringing in plates, food and all the trimmings of a fine feast. My body craved for food after repairing itself, I'll have to refrain from gorging myself like an animal; since I'm supposed to be healed from the prayers made by the warrior maiden.

The dauphin asked the warrior maiden to say a prayer before we started, she reached across the table to grasp my hand as each of us grasp the hand next to us before she began blessing the food. As she began praying, I felt a power that forced me to release my grip with the maiden d Arc. Fortunately, everyone's eyes were closed but mine and the warrior maiden as she looked at me with fear in her eyes. She finished the blessing and we all started to eat. Again, I began to wonder what she knew of me other than I was controlled by the moon and had fought alongside the crusaders in Jerusalem, against the Muslim horde of Saladin. I'll have to wait and see if she will be forthcoming about this latest encounter with the divine. I can't help but thinking about what the dark master said about misconceived notions during this time of man in this age of advancement.

I ate until I got my fill and a plan came to me. I took my goblet, stood up and said, "To Orleans, may she continue to remain French and to the Dauphin Charles VII, may he get coronation as king of France , "sant'e" As everyone was raising their goblet, I faked passing out by falling onto the floor, unconscious. I could hear the people scrambling around me, picking me up and taking me to bed. I could hear the dauphin's voice saying, that they had been pushing the limits of monsieur le Stone, despite of his healing by God, after all he is still a man. I was gently placed on my bed, and I could hear the footfalls of individuals as they left the room. Not everyone was gone from the room, I heard Marie saying that she would go a get a cloth and a bowl of icy water, saying that I could have a fever.

I felt a gentle touch my forehead and it wasn't Marie. By the sound of Marie's voice, she was across the room. Maiden D arc said," Yes Marie! That would be a great idea, he does feel warm to the touch." I heard the door close and Maiden D Arc leans in close to me and whispers, "You can wake up now. It's only you and me in the room." I lay there motionless and even slowed my breathing down and as I concentrated more, I was able to slow my beating heart down. I heard the door open, and Marie came in. Maiden D Arc said," Thank you Marie, I 'll stay with him until he awakens." Marie answers, "As you wish Maiden D Arc," and closes the door behind her. I felt a cold rag being rubbed on my face and on my neck. The maiden whispered, "You cannot leave me David Le Stone because I want you for myself. I felt pain just as you while we were holding hands during prayer. My body aches for you to be inside of me," and she touched my man parts. I grabbed her arm and whispered," Not here, Maiden.

It is too dangerous for you to do such an act. You must retain your purity; you are a vessel of God, and I am not." I released her hand and she whispered, "Do you not find me desirable?" I said, "Yes, but this kind of talk can wait, when we won't have the problem of someone of listening to this conversation." She bent down and kissed my hand and said," I forgot how much older and wiser you are than me, monsieur le Stone. I'll have to restrain my feelings for you, while in the company of others." I told her that I would do the same and said that maybe I could be better tomorrow. The maiden said," I suppose even the immortal needs to rest." I told her that I had only heard that word used twice since I've been alive and asked her what its meaning is. "You cannot die." She replied. She stood up from a kneeling position and in an un-hushed tone said, "I will check in to see about you tomorrow monsieur le Stone.

I also need to get my rest and may you sleep soundly." I replied, "likewise to you, maiden d Arc." My keen hearing didn't pick up anyone outside the door but, my gut feeling tells me to be careful about who to trust, and who not to trust. I'm hungry. I should've faked passing out after I ate some food yet, I don't know why such a notion popped into my head? The maiden is smitten by me and is it because of what I am, or does she want what I have? The dark master placed me in this age of man but yet, he told me not to help the warrior maiden. I just know that something is going to happen, and I will be powerless to do anything about it. I began to think about the time before any of this and drifted off to sleep. I find myself in a different place and a familiar voice saying, "Well Monsieur le Stone, do you think the prayers from warrior maiden can get you a pardon from the high court. Let me answer that for you, no. I brought you from the dust and I own you but, I didn't come here to get myself all worked up. I told you not to aid the warrior maiden and yet you sought her out." I blasted back at him by saying, "You placed me here for some reason to amuse your twisted tale that you've created so, you knew that I would do the opposite of your wishes."

The dark master chuckles and said," This is all a tale, but I did not create it, I only embellished it by pulling you from the dirt and gave you a new life." I interrupted him by saying," A life of horror, killing and eating people as I stay the same. I have a come to the conclusion that something is going to happen to the maiden d' Arc. She like every female that has been exposed to me, is drawn to me like a moth to a flame. Part of me is still human and I am subject of weakness when it comes to dealing with women. I know there is no sense in asking you, what is going to happen next. Is there?" The dark master said, "You are making someone jealous because the maiden is spending more time with you. In three weeks, the full moon returns, I expect your tribute as we agreed." The dark master vanishes, and I'm awaken by the hand maiden Marie." Bon jour monsieur le Stone, I have brought you some breakfast." Said the hand maiden Marie.

I placed my feet on the floor as I sat on the edge of the bed. Marie said," I could hear you having a conversation with someone as I approached the door. As I can see now, you were talking to someone in your sleep. I couldn't tell what you were saying because, you were mumbling." I said, "I was having a disagreement with my dead wife. I told her that I have no intensions of ravishing the young maiden Marie unless, she wanted me to." Marie giggled and whispered, "It is not only I that want to be ravaged by you, monsieur le Stone." I told her that I had better eat my breakfast so that I can heal up for such a feat. She giggled and told me that she would bring me something to eat this afternoon and if I am to be on my best behavior, possibly a bath would be in store.

CHAPTER 7

A SMITTEN MAIDEN

I promised her that I would be extra good. Marie almost bumped into Maiden d Arc, as she was leaving the room. My pardons exclaimed Marie, as they side stepped each other. Maiden d Arc said, "I see your up and eating some breakfast. Are you feeling better monsieur le Stone? I stopped pushing food into my mouth, swallowed it down with a sip of wine. I motioned for her to step closer and I whispered," You know that I can't stay much longer, don't you?" Oui, she replied. She told me to finish eating and she would take me outside for some fresh air. I gobbled up the food and drank half a flask of wine. I put on my boots and followed maiden d Arc through the halls of the castle, until we came to an opening. We walked out into the courtyard, which was still strewn with evidence left by the occupation of the English.

She told me that the Dauphin has asked for her hand in marriage and that she told him that she needs a little more time to think about this proposal. I said, "I made a mistake by coming here and now I've disrupted your plans to be the future queen of France. You already know about me because the heavenly host has told you so. I'm a danger to all that, coming in contact with me and well enough to take my things and go." I could see the tears welling up in her eyes and she said," How could I become like you? I want to be ageless and be with you, forever." I told her that she didn't want this because I don't want it and didn't ask for this. During the conversation, I looked up and saw that we were being observed, it was the French Dauphin Charles peering from a balcony. I then said, "Dear maiden, jealousy can make people do stupid things and I just saw the eyes of jealousy. Don't turn around because he'll know that we have been talking about him."

I thought about walking her to the clump of trees in the courtyard but that would even enrage the dauphin more. I told the maiden that because of her divine influence, is the reason I killed several hundred English to be here. I said, "I was hoping that your gift from Heaven, would provide me some haven of peace from what haunts yet, there is no escaping he that cursed me." My sensitive hearing caught the sound of footfalls approaching from behind. I slowly turned and it is the Dauphin Charles. I bowed my head in reverence to Charles and said, "The maiden has told me of your proposal to her and I offer my most humble congratulations my future king, and I have also told the maiden that I am well enough to put my killing skills back to work. I am grateful to the both of you for getting me back on my feet again."

Before I could say anything else, the dauphin's demeanor had changed from jealousy to elation. The dauphin said, "If you are thinking about leaving and fighting the English by yourself, I seem to remember that I offered you a job as a royal guard. If I'm to be the future king of France? I'm going to need the best of your killing skills to protect me, there are those that wish me dead. Don't you want to serve the future king of France and keep France free from tyranny?" I bowed my head and told him yes. The dauphin sent another servant to fetch the hand maiden Marie. The dauphin said, "You are pushing yourself too hard to wellness. I need you healthy in order that your killing skills will be at its full potential. I have summoned for Marie to take you back to your room, you need to rest my royal guardian. Come let's walk to the shade of trees, the summer sun in France can be very unforgiving." I walked with them to a clump of trees and was about to sit down against one and a voice said, "Don't sit down, I won't be able to pull haul you up on your feet."

I said, "I am merely waiting for an angel from Heaven to rescue me." Marie put her arm around my waste, leading me back into the entrance of the castle. She was scolding me the whole time as we were going up the stairs. I told her that it wasn't my idea to go outside and didn't have a choice in the matter. We arrived at the door of my room, Marie closed it and said," I know it was the maiden d Arc. I don't blame her for wanting to spend time with you only if it is brief." I walked over to a chair by the table and sat down. Marie told me that she is going to bring a bucket of water and soap to wash away the stench. I laughed at her comment as she exited the room.

I sat there at the table to relishing the moment, just experiencing what it feels like to be elevated above the average person, the man inside the castle instead of the man outside the castle. I know without this curse; I would be a part of the desert sand by now. There was a knock on the door, and I said," En tres." It was Marie carrying a bucket of water, she sat it down, closed the door and locked it. I could see that she was winded, and I told her to take a rest. Marie told me that maiden d Arc had asked her where's she going with the soap and water? Marie said, "I told her that I was bringing the soap and water for you to bath. The maiden told me to bath you and regrets that she couldn't be here to do it herself. So, go ahead and undress monsieur le Stone, I'm sure she won't let me be in here with you alone for any length of time, she longs for you and so do I." I stood up and began removing my clothing, I had turned my back to Marie and dropped my pants to the floor. Marie told me not to be shy and that she had seen a man's body before.

I asked her when she saw a man's body and she told me that she saw a naked corpse. Marie began washing my back and noticed that my scars were gone. Marie said," What happened to the wounds that she had tended? Turn around and let me see the front. Your guts were all but hanging out of your stomach and there isn't even a sign that you were injured." I thought fast and said, "The maiden asked God to heal me and the scars are no more." Marie began wiping my face with the cloth and began kissing me, pressing her body against me. I was already aroused as she began fondling me. She said," I want you inside of me David." She got the chair and pushed me down onto it, lifting her dress and straddling me at the same time. She began to whimper and moan as I thrust deep into her.

I remembered what the dark master said that if I plant a seed in a woman, the child will be as I am. Marie was in a spasm of ecstasy, and I pulled out of her before my fluid came out. Marie asked why I did such a thing and I told her that she would be shunned as an unwed mother. I said," You deserve more than being a hand maiden and you don't need the burden of a child to raise also." Marie began to get angry with me and said, "In other words, I'm not good enough for you is that it?" To calm her down I grabbed her and began kissing her, she calmed down. I stopped kissing her and said," Are you okay now?" Marie said, "Forgive me monsieur le Stone, it is my fault. I should have known better and I lost control. Please let me finish cleaning you up." I took the cloth and finished bathing myself off. I placed the cloth on the buckets edge and took Marie's hand and told her," Suppose I'm killed in battle and you're with child, would another man treat my child as his own?

Would another man be able to fill your heart and replace my memories from your mind?" Marie said," I would make you a good wife David le Stone but, you are right. I would be at the mercy of the world if you died on the battlefield and so would the child." My sensitive hearing picked up a sound at the door. I held my finger to my lips and said," I think that I dirtied up the water enough for today, can you wash my hair tomorrow? I think I need to lay down." Marie understood that someone was on the other side of the door. She quickly wiped the insides of her legs and placed the rag in the bucket. She said," Yes, monsieur le Stone. I will return later with some food and I will wash your hair tomorrow." She then leaned in and whispered in my ear," I love you David le Stone, for you are an honorable man."

She kissed me on my cheek, walked to the door, unlocked it, and opened it to reveal the maiden standing in the doorway. Marie bowed to the maiden and left the room. The maiden came in, closed the door, and locked it. I almost had my shirt on and the maiden asked me to raise it. She looked at my back and touched it with her hands, she too was amazed that there wasn't any scarring. She said," How did you explain the missing scars?" I asked her is it wise to be behind a locked door with another man besides your betrothed?" She said," My betrothed has left the castle and will be back before dark. Now, what did you tell Marie?" I explained to the maiden that I told Marie that the maiden's prayers had healed me.

The maiden was now facing me, pressing her body against mine. She stuck her hand down my pants and said," One part of your body wants my attention," as she gently fondled me. I said," Do you think this is wise? Maiden!" She said," A messenger from Heaven told me that an heir would be born with your same traits but different from you and will hold high regards in Heaven." I asked her how would she explain the pregnancy to the dauphin since she's supposed to be a virgin? The maiden said," I'll seduce him, the same way that I'm seducing you. Get undressed because I'm aching for you to the point I could scream." I said, "Don't do that, it would raise suspicion." The maiden took off her clothes, laid on the bed and I found the strength to ravage the maiden. She likewise managed to drain all the remaining seeds that I had left in me.

To my sensitive nose, the room smelled of sex. I quickly put on my clothes as the maiden did the same. I asked the maiden did she smells the spilling of seeds in the room? The maiden had brought with her a small bottle of perfume and placed some on her and then lit a candle on the table. She tore a piece of cloth from her dress and placed it above the flame. The cloth burned quickly the smoke masked the bodily fluids. The maiden unlocked the door to my room, got the chair from the table and sat it next to the bed. She told me to lie back on the bed and rest. She then said," Will the dark one visit me because of the joining?" I was shocked by her question. I didn't even ask her how she knew; I simply told her that she had crossed a bridge to no return. I said," Whatever he offers you, don't accept? He has been here for eons and knows our weaknesses." She then said, "Did you ever get a woman pregnant, in your travels? I told her that I didn't allow myself to get close because of what I become.

I said," That's enough about me, do you think you'll be able to curb your desires for me? In 2 weeks or so, I'm going to have to disappear or everyone in this castle will be dead even you." She said, "You would kill me and my child?" I said," I wouldn't but the beast will. He will be killing two maybe three nights in a row, that' why I have to leave." Tears began to flow down her cheeks as she asked if I would return after it's over? I told her that she's been in my room for too long already and I my mind is awash with all the things that could go wrong. She got up and leaned forward and softly said," I love you, whomever you are?" As she was walking out of the room, I told her to remember what I said. She nodded her head and left the room. I lay back on the bed, propping my head with my arm, I'm alone to battle these thoughts in my head.

I let desire take control over me today. What if both young women become pregnant? Is this what the dark master had planned from the start? My weakness has corrupted two young women and one of them is a messenger of God. The maiden has undoubtedly been tempted by the dark one already or at least she's been warned and decided to disregard it by today's actions. Now, I'm wondering what's going to happen, after the two women find out about each other? I'll have to watch their reaction to each other as they interact, this could be a problem. I'm again at war with my thoughts, the dark master wants me to be at war with humanity and anything connected to the creator, before I could form another thought came a light knock at my door. I gave a response to enter, and it was Marie with a tray of food. Marie gingerly placed the tray on the table and without looking at me said," I'll be back monsieur to get the tray." I told Marie to stop in her tracks.

I got up and walked over to the table and asked her to join me. I held out my hand, she grasped it and sat down at the table. She said," Monsieur le Stone, I just passed the Maiden in the hall, she looked flushed and was in a bit of a hurry. Did she force herself upon you like I did? I don't blame her because, we both love you." I spoke in a whispered tone. I told her to stop that kind of talk because the dauphin can have all of us killed. The dauphin only wants one thing and that is to be king, no matter the cost or who dies in the process. I exclaimed. I began talking in a normal tone and asked Marie what she'll be doing today besides bringing me food and sharing her company with me? She poured wine from a bottle into a goblet and handed the goblet to me. She said," Well Monsieur le Stone, I'll be washing your soiled clothes as well as the maiden d Arc and the dauphins by the river Loire,' after I clean up today's eating utensils." I told her that I should accompany her to provide protection from a possible raid by the English.

Marie said, "That would anger the dauphin if you were to do this, I'm replaceable and you are not." I told her that I would be held responsible plus I need to get some exercise to build up my strength. I asked Marie had she eaten and if she was hungry, I would share what she brought? She told me that she had eaten earlier and was appreciative of my gesture. I began stuffing meat and cheese into my mouth, washing it down with wine, my body needed replenishing after today's events. Marie sat patiently watching me eat, pointing at her chin indicating that I had food on my face. I wiped my mouth with my hand as she giggled innocently. I look at her and smiled but deep down inside, I feel like how long my time will here last? I finished the food on the plate and drank another goblet of wine. Marie gathered up the plate, eating implement placed them on a tray and said," Monsieur le Stone, I've been thinking.

You should stay here. I'm not altogether certain that it's safe to go beyond the castle." I asked if that's the case, why take such a risk for washing someone's clothes in the river Loire'? I had almost got my other boot laced up, then there's a knock at the door. I said, "Entrez vous." Maiden d Arc entered the room and said," The Dauphin has returned with commander Dunois, and they want to speak to you." As we were walking down the corridor to the stairway, I asked her did she have any idea what I was walking into? She told me that it's probably about where the English are moving to then, in a faint voice she said," I had a disturbing vision after our meeting today. If we get the chance to talk in private? I'll tell you about it."

We got to the bottom of the stairs, walked into the great hall and there with the dauphin, were other men dressed in adorned battle dress. As we drew closer, the dauphin sees us and said," Here is the maiden d Arc and monsieur David le Stone. Let me introduce you to them." At that moment, a familiar face makes his presents known, that face belongs to Andre St. Claire. I bowed my head in reverence to the dauphin and at the same time, Andre realized his friend wasn't dead and bolted forward, hugging a friend that he had written off for dead. Andre said," When I heard the name David le Stone, I thought my ears were playing tricks with me until I saw you. It is a miracle that we meet again." Andre then said, "Forgive me dauphin for being overzealous, please continue." The dauphin said," It appears monsieur le Stone doesn't need an introduction according to your field sergeant, commander Dunois?" Commander Dunois speaks up and says," My field sergeant told me about the swordsman that left many dead English soldiers in his path." The commander reached out his hand and I shook it. From that moment on, I had joined up with an army of French soldiers using the battle plan laid out that day from the meeting with the commander and the Dauphin. First, we went upriver to battle with the English to free the nearest fortification and succeeded, went down river past Orleans, broke the siege and returned to Orleans. Many English fell at my sword, I proved my allegiance as well as my skills as a warrior. I initially thought that my friend and I would be killing the English side by side? Andre has many men at his disposal as he watched from horse back just as the royal commander and the maiden d Arc.

The days have been used up during the raids on the English. I have five days before the beast takes over for three nights, I need to get clear of the chateau…. or people will die. I no longer have a room upstairs to rest instead, I have a room near the servants of the dauphin. I should stop complaining because I know what it feels like to sleep on the ground. I am now a royal guard in service of the dauphin, the field soldiers are camped outside the fortification and many are sleeping on the ground tonight. My stomach is full, from eating and drinking with the royal court this evening. I saw that the dauphin is showing favor to the maiden, but not as a show of affection between lovers; more like equal warriors. It could be that he doesn't want it known that a royal has fallen for a commoner. I feel that the maiden's expectations are clouded, I could be wrong. I was just about to drift off to sleep when I heard a light tapping at my door. I got up and went to the door, it is the maiden. She quickly came into my room and closed the door and locked it.

She whispered in a soft voice," I can't stay long but, I have to tell you that I was visited by someone in my sleep. He told me that he could grant me a gift greater than what I carry growing inside me." "I hope you didn't except his offer," I exclaimed. I said," You've stopped listening to the heavenly host, haven't you?" She nodded her head to signify yes, and told me to watch. She reached out her hand as to grab the wine bottle from the table, that is on the other side of the room. To my astonished mind, I watched as the

bottle floated to her hand for her to clutch. I could see in her face that she has tasted power and is drunk on it.

I took the bottle from her hand and said," I've brought the darkness with me and I see that you've embraced it. You cannot let anyone else see what you can do, there could be consequences." The maiden then said, "Before I met you, I dreamed of becoming queen of France but now, that is so short sighted of me. You and I could watch empires rise and fall together; you know this don't you?" I took her by the hand and led her to the far end of the room away from the doorway. I said, "You are putting us both in a dangerous situation, if the wrong person heard this kind of talk. In four nights from now, I need to be far away from here or people are going to die…. and I don't mean only the English." The maiden placed her hand over my mouth to stop talking and she began kissing me. I slowly pulled away from her and told her that she must return to her room, before the dauphin starts looking for you.

She said that she had left the dauphin in his room and that the dauphin was pasted out drunk from wine. The maiden said," I'm not leaving this room until I get what I came for." She pushed me down on the floor and I felt like a rabbit pinned under the paws of a fox. I said," What if Marie comes knocking on my door and I don't answer?" The maiden quickly sat up and said, "What do you mean by this?" I told her that Marie is jealous of her just as the dauphin is jealous of me. She leaned back down and whispered in my ear saying," I could kill them both using the gift that the angel gave me. Now stop talking, I want you inside of me." The maiden rode me like she was on a galloping horse. After she drained me of my fluid, she collapsed on top of me. After a long sigh, the maiden said," You belong to me and if I smell a trace of the hand maiden on you, she will surely die." I told her if she struck a deal with the angel, we no longer belong to ourselves, but to him. I said," You do understand who the angel is, don't you?"

"Yes!" She replied. She told me that she had been forsaken by the heavenly host because of our union. I told her that when I came to this place in time, I was told not to help the warrior maiden. Being who the angel is, knew exactly that I would seek you out. It seems now, that we have played right into his hands." Have you got a plan to get me out of here in four days?" I asked. The maiden told me she had a partial plan worked out in her head and would run it by me tomorrow night, when everyone is asleep. She got dressed as I got up from the floor, pulling my pants up and sat on the edge of the bed. She sat beside me, I turned to her and asked her, "Did the dark master tell you that you have to pay homage to him?" "Yes!" She replied. "I'll tell you more tomorrow night, get some rest and dream about us outliving all of this." She kissed me and whispered," Goodnight my king." She walked to the door, unlocked it and peered out to make sure that no one was in the passageway. I got up, locked the door, and turned around to see a figure sitting on the edge of my bed. I was reluctant to walk any closer and the figure said," Come sit, we have much to discuss." I said, "What if a guard walks by my door and hears someone talking?" He said that the guards are upstairs and, in the court, besides, no one will hear our conversation but you and myself.

I sat down and said," You've clouded her judgement just as you did to me and now, she thinks that we could team up and be a ruling family that never dies. What kind of ideas did you place in her?" "First of all, she was warned to stay away from you by the upper management. Second, she knew all too well what you are, and it was free will that she wanted to lay with you despite the consequences. The maiden's thirst for power is a driving force to want more than what this time has to give." I asked, "did the maiden want to know my true identity? The dark master told me that the maiden was told of my real name but excepts me as David le Stone. The dark master said," Enough about the significance of a name, in four nights you know what's going to happen to you.

The dauphin and Dunois will be on their way to Reims, the

dauphin's plan is to be coronated king of France, no matter who must die for him to get there." I said, "What of the maiden, what happens in four nights for her?" The dark master told me, that her power would increase exponentially during a full moon, and that she will be the only one that will be safe from the beast…. the only one. "Remember, if you want to stay in this time and be with the maiden, you both will have to pay homage to me." Before I could say anything else, the dark master disappeared like yesterday's sunlight. I laid my body down on the bed and began thinking, wondering what kind of predicament the maiden had gotten herself into. I replayed in my mind, the ability of the maiden to summon objects through the air to her without speaking. All she had to do, was merely reach out for it and it floated to her. My body and mind were tired and I drifted off to sleep. In the dream, I wasn't being confronted by the usual visit by the dark master, this time I'm changed into the beast and killing.

The beast is laying waste to dozens of men and hears a voice calling, "Come witness the power Israelite, come see." The beast slashed his way through countless bodies towards the calling in the night. Just as the beast was about to pounce on his next victim a black cloaked figure grabs the victim and drops the body on the ground. The beast reaches out and a pale white hand clutches the beast mighty claws and reveals itself with its free hand, moving the hood away from the face. The beast doesn't strike but, looks into the face of pale innocence, it is the maiden. Her eyes are closed, and she says with a fanged, blood drenched grin," I never realized how gratifying killing was until now." She opened her eyes and they were the color of burning embers. She releases the beast and says," Kill everyone my love, no survivors." I am awakened by a knock on my door, I got up and unlocked it. I opened the door, and it was my friend Andre st Claire. Are you going to sleep all day or join me for breakfast?" Said Andre. I said, "Killing takes a lot out of a man, especially when he's not as young as he used to be." Andre said," I saw you in action and I'm glad that we are on the same side." I sat down on the edge of my bed, grabbed my boots and slid them on. Andre told me to follow him as we made our way to the main kitchen.

There is a room that connects to the kitchen, he tells me the servants eat here. There were a few royal guards already here and as Andre walked in the guards stood up, Andre told the men to be seated. We sat down at another table and I could sense all the eyes in the room was on me. To break the tension I said, "I think that I should eat with the soldiers of the field, since I'm not dressed as a royal guard or have rank as you do sergeant St. Claire." "According to commander Dunois's recommendation to the dauphin, your skills would be wasted as a royal guard. I told the commander about our chance meeting and how we were able to infiltrate the English soldiers by dressing as them plus, your ability to speak their language fluently, gives us an advantage." I said," You want me to be a spy?" Andre leaned forward and said, "More than just a spy, an assassin."

I told Andre that I'm already an assassin and that I'm killing every English soldier within my sword's length. Andre explained to me that I was to follow behind the English, acquire an English soldier's clothes, the same way that he and I did before….by killing. Andre said," David, you are to work your way into their ranks, find out who is planning the attacks, assassinate him and return to us. By doing this, you would be cutting the head off the snake, the remaining ranks would scatter and our army would be there to obliterate them." I told him that I would run the risk of being recognized and I would have a far better chance of observing during the day and move in for the kill at night. As we were talking the maiden sat down at the table and said, "Monsieur le Stone, I will have two groups of men following you. We would give you ample space so that, we wouldn't be noticed by the English.

The plan is to flank them on the left and right, a scout reported that the English are moving towards Patay. It's a fortified stronghold that we must prevent them from overtaking. This could cause a problem of getting supplies to Orleans as well as Patay, it is imperative that we cripple the English before they can get reinforcement. Do you have any suggestions since; you've been among the English and have a sense on how they operate?" I told them that the English are accustomed to fighting in open engagement in the daytime so that, the generals can direct the fighting by horseback from the rear of the action and runners are dispatched to the field commanders with instructions. I said," Our best tactic would not be to engage on the open battlefield but, to attack at night and during the day, lure them into the forest and set up kill zones."

Andre said," What do you mean kill zones, monsieur le Stone?" I told him, "Imagine a circle with an opening in it. The circle would be a group of men, concealed in the forest and to the edge forest, a couple of men on the edge of the forest draw the attention of the English and trick them into following them into the center of the kill zone. This could be accomplished at night with torches, the men hiding would light there torches only when to spring the trap, come out with swords swinging." I said, I do not know the surroundings that lead to Patay, I'm hoping that there is forest and a lot fewer open areas." Andre said," When did you dream up this plan of yours?" I told him while I was listening to him and the maiden's plan to flank the English. Andre then said," I hear that a captured English soldier spoke of a demon in the forest that was killing his men and he was lucky to get away." I then said," Was the forest demon only killing the English? And if so, we may need to recruit him."

All those around the table began to laugh at my comment as I caught a glimpse from the maiden, as she was looking straight at me. Am I to go on this journey to the afterlife on an empty stomach? I asked. The maiden said, "No! You'll be fed and you'll be sending the English to hell." We all laughed at her comment as hand maidens were bringing in food, wine and placing it on the table. I was looking for the hand maiden Marie to walk in with something and she never showed. After we ate and had our fill of wine, Andre placed a map on the table and unrolled it, placing a wine goblet on each end to hold it flat. Andre pointed out our location and the location of the fortification at Patay. Andre said, "Monsieur le Stone, the English is at least one day and a half from reaching Patay. I'm having a horse out fitted with provisions for three days of food and wine. I also have a surprise to show you that will be added to your arsenal of weapons to choose from." I followed Andre through the maze of passageways until we reached the stables. Two men were just finishing up placing the last pack roll on the horse when, the horse became nervous as I approached, pulling at the reins to get away.

I saw what was happening and I grabbed the horse's bridle, walked up to him and held my face next to his, saying," Be calm my friend. You have no reason to be afraid of me." The horse calmed down and stood perfectly still, I released the bridle and rubbed the horse's neck. Before the men watching this could think, that this was some kind of witchcraft, I told them that it is a tool that my grandfather taught me as a boy. The animal must feel that they can trust you, sometimes it works and sometimes it doesn't. This time the animal felt at ease with after we bonded. Andre said," David le Stone, you never cease to amaze me, you are truly a gifted man." Andre went over to another horse and retrieved something from a pouch. He brought it over to me and asked did I know what it was? I told him that it looks like a small cannon ball.

Andre told me that it is called a grenade and told me to follow him outside the walls of Orleans. I said, "Am I to use a sling to throw the ball at the English, the same way as Goliath was felled by David?" Andre laughed and said, "You could get more distance that way, with practice I suppose but, let me show you it's real purpose." Andre takes out a piece of flint, his knife and a small bit of dried moss. He struck the flint with the knife, creating a spark to get the moss smoldering. He picked up the moss blew on it to catch up a small blaze, he picked up the round object, lit the fuse and threw it as hard as he could away from us. The object hit the ground and exploded with a loud report. Andre told me to follow him to where the object exploded and once, we got there; a significant depression was in the ground. Andre told me that anyone around this explosion, would have been obliterated. He told me that it is especially important to get rid of the object as fast as possible.

As we were walking back to the stable, he said, "I owe you my life my friend so, come back to us in one piece so that we can drink together and have our way with the loose women of Orleans." I got on my horse, rode to the huge iron gate of the city and waited for it to be opened. I heard Andre yell, "Go sparingly on the food and wine, you only have 3 days' worth." I waved my hand as I left through the mighty gate. I plotted a course towards Patay based upon a picture in my head of the map. It will be midday soon and I want to get myself and the horse out this heat, I headed for the tree line on the right. The field was littered with piles of dead English soldiers that had been doused with oil and burning. I began to notice that the field on which we are walking on is pocked marked by cannon blast until we had gotten to a point, which meant this was the maximum range of the cannons from the fortress. I urged the horse to walk into the forest, the shade was a dramatic change from the sun beating down on my back. I stopped the horse and got down from his back, I want to save his strength.

The horse is already heavily laden with a lot of weight, he doesn't need the additional weight of me on his back. Besides, I need to walk ahead of him to make sure that he doesn't get hurt by stepping in a hole, a lame horse is no good to me. Walking through the forest, I can open my senses to my surroundings, to really absorb what's all around me. My sensitive nose caught a familiar smell, it is the scent of death. The wind is blowing directly in my face, there is a human corpse somewhere up ahead. The horse and I kept walking, and the scent grew stronger. Up ahead I could hear the carrion eaters squawking, the scent is overpowering, and I could see the remnants of dead English soldiers that perhaps drug themselves into the forest edge, away from the battle and died there. I decided to guide the horse deeper into the forest because the stench is overwhelming, we kept moving deeper and I made the turn towards Patay.

The wind has lost its strength because of the density of the forest, the smell of death grows faint as we continue to move towards Patay but, my mind harkens back to the dream about the maiden. Her thirst for power has clouded her thoughts and she doesn't know the consequences of dealing with the dark master; to him we are mere game pieces to move on a board for his pleasure. The horse began to get restless as he and I sensed that we were being followed. I moved the horse behind some thick brush to hide his presence and I began to slowly backtrack, concealing my movements until I can get an eye on who or what is following us. I could see movement but the thick underbrush made it difficult to decide. I had drawn my sword, with my back against a large tree, I wait until the culprit passes and make a surprise attack. I listen and wait and then a familiar voice says," No need to draw your sword, monsieur. You are among friends here." I slowly leaned out to peer with my right eye and saw that it was four wolves.

I stepped out, sheathed my sword, and said, "I know my friends can't be hungry, with all the English bodies strewn across the field and in the forest edge." The lead wolf says," No, we are not hungry monsieur. One of my scouts saw you and alerted me of your presence in the forest. I've come to tell you that my father is dead, he was killed by an English soldier two days ago. When I met you, my name was Star and with the death of my father I am now King and like you we are at war with the English." I told him that I am sorry for the loss of his father and said that he was a wise leader. I then said," King, there will be French scouts moving behind me in the forest and I am going to launch a surprise attack on the English. I am proud to have such skilled talent in my midst. First, I must go and calm my horse before he sees you, he is carrying much needed weapons and I don't need him to fall into English hands."

King said," Go ahead and let the horse know we mean him no harm." I nodded in reverence to King and made it back to my horse. The animal was shivering with nervous energy. I walked to side of the horse, patting the tense muscles in his neck, and saying," It is alright my friend, we are about to have company with us and they won't do us any harm. Don't you trust me?" The horse snorted and nodded his head. I was about to give a hand signal to the wolves to come forward and they were already with us. I had the reins in my hand and I said, "King, since we are in your territory, can you tell me what is up ahead of us?" King told me that he and his pack are beyond their normal hunting grounds and as we were walking, he told two of his scouts to go ahead of us and report back with information. King was walking beside me and said, "I was angry with you and blamed you for my father's death until my mother brought something to my attention.

She asked me did my father trust you, the man beast? I told her that my father felt a closer kinship to you than any other wolf in the pack. My father told my mother that you are a lost being that is trapped between two worlds. Do you trust us animals more than you trust humankind?" Without any hesitation I said, "Yes! And do you know why I trust you more? Suppose I tell you that I'll fight to kill every English soldier there, by your side until the last man or wolf is standing? Would you take those words as a true and honorable statement?" King said," I trust you without thinking about it, especially when it came to my father's feelings about this." I said, let me rephrase this, what if I met you first instead of your father?" King said, "My instinct tells me that you are something unnatural to humans but more attuned to the natural world that is us, the animals."

I said, "The key word here is instinct, you act upon it without having to think about it first. As man thinks about the action itself, his mind is already at work throwing up barriers, asking itself questions, instead of using the natural built-in instinct to face the challenge head on. I have only met a few men in the centuries that I have lived to say that they would fight to the last man standing next me." "Centuries?" asked King. I told him, "Yes, centuries." Then as if we, the horse, King and I were all just one animal, in one mind just stopped walking and were testing the air with our innate sense of smell. I said, "The smell of wood burning means there are English soldiers not too far away." We only travelled a bit farther when, the two scouts return. They approached King, bowed in submission, and told him about their discovery. I heard the conversation but, in regard to my ally King, I would let him convey the message. King conveyed that there is a regiment of English soldiers camped up ahead, lying in wait for a surprise attack on the French army as it moves towards Patay.

I asked the scouts did they see any English commanders at the camp? The scouts turned to look at King, as asking permission and King told them to speak up. The scouts told me that there were three men on horseback that were there, and one rode ahead as the other two stayed behind. I told my companions, that we should stop here and wait until the sun goes down. A scout said that there is a stream not too far and it isn't too close to the English I said," Lead on my brothers and we shall follow you." We had gotten to a point in the forest that the under growth was very thick, I had to draw my sword to clear a path for the horse and myself. We finally arrived at the stream and the horse almost ran me over getting to it. The wolves were taking turns lapping up the water as the other was a sentry. I began to look around to see if there were footprints left by men near the stream, only animal tracks are there. The horse was gulping water like there was no tomorrow. I told him to slow down, so he wouldn't cool down to fast, it could kill him. Though we have been walking in a shaded forest, the heat of the summer sun still penetrated through the trees.

I walked up to the horse, unstrapped the bundles, to relieve the weight off the horse and began looking through them. My wolf brothers are waiting and watching me as I pull things from the leather bags. I found bread, cheese, a bottle of wine, a wineskin of water, some apples and several pieces of dried meat. I cut an apple in two halves and gave it to the horse. I gave the dried meat to my wolf brothers. King said, "Monsieur, it appears to me that they didn't pack nearly enough for your mission. It would be a suicide mission for the ordinary man but, you are no ordinary man." I took out a small loaf of bread, some cheese and a bottle of wine. I asked the wolves would they like some bread and cheese? One of the scouts walked over to smell the food as I held it out, he sniffed and sat back down on the ground. "I suppose you would prefer a nice plump rabbit for dinner, wouldn't you?" They all flicked out their tongues as an indication of a definite yes. I ate bread and cheese, followed by a copious amount of wine. The two scouts scampered off into the forest and I made an assumed comment to King, that the scouts have left to go hunting. King told me that he had sent them ahead, to wait on us after the sun goes down.

Just three kilometers southeast of David le Stone and his canine partners, is a group of fifty to a hundred French soldiers moving towards the fortification at Patay. Heading the group is Andre St. Claire and at the rear is the warrior maiden, Jean d Arc. The group has set up camp for the night and waiting to find out, if David le Stone was able to cause any damage to the English. As the sun begins to sink below the horizon, the mind of the warrior maiden becomes awash with visions of movement through a dark forest. She first begins to think that it is something coming towards her until, realizes that she is linked by thought to David le Stone. She sits down on the ground and closes her eyes and soon, all but slight noises outside her tent are heard by her ears. Her concentration was broken when a voice outside her tent called her name. "Maiden d Arc, we have food. Please come and join us." Said a soldier of the royal guard.

The maiden replied that she would be right there. The link had been broken between she and David so, she decides to go to get something to eat. She sees Andre and asks him how many men are guarding the perimeter around camp? Andre told her there is fifteen men staggered about the camp in a huge circle and will be routinely relieved during the night by fresh sentries. Andre said," Go and eat, don't worry, I have this under control. Commander Dunois gave me absolute orders that your safety came first above everyone else so please, don't make my job any more difficult than it already is." The maiden said, "Responsibility is a powerful word and so is friendship, your friend David is on a suicide mission. A mission that was given to him that, you knew that he couldn't turn down.

Was it the Dauphin's idea, in hope that David wouldn't return?" Andre said, "I assure you maiden d Arc that, I would rather be walking into an ambush with David than to be here, not knowing what's to become of an exceptionally good friend." The maiden said, "I'm sorry Andre. For the brief time I've known David, he's left an impression upon me. He is twice, maybe three times the fighter than any of us and I've got a feeling that he'll surprise us, and then we'll be able to breathe a sigh of relief the minute we see him again. Let's go get something to eat before I get teary eyed for falsely accusing you of abandoning our friend." The maiden told Andre that she would get her provisions from her horse and join him by the campfire. The maiden didn't have to far to get to her horse, it was tied out to a tree near her. She was still entranced about the experience she encountered before she was interrupted. She grabbed her pack from the horse, took out bread, dried meat and a vine skin and made her way towards the officer's campfire. As she approached the fire the men stood up to be courteous. Andre said," Would you bless our food before we eat?"

The maiden bowed her head, blessed the food and asked the Lord for a quick victory over the English. She sat down on the ground and began eating the dried meat and bread, while she listened to the men's conversation around the campfire. She drank from her wine skin and started to watch the flickering of the fire as she started chewing on a piece of bread. The conversation of the men became unintelligible, just a dull murmuring of sound as she became fixated upon the fire. The fire began to take on a shape as it flickered, the shape became a face. Her pulse quickens as she looks away and then looks back at it. The face began to speak to her in her mind's ear telling her," Jean d Arc, in three nights your power will show itself, remember your promise to me." The face disappeared into the flame as Andre distracted her with a question. The maiden said, "Forgive me Andre, my mind was elsewhere. What was your question again?" Andre said, "What do you see when you have these visions?"

The maiden told him that it is sometimes a messenger that comes to her and sometimes it is a message that she hears in her mind. He asked her did she have a vision about their mutual friend? The maiden said, "We'll be awakened from our sleep tonight by an explosion, two kilometers ahead of us." "Bad night for the English or for David?" Asked Andre. The maiden told Andre that they would meet up with David tomorrow afternoon. Andre smiled and continued to eat and drink. The maiden realizes now that the dark master can connect to her anytime and anywhere, she knows there isn't any backing out now. The maiden continues to eat and drink, talks of battle plans for tomorrow's march towards Patay. As time passes, everyone disperses and goes back to their own resting spot on the ground. A couple of kilometers northeast of the royal army, David has been informed by the scouts about the status of the English camp.

David told King and his scouts that he is going to take the horse in within a half of kilometer of the English, he's to take the explosives from the horse and strategically place them, at the perimeters of the English camp once he sees the layout of the camp itself. David said, "I want you my forest brothers to wait until all the explosions have gone off until you move in. The English will be so distracted because the bombs will be coming in on them from different directions as I move around them. I'll go in with my sword to kill as many as possible, but the objective is to kill the leader or leaders of the English. I want you, my brothers to know that it is an honor to fight by your side." King chuckled and said," We just want some fresh meat so now, let me avenge my father." King sent the scouts ahead as I grabbed the horse's reins and began walking through the darkness of the forest, as a semi-full moon splashed its light through the canopy of ancient pines and oaks. The horse is a little jittery because he is unsure of his footing, I assured him to trust me, pulling him forwards.

The wind is blowing in our faces, the smell of burning wood is heavy in the air. My sensitive ears were picking the sounds of the nocturnal creatures of the forest, as the scurry about on the ground and in the trees. An occasional owl screeches in the distance, announcing his presences to the prey that he is on the hunt. We are also hunting so to speak…. the English. We continue walking as I must sometime, hack through underbrush to clear a path for the horse. I hear a yelp just up ahead and King tells me that the scout alerts, that we draw near to the English. I unpack the horse and tell him, that he has a choice to stay here and wait for me, or at daylight he can head west and run into the French army which is behind us. The horse pawed at the ground with his hoof signifying that he will stay. I reached into the other pack and found an apple.

I cut the apple in halves and fed them to him. Before I left, I made sure that I had everything with me, a small clay bowl of pitch, a large piece of flint, the strike and dried moss. I have the five bombs with me, and I've only had experience using them just once. I patted the horse on his nose and told him that I would be back. I grabbed the bag of mayhem and made my way towards the English. As I got closer, I could see that the English were not camped close to the forest edge. I guess they fear a surprise attack and are grouped out in the open. I'll have to rethink my strategy, about throwing the bombs at this distance. At the outer perimeter of the camp, there are guards near flaming staff torches. The semi-full moon isn't helping much with concealment either, I guess I could prepare for a first strike. As I was observing the camp, I noticed there was little to no movement of men in the camp, they are asleep for the moment. I tied off the bag of explosives to my waste and proceeded with my plan of attack. Due to the excessive light of a semi-full moon, I had to keep my body low to the ground by crouching and even crawling towards the nearest guard.

As I inched my way across an open field, an opportunity happened, and I took advantage of it. A cloud blocked the moon, I got up and ran. The guard had his back to me and with my sword I lobbed off the guard's head. I took one explosive from the bag, pulled up the flaming staff and slowly walked towards the camp with it. I got a full scope of the size of the English army, by the number of unattended campfires. I put out the burning staff, since the clouds are in my favor and began looking for the commander's tent. I could hear some men even snoring as they slept, while I was about seeking my target. I must hurry and decide before I'm found out because I'm in the middle of about two hundred or so sleeping English soldiers. I found a wagon, it contained wooden kegs labelled "cannon powder." I made my way over to a smoldering campfire grabbed an ember with my bare hand, touched it to fuse and lobbed it into the wagon.

I didn't hang around to wait for the explosion, I pulled some explosives from my bag, lighting them and throwing them in random directions as I was running. The first explosion was massive, making all the others insignificant in comparison. The men that were startled awake from the explosions were on to me. I must fight my way out of the camp, make it back to the forest. My fingers no longer give me pain from the burning ember. Now, they must grip a sword and slash through human flesh just as, the half-moon has sliced its way through the clouds again. I could hear my four-legged friends mounting their own attacks upon the English. I felt the tip of an English blade pierce my back as they move in. An opportunity presented itself, a smoldering campfire was near and I pulled the bag free. I lobbed it onto the fire, men scattered as I made my way towards the forest edge. A couple of English arrows found their target, one in my shoulder and another in my ass. I pushed on into the forest to find cover, I could hear men shouting," Get torches and go after the bastard."

I have to keep moving deep enough into the darkness, so that locating me would be even more difficult. I got an idea, I stopped running and crouched behind a clump of dead trees. I grabbed the arrow that was stuck in my ass, clinched my teeth, and snatched it. I howled like a wolf, a long vocal tone" Aaaawhoooooo…." I waited for a moment, listening to see if men were still in my pursuit. I looked to where I came from, flaming torches were not getting any closer. I howled once again, and I heard a four-legged friend join in the chorus, judging by the sound my friend was close. I stopped howling and then there was three distinct barks and short yelps, they are making their way towards me. The arrow was in perfect center of my back. I could just get two fingers to grip, but not enough grip leverage to move it. As I was trying to reach it with my other hand, up walked King. King says," Looks like the English gave you a going away present, do you need some help?" I asked King, "did anyone get hurt besides myself? One of the scouts blurts out, "The English got hurt." While I was laughing at his comment, King grabbed the arrow with his teeth, a quick snatch with his muscular neck and the arrow is out. I howled in pain as the wolfs yelped in joy, they are glad to see me.

I stood up and caught my breath, I'm bleeding from my ass and it's running down my back. I'm up again, the healing has started I know this because I'm craving something to eat. In two nights, the change happens. Now, my body needs food in it. I hope my horse is still there waiting for me, I wouldn't blame him though, if he up and hauled ass on me. King walked within a couple arm's length from me, as we go towards the stream. My senses are getting keener, I can hear the scouts up ahead darting in and out the underbrush, flushing animals from their sleep. The wolves aren't hungry because they're on a mission, to help me find my damn horse. A few moments go by, and a single yelp indicates, he's found something. I watch as King goes in that direction, as he turns back to check on my progress.

I'm moving but unable to keep pace with the wolves. I caught the scent of water, that hopefully means we're getting close to where I left my horse. I continued forward until I found all of them…… at the stream. The wolves were taking their turn at lapping up the water, washing down tonight's kill. I patted my horse and thanked him for his loyalty. I checked around in the bag for something to eat, found an apple, a chunk of cheese and my wineskin. I cut the apple into pieces and fed them to the horse. Unlike men, animals can sense a man's true intension before it is acted upon. Tonight, the level of trust between me and the animals are engrained. I drank some wine, ate the remaining chunk of cheese and eased myself down onto the ground. My body still hurts from the injuries inflicted upon me from the arrows of the English soldiers. King sat down on his haunches and said,"

We might as well rest here for the night, tomorrow my scouts and I will return to our families. Tonight, with your help man beast, we have killed many English and have eaten of their flesh, the death of my father has been avenged. I will pass down the story of my father and tonight's events to my young, about the man beast that knows the heart and mind of an animal." I said," I will miss you my friends and I fully understand about returning to your home. I know you are all tired, just as I am. I am going to lay right here, go to sleep and I will see you off tomorrow." Just as I was about to close my eyes; I heard a voice in my head. The voice wasn't the dark master, it is a female voice, and it began as a soft distant whisper. I closed my eyes and began to focus my mind on the voice and I heard the voice say," I can feel the wounds that the English inflicted upon you my love and they will feel my fury."

I opened my eyes because, the voice was so clear as if the person was here talking to me. I suddenly recognized the voice; it is the voice of the maiden and she is showing me her new gift. I closed my eyes and only thought of getting some rest, I only focused on the sounds of the night in the forest. I drifted into sleep to find myself in bed with the hand maiden Marie. We were in the throughs of ecstasy, when the maiden came in with a sword and lobbed off Marie's head. The headless body still grinding against me until the maiden pushes it off onto the floor. The maiden stood there as the blood ran off the tip of the sword, her eyes glaring as if embers from a flame and she tells me, "I am your only lover, Marie doesn't love you...she could never love you like I can." "Is that the reason I didn't see her in the dining area, because she's dead?" I asked?

The maiden then changed into the dark master and he began to laugh. The dark master said," It is only a dream besides, you and the maiden are bound together now. She wants a real taste of power, and she shall have it in two nights." I said," Will she be like me, more animal than human during the full moon?" The dark master said, "She desires to be with you, no matter the cost." The dark master vanishes and I am awakened by the sound of thunder in the distance. I manage to fall back asleep and this time there isn't any dream, just drifting like a ship without a rudder. Before dawn, an owl makes his presence known and I awake to find only the horse and I are at the stream. My four-legged friends have gone and today is a new day.

I went to the stream, crouched down to wash my face and the arrow wound in my ass reminded me that it is still there. I cupped my hand and drank from the stream, I filled my stomach with water, knowing that I have nothing left in the provision bag. I walked over to the horse and told him to get water because I didn't know what was ahead of us. The horse walked over to the stream and began to drink his fill of water. I looked at the tracks on the ground, until they faded into the forest as I patiently waited on the horse to slake his thirst. My body needs food to complete its self-repair from the damage done to it, plus the body knows that it is only days away from the change. The horse raises his head and steps back from the stream and looks at me. I said, "The light of the sun is almost here, come let's meet up with the maiden's army. Maybe we can get something to eat from them before we go into to battle. What do you think?" The horse paws the ground with his hoof and motioning with his head, turning left to signify the direction.

Before moving, I strained to listen for any out of the ordinary sounds coming from the surrounding area. I could hear movement of men and horses from the south of us and it sounds like they are coming our way. I patted my horse on the neck and we made our way towards the noise. I carefully led the horse through the thick underbrush, the sun is rising to meet the clouds. The horse and I would walk for a distance and I would stop him, listening for a known friendly language…French. I did hear French being spoken, and I realized that there are soldiers in the forest as well. I didn't want to run the risk of getting another arrow in me. The horse and I stopped moving and I made my presence known by saying, "Viva le France!" A French soldier said, "Don't move monsieur, what is your name?" "It is David le Stone, the man who woke you up last night from blowing up the English camp." I replied.

The French soldier told the archers to lower their bows as the group made their way closer to me. My horse and I waited for the men and the French soldier walked up to me and asked if I had been injured in last night's raid. I told him that two English arrows had found their target, one in my shoulder and the other in my ass. The French soldier said, "We thought that you wouldn't survive a dangerous mission, and yet here you are." He asked me how far away the English are from here and I told him that it is at least 1.5 kilometers. I told him that the forest opens to a clearing, that's where the English are and the second group of English soldiers are to the left, a half a kilometer camped in a hedge row.

The French soldier asked me could I ride my horse and he realized what he said, then said, "Forgive me for not thinking of your wound to your posterior monsieur le Stone. Let me lend one of my men to take you to the physician." I agreed to his gesture as we walked out of the forest and into the oncoming French royal guard. As we exited out into the clearing, the French guard yelled, "Viva le Stone!" as they filed by us, men on horseback and men on foot, carrying all manners of weaponry heading towards the English. I was injured and I had to act injured. I was holding onto the horse's saddle to steady myself as I limped out into the opening. The soldier that is with me told me to stay put, he would locate the physician.

As I was standing there, General Dunois approached by horseback. "Bon jour monsieur, Le Stone. It is good to see you among the living. By the sound I heard last night, I was worried. Are you all, right?" I turned around to let him see my back side. The general asked how large was the group of English soldiers before I blew them up? I told him about one hundred men or so and there is another group of English troops one kilometer to the left that is camped in a hedgerow. The general told me that the maiden d Arc's soldiers are flanking the English as we speak. The general said, "Now get yourself patched up and I pray

I see you inside the fortress at Patay." I bid the general au revoir, as he nudged his horse forward.

A horse drawn wagon led by the soldier, that escorted to the clearing to fetch the physician. The soldier yelled back at the wagon driver, "Here he is physician, you'll do well to take care of this man or your apprentice will be taking care of you." I thanked the soldier and told him not to kill all the English, but to save a few for me to kill. The soldier laughed and told me that he would save a few for me in Patay. The physician and his apprentice had climbed down from the wagon and approached me. The Physician asked, "Where are your injuries?" I turned around so that the physician could see my injured back and my ass where an arrow had pierced it. The physician told his apprentice to help me to the rear of the wagon. The apprentice, a youngster of a man, gingerly helped me to the rear of the wagon, he let down the gate and pulled out a makeshift operating table. I could see that it had been used before me, the cloth and wood construction still stained from dried blood. The apprentice assembled the table, helped me remove my upper garment and told me to drop my pants, as he helped me onto the table.

I could hear the physician gathering things together inside the wagon as he was preparing to work on me. The table smelled putrid; the smell of death had been slathered upon it. The apprentice gave me a flask of wine to drink from it and told me to drink heavy from it, because of the pain from the treatment will be almost as bad as the cause of the injury. The physician came from the wagon with two clay bowls, some cloth and a wooden box. He sat the items at the edge of the wagon gate, came over to the table and examined my wounds. He told the apprentice to rinse the wounds with water and apply the ground yarrow root to the open wounds. I lay there waiting and anticipating the pain that was foretold, so far it hasn't happened. I watched as the physician began opening the wooden box and drew from it an unusual device. I asked the physician, "What manner of tool is that used for?" The physician told me that it is used to draw the wound closed so that it may be sewn back together. I thought to myself, here is when the pain part comes in.

The physician told me that he would repair my ass first because it is the most sensitive of the two injuries. The physician told me to remain still despite the pain and that he would be quick about it, as humanly possible. I felt the teeth of the tool clinch onto my flesh, it felt as if the jaws of a lion had bitten down without regards to releasing. The apprentice was right, the pain is far worse than the arrow. I grabbed the sides of the table and clinched down hard with my hands and I felt the needle being pushed through my skin as the physician tugged at the silk that ran through the needle. The physician stitched up my ass and unclamped the jaws of agony tool. The apprentice smeared honey upon the silk stitches and the physician asked me did I needed another drink from the wineskin? I said, "Do horses sleep standing up?" The physician chuckled and handed me the wineskin.

The physician said, "You may need to hold onto that wineskin, your shoulder blade is showing itself out from the wound." The physician told me to put my hands behind me, the apprentice quickly lashed them together with a rope. I angrily asked, "What in the hell are you doing to me?" The physician answered, "This procedure helps to pull the skin together on back wounds, be still so that I can work." I was helpless at this point and just laid there, gritting my teeth as I felt every needle stick and tug of the silk chord, as the physician worked on me. I could've hidden in the forest; my body would've healed itself by tomorrow morning, but I am extremely hungry. My body knows that a change is coming after tonight and needs food. The physician tells me that he is almost finished, and I felt the last sensation of a needle stick running through my skins, as the physician pulls the silk chord taught as it is tied, my hands are untied and I felt like my skin was going to tear.

The physician said, "Monsieur le Stone, I advise that you stay here with your horse and let the main battle group assault the English, you have more than proved yourself as a valued asset. I'll leave you some food and the apprentice will fill your wineskin." The apprentice helped me up from the makeshift operating table as the physician took his tools back to the wagon. I said," Who is going to protect you and the apprentice as you approach the battle ahead?" The physician said," Are you able to ride with your stitched up ass and swing a sword without destroying my handiwork?" I told him that all I need is some food for energy and that I can swing the sword with my good arm. The physician told the apprentice to get me some dried meat and cheese from the wagon. I was steadying myself by the horse, fully playing the part of an injured man.

The apprentice brought me the food, I took a big bite of cheese and a long swallow from the wine skin. The apprentice gave me a leg up on the horse and bounced right onto my sore ass. I waited for the apprentice to get on the wagon, and I followed beside it. I took the dried meat from my pouch to chew on, it helped take my mind off my sore ass. In the distance, I could hear the battle taking place. I took a quick scan of the area around us; I didn't see or hear any possible threats. I finished off the last of the cheese, meat and wine; I am still hungry. I am once again making my way into a battlefield. This brief moment, gave me time to reflect upon just how many men that I've put to death through the centuries, and how many more will I lay waste to before all of this is over.

The thing that concerns me the most is, where will the beast wind up tomorrow night as well as the abomination that the maiden d Arc will become. I played right in the hands of the dark master, he told me to stay clear of the warrior maiden and like a fool; I did just the opposite. I guess it doesn't do me any good to try and outthink him, he has been observing us humans since the garden of Eden. We know how things turned out for Adam and his bride, because of temptation by the dark master. A kilometer up ahead are two separate divisions of the royal French army, general Dunois is going straight up the middle into the English and maiden d Arc is flanking the English on the left. The maiden's forces aren't suffering more losses than the general's force, due to David le Stones late night raid, crippled the English. General Dunois men were able to kill and capture many English soldiers except, for the ones that retreated from the fight and headed toward the English forces at Patay.

The general made a decisive move, that helped to vanquish the English engaged with the maiden's forces. The English were caught in the open and were afraid to take refuge in the forest, due to an encounter with as the English put it, a demon of the forest. The battle is over, the wounded are carted away back to Orleans and a detail of men were assigned the duty of burying their fallen companions, while the dead English soldiers are piled up, dowsed with tar, cannon powder and set ablaze. There were many piles of humanity left to burn like an abandoned campfire, left to burn out until all the fuel for the flame is gone. The French forces march back to Orleans with many captured English soldiers to be hanged because Orleans barely support its own much less the enemy that ravaged her. On the way back to Orleans, I saw a lone rider waiting for me. I am a half of a kilometer away and the rider removed their helmet. I knew who it was without the removal of the helmet, it is the maiden.

She waves me forward, wanting me to put my horse into a gallop. I nudge my horse into a slight gallop, told him not run to hard and save his energy. The horse snorted and sprinted towards the maiden. My ass is taking a beating from bouncing in the saddle, I stand stiff legged in the stirrups to relieve some of the pain. My horse slowed down as we got closer to the maiden, and I realized why my horse is so interested in getting closer to the maiden, her horse is a mare in season. The maiden said," It is good to see you again monsieur le Stone. I noticed you standing in the stirrups, are you injured?" I told her what had happened, and she laughed so hard, she almost fell from her horse. I said," Let's start moving towards Orleans, because my horse is interested in the mare that you are riding." "I don't blame him, because my body aches for you.

I want to have my way with you right now but, our time together is only one night away." Said the maiden. As we were riding side by side, I asked her what did the dark master promise you after you swore allegiance to him? She said," To live forever just like you except, I won't be losing my beauty. I told the dark master that would be the only way I would swear allegiance. I said," He wanted you all this time because you are or were God's special elect. When I arrived in your time, he told me not to seek the warrior maiden. He knew I would do the opposite, because he knows that given the chance, I defy him and he sends me forward into time, into another no-win situation. What else did he tell you?" The maiden said," My new master said that the dauphin will be king, and the dauphin lied about marrying me. He said that I'm not royal blood and the royal family wouldn't permit a peasant girl marrying into royalty."

I said," You do know that the dark master is the prince of lies, don't you?" The maiden's face had tears and rage painted on it. She said, "Tomorrow night I will test my powers, you and I will unleash havoc." I said, "There are too many innocent people in Orleans." The maiden said," How many innocent people has the beast that you become have killed. How many more will die that you will come in contact with? Don't you see, I love you and I want us to be together forever. We will never grow old nor die. Aren't you tired of not having someone with you, I know you have outlived many people that you've grown attached to, we are destined to be more than just some king or queen. As empires rise and fall, we will be able to walk through the ashes because we are immortal."

As she went on talking, I thought to myself … I have been lonely through the last few centuries. I'll have to wait to see after tomorrow night. By now we have gotten closer to the French army and nearing Orleans, our subject matter changed to talking about the surprise raid I did on the English. The troops began splitting up into groups on either side of the entrance, that leads over the river, filed their way down the boulevard over the river Loire, surrounding the fortress of Orleans. As we pass through the main gate of the fortress, I could see sort of a construction happening. I asked the maiden what is being built? "A gallows." She replied. She saw the puzzlement in my face and told me that it is for multiple hangings at one time. I told her that I've have never witnessed a hanging before, but saw how the Romans used crucifixions. I followed the maiden to the stables and asked the maiden to help me off my horse.

She looked at me kind of puzzled and realized the charade must continue, as someone that is a normal person. General Dunois saw what was going on and told the maiden that he would help me. The general walked over and said," Monsieur le Stone, ease your right leg over to my side, lean forward on the saddle and slide down on your stomach as you hold on to the saddle. We don't want you to bust any stitches that the physician put in do we?" I told him that the stitching hurt almost as bad as the arrow and the English blade, that I received from the night before. The general called over a soldier and told him to help lift me up, in order to carry me. I told the general that carrying me wasn't necessary and to just help me to my room.

The general said," That I can do and I will get someone to get you cleaned up and bring you food. You saved a lot of lives of my men monsieur le Stone, the dauphin asked more of you than I would've." "We were both just following orders." I replied. I hobbled into my room and eased myself down on the bed, it feels good to lie down. The general shook my hand and told me that he would send a hand maiden to freshen me up. My body knows that it's only one night away from the change, my stomach is needing food, every muscle in my body aches. It is always like this, just before the full moon beckons the beast. I was lying there trying to relax and take my mind of the hunger pangs and there is a knock at my door. I told them to enter, and it is the hand maiden Marie.

She closed the door, walking forward with a basin of water, a cloth and a joyful smile. She said," Where are you injured monsieur le Stone?" I rolled over onto my side, told her that I got an arrow in my ass and the tip of an English blade in my ass. She asked me could I stand up long enough to get onto a chair so that, she could give me a bath without getting the bed wet? I told her that the chair needs to be closer to my bed, she fetches a chair and places it by my bed. She asked which arm is injured so she pulled me up with my good arm. I sat up and eased my legs over the side of the bed and Marie pulled me up, sat me in the chair. She helped pull my top off, examining the physicians stitching job and began washing off the dirt from around it. She gingerly cleaned away the dirt from my upper body.

The coolness of the water is a relief from the sultry summer in France. She said," Can you lean forward, so that I can wash the

dirt from your hair?" I leaned over as she took the cloth and squeezed the water over my head. I could see colors of the creek mud falling to the floor. She ran her finger through my hair to remove the remainder of the outside elements and squeezed more water over my head. She rang the water from my hair and said," I want you to stand and drop your pantaloons and hold on to the chair as I clean you up." I said," What if someone walks in on me, and I here bare as a newborn?" Marie said," They or whomever it is, should knock first and I'll cover you with a blanket.

Stop worrying, be still and I can finish getting you cleaned up. I don't want your injuries to get infected." She softly said that she's glad that my important part didn't get injured as she gently washed me. Marie finished cleaning me up, helped me put on clean clothing and helped me back to bed. She leaned over and kissed me and said," The maiden has all but implied threats against me to stay away from you. She cannot have the dauphin and you; you are just a trophy for her. I love you David le Stone, she only loves herself and a title." I whispered to her to be careful of such talk, it is treason and could cost both our lives. She grabbed the wash basin and was heading for the door, and someone began to knock. I shouted," Entrez vous." In the doorway is the dauphin and the maiden, I told them to please…. come in. As Marie bowed in reverence to the dauphin, I could see the subdued scorn in the maiden's face.

I asked Marie could she bring me some food because I'm starving? Before she could get a word out, the dauphin said," You will be eating at the table with me, monsieur le Stone. According to my generals and the maiden, you pulled off a spectacular ambush on the English and saved possibly a thousand French soldiers. It wouldn't be proper to have a celebration without the guest of honor, would it? I'll have two of my personal guards place you in a chair with a cushion of course, carry you to the dining hall." I told the dauphin that I will be there on one condition, that he doesn't keep me up to late, I need to get my rest. The dauphin chuckled at my comment as he let the room first, the maiden grabbed the door and winked at me as she closed it. I thought to myself, Marie's conversation was probably heard, not by the dauphin… the maiden.

Marie may have just brought the shadow of death on her. I can't help but think about the dream I had about her being beheaded. Is it a foreshadowing of what's to happen or just another twisted drama put together by the dark master. I lay there on the bed, trying not to think about anything because I know somewhere in the background the dark master is waiting for something to happen, and more than likely it's me that somehow pisses him off. I was at the point of almost falling asleep, when I was startled by a knock on my door. I said, "Entre." Two royal guards came into my room and said," Pardon, monsieur le Stone. We have been tasked to bring you to the dining hall, can you sit up in the bed?" "Oui." I replied, as I grabbed the side of the bed with my good arm and pulled myself up. Though my pain is gone I have to continue the charade.

The two men helped me to my feet, one man held me steady as the other grabbed a chair. I told them before I sit down, would one of you fold up the bed cover and place it in the chair. One of the men asked me what had happened and I pulled down my pantaloons and showed them. One of the men said, "Did the arrow cause that much damage or was it the physicians handy work?" I told him that the physicians needle hurt a lot worse than pulling the arrow out of my ass. The other guard enquired about my arm; I showed them where the English blade went into my back. I readjusted my clothes and sat down in the one guard got in front of me, the other was behind me, as they lean my chair back, picking up the chair and made their way out the door. I said," I don't feel like I deserve this royal treatment, I'm a soldier just like you men are and nothing more.

One of the guards said, "You weren't supposed to live through that attack." The guard behind me, told him to be quiet or they would be sent on a suicide mission. In a faint voice I said," Let me guess, I'm more popular than the dauphin?" "Oui." Replied the guard in front. The talking stopped as we were nearing the dining hall entrance, and I said, "Here goes another nail in my coffin." The guards snickered because they knew what I was talking about. We enter the great hall, men stand clapping and cheering, the dauphin at the end of the table was also clapping no cheering. The guards set me down at the empty spot near the dauphin and the maiden. The men sat down, and I asked permission to speak from the dauphin. The dauphin told me that permission is granted. I grabbed the table with my good arm and pulled myself up, standing and steading myself. I said, "I am humbled by this gesture by my brothers in arms and offer my gratitude to the future king of France. I want to give thanks to my brothers that didn't make it and to offer this prayer. Oh, Creator of this world we stand on. We ask that you grant my fallen brother's entry into your world that is without pain and suffering, and to let you know that they fought against tyranny and enslavement. Please watch over the people at this table and camped around all of France, in thy name I pray. Amen." I eased myself back down in my chair and for a brief moment, I felt as if all of Heaven was listening.

The dauphin said, "The warrior speaks like a priest, you never cease to surprise me do you, monsieur le Stone?" The dauphin told the hand maidens to pour the wine. The men started passing platters of food around the table after the dauphin got served first. I am starving, the smell of cooked meat has peaked my cravings even more. A field sergeant next to me held the platter of fresh vegetables, while he pushed vegetables onto my plate until I told him to stop. I thanked the sergeant as he passed on the platter, I'm waiting for the meat platter. As platters are being emptied, the handmaidens are bringing in more food. I wait to see if Marie is part of the foray of food? She surprised me by setting a platter of bread and cheese close to me so that I can reach it. I said," Merci." "De Rien." She replied. After that moment, I heard the other men at the table be more courteous to the hand maidens except, the dauphin and the maiden.

I had my plate filled a couple of times, with several goblets of wine in my stomach. By now the men have filled their stomachs with food and are consuming more wine. The hand maidens have started clearing the table of the main course, leaving only the bread and cheese. The general across the table from me asked a moment-by-moment explanation of the ambush on the English. I began telling them about trapesing through a dark forest, pulling a horse loaded with explosives with little to no visibility. As I was talking, another voice in my head, a female voice saying," You were sent on a suicide mission, they didn't know you're immortal. They will all pay tomorrow." I looked over at the maiden, she stood and raised her goblet and said, "Stand up fellow warriors. I propose a toast to a man that was given an impossible task and yet he beat the impossible odds to make it back to us. Viva le France." The men raised their goblets and shouted viva le France and turned up their goblets. I said to myself if the dauphin is already threatened by my presence? He will most surely find a way to rid of me after the toast from the maiden.

I thanked everyone and I asked the dauphin could I be excused to go back to my room. The dauphin said, Of course, monsieur le Stone. I'm sure the injuries are painful from getting stabbed, shot in the ass with an arrow while running from the ambush." I pulled myself up with my good arm, I bowed to the dauphin in respect and slowly started to hobble away from the table. The dauphin told a guard to help me to my room and another came with him. They put their arms around me, taking the weight off my legs as they carried back to my room. The guards eased me down onto my bed and one of the guards said, "I don't understand monsieur le Stone, you are a hero to me and others." Before I could say anything, the oldest of the two guards said," Monsieur le Stone has stolen victory from the dauphin and his generals and though they praise monsieur le Stone, they wish him dead at the same time.

I know that monsieur le Stone didn't win the battle all by himself, it is what's to be remembered and talked about in days to come, that the dauphin and his generals hate the most." The eldest guard then turned to me and said, "Monsieur le Stone, you no doubt probably saved our lives last night. I suggest that you need to leave this place as soon as you can, even if you don't wait to heal up. I fear for your life as long as you stay here. We must get back to the dining hall and please heed my message." I thanked the guards for getting me to bed as they closed the door to my room. It seems now, I have worn out my welcome. In the dining room, many of the men have left the great table, including the maiden.

CHAPTER 8

A SCORNED DAUPHIN

The dauphin and his generals are discussing the next campaign to rid the English and Burgundy armies between Orleans and Rouen. One of the generals told of the heavy encampment of the English there, from information given by a scout's return from that area. The dauphin said, "I want a meeting with the commanders in here in the morning." The dauphin turns and walks to the stairway, he's a man full of scorn as he makes his way to the maiden's room. He knocks and a female voice says, "Go away! I'm trying to get some sleep." The dauphin tries to open the door but it is locked. The dauphin says, "Open the door, Jeanette. Is that the way you should treat your fiancé?" The maiden opens the door and allows the dauphin to come in. The dauphin expecting to see the maiden in her night clothes, finds her fully clothed. The dauphin said, "I heard you say that you are trying to get some sleep, yet your lamp is still burning and you are fully clothed.

Are you planning to go somewhere?" The maiden said," I had finished praying before you arrived at my door, I didn't feel like changing my clothes and as far as me being your fiancé…. you have been leading me on this whole time. I am not royal blood and I've never heard once announce me as your intended. I may be a young peasant girl but not a stupid peasant girl. I'm a good luck charm to you because of my visions from God." The dauphin said," What has your latest vision revealed?" The maiden said," The latest revelation is that you may or may not be the next king of France. Your destiny is not preordained and everything you do from here on out is based solely on your own actions. In the message I received, it was revealed that you are no better than the English king, you do not care for your subjects or France. You are only seeking power for you."

The dauphin made an attempt to back hand the maiden, but the maiden is quicker and overpowered the dauphin. The dauphin said, "I could have you hanged for this and have you friend David le Stone hanged for treason." The maiden said," Treason! On what grounds for treason?" The dauphin said, "For conspiring to overthrow my ascending to be king as your accomplice." The maiden released the dauphin's arm, that she had twisted behind his back. She said, "Do whatever you want to me but, monsieur le Stone has offered up more than his loyalty to you, he offered up his life to save many in the raid….by himself." The dauphin said, "If you want to save monsieur le Stone and yourself, I'll expect full submission from you and I won't require you to go on battle campaigns. Are we in agreement?"

The maiden bowed her head and in a faint voice replied," Yes." The dauphin went to the door to only check that it is locked and stood before the maiden, told her to get down on her knees and start sucking. The maiden was very repulsed by this and yet she did it anyway, then removing her clothes and allowed the dauphin to enter her from behind. During this humiliating experience, she could only imagine that it is David doing this to her and the revenge she plans on releasing tomorrow night the full moon comes. Downstairs in his bed, David had been awakened by a touch on his shoulder. A candle has been lit and he sees Marie in the room. David said," I didn't hear you come in." Marie turns her back towards David, dropping her tunic onto the floor, jutting out her bare bottom suggestively and saying, "Don't you like what you see, David? "Yes, I do." Replied David. Marie turns around and changes right before his eyes into the dark master. The dark master said, "I really had you going, didn't I? The dark master chuckles and told David that the maiden had given into the dauphins demands. I asked what the demands are and what are his reasons. The dark master said, "The dauphin has threatened your Jeanette into full submission to keep you and her from being put to death. We both know that you can't die by hanging and the maiden knows the dauphin has no intention of marrying her, she is only his source for sexual release. Right now, the dauphin is upstairs releasing his jism into her ass. Just remember you still owe me my sacrifices tomorrow and she'll be acting out her revenge."

The dark one disappears into the night and the candle goes out, just as a light knock is heard at his door. "Entrez vous." I replied. In walked Marie carrying a candle and she lit the candle on my table and put her candle out. She locked my door and came over to my bed. I said, "What is wrong Marie? Are you okay?" She laid beside me and said," I fear for you, my dear David. If you were well enough, I would take you from this place and we could start all over somewhere else." I asked Marie how far away is her family from here? She told me that it is a day's ride from Orleans. I told her that she must leave tomorrow morning, dressed in men's clothing and go to your family's home and stay there for three days.

Marie said, "I won't go unless you go with me." I told her to wait for me and I would find her. She kept enquiring about what was going to happen in the next three days? I told her to trust me and to get me a sword, while everyone else is sleeping. She kissed me and said she wouldn't have to go far to get one. She got up and left the room. I waited with anticipation, hoping she gets back without drawing attention. It was only a short while, that she soon returned to my room with a sword. She locked the door and brought the sword to me. I placed the sword by the bed and out of view. She saw me use my injured arm, when I hid the sword. She took off her clothes dropped them in the floor and blew out the candle. I slid over to give what little room there is, in this very narrow bed. Marie said," I thought your arm was injured?" I told her that I'm not totally helpless, I have to appear helpless in the eyes of the dauphin and his closest generals. I said," Let's stop talking and enjoy tonight, because tomorrow I want you gone to be with your family. I promise, you'll be seeing me in three days."

Marie then said, "You won't be letting the maiden have her way with you, as I am now… will you? I told her to stop such ridiculous talk. Marie stayed with me until almost daylight. I made her promise to leave Orleans, I know she won't listen. My sense of smell has caught the scent of rain in the wind, it will be raining soon. My body already desires food, the pain from my injuries have gone and my acute hearing picks up the sounds of a new day. My mind is awash with probabilities, mass rampaging killings on the guilty as well as the innocent. The fires of hell have been stoked into the mind of the maiden. I know not of the extent of her power she'll possess but I'm certain that she'll strike down all those whom have crossed her. I know of two targets, that is the dauphin for using her and Marie because, she knows Marie is drawn to me. I can hear more movement outside my door and men talking. The men burst into my room and one of them said," Monsieur Le Stone, you are to be confined to your room and a guard posted at your door. No one is to enter or to leave without permission."

I said, "What have I done to desire such treatment." The guard said, "The show of disrespect toward the dauphin last night when you turned your back on him. Such an act could be interpreted as show of treachery." I assured the men, that no such meaning was suggested, the wine and his comment prompted me to be defiant. If you were there to see it, and if you had the backbone, you would've done the same." The guards told me that they are merely doing what they're order to. I told them that I am injured and pose no threat to them. I merely asked them to get me some food because I'm famished. The guard told me that he would get some food brought to me and apologizes for this treatment. He said," The dauphin is jealous of your lone accomplishment as are his generals; I don't think they expected for you to live through that raid. He doesn't want people glorifying you instead, he wants all the glory for himself." Another guard said," Hold your tongue or we'll be under arrest for treason ourselves. If someone hears this kind of talk?"

I said, "I could make your life and the dauphin's a lot easier to bear, if you get me food, bring my horse to my door, I will disappear like yesterday's sunshine." The two guards looked at each other and one said, "What do we say when asked about you, when we were sent to guard you?" I told them to give me enough time to leave Orleans and tell your superior that you spent time looking for me. As we were talking, the rain began to pour from the sky. I then said, "Forget the food and get me a horse, I will cover myself with this blanket, get on the horse and be gone. The oldest of the guards told the youngest, to go and get a horse and bring it close to the room and walk away. The younger guard hesitated and before he could utter a word, the eldest guard told him to go, that he was wasting time. I raised myself up on the bed, eased my legs over the side and reached for my boots. I put on my boots as quickly as I could and thought about the sword.

An idea came to me in a flash. I told the guard that I am going to save him from the gallows, as I acted like I was reaching for the blanket. I clenched my fist and backhanded the guard with all my might. I knocked him to the other side of the room, he was unconscious. I grabbed the sword, threw the blanket over me and headed out the door. A horse was there in the courtyard waiting for me. I began walking towards it and a familiar voice from the upper balcony said, "Where are you going? "I kept on walking, ignoring the maiden. I got my hands on the reins, put my foot in the stirrup and nudged the horse towards the gate. I wanted to make the horse run but, it would draw attention of the soldiers on the fortress wall. At the gate a soldier stops me. He asked me, "Where are you going?" I stared into his eyes and told him to tell the gate keeper to let me pass. I leaned back into the saddle and the soldier yelled," Let him pass." I waited for the massive doors to open and I nudged the horse to pick up the pace.

I know that the maiden will be following me. I didn't cross the bastille bridge instead, I headed to Janville. I heard that name at the table in the dining hall, the English are there as well the beast. I will do my best to direct the maiden's anger towards the pursuit of the dauphin. I know by staying in Orleans, many innocent people would die plus, a real possibility of someone finding out that I am the beast. The raining is beating down and resonating through my skull even though I have a blanket covering. The sound of the rain is loud but, not so loud that I couldn't hear that voice behind me saying," Stop! Come back!" I continued forward and I heard a single galloping horse, getting closer from behind. I pulled back on the reins to slow my horse, the maiden in a hooded cloak rides up beside me. She said, "Where are you going?" I said, "I'm going to kill the dauphin, the people of France deserve much better. Don't you agree?" The maiden said," He's destined to be king. I saw it in a vision."

I asked her did she have the vision before or after her encounter with the dark master? "It was before but, what does that have to do with anything?" She asked. I told her that the dream or vision is not a guaranteed outcome, but only a possible scenario. I said, "I dream or have visions about stuff all of the time and the outcome in real life doesn't match up." The maiden said," Let's head into the forest and get out of the rain. She nudges her horse into a quick gallop and my horse followed suit. I thought to myself, I saw the hooded cloak she is wearing in a dream. The only difference is the color; the color was black and not brown. We continued into the deeper part of the forest; the trees shielded us from the rain somewhat. I saw a couple of dead trees leaning over and I told the maiden to stay on her horse, while I build a temporary shelter. She didn't listen and told me that we are a team now. She climbed down from her horse and began to gather tree limbs to help build a lean to from the dead trees.

In After a short while, we managed to build shelter from the rain. Both of us were soaked to the bone, the shelter wasn't completely waterproof yet, it was better than total exposure to the rain. We got underneath the shelter; the maiden removed her cloak, and I took off the rain-soaked blanket and placed them to the side. The maiden said, "I'm afraid of what is going to happen to me tonight." I told her that the change happens before it gets dark. It begins just as the moon starts to rise to the horizon, the change begins. In some cases, the full moon is visible during the day, and you'll be affected by it. She said, "Is it painful?" I said," It is for me because my whole body is transformed into a different creature than what you see know." She said, "I want the dauphins head ripped from his body and slaughter his generals. Do you know what that bastard did to me last night?

I knew what happened because the dark master had paid me a visit, I didn't elaborate about it and listened. She said, "That bastard told me that if I didn't totally submit to him, you and I would be hanged for treason, conspiring to overthrow his rise to power. He made me get on my knees and suck his cock and he entered into my ass like I'm a dog. As it was happening, I only thought of you doing to me to get through it. "I asked her does her body feel any different today than yesterday? She said," My energy level is unbounded and my body craves more food, even though I had a large meal this morning." I told her that at least she got to eat and the dauphin had a guard placed at the door. I said, "That is why I chose to leave when I did. The dauphin planned on doing away with me regardless of your submission to him. The maiden said, "I shouldn't have made that toast just for you, that enraged him."

I said," The two guards that came to my room were sympathetic towards me. They knew I was sent out on a suicide mission and wasn't supposed to survive, and I was a symbol to the victory instead of the dauphin and his generals. As A matter of fact, they helped me to escape, one guard obtained me horse while the other guard stayed in my room. The guard that got me a horse, had tied it outside my room came back and I told him to leave. The older of the two guards, I knocked him out and left him on the floor. By doing that the suspicion of aiding me would keep them from hanging." The maiden began hugging me and crying and she said," There is good in your heart, Judas Iscariot." It surprised me by her comment, and I asked her how did she know? She said, "The heavenly host visions told me to avoid you because of what you did." I told her that I had been set up by listening to the prince of lies. Three days after I was resurrected, my teacher appeared to me in the flesh. He told me that all of my sins would be cleansed if only I repented.

I told him that I cannot forgive myself for what I've done and I deserve this damnation. The maiden," You actually were in the presence of Jesus?" I said, "He showed me marks left by the Roman nails, the lash marks on his back and the markings left by the crown of thorns. I was moved to tears at this sight before me." Tears fell from my eyes as I was telling her this. I told to her that Christ walked the earth for forty days before he ascended and on the thirty ninth day, he reappeared to me again. He said, "Judas, it is never too late." He placed his hand on my shoulder and disappeared. The maiden sat there with this amazed look in face and said, "I'm sitting here with one of the twelve apostles of the Lord." and she begins to cry. She said, "I only thought that I was chosen by God and yet, I'm just small piece of the puzzle compared to you Judas. You knew the Lord, walked with Lord, witnessed healings and the raising of Lazarus from the grave." Before she continued rambling on, I told her that my own greed, envy, and jealousy clouded my reasoning.

I left myself wide open for the dark one to further cloud my mind for thirty silver Denarii, payment from the Sanhedrin priest that were no better than Satan himself. They felt threatened by the Lord and the Romans at the same time, just as the Dauphin and his generals feel threatened by us. The maiden began kissing me and slowly pushed back onto the wet ground. She laid beside me and began fondling my man parts. She said, "I loved you from the first time I met you. I knew something was special about you. I couldn't pinpoint what it was. Now we are bound to each other and the

Dauphin shall feel our wrath as well as anyone else that gets in our way.

CHAPTER 9

A NEW PREDATOR

The maiden slid down my pantaloons, she pulled hers off and mounted me. We made love like two wild animals until we both collapsed into each other's arms. We took off our clothes, removed ourselves from the shelter and let the rain cleanse us. I watched the maiden as she turned in the rain as the water trickled down her body, I noticed that her breast had increased in size and the curves of her hips were also enhanced. I walked over to her and cupped her breast. I said, "Have you noticed anything?" She said, "They weren't like that this morning. I hope they remain like this to please you." She also made notice that my injuries are gone and said," Will I heal quickly like you?" I told her that the healing process happens at a much faster rate once the time shortens before the next full moon, just as it will occur tonight. While we were admiring each other's bodies, an unsuspected visitor showed up. "You two remind me of Adam and Eve when I first met them." Said the dark master.

We were scrambling to gather our clothes and told us that it is no bother. He said, "I thought I would pop in to see how you two are doing and I find that you have been doing each other. I've come to inform you that you only have a couple of hours until the change begins and I expect the sacrifices made to me, to be nothing less than spectacular and a symbol to those that see it. Do we understand each other? The maiden said, "What kind of symbol do you speak of?" The dark master said, "David, I mean Judas. Do you want to explain to her? I said, "The symbol is to be a five-pointed star which represents the morning star, it could be bodies placed to make the shape, the bodies to be carved with the shape or even a building marked in blood with the shape." The dark master said," That is correct my pupil and don't want to hear of any more talk of redemption because there isn't any, the upper management has written you off as a loss. Remember this, a noncompliance means one or both of you will be sent hurdling though time to start all over again." The dark master disappears, leaving us naked and confused.

The maiden told me to stop calling her maiden and address as Jean or Jeanette, which is her real name. She walked over pressing her body against mine and whispered, "You are my master and I only submit to you." She began to get on her knees and was about to place my man part in her mouth and I stopped her. I told her that she wouldn't need to do that anymore and I would prefer to enter the place that God had designed for her. She began kissing me on my lips, fondling me until I got hard. She pressed me against a tree and mounted me, bouncing up and down in the throughs of ecstasy until we both exploded. The rain had stopped and I said, "You have all but drained the energy from me my dear Jean. I could eat a whole roasted pig by myself." "I could eat two roasted pigs." She replied. I said," We need to get a move on towards Janville, if we are to intercept your ex-fiancé." Jean said, "I will cut an X across his yellow back." We got dressed and climbed onto our horses and I suggested that we use the cover of the forest because I have a feeling someone is hunting us from Orleans. We continued through the forest for several hours. I looked over at Jean as she is riding besides me, I notice that she is rubbing her jaw.

I asked her if she is feeling any pain in her jaw and anywhere else in her body? She told me," Yes! Is it a sign for the change?" I said that it is a sign that the change is coming soon and she asked me did I have any of the symptoms? I said, "I have been feeling the aches for the few minutes or so. Have you picked up any smells or sounds?" "Yes, I smell meat cooking and I can hear English soldiers talking just up ahead even though I can't see them for the forest. Judas, I'm afraid and excited at the same time. You don't think we'll attack one another, do you?" I said," The beast will know who you are. Remember, you were seeing through my eyes when I raided the English, you have a way of linking minds with me because you are carrying my child.

The beast would not harm you because of his offspring." Jean said," How long do we have before the change completely takes over?" I said, I could be an hour or two hours. The minute the pains intensifies, the change is upon us and the pain doesn't stop until we are transformed?" Jean reaches over to me and I took her hand. She said, "I love you Judas, or do you want me to call you David?" I told her that I love her and that it would be wise to call me David, especially in mixed company after we're normal again or should I say in human form." We rode a bit further and I too could hear the English, they aren't too far ahead of us, and they're camped in the forest. I said, "We must stop here. I told Jean to take her cloak off the horse. She looked at me in a surprised manner and I told her that she would need after she changed back to human. I told her that there would be a possibility that she could be naked after she changes back to human form. She said, "That'll be embarrassing."

The English are camped in the forest, and we don't need to be so close to them while we change." She asked me why? I told her that the change feels like your whole body is being ripped apart at least for me and the English doesn't need to hear screaming in pain coming from us. We got off the horses and told her to watch what I did. I walked in front of my horse, grabbed him by the reins and told him to look at me. The horse resisted at first until he settled down, I told him not to fear me and to go back into the forest and stay there until tomorrow morning. I asked the horse did he understand me. The horse snorted and nodded his head. I released the reins and waited. The horse hesitated for a moment, I pointed in the direction we came from, and horse began trotting away. Jean grabbed the horse's reins and began to repeat what I did. The horse became frantic and tried to pull away. I grabbed the reins and looked into Jeans face; she is changing faster than anticipated.

I got the horse calm and sent him to follow the other, he began to run away. Jean is frantic. She said, "When I looked into the horse's eye's I saw food and the horse knew it. What makes me different from you? I said, "I don't know but, I'll hold you as long as I can before the change takes me over. Jean says, "It hurts David! It hurts!" As I feel her fingernails dig into my skin as I wait to see if hair appears on her arms. I saw no signs of fur instead; her skin color turns deathly pale. I had no choice but to release her, my body is racked with extreme pain. I fall on the ground screaming as my body is being changed into the beast. Within a matter of moments, the change is complete, I'm seeing through a distinct set of eyes now and I get up onto my feet. The beast realizes that he is not alone and sees something that he doesn't recognize. The beast growls and moves towards the figure. The black hooded figure removes the hood and begins to talk to the beast. In a different female voice, the new creature says," It is me Jean, my love. Can you speak to me?" The beast growls but does manage to say, yes. Jean then said," Do you still find me beautiful?" As she opened up her cloak to reveal a naked muscular body. She saw that the beast was getting aroused and covered herself. She said," Let's feast ourselves on the English and once we are full, we can pleasure ourselves, what do you say my love?"

As the two transformed creatures move towards the English encampment, Jean finds out that she cannot venture into sunlight. The sunlight burns her pale skin and has to stick to the forest shadows. The beast isn't affected by it and continues on, stopping momentarily to smell and listen to his surroundings and noticing how Jean glides over the ground effortlessly. The beast's senses tell him that nightfall is coming and he nor Jean will have to use the cover of the forest to hide. The senses of the beast are being flooded with smells and sounds, his hunger for flesh can hardly be contained. The beast slowly approaches the edge of the camp, concealing himself behind thick underbrush. He begins to survey the layout of the camp as well as spotting an easy victim to drag into the forest, without alarming the camp.

He spots an opportunity; a lone English soldier is building a fire and has his back to the forest. The beast makes his way towards him and sees that Jean has beaten him and he watches her. The beast crouches down as Jean gets the attention of the soldier by putting her finger to her lips and opens her cloak to reveal her beautiful body and walking back into the forest. The soldier gets up and walks towards the direction of Jean. The beast gets curious and gets closer for a better look. Jean has opened her cloak and as the soldier moves in thinking to ravage her, Jean looks at the beast, exposing very pronounced canines and buries them deeply into the neck of the soldier. She pushes him onto the ground, the soldier tries to scream, she muffles his scream by placing her powerful hand over his mouth and continues to feed. The beast begins to look for another potential victim, he moves to another location and catches a soldier off guard that had been gathering wood. The beast rips off the head of the soldier and feast upon the softer parts of the human body, the lungs, the heart and the liver. His hunger not yet satiated, he watches from the cover of the forest. The beast not only is searching for prey, he searches the recesses of the mind of the beast, trying to make sense of what is happening. He thought himself to be an apex predator and finds another kind of predator in his midst. The new predator doesn't share the same outward appearance as he but has observed a deadly skill.

A skill likened to that of a spider instead of a web, she uses her body to lure men to their deaths. The beast continued his hunt until another unsuspecting soul is harvested. As the sun's rays began to diminish into the shadows of night, the hunters could pick at will. A few English soldiers fought back with swords, spears and arrows and found no weapons could stop the creature's onslaught, they are helpless, they are food. Jean has gorged herself with the blood of the English and begins to just snap their heads off, marking their bodies with a five - pointed star in blood. She is following her new master's wishes. Many English have fled the area, hoping to escape the demons of the night. The beast rolls the bodies of the dead onto their stomachs, using the talon like nail of his index finger and carves a five-pointed star into the backs of the dead.

For many hours, the two creatures of the night continued on with their binge killing of the English, stopping only to mark the dead in homage to their dark master. As the night was on the verge of giving into the day, the two creatures of the night started to feel the powers of the moon loosen its grip upon them. The creatures then sought refuge into the forest to hide themselves for the change to come. Jean and David had gotten separated during their feasting on the living and are separated still, each suffering the pains of changing from beast to human and both are disoriented of the surroundings. Jean has no shoes and totally naked except for the hooded cloak she wears, that now is blood stained and the taste of blood is still in her mouth. David has no shoes and no shirt with blood spatters on much of his body.

He hears a voice, turns to see where it's coming from, no one is there. He hears the voice again and realizes the voice is inside his head and it's Jean. David said, "Where are you?" Jean replied by saying that he didn't have to speak but only to quiet the mind and speak in thought. David relaxed and thought of nothing else but to a singular message," Where are you?" Jean said," I'm in a hedge row and there are English soldiers not too far from me. Can you sense my location?" I continued to focus my mind in a way that is new to me, using my mind's eye I saw her location. I thought quickly, removed the clothing of a dead English soldier, I grabbed his sword and began walking towards where Jean is. I was holding my side to pretend to be wounded. I walked over the dead scattered field in Jean's general direction and staggered into the hedge row, just below Jean's location. My plan worked. The five English soldiers are drawn to me a speaking to me saying," Don't go into woods! The blood sucking demon is in there." I said," Come help me! I don't have the strength to make it!"

I quickly dispatched the five soldiers, just as Jean walked up. I told her to see if she could fit into one of the dead soldier's uniforms. She looked at me and said, "Dress like the enemy?" "You do want to get closer to the Dauphin...don't you?" I spoke. Jean said, "You never cease to amaze me, my darling." She quickly got dressed and we made our way back in the direction of the horses. As we were walking Jean grabbed my hand and said," I was afraid at first, when this creature had taken over my mind and body. I felt its power coursing through my being and its insatiable thirst, the craving for blood. The first time the creature fed, it became stronger with each feeding until the bloodlust stopped and the pleasure of just killing started. Is that how it is for you?" I said," At least you get to keep some semblance of your human form but, for me it is an agonizing change.

My mind no longer belongs to me when the beast is in control. What did the beast do when you encountered it? Did it not try to attack you. I only remember bits and pieces of what happened last night. Do you remember everything?" Jean stopped walking and faced me. She said, "I do remember everything. The one thing that stands out above all last night is when, you the beast approached me. You approached me in as to attack, you growled, barring your teeth and claws. I asked you did you recognize me, and you hesitated for a brief moment. I asked can you answer me then, something amazing happened. You answered yes in a half growl but, it was you. I was able to pull that part that is hidden deep inside the beast that is you. I don't know if the beast knows that I may be carrying its child or that we are bound by the same master, I don't know. I do know this; I love you and have since I first met you."

I told her that when she met me, I had just finished my last monthly change and that all females are drawn to me for some reason. She said, "I'm not just some female now and my body aches for you. We are alone and I want you inside of me, where you belong my love." We took each other's clothes off and ravaged each other's bodies in the forest like two wild animals. After we both released an explosion of ecstasy, we lay collapsed upon each other. I thought to myself that I wanted this woman dead and now I feel drawn to her like a moth to a flame. Jean kissed me and said, "We belong to each other, remember my love." She got up and put on the English soldiers clothing and I did the same. An idea came to mind and decided to try it. I put my two fingers in my mouth and let out two long whistling sounds and I waited. Jean looked at me and smiled and said," I hear two horses coming our way."

We walked from the forest and into a clearing, the horses were in a steady gallop coming towards us but, they weren't alone. I could clearly see that some French cavalry was trying to catch up to the runaway horses. I told Jean to give me her sword and step back into the forest, to stay out of sight. She wanted to engage them but I forbade it. She threw me the sword and hid into the woods. The horses stopped in front of me, and I pointed towards the forest, they complied. The

French soldiers hastened their horses towards me, with swords drawn they charged. One was able to land a slash to my left arm, but I also removed the arm of a Frenchman. He fell from his horse and the others turned to charge at me again. I ducked the charge and threw my sword into the back of the rider. Only the one-armed Frenchman remained and I made quick work of him, felling him like a woodsman's axe to a tree. I knew that the French weren't too far behind us, and we are dressed as English soldiers and one of us is a woman.

The hedge row has little to no concealment of us and we'll have to move. Jean with her fast thinking, cut off the bloody clothing of the Frenchman, wrapping her head to conceal her long hair, leaving one eye exposed. I said," You are changing in more ways than you realize. You've learned to adapt and overcome." "I've learned from the best." She replied. We nudged our horses forward and they instantly went into a fast run towards the forest. After entering the forest, the density of the undergrowth slowed our pace considerably. I was constantly sniffing and tasting the air, all of us will need water to replenish. I told Jean that we need get off the horses and walk them for a while, to cool them down slowly. She got down off her horse and said, "That's another reason why I love you so, Judas. You have compassion even for the horses." I said," Do not call me by that name, that man chose greed over compassion and knowledge of that man has cost you greatly. Please call me David, though it isn't my real name, it still pains me greatly." "I'm sorry David, it won't happen again." She replied.

As Jean and David were on the search for water, an English soldier gets up from among his fallen brothers. He vaguely remembers getting attacked by something and could feel as if all his life force was being drained from him. He touches his neck and there are two puncture wounds, no blood is oozing from them. He feels no pain except, the brightness of the sun is burning his eyes. He shields his eyes with his hand as he turns towards the last known English camp. He walks tirelessly until he finds a campfire only smoldering, surrounded by corpses of dead English and French soldiers alike. He examines the dead to see if they bear the mark, some have their stomachs and throats torn open. While others have puncture marks in the neck plus the necks are broken. The English soldier searches his mind from what happened last night, he was attacked from behind and something happened that, he cannot yet understand.

He only knows that there is something different about himself, his body needs nourishment and that the sunlight makes it impossible to see. The English soldier goes into the nearby forest to escape the blinding sun. He finds shade, protection form the sunlight and lays down to go to sleep. David with his specialized sense of smell, has located the direction of a nearby stream. David leads the way towards the stream. As the stream comes into view, they find themselves in strange company. David's instinct knows this stranger dressed in a different period of clothing. The stranger says," You two have become quite a pair, marking your victims paying homage but, one of you made a mistake." I said, "Stop toying with us and just tell us what you want." The dark master said, "I told the maiden that after she feeds, she's to snap the neck of the victim or there would be consequences." "I did as you asked." Replied Jean. The dark master said, "There is one that you let slip by sweet Jeanette." Jean said," The consequences is that he becomes like me on the full moon, is that it?" The dark master said," Every night he will feed and everyone he feeds on will feed." I said, "Isn't that what you wanted? A hell on earth?" The dark master pointed his finger at me and said," You did not heed my warning." I said," Did you fully disclose to Jean the consequences of this contract between the two of you?" The angry dark master said," She did not ask?" He just disappeared.

David leans down to scoop up a drink of water with his hands and begins to wash away the blood stains on his face from the night before. As he walks towards the horses, we saw Jean remove her top and began cleaning herself. David walks over to the horses, searching for something to eat in the pouches, that are tied to the saddle. He found nothing on either of the horses to eat. He listens as Jean is washing herself in the stream until, he doesn't hear the splash of water on the surface of the stream. David turns around to look and Jean is standing right in front of him. David said," I didn't hear your footsteps. How is that possible?" She said," It must be that my feet are wet." David looks at the ground behind her and doesn't see any signs of footprints. David said, "You must be careful with this new power. There will be times that can't use it because someone will see it and your secret is no more." She said," Only used pure thought to get me here with you, my feet never touched the ground." I said, "That is amazing but, it came with a terrible price." I told her that I didn't find any food on the horses, and she told me that she wasn't hungry at all. I wasn't really hungry myself but I could eat something.

I lead the horses down to the stream so they could drink. I sat down on a large rock and Jean sat beside me, leaning her head on my shoulder. She says, "I know what you are thinking. You are thinking that we should stop pursuing the dauphin and get the hell out of France." I said, "You are close but, we have to stop the cycle before it starts. There are two more nights of the full moon, we'll be feeding as well as the English soldier. Do you think you can find him or control him?" "I possibly can once I change but, you know as well as I do, the hunger comes first. I'm sorry that I messed up David. I'm like an animal when I become that creature." I told her that I totally understand and that she shouldn't beat herself up over it. I said," We cannot change the past but perhaps we can alter the future." She asked what I meant by that? I told her that after these two nights, we make our way to the coast, get on a ship going to England. She said, "My home is in France, and I want us to be king and Queen of France instead of the spineless dauphin." I said, "We'll be alive after the dauphin's bones have turned to dust besides, in the next two nights, the countryside will be awash with creatures that come out at night and sleep in the day.

We don't have a choice but to keep moving because, there won't be anyone left for us to feed upon." She said, "Janville isn't far from here, we might as well go there. I hope the dauphin is there so that, I can kill him myself." I told her that we might Leave the horses here as well or they'll become our first meal. I took her by the hand, crossing over the stream and the horses began to follow us. I walked over to each horse, making eye contact, telling it that it shouldn't follow and to stay here where there's water. I patted them on their necks and joined Jean on the other side of the stream. Jean said, "How do the animals feel about me?" I said," They fear you the most because the beast in me prefers humans over animals. They know that blood courses through them and you desire blood, any kind of blood." I asked her when she met with the dark master, what was actually requested from the dark master?

She said," I told him that I didn't want to ever grow old and to live forever like you." "What did the dark master say?" I asked. She said that the dark master asked her did she thirst for power? Jean said, "I told him yes and what would I need to do to gain such power?" She then told me that the dark master took his fingernail, made a cut on his hand and told her told drink the blood. She said that the dark master told her that there is power in the blood, and she would change during the full moon. She said," He told me after feeding to break the neck of the prey but never explained why. He did tell me that the urge would be strong after the full moon's influence is over, and that if I gave in to the urge, I would never see the sunlight again." I said," That explains why you aren't hungry for solid food." She said," I'm not so hungry that, I cannot control myself and take a bite of you, my love."

I said," I'm already worried about the mixing of our blood with the child that you carry." She laughs at my comment and tells me that the child will be more powerful than either of us. I said," The child is even more the reason to get far away from this place as we can cause, tonight and the next, there is no telling how many people will be turned. The numbers would only increase night after night." She said, "It is my fault, I got careless. We will need to stay after the full moon phases are over to destroy the creatures. We know that they sleep in the day and that's when they are vulnerable." I said, "We'll have to somehow gain the trust of the people of Janville after we kill off the remaining English that haven't been turned." Jean said, "We just have to make sure that we somehow get inside of Janville, we will need French clothes to make the next plan work."

As I started walking forward, she took my hand and squeezed it lovingly. She said, "This is hard for me to ask but, it has been on my mind since, I found out who you really are." Before she could utter another word, I said," I know what you are going to ask me. You want to know what it was like to be in the presence of the teacher?" "Yes!"

She replied. I said," He was the kindest man to walk this dirt, that I'm not even worthy enough to lay on. During the forty days after his resurrection, he came to me and said that it wasn't too late to redeem myself. All I would've had to do is to ask for forgiveness. I told the rabbi that I can't forgive myself, for what I had done to my best friend. To speak of this causes me great pain. I know that it happened centuries ago but, to me it was like yesterday." She saw the tears falling down my cheeks and said, "I'll never mention it again and I don't want you to think that you are the cause for what I am now. I made the decision on my own and I want to be with you until the end."

We continued through the forest; I could already feel the effects of the oncoming of the night. My jaw is starting to ache, and I could feel Jean's grip get tighter upon my hand. She said, "It isn't dark yet and the hunger is starting to change me. I know you are feeling the change is beginning." I released Jean's hand before I crushed it, my body is racked with pain as I collapse on the ground. The English soldiers clothing is being stretched, becoming tattered remnants of unrecognizable clothing. My senses are super keen and in tune with my surroundings. I stand up and see that Jean is completely nude and as I approach her, she reaches outward to her side and the black cloak appears out of nothingness. She wraps herself in the cloak and says to the beast,

CHAPTER 10

HORRORS IN JANVILLE

"Are you hungry my love?" The beast in a gravelly voice answer tells her yes. The beast tells Jean that men are close. Jean says, "I'll draw them into the forest for us. There is still too much daylight for us to be out in the opening, be patient my love Jean makes her way ahead of the beast, staying in the shadows of the forest. The beast moves without noise, watching, listening, and testing the air with his nose. Jean stops away from the edge of the forest and begins yelling in French," Aide-moi! Help me!" She repented it a few times and it didn't take long before someone had taken notice. A group of English soldiers go into the forest but, they didn't come out. Out in the opening, an English officer takes notice that his men did not return form the forest. He sends more men to investigate and hears screams of the men being slaughtered. The officer struggles to make sense of what is happening to his men.

He gathers up his subordinates, tells them to line men up at the edge of the forest and to kill anything that steps out. By now Jean and the beast have fed on many men that lay scattered about the forest. The men at the edge are nervous, the forest is silent except for the wind whistling through the branches. The officer at the rear calls out to his subordinates, "Send in three men, five meters apart and five meters inward. Tell them to report from where they stand." Three men are chosen, they draw their swords, walk to the edge of the forest and they proceed forward at the same pace. They stepped off the five meters and stopped. The men are in sight of each other than the exception of trees blocking full view. They look around and see bodies scattered about the ground. One soldier yelled out, "I see dead men out here." He was about to utter some more words but, was cut off abruptly. One of the two remaining men saw movement but, unable to determine what he saw. He said, "There's something in here."

The beast attacked the soldier but also felt the soldier's blade. The soldier's blade did nothing to slow the beast, the beast severed the soldier's head, ripped open his chest and feasted on his heart and lungs. The remaining soldier ran back to the clearing, screaming that the forest demon has followed us. The officer told his men to pull back and to light the forest on fire with flaming arrows. Torches were prepared with black tar, arrows wrapped with cloth, dipped in the tar and sent flying by the archers. The beast and Jean have joined back up, the beast sniffs the air and in a gravelly voice says," The clouds will bring rain." They didn't stick around to wait for the rain, they went deeper into the forest and towards Janville. The English troops waited at the edge of the forest, for the forest demon to run into their barrage of arrows. The forest has now turned into a blaze, the intense heat has pushed the English back, still no sign of the forest demon. The English did not realize that they are being observed at their rearward position. Another predator is hunting and it hungers.

The English predator walks in to join his compatriots, he is recognized by one of his comrades. The predator walks up to his friend, with arms wide open in a gesture for a hug, his friend is held in a death grip. The predator sinks his teeth deep into his friend's neck, draining the blood from his body. The night's newest predator drops his friend's limp body on the ground. The other soldiers are watching the tree line as the forest blaze grows, the transformed soldier wipes the blood from his mouth and moves to his next target. The officer on the horse. The transformed soldier loathed the officer while he was once a walker in the sunlight. He couldn't control the hunger to slay his friend and to drain the officer would be a vengeful killing. The horse became nervous, knowing that a predator is nearby. The officer was still unaware and trying to calm the horse. he's knocked from his horse. The transformed soldier rips open the officers throat, as the heart pumps its last beat, the newest creature of night becomes stronger.

The English creature was seen attacking the officer, men are rallied to defend the fallen officer. The sun has faded now; the English creature met his brethren head on. Swords are not effective and the English creature slaughters unabated. Jean and the demon of the forest as named by the English, have also laid waste to the English as they make their way closer to Janville. Jean has been dutiful in remembering to snap the neck of the blood drained men, the beast simply decapitates and moves on to the next victim. During this mass slaughter of humanity, something unexpected happens. The turned English soldier sees Jean and makes his way towards her. Jean is feeding and stops. She snaps the neck of the victim, knowing that someone or something is approaching from behind. She turns and the transformed soldier is standing face to face with her. The transformed soldier said, "You made me stronger than I ever thought achievable as a man. I am now a creature that I thought was only a myth, the undead, the drinker of blood, a vampire. You are different from me what would happen if I drank your blood?" Jean opened her cloak, exposing her pale beautiful body in the moon light.

She said, "Have a drink." She gently places her hands on each side of the soldier's head, gently pulling him towards her neck, then tears his head from the body. She knows there will be others to contend with. The hours of the night will continue with carnage now, inside the confines of the chateau at Janville. Jean and her partner of the night managed to scale the wall unnoticed. They find out that Janville is in the hands of the English and there are no signs of French occupants. The drizzling rain has stopped, and the moon begins to uncover itself from the clouds. Jean and her partner are at ground level and see that little activity is happening except, the occasional movement of a few English soldiers on patrol. The hunger is still strong, the desire to feed pushes them both to begin the hunt again. The two split up, staying in the shadows and catching the unaware soldiers to feast upon. This went on until the village of Janville was littered with the dead.

The night begins to give in to the day and the partners of the night must seek refuge from those that remain alive. The alive that lay in their beds sleeping, oblivious to the harbingers of death will feel the sting of reality at daybreak. Jeans transformation is subtle than that of her partner's pain riddled body, as it returns to that of a normal man of flesh and bone. Jean has slipped silently into a dwelling and her cloak of the night, her fingernails have receded and likewise, per pronounced canines. She is without clothing and listens for movement in other parts of the dwelling. She needs a weapon and finds one, it's an English dagger left on a table. She moves about, noiseless as a cat. She stops for a moment at a door and hears the sound of snoring going on. She slowly opens it, sees two beds, they are four people in this room. Jean also sees English soldiers clothing on the floor.

A young girl raises her head and sees Jean. Jean gave the girl a gesture to be quiet by placing her finger to her lips. The girl complies as she watched Jean stick the dagger into the soldier's throat, this would prevent the soldier from alarming anyone. The young girl points to the other bed and holds up two fingers. Jean nods and moves to the other bed. Evidently, the English soldier is a light sleeper and sits up in the bed. The soldier thinks that he can over power the woman with the dagger, he was sadly mistaken. The girl that was sleeping with the soldier starts to panic. Jean grabs the girl by the throat and ask, "Are you English or Francais?" The girl squeaks out the word Francais and Jean releases her. Jean asked the girls did they want to continue to be whores for the English or do they wish to regain their dignity? One of the girls said, "The English over ran Janville and now more are pouring in since their defeat at Orleans. Who do you think you are, the maiden d Arc?"

Jean said, "I know her well and she gave me inspiration to kill as many English as long as I have breath in me. Now, are there any Frenchmen left in Janville?" One of girls told Jean that there are a few left and they are tied up in the church. "How many is a few?" Asked Jean. The told her maybe twenty or more men and then said,"

The English hang one man a day that they "the English" remain in Janville." Jean says, "I cannot continue to walk around naked holding a dagger. One of you get me clothing and if you try to betray me? The other girl will get the same as the English soldiers that you two fucked last night." The girl said, "I will get you some clothing. Please don't hurt my sister, she's been abused enough as it is." One girl leaves the room as Jean stays with the other. It isn't long before the girl returns with clothing for Jean. The girls watch nervously as Jean gets dressed, not knowing what Jean has planned. Jean now wears the peasant girl clothing, that she wore before the visions, messages from the Heavenly host turned warrior. Jean said, "Is there somewhere in this house we can hide the dead soldiers?" The girls told her, there is a hidden cellar that, their father built before they were born.

One of the girls tearfully told Jean that the English took their father and doesn't know if he is dead or among those tied up in the church. Jean said," The English will be panicking shortly, after they find all the dead English on the fringe of Janville." Jean helped the girls remove the dead from the room and toss the bodies down the cellar. They quickly concealed the cellar door, cleaned up the blood and waited for Jean's next plan of action. Just as they were about to take a sigh of relief, an English soldier came into the house asking, "Where are the soldiers that stayed here last night?" Jean spoke up and said, "They are still asleep in that room." The soldier starts to open the door; Jean throws the dagger that she has been concealing at her side. The dagger finds its target and is buried in the back of the soldier's skull. Jean tells one of the girls to stand outside the door and signal by tapping twice if someone is coming in. The girl goes out and closes the door behind her while, Jean and the remaining girl hid the body in a closet. Jean knows that she just can't stay in that one location.

On the other end of the village, David le Stone finds himself in midst of chaos. The English have discovered the bodies and talk of the forest demon is rife among the terrified English. David's clothes are tattered and is confronted by an English officer. The officer said," What is your name, and did you see what happened?" David said," Stone sir. I barely escaped with my life. It was dark when we were attacked and I don't know what it was. I know that it is strong, and I left my sword stuck into it. My friends were not as lucky as I, they lay out there on the ground." The officer asked the number of men in my group, and I told him fifty or more men. He told me to get a change clothes and start rounding the soldiers by going from house to house. I didn't know where to go to get clothes so, I walked up to first dwelling I came to, opened the door, and walked in. I was almost knocked to the ground by an English soldier as he was walking out. The English soldier asked what happened to me? I told him about being in battle with something in the dark and I managed to escape it. By this time more soldiers in the dwelling came forward to hear what I was saying. One of the English soldiers said, "It had to be the forest demon that I've only heard about. Where is your sword?"

I told him that I buried it into the creature's chest at the same time, another soldier thrust his sword into its back. I then said," The swords only enraged the creature, he simply pulled them out and began ripping men to pieces. I had no weapon, and I ran through the forest blindly to get away. I lay hidden until daylight to make it back here. The clearing around Janville is littered with the dead and dying." I could see the fear in the men's faces as I spun the tale of last night's terror. I asked the men could I get some more clothes? A much younger soldier told me that replacement uniforms are scarce. He said, "You may have to rob one of the fallen brothers, they no longer need them." I told the men that an officer told me to gather men house by house and to meet in the courtyard. I asked if food was scarce like the uniforms. Another soldier told me that there is cheese, meat, and wine in the next room. I thanked them as they filed out of the house and I made way to the food. The beast may have gotten his fill last night but, my daytime body is starving.

I sat down at the table and started eating and started thinking about Jean. As I was cutting off a hefty piece of dried pork with a knife, I heard a soft voice in my head. The voice told me that she is close. I closed my eyes to focus on my thoughts and suddenly as if, she was standing next to me whispering in my ear. She said, "Tie the food up in a cloth and walk out from the dwelling and stand there." Jean went to the door, told the girl to come inside and as she walked out, David saw her. He avoided the crowd of men in the courtyard and walked towards the dwelling. Jean went back inside and told the girls that a friend was coming. While Jean was explaining that a friend is coming, the door opens and in walks David. The girls wore the face of fear once they saw David's tattered English soldier's clothing.

Jean recognized their fear and put them to ease. David placed the cloth bag of food on a nearby table. David said," We don't have long before the English start rounding up everyone from inside these buildings." As he was speaking, he caught the scent of something familiar and said," I smell a dead body in this house." Jean told him that there is a dead soldier in the bedroom and two in the basement. David said," Is there a back door to this house?" One of the girls said yes. David told everyone that they cannot stay in this house and cannot go out the front door. The English don't need to find the dead soldier in the bedroom nor those in the basement, we need to go now! David followed the girls to the back door as Jean hid a dagger in her clothes and grabbed the food bag.

David slowly opened the door to peer out and assess the situation. David didn't go unnoticed; he was spotted by an English soldier. The soldier said to David," What are you are doing?" Using his free hand, David motioned for Jean and the girls to go back. David told the soldier to come and look at something, the soldier blindly walked into the house only to be met with the swiftness of Jean's dagger slicing threw his throat. David once again looked out of the door to seek an outlet. This time it looked less promising; more English are moving about. David said, "I think I have a plan." He took the garment from the dead English officer and put it on. He asked the girls where is the French being held? The girls told him that the cathedral is at the end of the village. David grabbed a sword and instructed them to walk in front of him as they went out the back door. He told the girls to lead them to the cathedral.

On the way to the cathedral, an English officer asked David what is he doing? "I'm taking these French women to be locked up with the remaining French in the cathedral, until we can control whom or what is killing my men." Replied David. The English officer agreed with David and David continued to follow behind the women on the way to the cathedral. The cathedral entrance wasn't guarded, the youngest girl in front opened the massive doors and we walked in. An English soldier started to ask a question until he saw that I had an officer's garb on and he waved us through. I could see that the French prisoners were bound, men, women, and children alike. I had to think fast, and I whispered to Jean to follow my lead. I told the women to get down on your knees with your hands at your back. I called the three soldiers to come over, bring some rope and bind the prisoners. I had to get all three in close, so that they can be swiftly dealt with.

One by one they came over and as they were tying up the women, I lopped off the head of one, stabbed another in the chest and broke the neck of the third with my bare hands. I told Jean to quickly cut the bindings of the captive men and told everyone else to be quiet. The freed men took the swords of the dead English soldiers and waited for my instructions. Jean told the remaining captives to patient but, one person is objecting to what is happening the priest. The priest said," How dare you commit murder in the house of the Lord." Jean quickly made her way over to the priest and stuck her dagger to his throat and said, "You probably told these people to give up peacefully didn't you, you led your own people to the gallows. You make me sick." The priest said, "I know who you are maiden d Arc. The English would love to put a rope around your neck. You are a heretic. You are no messenger of God." Before the priest could say another word, Jean knocked the priest out with a well-placed punch to the head. Jean said, "Does anyone else disagree about being rescued?" Jean could hear murmurings about her actions and heard some woman saying she is just the Dauphins whore. Jean said, "David, I beginning to think some of these people aren't worth saving. I just heard a woman in the corner of the room say that I'm just the dauphin's whore."

The guilty woman said," How could she have heard me when I only whispered it to the woman beside me? The priest is right she's a heretic and probably a witch. Only a witch could have such an ability." Jean was about to explode in anger, and I grabbed her arm to stop her.

I told her to focus on helping me get us out of here. I told the freed men to put on the English clothing as Jean and the two girls removed the dead bodies from sight. Just as the men were finished dressing, two English soldiers came in. One of the freed men thrust his sword into the side of the English soldier and quickly shut the door. The other soldier managed to shout, "Help!" as a thrown dagger stuck into his forehead by one of the freed men.

The Frenchman said, "If the English heard him, they will be in here soon. What is your plan monsieur David? I said, "Untie as many men as possible, take the weapons of the dead soldiers. We won't be able to take them on all at once but I need two men standing guard outside the door, one of you must be able to speak English fluently for this to work. One of freed men spoke up and proved to me his language skill. I said, "We must move quickly for this to work, once you two men go outside the door to stand guard, I want you to assure any inquisitor that things are under control. If they insist on coming in, let them and we shall take care of them. In the case no one heard anything, just stand on guard outside the door and wait. I'll come outside to brief you for the next stage." The two men exit the doors of the cathedral, I put my ear to the heavy door and listened. I could hear the English but, they were not in the least concerned about the occupants of the cathedral. The freed men inside were pushing me for an answer about the plan. I had nothing to tell them at first until, the map of the plan unfolded in my mind. I told the freed men to stand out of sight the opening of the doors on each side and wait for three to four English soldiers to come in. I said," Try not to bloody up the English clothing because you will be wearing them. You'll need to move the dead bodies out of sight or they will alarm the others.

The guards outside will knock twice if more than 10 men are coming." The men got into their position and I walked towards Jean, to tell her what I'm going to do next. I went up to Jean and she grabbed me, gave me a long kiss on the mouth. I said, "What was that for?" She said, " I love you, David le Stone and you are a brilliant man. I told her what I was going to do once I left the cathedral, she had to stop herself from laughing out loud. She said, "That will surely draw them in but, how are you going to keep them from rushing the door?" I told her to tell the Frenchmen that after they take the English soldiers clothing, the same number of men are to exit the cathedral and to be adjusting their clothing as they walk out. In the event that an English soldier ask them a question, tell them to say nothing. Tell them to imitate the movement of love making, the English will not have a problem of interpreting that. Jean snickered and told me that she'll have the two girls undressed, waiting down by the altar.

She said, "Catching flies with honey." I made my way out past the large cathedral doors and heard them close behind me. I saw a group of ten or so soldiers talking among themselves. My sensitive hearing caught the conversation about the forest demon being responsible for the deaths, on the other side of the wall. As I was walking up to them, I was adjusting my clothes. I said, "I just had two French girls at once inside the cathedral. If the forest demon kills me tonight, I'll have a memory to take with me." The English soldiers are very attentive and asking questions. I told them to be discreet about it and not go rushing to the cathedral at once. I suggested that three men go and the rest to wait until the other three have come out, before entering the cathedral. One of the soldiers asked, "What about the guards at the door? Will they let us pass?" I told him to say, "David sent me." I kept on walking and observing the number of English soldiers moving about.

A rough estimation to about 30 or so soldiers that I can see. I went over to a group of soldiers and pulled five or six men to the side and told them what is going inside the cathedral, pointing the group of men that are next. I told them to stay put, not to draw attention and wait until they see those standing over there come out of the cathedral. One of the soldiers said, "This sounds too good to be true." I told him that the girls have heard about the forest demon also and want to go out with a bang, so to speak." The soldiers chuckled a subdued laugh, and making remarks about drilling the French girls. I walked over to a dwelling and opened the door. I checked to see if anyone was in here besides myself and cracked the door open to peer out at the front of the cathedral. I watched for a while as men walked out being replaced by the French dressed as English soldiers. I was thinking to myself, how long will this farce continue before something happens. I have a gut feeling that I should go to the cathedral…. now. I closed the door to the dwelling and ran to the cathedral. The fake guards let me in, and I could see different kind of fear in the eyes of freed villagers.

A French girl ran up to me and said," You must follow me, there's something wrong with the maiden." She took me to the back of the cathedral where the dead English soldier's bodies are. I asked the French girl," What has happened?" Before the French girl could answer, I heard Jean from a darkened corner of the room say, "They are afraid of me. I have failed you David, my love. I could not control the hunger and I was seen feeding on the dying." My mind was spinning. I know that it has been many hours since daybreak and I haven't felt the usual sensations before I change. I walked closer to the dark corner and held out my hand. Jean said," You have to come closer; the sunlight burns my eyes." As I got within arm length of her, she pulled me to her with great strength, wrapping her arms around me, nearly stopping me from taking a breath. She started weeping, telling me that she has really messed up. She said, "I tried to eat some food but I only vomited it back up. My body doesn't want food, I tried to fight the urge and I gave into the craving."

I said," We must get out of this place before this gets out of control in here. You know what is going to happen soon and there will be more creatures of the night coming to feed. is there a back door to this place?" Jean told me that the door is all but blocked with dead English soldiers. I told Jean to stay put until I can put a plan together in my head. I got the attention of one of the French girls that, has the cheese basement. She came over and I told her that she and her sister are to get in the cellar and not come out until daylight tomorrow. She was about to ask me a question, I grabbed her, looked her in the eyes and said," Get access to the back door and flee to your home once you hear me yell out," Stop! Don't make me kill you!" I told her to let me know when the door has been cleared for her and her sister. I went back to Jean and explained what I had planned. She said," I know how to play dead since, I am almost anyway." I told her that it pains me to have to it this way but, it will be the only way to get past the gate. Jean said,

"Don't miss! Make it count." She kissed me and I could taste the traces of blood from the soldier she had fed from.

One of the French girls said, "Monsieur, we are ready." I told Jean to start making her way to the doors hurriedly as I unsheathed a dagger. She burst through the doors, knocking down the fake guards and at a full run. She had gotten about 10 meters when I yelled, "Stop! Don't make me kill you!" I drew the dagger and released it. Jean was about 20 meters when she fell. The dagger found its mark into her back. I ran up to her, ahead of any nearby English soldiers. I pulled the knife from her back and rolled her over. I placed my arm under her neck and said, "Why didn't you listen to me?" "I wanted to be free." Replied Jean. She grasped the front of my clothing and collapsed. By this time, soldiers are gathering to see the drama unfold. An officer broke up the crowd and asked me about what had happened. I made up story about her cleaning my wounds after we left Orleans. I asked the officer, could I give her a decent burial outside the gate? The officer began telling me a response I wasn't looking for. I stood up, looked him in the eyes and said," I need a spade to dig her grave outside the gate." The officer turned and ordered a soldier to fetch me a spade. I picked up Jean, threw her over my right shoulder and waited for the soldier carrying the spade. I looked past the soldiers peering at me and I saw the French girls close the door of their home. The soldier walked up with the spade and asked me did I need assistance? I told him that I owed her this final duty and I thanked him for the offer. As I was carrying Jean towards the gate and waiting for the gates to open, I could feel the tightness in my jaws begin and I must hurry.

The gates slowly opened, I felt like running with her but, it would draw too much attention. I began looking for some cover and there are three solitary trees, I made over to them. The sun is sinking down but darkness has not arrived. I get to the back side of the trees, to somewhat block the view of anyone watching from the wall. I gently laid Jean on the ground, and she said," That was a well-placed throw my love and a brilliant plan. I know the change is coming but we can't stay here." I started digging a hole in case someone can see me. As I was digging, I asked Jean will she be able to control me? Jean said," Yes! I'll be even stronger as the sun goes down. I can even feel the awakening of the others, the walled city will bleed tonight." I could feel my body start to ache, I continued to dig to slow down the process if I can fight it. Jean said, "He is here. I have summoned him." I stopped digging and turned around, a man dressed in clothing unlike I've ever seen. I knew, it's the dark master. He said," Looks like Janville will be up to their necks in vampires, pardon the pun." Jean said, "I've never heard such a name before." He said,"Janville is where the term will be born. So, I gather that you two want me to get you out of here? What will you do for me David le Stone if I do this?" I said, "I'll do whatever it takes not to piss you off master." He said, "That is a very good answer." He snapped his fingers and instantly we are in a forest.

The change has taken over the both of us. The change for Jean is more subdued than it is for me. She kneels and places her hands on me, it does little to take away the pain until the transformation runs its course. The beast opens its eyes and growls until it realizes that it is Jean by his side. Jean said, "It's okay David, it's Jean. I don't know where we are but, our bodies need food. What can your magnificent sense of smell and hearing tell you?" The beast stood up and began sampling the air with his nose and listening for signs of people, signs of food. The beast has caught a scent, he points with his talonlike finger and says in a gravelly voice," This way, follow me." The beast springs forward with the effortless movements of a mature deer. His sensitive nose is constantly testing the air as he moves. Jean's movements are just as swift, staying just behind the beast as he plows through underbrush, leaping over dead vegetation, the hunger is in control.

The sun has dipped even lower in the sky, being overtaken by the night. Jean watches as the beast slows down his pace and sees him going into full stalking mode. Jean also is picking up the scent of wood burning and faint voices travel on the wind. The two predators of the slowly approach the edge of the forest, keeping themselves hidden as they peer out at a village that's unaware. Tonight, is the last night that the face of the moon will shine until many weeks from now. The beast has acquired a target, as his muscles tightened waiting for release like a spring, Jean grips the beast's massive arm. She says, "David, I mean

Judas. Whatever happens to me, I made this choice. I had a vision come to me as the dagger pierced my body. I saw myself never being able to walk in the sunlight again. I wanted power and to live forever with you. I only thought that my will is just as powerful as yours, it is not. I let the craving control me instead of me controlling the craving. The worst part is that I fed on a dying man inside the church

" The beast says," Are your cravings stronger now? If they are? You must own what you are, time doesn't go backwards. Own this power because you cannot give it back. We aren't regular people anymore; people are food to us." Jean released her grip and said, "You are right! Let's own tonight together, my love." The two apex predators of the night did indeed, own the night. Each one had their own approach to the art of killing but, regardless of their technique, it was the craving that controlled both. There wasn't any preference of their choosing being it man, woman, child or infant, opportunistic killers just fed as the night before, until the coming of the dawn. The night creatures found each and refuge in a cottage that they had visited earlier. The occupants, a family of five had been slaughtered like cattle. The cottage permeated with the smell of blood and shredded flesh; the night creatures once again returned to their human state. Both are nearly naked, blood stained and in need of clothing.

David hears the too familiar tongue of English soldiers outside the cottage. He had to think fast before the English came in. He smeared blood upon his body that he wiped from the floor, the blood of a nearby victim. Jean saw what he was doing and did the same. She quietly whispered," We'll play dead until they move on." They barely had enough time to place themselves in position when, the door is pushed open and three English soldiers came in. The soldiers began pushing and prodding the bodies checking for signs of life. I made my breathing so shallow and slow that, the movement of my rib cage nearly undetectable. A soldier rolled me over onto my back, my body totally relaxed, limp and lifeless. The soldiers moved their attention to Jean, lying face down in the corner. A soldier rolls her over and starts looking at her body for wounds. The soldier says, "I don't see any markings or wounds on her yet, she feels cold to the touch." The soldier began fondling the breast of Jean as the other soldiers laughed.

One soldier said," I think that's the first time you've ever touched a woman's breast before, isn't it?" I'm thinking to myself, the situation is going to get out of control. The third soldier in the group said," I bet he hasn't done the deed with a female either." The soldiers were chuckling as the shamed soldier began to probed Jean's female organ. Her body flinched and the frightened soldier withdrew his hand saying," She's warm inside, she isn't dead!" Another soldier said," If she isn't dead, only knocked out let me show you how to do the deed proper." As the soldier was about to penetrate Jean, she sat up, snapped the soldier's neck. I sprang up and a soldier stuck is sword into my ribs as the youngest of the three escaped. The soldier wielding the sword is in shock because I'm not collapsing onto the floor. Instead, I pull the sword out and lopped off his head swiftly, fluid motion. Jean said," More will be coming, I don't think putting on the English clothing is going to work this time. What do we do?" I said, "Fight until we cannot fight anymore. What are they going to do, kill us?"

Jean smiled, picked up a sword and told me that she loved me. I told her that I will always love until the end of time. I could hear the young soldier screaming," There is witchcraft in the house! The dead have awakened!" He kept repeating it over and over until he stopped. An officer had grabbed the young soldier and slapped him. The officer said," Calm yourself…. tell me. What have you seen?" The young soldier told the officer about the incident that he had witnessed. The officer sent soldiers to block any possible exits to the dwelling. As the English soldiers got into position, the officer called out, "Surrender or I'll send my men in to kill you." David grabbed the headless body and began going to the doorway with it. Jean spoke in a low voice," What are you doing?" "Watch and listen." David replied. David placed his body directly behind the headless body, standing upright and began talking to the English soldiers. David said, "I should've stayed in England and I'm in France instead. You bastards took me from my home and now I've lost my head. " David tossed the body into the crowd of soldiers, knocking many to the ground and returned to Jean's side. Jean laughingly said," I wished I could've seen their faces, you are diabolically brilliant." I said," Let's take a few of them out of the equation and we let them stab us with their blades, we cannot die that way…. remember." The English began pouring into the cottage.

We killed as many as we could until, there was no more room to fight. I felt the cold steel of their blades piercing through my body and I collapsed on the floor. I closed my eyes, feeling the soldier's boot as he kicked me in the head. I heard the soldier saying," They look very dead to me lads. I don't see any sign of witchcraft. I think these two have made their last stand and the use of the headless soldier was very crafty. The dead man did that to buy a little of time. He and his wench were in a no-win situation and they lost. Get our men out of here and bury them and as for the so-called witches, just leave them here to rot. We are moving on to Rouen. I lay still, listening as I heard men dragging the bodies of their dead comrades across the earthen floor. I've slowed my breathing down, very shallow breaths to restrict the movement to avoid detection. I didn't know what kind of condition Jean was in, I just know that I'm lying in a pool of my own blood. I could still hear movement going on outside. I dare not move or make a noise because, at any moment some curious soldier could walk in. My mind began to drift, replaying images of what transpired on that day.

A moment that will forever haunt me until the end comes for me. I must have fallen asleep as my body was repairing itself because, I was awakened by Jean. Just outside the small village, a small group of English soldiers have been delayed. An English soldier has gotten the attention of his commanding officer. The soldier tells the officer that the dead woman in the cottage bears an uncanny resemblance to the warrior maiden. The officer ask the soldier," What reason would the warrior maiden be doing here and where did you see her last?" The soldier said, "I saw her in Orleans and I'm telling you that the person in that cottage is her or she has a twin. Dead or alive she would be a great prize for General Falstaf in Rouen. The general would recognize her and you would gain much favor with the general." The officer said," What do you expect to gain from this, if in fact the woman is indeed the warrior maiden?" "I'm just a soldier, maybe a higher rank if the general proves me right. The worst thing that could happen is we just brought a corpse with us to Rouen. In fact, if she isn't the warrior maiden, you can simply blame it on me."

The officer said, "Take two men with you, build a proper coffin for her, you have one hour to do this or get left behind with your dead warrior maiden." The officer walks his horse over to the shade, opens his pack and retrieves the hourglass, flips it and places it on the ground. The sand begins trickling down as the officer tells the rest of his men to find shade and wait. The soldiers began walking back to the village with a horse drawn wagon. David hears them coming back and tells Jean to lay back down in the same spot the attack occurred. Jean whispers, "Something doesn't feel right about this." I whisper back to her telling her to stay quiet and remain still, they'll be gone soon." I could hear the soil beneath the wheels of the wagon being crushed along with the hoof falls of the horse. The wagon stops in front of the cottage, two soldiers enter blood spattered room they pick up the body of Jean and place her in the wagon. I lay there motionless and helpless. I hear a voice in my head saying," Stay!" I don't understand why they are taking her. I hear the soldier that is tending the horse say," Find an axe, some rope and we'll build a box from doors."

The same soldier found a blanket and rolled Jean's body in it. The other men began breaking up doors for the bottom, the top and the sides of the makeshift coffin. The men that were tasked to making the coffin asked, "How are we to attach this together without nails?" The soldier grabbed the body of Jean placed her on the ground. He grabbed the rope and slid it underneath the bottom of door section and told one man to place the sides upward. The soldier pulled the rope to meet in the middle and cut it. He repeated this until he had two ropes to surround the sides and two ropes for the full length. They placed Jean's body on the bottom section, one man held the two side in place as the other placed on the lid. The third man brought the ends of the two ropes together and tied them securely. The same was repeated for the ends of the box, capping off and securing it with ropes. The placed the makeshift coffin in the wagon and headed towards the commanding officer and what remains of his company of men. The officer said," I must commend you on your speedy delivery of the supposed maiden all wrapped up in a box, less than an hour." He'll yelled to his subordinates to get the men moving towards Rouen. I strained to listen, waiting for the sound of movement, voices, anything for a sign. I began to take in deeper breathes, I tried to raise my body from the floor, some unknown force kept me pinned down. I tried fighting it but, the force is much more powerful than I. The more I fought, I could feel my strength being pulled from me.

My energy gone except for the ability to breathe and open my eyes. I had gotten to the point that I couldn't hold my eyes open, I gave in to sleep. I found myself walking in the presence of the eleven disciples. "Where are we going, my brothers?" I got no answer and I asked again, still no response at all. They would not even turn to look at me, looking forward, walking forward. I even tried to slow them down, only to get pushed forward by the disciple behind me. I try to peer to see where or what, we are walking towards. There is no terrain to speak of, just a void of light blue haze. I know that I have feet but cannot see them. I say out loud, "I must be dead and being led to judgement?" A soft calm voice answers," No Judas. This isn't about you." The disciples have vanished and a shapeless form appears in front of me. I was about to speak and an unseen hand is pressed to my mouth. I dropped to my knees and bowed my head. I looked up and the shapeless form has transformed into an armor-clad man of great statue. His armor shimmered with brilliance brighter than gold. I thought to myself, he must be a warrior angel. The armored being said," You are correct, Judas. I am the one that was directed by the Father, to cast out the dark one and those that followed him.

I am the archangel, Michael. I was sent by the one you betrayed, the lamb that you marked for slaughter. It was me that held you steadfast on the floor that is covered in blood. I was tasked to give you vital information that, it is the dark one that got the English officer's ear. It is the dark one that helped bind Jean d Arc into the box and is giving her over to the English. I am here for you to release her, and I don't mean freeing from the box or the cage, she is going to be put in. Do you know what I'm talking about?" Tears began to well up in my eyes and I said, "You mean freeing her soul from eternal torment, don't you?" The warrior angel said, "Yes." I said," Why did the dark one turn his anger on her?" The warrior angel said," He is doing this to hurt you. He doesn't care about her. He knew that she would be drawn to you like a moth to a flame. He told you not to seek her, he might as well tell you, not to eat when you are hungry. The dark one grew tired of your devotion towards her and not him. This is about redemption, Judas. Remember when the lamb came to you in the desert. Remember what he said to you, you can save her." I was awakened by a fly crawling on my nose, and I wasn't bound to the floor, I can move. I moved cautiously to the door opening, stopping at the threshold, and listened for any movement. I could hear songbirds and I caught the smell of fresh air as it whisked by. I heard no sounds of people and made the decision to venture out. The remnants of the tattered clothing, I wear is still wet from blood of the soldiers and my own. I walked to another dwelling, carefully opened the door and walked in. I need food more than I need clothing; I am weak from the blood loss. My instincts push forward, searching for something to fill my empty stomach.

The front room had nothing to offer, just shambles of broken furniture, the smell of urine and defecation in one corner, left by the English. I went into the next room, found a piece of bread on a table. I picked it up, it was dried hard as a stone, I bit into it anyway. It is food. I looked around and the room had been ransacked. I left the dwelling, searched a few more and did find some clothing. The clothes weren't made for a man of my build, someone much larger. At least they weren't smaller and I room to move. An idea came to me and I located the graves of the dead English soldiers.

CHAPTER 11

1431 A VAMPIRE BURNS

I robbed them of their shoes, they no longer need them. I took their swords and some even had wineskins. I began walking in the direction that they took Jean, my Jean. I now know for certain that, both of us have been tricked. I have to reach Rouen, the English don't realize what they have in the box. Jean will be hungry and her wrath will go unchecked. The dark master is somehow going to make an example of her because of me. I continued, following the edge of the forest and staying out of the open. The dark master knows I'm coming but, the English don't have a clue at least, not yet. My body is craving food, that piece of hard bread is a distant memory. I uncorked the wineskin and drank from it. I wanted to drink all the liquid from a nearly full wineskin but, I needed to keep my mind sharp. I corked the wineskin and pushed on. I don't know what I'm walking into. I just know that I have an obligation to fulfill, no matter the cost.

The wind has carried the scent of a large settlement not too far ahead. I make my way up to a rise in the landscape, I see before me a scattering of buildings and English troop movement. I may have 3 to 4 kilometers before I get to the supposed city of Rouen. I stand on the hill, close my eyes, and quiet my mind. I'm hoping, just maybe, that I can reach out to Jean. I begin calling her name in my head and listen for a response. I wait as the wind brushes over me and I hear a faint, weak voice saying," I'm trapped! The hunger is more than I can bear. Come and find me. Please hurry!" I open my eyes and see that the forest edge has been taken over by civilization. I might as well just walk right into the fray, to them I am a nobody. I need to blend with rest of the people, don't draw attention to myself. I'm hungry and have no money. I can trade these weapons for food if I must. I continued to walk forward, acting like I've been here before, confident and peering forward. In my heart, I feel as if I'll be absolutely powerless to change the outcome that I want. I want to free Jean to be with me, she understands what and who I am. The warrior angel told me that It's not about me. As I get closer to the city, more people are milling about from place to place. I smell food and my stomach desires something to fill it. I begin to listen to people's conversation's, trying to pick up on the prevailing gossip. The English have a heavy presence here, the English soldiers are checking a farmer's wagon for hidden renegade French fighters.

I continue walking towards the strong smell of food. English soldiers are going in and out of the dwelling in front of me. I walk inside and two soldiers greet me. One the soldiers asked me," What are you doing? Only soldiers in full uniform can eat in here." My garb is a mismatched combination of peasant and English soldier. I look at their clothing and I don't see much of a difference. A thought came to me and I said, "Do either of you want to find out who is the better soldier? You can let me get some food and you won't get hurt." The soldiers began to push me towards the door and were stopped by an officer. The officer said, "You men let the soldier get some food and after he eats, we'll see which of you are the better soldier." The soldiers let me through, I observed what the other men were doing to get food. They sat at tables as peasant woman placed bread, cheese, wine, and a large tray of some cooked animal quarters on the table. The men were slicing meat with their daggers, pulling meat from the bone with their hands. I sat down on the end of the bench; an older peasant woman sat a goblet of wine in front of me.

The man next to me knocked it over in my lap saying, "Excuse me mate. I didn't see you." The men across the table were laughing. I gave the empty goblet to the woman and asked her to refill it. I took out my dagger and as I reached out to cut a chunk from the cheese block, the soldier across from me made an attempt to stab my hand. I slammed the pommel end of my dagger against his hand, causing him to release it. I took his dagger, and I felt the tip of something sharp in my side. The soldier beside me said," Give him his blade back." I told the soldier to withdraw his blade or he would have a dagger in his skull. The soldier held the blade tip at my side and said," You're not that fast, now give up the blade." In an instant, there is one less man at the table. The soldier had a dagger in the center of his forehead and was laid out on his back. The officer was watching this unfold and stopped the rest of the men from attacking me.

The officer said, "Go ahead and eat your fill. When you finish? We'll see how good you are with the sword." The woman returned with a full goblet of wine, I am mad hungry and began stuffing myself with meat, bread, cheese and gulping down the goblet of wine. The woman left to retrieve a wineskin to refill the goblet. Most of the men had left the table and were grumbling under their breathe about me killing one of their comrades. The woman returned with a wineskin, and I told her to leave it on the table. I continued to gorge myself with food, taking a moment to wash it down with wine. I ate until I couldn't eat anymore, I drank the remainder of the wine from the wineskin and belched out a loud burp. I am ready for whatever happens next. The English officer said, "What is your name soldier?" "David Stone." I replied. The officer said," Alright, David Stone. Let's see if you can move as fast with a full stomach." The officer motioned for me to walk out first. I walked out into a crowd of angry men, wanting blood, wanting vengeance. I got to the center of the wagon path; a man runs up to the officer saying, "Captain Harland! That man is supposed to be dead."

The captain said, "He'll soon meet his maker after my best swordsman finishes him. Now stand back! You've had too much wine." Another man steps forward and says, "He's right captain Harland, I was there. We ran he and the maiden through with our swords. He shouldn't be alive, it's witchcraft... it has to be." I raised my clothing, exposing my stomach and my back as I turned around, for all to see.

The captain sees no sign of any wounds. The captain says," Where is my swordsman?" A tall man pushes his way through the crowd and says," I am here, Captain Harland. Is this the man that is faster than lightning itself?" "He's extremely fast with a dagger but let's see how fast he is with a sword." I said, "I know what I'll get if I lose. What will I gain if I beat your best swordsman?" "That's to be determined if you win but, my swordsman has never lost." Said the captain.

As the swordsman approached me, I asked his name. The swordsman said," My name is Death to those who oppose me." I told him that I'm going to change his name......to dead. The swordsman made the first swipe at me and I dodged it. We were closely matched as fighters, and I decided to take this to the next level. I bent down... acting as if I'm out of breath, the swordsman lunged at me. I side stepped his attempt and lobbed off his head. In the same motion, I grabbed my dagger and threw it into the stomach of the captain. I didn't want to kill him. He will be the one to give the next order. The captain yelled out, "Lock him up next to the box that supposedly contains Jean d Arc. Get me to the physician.... hurry!" I didn't make it easy for the men to capture me, I sent men many to their deaths until I was overwhelmed by so many men.

My only weapon was stripped from my hand, as they kicked and clawed at me while I was being dragged into this guarded building. The men threw me into a barred cell and slammed the door shut. The guard locked the door and said, "You'll hang for this, David Stone." "At least I got a full stomach before I go to the gallows." I spoke. The room was dimly lit by one lantern, it was flickering as the guards walked past it. I wasn't alone in the cell, there are three other men in here. I sat down in the corner, leaning on the bars that separate me from Jean. She knows that I'm here I can feel her thoughts in my mind. She is weak, too weak to breakout from her makeshift coffin. One of the men in the cell tells me, "You should come over here with us. We have been hearing a voice from the box." I said, "You've actually heard a voice from the box speak to you?" Another man said," Not with our ears but, within our minds." "What does the voice say to you?" I asked. One of the men said, "If we release her, she will grant us a gift. We have no way of releasing ourselves." I chuckled and said, "You men must had drunk some bad wine or eaten spoiled food, to be talking such crazy talk. I don't want to hear any more of your wild stories, I just want to sit here and await my fate at the end of a rope." I closed my eyes, relaxed my mind and she appeared to me. She's not the bloody mess that was lying in the room with me, she's beautiful and dressed in a flowing black cloak." You have taken a significant risk to be here with me." She spoke.

I told her that I'm here to save her and before she could reply, my concentration was broken. A guard and a high-ranking officer entered, the guard opened Jean's cell and the officer told him to cut the ropes loose. I watched as the guard cut the bindings from the makeshift coffin. The sides fell away and the guard removed the lid that rested on her body. The officer leaned over to look at her blood-stained naked body and said, "It is the warrior maiden! I was hoping to do her in myself but fate has dealt her a different hand." No sooner than he could say the last syllable of the last word, she sprang up, sinking her teeth into the officer's neck. The guard tried to pull Jean away but was knocked unconscious. The men in my cell were yelling, out of fear for their lives. Jean takes the key from the knocked-out guard, unlocks my cell and enters it. The three men were cowering in a corner, Jean goes over to them and said," Who wants to live forever?" The men didn't answer quick enough for her and she began to feed upon them. She didn't snap their necks after feeding, they will become seekers of blood themselves. Jean was finishing off the last of the prisoners in my cell and I heard a noise behind me. The guard had awakened, ran to my cell door, closed it and removed the key. Jean was furious and began shaking the door, trying to trip the lock, the lock didn't budge. I remembered something that the dark master told me when, I arrived in this time. He told me to be careful about my actions because people can be burned at the stake for witchcraft.

The guard came back with an officer and more guards, they had to see this for themselves. The officer came over to the cell that I am in and said, "Has the demon-witch hurt you…prisoner?" I told him that she must be full from feeding on the four men and is now in the dark corner. A guard raises his lantern and sees teeth and glaring red eyes staring back at them. The officer said," Prisoner…if you survive tonight, you'll be hanged, and the demon-witch will burn at the stake. Do have any last wishes?" "How about a full wineskin to kill the pain?" I replied. The officer said, "You shall have it." He told the guards to remove the general's body from the neighboring cell and bring me a wineskin. I just sat there and waited until they were gone. Jean came over to me and began kissing me. I could taste blood of the men on her lips, her naked body felt cold to the touch. I got up and took clothing from the dead men and dressed Jean. She joked about how ungainly the clothes fit her. I said," Jean. I had a visit from a Heavenly host. I am here for redemption, and it is not min. Your redemption. You can prevent your soul from going to hell. You have to get on your knees and ask forgiveness from the lamb, repent your sins, forsake the dark master and the rest is up to the lamb to accept your plea." Jean said," What about you…. Judas? Didn't you tell me that the rabbi said…. it's never too late to ask forgiveness?" I told her that it is too late for me and that I couldn't ever forgive myself for what I did to my teacher. I heard footsteps coming and I told her to stay in the corner. I watched as the guard with the lantern enter the dark building, making his way towards the cage. The guard held up his lantern to see the layout of the cage. I think mostly to see where Jean is.

He threw the wineskin at my feet and quickly left. Darkness fell upon room again but the darkness has no effect upon me nor Jean. We are accustomed to the night. Jean returned to my arms and began weeping. "The Heavenly host warned me to stay away from you, I chose not to listen. The first time I saw you…. I knew in my heart that I loved you. It is not your fault; I struck the deal… not you." Said Jean. I told Jean that the three men will arise at sunset and will be seeking blood. Jean said," I can control them. don't worry." I told Jean that the men will be like starving animals, and they may even try to feed upon her. Jean jumped up and quickly dispatched the men by snapping their necks. She looked at me and said," Problem solved." I said," I guess we'll never know how the baby turns out…. will we?"

She started weeping and told me that the child did not survive the transition. I assumed that she was speaking about transitioning from human to vampire. I began consoling her, holding her tightly in my arms and said, "Your hunger will be stronger as the night nears. I love you so much that, I willingly give myself to you. I don't know if my blood will make you impervious to flame but, you know what will happen on a full moon. Jean said," I could never bring myself to do this. I love you more than I love this world." I told Jean that she has spoken a similar phrase that I heard from the teacher. He said," We are not supposed to love things of this world because they are just things with no meaning. Love is the key; you have to repent and express your love for the teacher."

I then heard a familiar voice from the next cell saying," The rabbi can't save either one of you. With one snap of my finger, the lock will open and you could be free." I said," There is always a consequence, when giving in to you isn't there? The dark master chuckled and said, "Oh yes! There are consequences. You both haven't been paying homage to me. Did you think I wouldn't notice? I'm the one that convinced the English officer to bring the warrior maiden's body here." I stood up and reached out to grab him. " Judas, you've lost your focus and that is to serve me." I said," We have been serving you. You've turned us into the ultimate killing machines." "Speaking of killing machine, the night approaches and the general will be hungry. I think I should approach the general with a proposal since, you two have disappointed me." said the dark master. The dark master disappears, leaving Jean and I alone with three corpses.

Jean pushes away from me, retreating to the opposite corner. I said," The hunger has started. Hasn't it?" "Don't go to sleep my love. I may lose control of myself." said Jean. I ask her if she ever fed on the dead before? She told me that's on her mind now verses feeding upon me. In another part of Rouen, General Falstaff has risen from the table, he was laid upon. He has attacked and fed from many victims. The dark one has appeared to the general and told him that the warrior maiden must be destroyed….and soon. The dark one cooked up a plan with the general. The plan is for the general to return to the table he had left from. The dark one possessed the body of an officer and the officer knocked on the door of the clergyman. The priest said," What is it my son?" The officer said," Priest! I beg of you to come and pray for the soul of General Falstaff. The witch maiden d Arc caused his demise, please come and free his very soul from damnation."

The priest told the officer that, he must get the Holy sacrament. The officer said," You do believe strongly enough in God without it… don't you?" The priest told the officer," Yes!" without any hesitation. The officer led the priest to the location of the general. There were no guards at the entrance but, there were signs of blood where the guards should've been. The general is laid out upon the table, the priest told the possessed officer that he had already given the general the last rites. The possessed officer told the priest to examine the teeth of the general. The priest cautiously approached the body of the general, gently raises the upper lip and gasped at the site. The priest said," We have to do something immediately. This body must be destroyed before it can make more of this kind. I have already heard of what happened in Janville. The vampire is a plague that must be destroyed." The general jumped from the table, disappearing into the night. The priest said, "Are there any others?" The possessed officer said, the source of the plague could be locked in the stockade. The officer orders another soldier to follow them to the stockade. The three men walk into the dimly lit stockade. The priest put a cloth over his nose because of the stench emanating from the stockade.

Jean withdraws from me and goes to the opposite corner. The possessed officer grabs the lantern, holds it to illuminate the cage containing the maiden, the three dead men and David Stone. The priest says to Jean, "Come closer my child, you have nothing to fear from me." Jean stands up, her hair hides her face but her clothing doesn't hide the splattered blood. As she draws closer to the lantern light, the priest says," What is your name child?" "What does it matter Priest? I must be a criminal because I'm locked up in this stockade." Replies Jean. "It matters to God, and we all answer to him." Exclaims the priest. The priest began removing the cross-bearing necklace from himself, holding it in his hand. Jean peeping through the strands of hair sees the cross and tells the priest her name. The priest says," Maiden d Arc, did you attack General Falstaff?"

"He killed thousands of my people." Replied Jean. "What of those three men and the one in the corner that isn't dead?" Asked the priest. She said, "The three men are English and the man in the corner isn't." The priest stuck his hand through the bars, holding the cross-bearing necklace. The priest then said, "Come closer and kiss the cross." Jean walked forward and acted like she is going to kiss the cross instead, she grabs the priest arm and began feeding from it. The priest began screaming in agony as a soldier retrieved the keys from a distant wall. Other soldiers began running into the stockade to see what the commotion is about. The priest is pleading for someone to pry Jean away. It took many men to tear Jean away and I was moved to the adjoining cell. The priest said, "This creature must be destroyed tonight! She must burn!" The possessed officer tore a piece of cloth from the priest clothing, and applied a tourniquet to stop the bleeding.

Jean began laughing hysterically and said," Your blood is stained priest! You're just a money changer and in bed with the English and you are going to hell." "It is you demon whore of Satan that is going to hell! I am sending you there tonight!" Replied the priest. As the men exit the stockade, the priest stops in front of my cell and ask," How did you escape her attacking you?" I said," I once was a faithful follower of the teacher until I killed a man." The priest asked me why did I kill the man? I told him that pride, lust for money instead of salvation was my undoing. The priest said, "You'll hang tomorrow. Do you want me to hear your confession of your sins?" "You cannot absolve me or anyone's sins, only the lamb of God or the God of Abraham can do this. You are just a man and imperfect; the lamb and the God of Abraham is perfect." I could see the sneer upon the possessed officer's face as I made my decrement. The priest said," Let's hope that the God of Abraham will be listening tomorrow as you swing from a rope." They all left the stockade, leaving Jean and I in our separate cells. I went over to meet Jean at the bars that separated us, she was already there. I placed my hands on top of hers and said, "Jean…. there isn't much time left. You have to ask for forgiveness and repent for your sins. You have to mean it in your heart or the words are meaningless." Jean got down on her knees, bowing her heading with her hands clasped together. She began pleading with the Creator and rebuking the devil. A quick flash of light illuminated the stockade, blowing out the lonely lantern on the wall.

I heard Jean crying and she said," I am clean again, I can feel the coldness of the night on my bare feet." She came over to the bars that separated us saying, "My heart is beating again, give me your hand." She placed my hand on her warm breast and I quickly withdrew it. She asked me what is wrong? I told her that I shouldn't have done that because she has been purified. Jean said, "I saw them!" "Saw whom?" I asked. She told me that two beings of light approached her and one of them placed his finger on her forehead. I asked her did she experience a flash of light when the heavenly host touched her? "Yes!" she exclaimed. I told her that I saw the flash also. Jean held my head against the bars and gave me a long passionate kiss. She said, "I won't ever see you again, will I?" I told her that maybe once I've done my penance, I'll be allowed to walk through the pearly gates. Jean said," I'm going to feel immense pain, aren't I?" I told her to look into my eyes and to repeat after me. I said, "The hotter the flame, the less pain I will feel." I told her to repeat what I said, while she focused on me. "Men will be coming to take you away. I want you to close your eyes and you'll see my face, begin repeating the phrase so that only you can hear what you are saying.

Before I awaken you, when you hear me say," Close your eyes, Jean!" then you begin repeating the phrase. Do you understand?" Jean answered softly," Yes." I'm going to count to three and you'll be fully awake….1…2…3." Jean asked me why I stopped kissing her. I leaned into the bars, placed my hands around her face kissed her and told her that I love her. She told me that she loved me and said, "We really put a hurting on the English, didn't we?" I could hear men coming and told her," Yes! We really wreaked havoc for a while." I held her hand tightly until the men came into the stockade carrying lanterns, ropes and swords scrapping the walls. A soldier opened her cell, while another threw a rope around her, and another until she struggled no more. Jean was yelling," I'm clean! I'm not a monster anymore! Tell them David

Le Stone, tell them!" I said," Close your eyes, Jean. Just close your eyes and it will be over. Close your eyes, Jean!" She stopped yelling and I couldn't see her as the men took her out of the stockade. I could only hear an angry crowd saying, "Burn the demon witch!" I sat down with my back against the cold bars. I was wondering does my condition save me from being hanged? Tomorrow could be the end for me, and I'll be one of the dark master's hell hounds. I sat there and caught a whiff of a large fire, hearing men yelling to burn the demon witch. I also heard the faint cries of men being the victims of General Falstaff, the victims will become the predator's tomorrow night.

As the people of Rouen along with English soldiers gathered, to see the warrior maiden burn and cry out for forgiveness, not a whimper was heard from the maiden. She was bound tightly around a large timber; her head had dropped down as the flames licked at her waistline. The priest watched and wondered about his own demise and the destruction of the general's body without causing an uproar with the English. The priest is already beginning to feel different; the maiden's cursed blood is already comingling with his. The priest looked for the officer that brought his attention to the general's body. The priest found a soldier and told him to accompany him to where the general's tent is. They made way towards the tent and found bodies with their throats ripped open. The priest said," I think we are too late." They ran to the tent where the general's body was lying in state, there isn't a body. The soldier with the priest is totally confused about the matter at hand. The priest told the soldier to quickly to draw his sword and cut off the arm above the bite mark. The soldier said, "I'll be damned to hell for committing such an atrocity to a man of God." "I'll be damned along with the whole town if you don't." The priest placed his arm on the table. Just as the soldier reared his arm to cleave the arm from its body, General Falstaff steps in. He grabs the soldier's arm and severs the soldier's head from its body. The priest begins cowering back from the general.

The general says," You've ordered the death of our queen and now you will serve me. Your God will no longer accept you into his kingdom." The general drained the priest dry and continued to prey upon others until dawn. The general found somewhere to hide from the oncoming daylight. As the general was wreaking havoc at first…. I thought of a plan to piss the dark master off. Is it even worth it? Every woman that I've grown attached to, was taken away from me. I might as well take the, "I don't give a shit attitude" and take care of yours truly if I survive the hanging tomorrow. I laid down on the cold floor, resting my head on my arm. I thought how beautiful Jean was before the dark master turned her into a monster. I finally drifted off to sleep but, a peaceful sleep it was not. The dark master shows up in my cage and says, "Get up Judas!" I acted like I didn't hear him. I felt the dark master's hand around my throat as he pushed me up the cell wall. He says," You robbed me of a soul that was mine and conversed with the enemy. Do you feel the tightness of my grip around your throat Judas? Does this remind you of something?" "Yes!" I said. "I should've never let you deceive me to give up the teacher. " The dark master throws me to the ground in a fit of rage and says, "Let's see if you are immune to hanging tomorrow?" Before I could give him a rebuttal, he disappeared into the night.

I found myself awakened by the incident and laid back down. I started thinking about all the people I knew, the people that I killed through the centuries, and I know there will never be forgiveness for me. I finally found sleep but, it didn't seem like I got very much of it. English soldiers came in, unlocked the cell, and carried me outside. My eyes had to get adjusted to the morning rays of the sun, as the soldiers escorted me to another building and sat me at a table. An English officer sat down across from me and said," The priest, General Falstaff and several men are missing yet, you survived being locked up with the demon witch Jean d Arc. I was outside the stockade last night, as I heard her yelling, "Tell them I am clean David le Stone. Who are you, David le Stone? Your answers can determine whether or not you swing from a rope or a free man. " A soldier steps forward, tells the officer about me killing a soldier at the dining table.

I thought for a brief moment about just telling him the truth and then I said, "I am a defrocked clergy that belonged to an elite group called the Knights Templar." The English officer said," Your kind was supposedly killed off but, that doesn't explain how you remained unharmed by the demon witch?" I explained to him that I'm not one of the original Templar's, their teaching was handed down to me. I told him what saved me from being attacked was, I explained to the maiden that I had been to Jerusalem, walked the same steps as the great teacher, stood on the ground at Golgotha where he was crucified and the supposed place from which he rose." The officer said, "That sounds like a fantastic tale that you've just spun. You still have not answered my question?" I told the officer that I had helped cleanse the body of the demon that held her captive. I said, "It only works when, you ask for forgiveness from your heart and not just by saying it." The officer had a more puzzled look upon his face and said, "The maiden went from screaming to silence, not a whimper was heard from her as the flames engulfed her. You must be a true holy man David le stone and yet, you are in the stockade.

You've killed our best swordsman, maimed, and stabbed a fellow English captain named Harland. Harland is also among the missing men. My men want your head on a pole, but I feel it would be a grave mistake. I heard you tell the priest, that you killed a man, his death weighs heavier than others. Who was this man and why did you take his life?" I told him that I killed a priest because his was molesting children, I had been following him from village to village, getting evidence was hard to do. The children had been threatened speaking about it, so one day came and I caught him in the act. A young boy, eight or nine years old or so was kneeling down and sucking on the priest private part. The priest had his head tilted back, his eyes closed and I lunged forward, slicing off his head from his body. The little boy called me a murderer, the boy had been led to believe what he was doing was okay, it was blasphemy. I had been on the run ever since I was caught. I said," So here I am at your mercy. Those children were at the mercy of that twisted man's desires, that man people called a priest."

The English officer sat back into his chair pondering the words that spewed from my mouth, the second part of my story just sprayed from my mind like water from a fountain. The English officer leaned forward and said," What can you tell me about these blood drinkers?" I said," Does this mean I get to live?" The officer said, "Yes, I need to know how to fight this plague or whatever this is." He asked me where do these blood drinkers go in the daytime and how to kill it? I told him that I had encountered these creatures in my travels and found out that, they are to be completely decapitated. I said, "These creatures find a place during the day to sleep and out of the sun's rays because the sun causes them to burn. The first places I would look would be basements, attics anywhere that is dark.

Your men must be ready to take on a creature that is twice as strong as your strongest man." The officer said, "Was the maiden your friend?" I told him that I was her friend, that helped deliver her from the grips of Satan and yet, powerless to keep her from burning at the stake." The officer told me that he's going to get me some clean clothing, something to eat and drink rounded up. The officer walked out as the two guards, kept watchful eyes on me. I heard the officer tell a subordinate to fetch food, wine, and fresh clothing for the prisoner. I am barefoot, my clothing is blood stained from Jean's attacks in the stockade. I can still smell traces of her scent from where she touched my clothing. That is all, of the physical evidence of her that is left, and that will be gone once I change clothes. A pair of hand maidens and a soldier enter the building. One hand maiden places on the table a wash basin, soap and washing cloth. The other maiden placed at the end of the table a bowl of stew, by smell of it with a spoon and wineskin. The soldier dropped the clothes and shoes on the ground. The officer saw what he did and told him to place the clothes on the table and take the maidens away. The officer said," I would like to be able to trust you, leave you to clean yourself up a bit in private but, I cannot let my guard down, as of yet." The officer told the guards to alert him once I had gotten cleaned up and changed. In my position, there was no need for modesty. I stripped off my blood and dirt-stained clothes, grabbed the rag and soap and began cleaning as best I could. I was being careful with the amount of water that I was given, I was doing more wiping of the extremities. I saved most of the water to wash my matted hair that was riddled with everything, rinsed it and shook it out like a wild dog.

I began getting dressed and felt almost like a person again. One of the guards stepped out, to alert the officer that I had finished bathing and gotten dressed. I sat down and waited. I could've taken the assumption to begin eating without permission, but I chose to show the officer that I am in control of impulsive actions. Anyone else that just spun a yarn 5 kilometers long as I did and starving on addition to that, would not be able to resist the food, at an arms-length away. The officer came in and I stood up in respect. The officer said, "Go ahead and eat David Stone. We can talk while you eat." I moved the bowl and the wineskin in front of me, bowed my head, uttered no words, and made the cross gesture over the food. I sat back up and began scooping the stew into my mouth. The captain said," David, I noticed that you did not say a prayer and did not make the sign of the cross on your body, why is that?" I stopped eating, wiped my mouth, and said, "The priest you speak of hear confessions of people's sins, then tells them to repent and they are absolved of their sins. The sinners need to ask only the teacher and the creator for forgiveness and not to continue to sin. The great teacher and the creator of the universe are the only beings that can forgive you or I."

The officer leaned back in his chair and said," David, that is a mind changing concept, and that kind of heretical talk could get you and I roasted on a stake. Let's talk about these creatures these blood-thirsty demons of the night. I said," If you find a lot of them in one place, set it on fire and as they come out, lop off their heads. Your men need to guard at all costs of not being bitten by those creatures or, they will turn into demons. The demons try to go for the throats of their prey. The throat is tender and major veins are located there." I continued to scoop up the meat and beans from the stew, picked up the bowl, drinking the broth. I then took the wineskin and drank from it. I offered the wineskin to the officer and said, "Good hunting… Captain Jonas and thank you letting me feel like a person for a little while."

The captain said, "How do you know my name?" I told him I heard the soldiers outside addressing him as Captain Jonas. I said," I see in your face that you genuinely care for your men and you'll be moving up in rank. Captain Jonas told the guards to escort me back to the stockade. One guard unlocked the door, I walked in sat down on the stone floor. I leaned back on the bars, waiting and listening for what happens next. I have food in my stomach, clean clothes, boots yet, I feel the weight of guilt for Jean's demise. Just as I was about to drown in pool of self-pity, I heard a lot of commotion from outside. I heard some soldiers saying that they found some demons. In the confines of the village Rouen, homes are being searched for the hiding places of the blood demons. Soldiers are finding entire families dead in their homes along with the predators that brought death to them. The soldiers were instructed to behead the victims, set homes ablaze in the event of a demon horde is hiding there. The villagers are caught between two worlds, an invasion by the English and something that takes over the body and the soul… the vampires.

I could smell the scent of burning wood and flesh, as the occasional wind blew down the hallway of the stockade. There's only one way in and one way out, no windows either. I know in a few hours the night will come, and so will those thirsty for blood. I had stuck my fingers in my ears to drown out the cries of the victims, as well as the screams of the vampires burning flesh. I could still hear the sounds travelling through my bones, no way of blocking out. I hear the sounds of men, running towards the stockade. One man unlocks the cage as the other grabs my arm, pushing a blade at my back. A soldier says, "Captain Jonas told us to fetch you. Don't put up a fight or we'll bleed you instead of the demons." After we got outside of the stockade, it was apparent that things are out of control. Buildings are on fire, people are running in all directions, burning blood thirsty demons are being fought out in the open. The soldiers hurriedly take me into a building and shut the door. I find out why, I was brought from the stockade.

A vampire had been captured and is bound up across the room from me. Its face is unrecognizable, until it spoke to me. "Are you ready to confess to me now? Sinner!" I said," I can release you from this and give you a far better deal than you gave the maiden. Priest!" Captain Jonas interrupted the war of words and asked me," I thought that the fire would destroy the demons?" I told him that fire flushes then out to sunlight, sunlight burns their skin. Captain Jonas said," I brought you here to see if, you can find out any other weakness, that they may have." I moved closer to the priest as he snarled at me like a mad dog.

I asked for a lantern so that I could show the captain something. A soldier handed me a lantern and I pointed out the area where the priest wore his rosary. Captain Jonas leaned forward and said," The rosary bearing the cross, has burned into the skin. Holy relics will burn them and possibly repel them. David, there are people dying because of these things.

The night will be here soon and if a decision isn't made quickly, this plague will own us all." I said, "How many cathedrals are there in Rouen?" "A couple maybe… I guess? Why do you ask?" asked the captain? I told him to round up as many women, children, and abled bodied men, placing them inside the cathedrals. He asked me did I think that this would work? I said, "I can think of no larger holy relic than a cathedral, can you?" I told him to hurry because the night is coming and the scent of blood is in the air. The captain asked me did I want to go inside the cathedral. I told the captain to place me back in the stockade, the creatures will be drawn to me but won't be able to get in unless someone gives them a key. The captain laughs at my comment and tells me that he'll be having breakfast with me if he survives the night. As the word was spread to the villagers, to make their way to the cathedral for safety, many didn't get the news because, they already belong to the night. Some people found refuge within the confines of the cemetery. The blood thirsty couldn't cross into hallowed grounds that had been blessed. The insatiable hunger drove the blood drinkers to find easier prey.

The soldiers are escorting me back to the stockade and we were attacked from the shadows. The rear guard is attacked, I jumped on the back of the creature, snapping its neck like a twig. The front guard sees that I've attempted to save his comrade. The rear guard is still alive, but he won't be human, the creature has bitten deeply into the guard's shoulder. The bitten soldier was pleading for his life and the other guard was saying," Why not lock him up, to see if he changes?" I said, "They stop being people after they change. They become an insatiable feeding beast that can't be filled. Do you have family back in England?" The guard said "Yes!" I told him once the transformation has taken him; he could drain every drop from your family's veins and feel no remorse. The guard took out his sword and lopped off the head of the other soldier. The guard hurriedly got me to the stockade, opened the barred door and locked it. The soldier got into the cage next to me and locked himself in it. I asked him. Why did he do such a thing? "Because Captain Jonas believes you and so do I. I don't want to become one of those things." Replied the scared soldier. I told him that those things will be coming into the stockade but, that cannot get through the bars. I said, "Do not make eye contact with them and stay out of their reach.

In fact, just keep your eyes closed the whole time and don't pay any attention to what they say. They want to drain you dry of your blood. They can mesmerize you and coax you into handing them the keys, do not look into their eyes." As I was talking to the soldier, a predator of the night came in. I told the soldier to shut his eyes and say the lord's prayer. The sound of the soldier saying the prayer attracted more inside the stockade. The blood thirsty are ridiculing the soldier and I told the soldier to pay no attention, keep praying. The blood thirsty were constantly trying to get the soldier to look upon them as I continued to antagonize them to come to my cage. The soldier stopped praying and I told him to repeat it until he could no longer speak it. I said, "After your unable to speak it, get on your knees and pray with the words in your mind."

An unfamiliar voice came into the stockade saying," You couldn't save our queen. What makes you think you can save this soldier from us?" I said, "What makes you more worthy than any of your blood sucking servants here?" The general pushed aside his subordinates until he was at the entrance of my cage. I continued to tell the soldier in the next cage to keep praying and not listen to the lies being spewed by the blood drinkers. I said, "Your queen drank from you, you are a direct source from her, why shouldn't your brothers and sister's share from the source?" "I am their new king and I was chosen by her. Besides, I know what you are trying to do, Judas… the fallen disciple." Replied General Falstaff. The other blood suckers were asking the general, why wasn't their gaze upon me ineffective? I had planted a seed amongst the general's followers. They begin attacking him and the general forced his way out of the stockade.

In my greatest of hopes, the general's subordinates wound drain him dry and sever the chord of the blood thirsty plague. At least for now, the blood thirsty aren't in the stockade. I told the soldier to relax, and I was prepared for the questions that are coming. I sat down on the floor of the cell and leaned back onto the wall. The soldier in the adjacent cell stood up and walked over to the bars that divided us. The soldier said," You are a true holy man, those creatures knew that you weren't afraid of them." I told the soldier that the night wasn't over yet. I said, "Rest while you can and be quiet. Hopefully, we both will be walking out of here in the sunlight." We sat there caged up, listening, and waiting for something to happen. Minutes went by and then hours, I was fighting the urge to go to sleep.

I stood up and moved around a little to combat sleep. The soldier in the next cage mimicked my actions, he understands the seriousness in this battle. We are not just fighting against sleep and the blood suckers; it is a battle of will. I'm not so much worried about myself but, I do care for the well-being of the soldier. The soldier put his faith in me to get through this. My sensitive hearing caught the sounds of men, women and children being slaughtered. Those that didn't make it to the cathedral are lost. The general had to dispose the subordinates that wanted to drink from him and be as powerful. The general had only one choice to make, he had to leave Rouen before sunrise. He knew that his kind would be hunted once the sun came up. The general took a horse and rode as hard as the horse could carry him to the next village. He rode into a small village near the river Seine, he's still hungry. He uses status as a general to take the command of a small group of English soldiers camped there.

The dark master has set the general on a different course. The general using his powers, directed two soldiers to bring him a young female. The soldiers went on their way without questioning. The soldiers went into a nearby pub and commandeered two women. The soldiers in the pub questioned the validity of their action. The soldiers told them a general directed this order. The woman questioned the soldiers and told them that the general would pay her generously. The woman stopped protesting and fighting with the soldiers. The soldiers arrived back with the woman at a horse stable. The general greeted her and told the soldiers to stand guard. The soldiers heard the whimpers of the dying girl as her blood was being drained from her body. The general wiped his mouth and covered the corpse of the dead girl with straw. The general went to the two soldiers and made them look into his eyes. He said, "You will not remember anything as I tell you to turn and walk away." The soldiers were compliant as they performed the general's instructions. The general climbed into the hayloft and remained there until the following night. The plan is to make it back to England, a port in the English Channel isn't far. In England, he could make those pay that sent him to France.

In Rouen, a new day brought with it more missing people, except for those fortunate enough to find sanctuary in the cathedral. Captain Jonas took a group of men to the stockade to see if David made it through the night. A soldier walked in first and tells the captain," There are two alive ones in here. sir!" Captain Jonas walks in and sees that they are locked in separate cells. The soldier in the cell next to David reaches through the bars and says, "Sir! I owe you my life and if it were up to me? You wouldn't be locked up like this." I shook hands with the soldier and watched him unlock the cell he was in. Captain Jonas approached my cage door and told me that many were saved by going into the cathedral and there are signs that many didn't make it. Captain Jonas said," Unlock the cell and escort le Stone to my quarters." A soldier unlocked the cage and told me to walk.

The captain followed from behind as we made our way to his quarters. The soldiers sat me down at a table as the captain sat across from me. I could see by the captain's face, that he is reluctant to tell me something. The captain took a deep breath and said, "The general is gone, a lot of my men are gone, those that are alive are afraid of the darkness. They that are alive are saying, that this didn't happen until you and the maiden came here. They want justice but, they forget how they got saved or how to combat these things." I said, "You could've told me this in the stockade that I'm to be hanged. Why bring me out of the cage?" The captain fighting awfully hard to maintain his composure said" Monsieur le Stone if there is a miracle left in you? I want you to do it, so those that see it cannot condemn you to death." I said, "I cannot walk on water or raise the dead just like the teacher from Nazareth. I know the difference between good and evil. By you being here along with the soldiers that escorted me to your quarters, you listened to my instructions and alive for it.

Those things that sleep in the day are evil and must be destroyed. You will have to repeat my instructions until those things are gone. If they go unchecked, all of France will be a place of the undead." The captain turned to one of the soldiers and said, "See to it that monsieur le Stone gets a hefty meal and bring a full bottle of wine." "Yes Captain!" replied the soldier as he hurried off. The captain said, "Let's change the subject matter for a moment. I am curious about the maiden and if she told you, how she became a demon of the night?" I realized that I could've mesmerized them and slipped away. Then I thought, this could be it. I would be free of this life. So, I went into telling the captain and the soldier standing guard, the first time that I met the maiden, before she was stricken with a curse. I told the captain that I had a brief encounter with her in Orleans. I said, "It was one of those strictly by chance meeting, that I knew would one day, that I would be forced to relive it. Orleans had been taken by the French and I was inside the walled chateau. I heard an angelic voice yell out," We have a holy man fighting here with us. He doesn't fear death because he knows Heaven awaits him." She yells out. "Viva le France!" She is pointing at me with her sword atop her horse as this was going on.

At her request, the dauphin invited me to eat at his table. I took the invitation and not knowingly, I was put on the spot. The maiden had a God given gift and it wound up being her undoing. While I was sitting across the table from the maiden, she stuck her hand for me to grasp. She held it for a brief moment and said," This man has walked on the sand that the Lord Jesus bled upon." Everyone at the table stopped eating and talking after she said that. The Dauphin asked her, how could she make such a claim? I stood up, bowed in reverence to the dauphin and told him," Yes, I studied his works inside Jerusalem for 10 years until returning to France." I sat back down and waited for what was to come next. The dauphin said, "Are we to take this for a fact, this could be a rehearsed parlor trick." The maiden asked for the Dauphin's hand and my hand, she told me to show the Dauphin the holy land. She was able to stream my visions of Jerusalem through her to the Dauphin. The Dauphin saw more than I wanted him to and I broke the chain. The dauphin said, "I saw it! I saw where he died! I thought all the Templars are dead?" The maiden calmed the Dauphin and told him that it was only a vision. By this time, a soldier has brought with him, a woman carrying food and a bottle of wine. The sat the items on the table as I continued to talk. The captain was glued to my every word as he watched the wine being poured. I said, "The maiden had stepped into dangerous territory, there was a priest present and he saw everything.

I was questioned by the priest and the priest had never been to Jerusalem, he felt threatened and condemned the maiden's action akin to witchcraft. The Dauphin much like your king isn't in control, the church leaders wield the power. The priest told the Dauphin to distance himself from the maiden and eliminate me in the process. During the night I was awakened by the maiden and told me that we are to leave immediately or face being hanged tomorrow. We narrowly escaped with our lives that night. The maiden and I were fugitives from the French army and hiding from the English as well. She was young, barely turning into a woman and I a middle-aged man, forced together and on the run. We had been staying in the forest and moving around, avoiding staying in one place too long. One day, we thought our luck had changed. We had found a dwelling and after entering it, there were traces of blood in a few rooms but, no bodies. We began scavenging for food to eat and there was food there. The day was almost gone and the maiden found some candles as I started a fire. I heard the maiden call for me and I saw that she was trying to fight off one of those things. I pulled it away from her and cut off its head with my sword. Those things had been hiding within the dwelling from the sunlight. The maiden was bitten by that demon of the night, she changed in two nights. I didn't see her again until she was brought into the stockade. You know what happened after that so, this means I get to eat my last meal.

The captain raised his cup of wine and said, "I raise my cup to you, monsieur le Stone. You have enlightened me in more ways than anyone that I've ever met. I am terribly sorry that things have turned out the way they have. "I told the captain not to be sorrow filled because I've witnessed things that people shouldn't have to see. I said," I may look like a middle-aged man but, I've struggled with just being alive more than several life times. You are doing me a favor by ending this. I just hope that I'll be forgiven for the things that I did and accepted through the pearly gates." The captain asked me did I have any last requests? I requested that I be buried outside the village and facing east ward. Why not in the church graveyard and facing east? asked the captain. I said, "Those that are buried in the church graveyard, aren't guaranteed entrance to heaven simply by being buried close to the church.

God exist in the hearts and the minds of men besides; the great teacher addressed his followers out in the open. You question about facing east is a reference to the final judgement. The sun rises from the east and the lamb with legions of his angels will descend from the east. I want to be aimed in that direction, to stand up and wait for my name to be called." A crowd had gathered outside and were saying, "Bring out the witch! He has brought damnation to us! Hang him! Hang him!" The captain said, "Take another big swallow of wine." I picked up the bottle and nearly emptied it in one gulp. I sat the bottle down on the table and a soldier put irons on my hands. They led me out of the building, through the crowd of people that were yelling and spitting upon me. I thought back to the time that I hanged myself and what happened afterwards. I don't mean the moment I met the dark one, I mean while I was dead. I just remember floating and seeing twinkling flickers of light, in a void of darkness. The soldier besides me continued to tug at my arm pulling me in the direction of destiny. We went around this dwelling until the gallows were in full view.

Many people were waiting, jeering at the me and some threw rotten vegetables, as they were yelling "Hang the witch!" The soldier nudged me towards the first step at the bottom. I collapsed, and the soldier helped me back up. I needed to show that I'm not ready to die then again, any normal person would be ready to relinquish their life like this. Each step up the staircase made me recant the good experiences I had through the centuries. As I stepped to the top and final level, seeing the hangman, the noose waiting, could this be the last time the creature won't own me on the next full moon. Captain Jonas had followed behind us and he walked me to the noose. Captain Jonas said, "Put in a good word for me, will you?" I looked him in the eyes and said," I will as long as you keep your promise." "I will keep my promise." Replied the captain. The captain said, "Are there any last words you would like to say to the crowd?" I yelled out at the crowd, "The great teacher from Nazareth died for you." The hangman placed a hood over my head and the next thing I heard was my neck snapping.

I wasn't dead nor alive, I felt the men release my limp body from the noose. My body was placed in the back of a wagon and driven out of the village. The captain kept his word, he followed the men by horse to ensure my wishes were carried out. The captain watched as the men dug my grave in an east to west orientation. The hole was dug, and the men placed me in the hole. The captain got down from his horse, placed two gold coins on my eyes and said, "Here is payment for the gate keeper monsieur le Stone." I felt the dirt being cast upon my body; I am powerless for the moment. I could hear the pounding on the soil as the men packed the dirt with their tools and then the sound of the wagon and horses walking away. My human mind is asleep, but my animal mind is in a panic. My body has been able to repair deadly sword wounds, broken arms, legs, and excessive blood loss, but this degree of damage has never been experienced, at least since I been changed.

The people of Rouen are preparing for another night of the creatures that sleep during the day. The men in the village and the English army have flushed many from their hiding places and eradicating them by decapitating. The women and children have been moved inside the cathedral, the night creatures cannot enter sanctified buildings or grounds. The villager's ability to go to sleep in the safety of their own beds, has been replaced by the horror of being drained of blood, and themselves changed into the living dead. Captain Jonas carries the responsibility with much more weight than before. He has no more superiors to guide him, the insights into this madness have been forcibly hanged and the light of day is fading. He and a group of his men were able to make it to the church graveyard. Torches were readied at the parameters, the men instructed not to look into the eyes of the creatures and not venture too close to the torches. The torches mark the boundary between being safe to being drained and transformed into something hideous.

The captain had appointed men to stand guard and keep watch over one another. The captain sat down at the foot of someone's grave-marker, a stone cross. The captain laid down on the grave, placing his hands over his ears, to mask out the sounds of the night. The day's heavy trial finally gave way to sleep for the captain, it wasn't easy. Guilt can weigh heavily on one's mind. As I lay in the ground, my mind is still at work. The mind of the immortal is telling the body to repair itself. In a matter of hours, my head is reattached to my spine. The moment it happened caused an instantaneous spark, my muscles and sense of touch is intact. I also find that it is difficult to breathe with soil encased around me. My arms being crossed against my chest, I pushed upward to loosen the earth's bondage. I finally broke free and took in a deep breath of air, I wasn't far from the chaos in Rouen. I could still hear it. I began walking in the opposite direction of Rouen. I need to put some distance between me and Rouen. I'm supposed to be dead according to the people that witnessed my hanging. At least, I found out that I can't be killed by hanging. Again, I'm walking aimlessly towards whatever this world throws at me. My heart still aches over the loss of Jean, but she no longer has to worry about being captive to this world nor the dark master. In two weeks, the full moon will have control over me. I need to find somewhere away from people. I continued walking, making my way into the forest and out of sight. I just wanted to be alone.

As the morning sun glistened through the above canopy of immense ancient trees, my moment of tranquility stopped abruptly. A voice, the familiar voice that I dreaded to ever hear from spoke to me. "Did you think I had forgotten about you?" Said the dark master. I turned around to see him; he was dressed in some unfamiliar clothing. The dark master said," Do you like these clothes? It will be the latest fashion in France after the revolution." I told him that I had already witnessed a revolution in France. I said, "I thought that you have gotten a new pet to control, general Falstaff." The dark master's demeanor changed as he began to unravel his rage upon me. As he was yelling, the ground trembled, trees were falling all around us. I screamed back at him saying," What do you want from me? I don't have anything left, that you haven't already taken." The dark master's rage stops, all sounds stop. The birds aren't singing, and the wind isn't moving, just silence. The dark master takes a moment and says," Everywhere that I placed you, you had the chance to take control. I only ask of you to pay homage to me. You did that very thing to start with and what happened? Did you think for one moment that I wasn't aware of your personal rebellion against me. I told you not to seek out the warrior maiden and she wanted power just like you. She embraced the power that I gave her and then, you denied me what was supposed to be mine…. her soul. I was in the crowd of people when you were spouting about your teacher. They still hanged you regardless of the people you saved from the vampires. The warrior maiden will be remembered in history but, you will be just a foot note." I reached inside my pants and pulled out my man part and said," How's this for a foot note?" as I urinated upon the dark master's shiny shoes. He grabbed me by my throat and threw me through another hole in time. I watched as centuries sped by until I dropped onto the ground.

I hit hard; my ears were ringing from the impact. I lay there for a moment just wondering what I will be facing. I was about to stand up and heard this loud whirring getting louder, as it was fast approaching in my direction. The object hit the ground and exploded near me, throwing me into the air effortlessly. I've experience cannon fire but, cannon balls don't explode like that. My ears were really ringing now after the blast also, hearing multiple blast of some smaller type of weapon firing in rapid succession. It is evident I've been dropped into the middle of a battlefield; the smell of death is heavy in the air. I began crawling towards the direction from whence, the large explosive weapon came from. It is evident that the other side is being outclassed in weapon strength. I might as well see if I can join the winning side.

CHAPTER 12

1915 A NEW WAR

As I crawled upon the pock marked landscape, I saw firsthand the result of a type of carnage, that lay waste to those caught in the open. The rain had turned this killing field into a soup of mud. My once dry clothes are no more than a soggy weight to drag upon the ground. I could hear this whizzing noise just above my head, as I continued to drag my belly through the mud. I found a large depression in the ground that had been blown out and crawled into it. The hole was partially filled with rainwater, dead men, an odd smell that was burning my eyes and lungs as I took a breath. I could no longer inhale the tainted air and crawled from the hole. From my vantage point, there were no trees or rocks to hide behind. The thought of stealing the dead's clothing and changing in the middle of this chaos is out of the question.

My body tells me, that tonight the full moon comes and the beast doesn't have any fear of his surroundings. I continue until I've reached some kind of metal barrier that is riddled with sharp barbs. I try to move it, but it is anchored in the ground. I have only one choice and that is, to crawl back far enough to give myself some room. I'm going to have to leap over the metal obstacle regardless of the outcome. I crawled back several meters and decided to make my run in an arcing move. Whatever weapon they are firing, I will be making it harder for the weapon bearer to line up on me by doing this. My only vulnerable move will be my landing on the other side of the metal wire obstacle. My sensitive hearing has picked two distinctive languages, one is French, and the other is different. I continue to listen as I plan out my run, the language is Germanic. Both sides have seen a moving object on the battlefield but I haven't seen them. I decided to make my move, I arched my body up and began running as fast as I could. I heard and saw the flashes of the weapon as it was spitting projectiles at me.

I felt the searing stings into my back and as I cleared the wire obstacle, I felt the searing stings of the projectiles going through my chest, legs and my stomach. I collapsed on the ground; the projectiles tore into me like small hot embers from a flame. I rolled over on my back, I opened my eyes and said to myself, I'm still alive. The projectiles, like modern arrows, have no effect on what lives inside me. I can already feel my body repairing itself, I'll just lay here and let the weapon bearers think I'm dead. The high-pitched sound of the large projectile as it travelled towards an unseen target, made an even louder sound as it connected to something. I could feel the ground tremble underneath me after every explosion. The great cannons must be to the rear of the fighting, their reach is far beyond any type cannon that I've experienced.

No castle wall could withstand this new killing machine that men have designed to kill each other with. I can already feel the tension in my jaws, the first sign of the transformation is happening. The sky is overcast with clouds of gray. The smell of rain mixed with burnt gun powder and rotting flesh floats with the wind. My body aches have now turned into excruciating pain. The constant firing of unknown weapons coupled with the barrage of explosions; my yell of pain is being drowned out. What feels like an eternity during the change, has finally subsided as the rain began falling in torrents. Laying on the ground the beast opens his eyes, springs to his feet and running towards his first kill. The constant firing has stopped because the weapon bearers are blinded by the rain. The beast has tasted the wind and knows where his targets are. The beast dives into the manmade trench, surprising his prey. A soldier does manage to shoot projectiles into the beast, but he didn't live to long afterwards. The beast manager to kill five or more men before he could begin to rip flesh from their bodies to consume.

He would hear men speaking as the trench channeled the sound to him like a roman road. He had eaten enough and went on a killing rage as rain continued to fill the trench with water. The beast had seen what the men were firing at with, he felt the burning sting. The projectiles mad him angry and at the same time, the pain was making him think about retreating. In the trench, he felt confined and was being fired at. The beast made the decision to leave the trench and go towards the rear of the fight, towards the big cannons. His hunger has been satisfied but his curiosity has not. He is in a strange land and continues to run, as sheets of rain pour down. His senses are acute, but he doesn't see the coiled wire in front of him. He hits it, it tears into his flesh, and he struggled until he has finally freed himself. The beast leaves dead men behind and a witness to the savage carnage. The frantic German soldier gets on the radio to alert the second defense trench. The soldier screams," Der teufel kommt! Der Teufel Kommt! (The devil is coming!) Another voice from the rear trench ask, "Was passiert? (what is happening?) The soldier in the forward trench is mortified from what he witnessed. He dropped the radio and began asking for forgiveness from God. He could not grasp how something could survive all those bullet holes and keep going.

Other soldiers had heard the commotion and came to investigate. They found one lone soldier on his knees; he is praying to God to forgive him. The men first thought that the soldier had killed his own brethren, until they noticed the dead had not been shot. Their bodies had chunks of flesh missing, claw marks of something that their mind could not comprehend. The soldier was asked what did this? He said," Der Teufel!" (the devil). The soldier pointed in the direction that the beast, or in his mind the devil had gone. The men looked at the side of the wooden lined trench and saw claw marks. A soldier placed his hand over one of the claw marks and saw that it was much larger than his. The men felt a different kind of terror other than being killed by machine gun fire by the enemy, something unexplainable was happening.

He senses up ahead another trench, by the smell of the presence of people. The wind and rain carry the odor of urine and excrement mixed with spent gunpowder. He also knows that the projectile spitting weapons are there also. He pushes on despite the outcome, the killer instinct drives the beast. He is full of anger from the sharp wire and is going to unleash his anger on anything in his path. From the rear trench, a German soldier looks through the periscope sight glass and sees something. The rain blurs the view, the movement of the artificial eye has gotten the beast attention. The beast lunges into the trench kills the soldier by decapitation. The beast hesitates for a moment and is hears movement coming towards him. He uses the dead body to somewhat cover his presence, he peers out with one eye. He surveys the situation. He hears the men talking about some message from the radio. The beast does not recognize such a word, but he hears a word that he does understand. der teufel; it's a Germanic word for the devil. Are they describing him?

Has man developed a way to relay a message other by courier, and have they been warned about me? The beast has spent much energy freeing himself from the wire and getting to this spot. He decides to catch the men off guard, they didn't have a chance. The beast gorged himself upon the fallen soldiers, but knows that he cannot remain in the trench. He knows that time has been ticking by and the change will come with a new day. The rain has not let up and he climbs out of the trench, he keeps moving. He knows that he can't be seen as the change happens. The big cannons have not fallen silent even in the rain, there are many of them placed several meters from each other. Each one raining down death and destruction, as each projectile makes contact and explodes. He must run, his legs must carry him faster than they've been pushed to His nose catches the scent of some type of vegetation not far ahead. The rain is slowing down, he pushes his body to the limit to seek somewhere to hide. The beast hears Germanic voices coming from a narrow hedgerow, he commits to the attack.

The men didn't have a chance, the men that were at a machine gun placement; are now dead. The beast feels the pains that signify the sun has begun it's rise. The beast has no control over his body until the change is complete and with the continued bombardment of the big cannons, no one will hear his screams from the pain. As the minutes tick away, the beast is no more. Judas must hurriedly change clothes with the dead Germans. Their clothes are soaked from the rain and Judas has taken notice of from his own eyes, the advancements that man has come in ways not only in the ways of killing, but the manner of their clothing. Judas swiftly finishes off the change by trying on the boots of the dead. He left their socks on because they were soaked. He remembered as the beast seeing the Germans throwing the exploding sticks at him.

Judas sees a way of destroying the evidence of the dead Germans. He puts the bodies close to each other and next to the projectile spitting weapon. He takes three of their stick bombs lays it on them, then taking one in his hand, pulls the string and throws it onto the bodies. The blast blows him backwards and steel fragments from the machine gun is embedded into his chest. A nearby German command station heard the blast, only because it's close proximity. An officer sent out a patrol to see what had happened, they found an injured soldier with shrapnel in his chest. The blast knocked Judas unconscious, and he was taken to a makeshift field hospital. The field hospital is only but a canvas tent to shield the injured from the elements. The German soldiers place Judas on a cot, taking him back to their post. Judas slowly opens his eyes and the pain from the shrapnel hits him. He sits up on the cot and begins clawing at his clothing. A nurse sees him and yells" "Halt! Unten!" (Stop! Down!), Judas understands and lays back down, as the nurse comes over to see why he was clawing at his clothing. The nurse saw right away the metal shrapnel is protruding through his jacket. She yells,"Kommt Arzt!" (Come Doctor!) The nurse places her cool hand upon my forehead and she gives a warm smile.

Though her clothing is blood stained, she has a face and manner of purity. I can feel that she genuinely cares not just for me but all the wounded and the dying in this place, a brief sanctuary from the fight. A man comes over and give the nurse instructions to start cutting away the clothing. The nurse gingerly takes a pair of scissors and begins cutting off my jacket, leaving a patch of the clothing intact with the shrapnel. The doctor nods at the nurse as she places a gas laden cloth over my nose. I struggled in refusing to inhale the gas. The nurse said, "Atmen." (breathe), as she placed her other hand upon my shoulder. I inhaled the strange smelling odor and I could no longer keep my eyes open. My will to resist is overtaken by this drug, my body is numb. I could hear the doctor and nurse talking for a little while and then, I find myself standing in the battlefield. I hear a familiar voice, I turned to my right and he is standing there. The dark master says, "Well Judas, you've found yourself in the beginning, of what's to be called the Great War. How do like my uniform? It was tailored just for me." I said, "What happened to your protégé, General Falstaff?" "He got larger than his ego and thought that he couldn't be brought down even by me." Replied the dark master. "I guess you really showed him, who the boss is?" I exclaimed. The dark master then said," You really know how to make me mad, but in a much unusual way. I've gotten over it and General Falstaff, I've placed you here to lay some groundwork for the future. This war pits some major countries against each other and from this war, many new inventions designed for killing will spring up like weeds after a rain in the spring. I'm going to let you set your own course. Just know that some people that you run into will be impacted, and that impact will be felt in the next war to come."

Like before, I was about to ask questions and I was awakened. I felt the cool touch of the nurse's hand on my forehead. She said," The shrapnel is gone and I'll get you something for pain because, though you're not in pain now, you will be. I was still groggy from the inhaled drug and I'm somewhere in Germania. I've been placed into a battle that I know nothing about. In the life before this, the French were at war with the English. Last night the beast heard French voices on the opposing side, as he was feeling the projectiles strike his body. I don't know which side won the last battle, nor do I know if I'm on the side of the oppressed or the oppressors. I do know that my chest is beginning to hurt like I've been stabbed multiple times. The nurse and the doctor came back to cot that I'm lying on and the doctor said, "What is your name soldier?" I hesitated, trying to think of a name. I looked at the doctor and told him I can't remember my name. The doctor told me that it is a miracle that I'm alive. He said that he removed the metal fragments from my chest, a bullet from the base of my skull, and twenty-seven bullets, that were scattered about from my back and legs.

He then said, "I'm not so much worried about your temporary amnesia for the moment. I've instructed my nurses to keep your wounds clean and your dressings changed. You could possibly remember who you are after you get a night's rest." The doctor pats me on the shoulder and walks away. The nurse lingers at my side looking into my face. The doctor calls to her, saying he needs her assistance. She tells me that she will check on me later. I know who I am. I also know what will happen if I stay here. By the sounds I'm picking up with my sensitive hearing is, there is a lot of activity surrounding this tent. I didn't plan on getting knocked unconscious by the explosive. I didn't know what I was playing with. I've got to get out of here! I grabbed the sides of the wooden cot and pulled myself upright. The pain is at the point of unbearable, it reminded me of the day, that Jean and I had all of those swords thrust into us by the English. I lost a lot of blood that day but, today is unlike then. I'll recover much faster today because, I'll change before it gets dark.

Another nurse sees me sitting up and frantically comes to my aid. She tells me to lie down or I'll bust my stitches and start bleeding. She gently eases me back onto the cot. I grabbed the nurse's hand and said," You must get me out of here! Something bad is going to happen!" She looked into my eyes and said," It's all right, you are safe here. We are far from the western front." She smiled and placed her cool hand on my forehead and said," You don't have a fever, just remain calm." I was about to force my will upon her then, I could hear explosions getting closer in the distance. A high pitched sound began that hurt my ears and someone began screaming,"Luftangriff! Luftangriff! (air raid! air raid!) The doctors began yell to the nurses to exit the field tent. I could hear the explosions getting closer along with this whirring sound from the air. I sat back up on the cot, swung my legs over the side. I realized then that I was naked except for the sheet that covered me. I saw men that were able to get up, naked or not scramble to leave. It is evident that we are not safe inside the tent. I wrapped the sheet around my waist, tied it off to cover my nakedness.

All around me are men, just waiting for deaths final call. I was almost at the doorway when, the first nurse was coming through the door. As we made eye contact, something struck that end of the tent and exploded. The nurse was gone, that end of the tent was gone. The cloth roof had partially collapsed and I thought to myself, here's my chance, I just need some clothes. I slowly made my way outside the tent, people were frantically moving about as more explosions are happening. I looked up into the sky and saw where the sound and the bombs are coming from. I say to myself that, man has developed a flying killing machine. As I was standing there looking at the flying machine, a nurse took me by arm, pulling me to a trench. I asked her what was that flying and dropping bombs? She said," It is a Nieuport, a French airplane! Is that the first time you've seen an airplane?" "Yes." I replied. She then looked at the bandaged areas and saw that for the moment wasn't bleeding. I asked her can she get me some clothing? She said," Once the bombing stops, I'm taking you back to the field tent. I want to make sure that your stitches are holding. I amazed that you were able to walk, judging by all the areas that are bandaged up. It looks like you were hit everywhere but your arms." I said," I guess I'm luckier than some of the men in the tent I left from, some had missing arms and legs. Not mention, those that were on the receiving end of a bomb."

The nurse asked me my name and I told her that, the doctor removed a bullet from the base of my skull. I said," The doctor me that the bullet may have brought about the memory loss." The nurse looked into my eyes and said," I can picture you with curly hair so, how does name Krause sound to you? It means curly hair" I told her that it is fine and I feel kind of exposed. She touched my private parts and softly said," If we were alone, I would give myself willingly to you." I made direct eye contact and quietly told her that if she got me a uniform, she would get her wish. She grabbed my hand and whispered we must go now while we have the chance. The entire area was filled with smoke outside of the trench, she pulled me at me and said that we must hurry. As I was moving, I could feel my muscles growing and strengthening. There is so much chaos going on that, the nurse and I aren't even noticed. I was desperately trying to hold on to my wrapping, as I kept pace with the nurse. We stopped between these two drab green tents and she told me to wait there for a moment. She went into the tent on the left and quickly came back for me. She said," There's no one in the supply tent. Let's go!" She took my hand and led me inside. There is shelves of cans, medicine, blankets, and clothing.

The nurse took a pile of blankets and placed them on the ground in the back of the tent. She eased me down onto the blanket and pulled down her undergarments, opened up her shirt and released her young firm breast. She untied my temporary garment and began caressing my man parts. It wasn't long before she was on top of me, bouncing up and down, like she was riding a horse. She squealed with pleasure as she climaxed. I was about to spew inside of her until, I pulled out, turned her over on her stomach and slid into her anus. I pumped a few times until I blew my juice into her. I couldn't risk making another me running around and killing, during every full moon. Both of us are euphoric and can't believe what we just did. She quickly cleaned herself and I then, she began looking through some pants for me to wear. She asked me did I want to be an officer or regular soldier? I told her we need to hurry, and it doesn't matter. She found a pair of pants and I put them on. She said," Here try this on!" The jacket was a little tight but, I was able to button it up. She found some socks and boots and it was extremely lucky that the boots fit. She had me sized up like a tailor. She then said, "You're in an officer's uniform and you need a proper name." She said, "How about Hans Engel?" I told her that I didn't feel like God's angel but, who knows what he has planned for me." I said, "Doesn't this come with a proper hat with this costume?"

She rambled through some crates and found an officer's cap. I took off my head bandage, put on my cap and said, "Before I leave you what is your name fraulein? She told me her name is Gerta Klein and asked me why I was leaving? I kissed her on her lips, gently grasping her head with my hands and said," Gerta, look at me." As I was looking into her beautiful blue eyes, I said, "You will forget this moment, you will forget my face. Do you understand me? Sit down and when I get to the tent opening, I'm going to say your name and you'll forget all of this. Do you understand?" She nods and sat down. I make my way to the tent opening and say, "Gerta!" I quickly moved away as far as I could without being noticed. I had to get away from everyone, best estimation I have an hour or so before the change takes place. I continued walking until I could get out of sight range in case someone is watching me. I could see smoke rising in the distance and smelled wood and flesh burning. My jaw is starting to ache, I must continue and get away as far as possible form the people I just left from.

I quickened my pace to a full on run and turned towards the edge of what's left of a forest. As I got closer, it became evident where the smoke was coming from. I saw a burned-out shell of what used to be a village. The brick-and-mortar buildings were just skeletons of what remained after the Germans pushed through. I cautiously observed everywhere around me, listening for anything. I left the forest edge and entered into one of the demolished buildings, there is bullet torn bodies in here. Men, women, and children were cut down like woodsmen fell trees. The smell of decay is rife, and I kept moving, looking to find somewhere to stash my clothes. I can feel my leg muscles starting to sting and I must find somewhere fast. I went into another bombed out building, I can't go any farther. I took off my clothes rolled them up with the boots and hid them under the caved in roof. As I was fighting back the change, I had to mark the outside of the building in a way to recognize it, once I returned as a man. I took a piece of charred wood and marked the letter V on the corner of the building. I made it back inside and collapsed on the floor, now covered in ashes and remnants of someone's life. The pains begin, as my body transforms into an apex predator.

A predator that has only a single mindedness to him, to kill and eat. The pain is gone, and I am looking through a distinct set of eyes again. I am no longer in control; a vicious mind is in control now. The beast lies still for a moment, listening and testing the air with his hypersensitive nose. He stares upward at a smoke-filled sky and gets into a crouching stance, peeping around a wooden beam, that once held the now caved in roof. He catches the scent of rotting flesh but, the beast yearns for a fresh kill instead. He's hungry and will feed upon the dead but, the urge of the kill drives him forward. He is cautious as he moves about because, he remembers the feeling of the bullets tearing through his body. He will make every attempt to avoid such an unwanted encounter. Not too far away, he hears the groans of the wounded and dying. He carefully makes his way through the rubble, as he continues to survey the terrain and listen for unexpected company. The beast is thrown off guard by a loud explosion and high-pitched whistling of the projectile as it flies over him. He now knows where one of the big cannons is and probably heavily guarded.

The hunger for food pushes the beast forward towards potential prey. He sticks to the shadows; the full moon is in an almost cloudless sky. He slips into a severely damaged building and discovers the dying and the dead peasants that were caught in the middle of this war. He finished killing people that were trapped by the building collapse, the rest were obliterated perhaps by one of the cannon projectiles. The beast feasted until he got his fill but, the satisfaction of killing wasn't satiated. He desired more. The beast is a killing machine, this burning anger compels him. It is an anger that the beast has no control over it nor has he tried to quell it. The trapped victims were too easy, and he seeks out to find the kill that is worthy of his rage.

The rage, is the beast anger directed towards the dark master for making him or is the anger directed towards man? The beast remembers, it has been man, that has robbed him of everything that was held dear to his alter identity. He growls to himself and a gravelly voice says," Man." The beast sees a vantage point, but he must cross out into the open, of what used to be center of this village. He clings to the shadows, blending with it, watching, and listening as he moves with stealth like movements. Just as he was about to round the corner of a building, he sees movement at the vantage point. A portion of a second level building stands as a sentinel and the beast sees the movement of the barrel of a weapon, sticking out from a broken window. The beast will have to rethink his attack. The fullness of the moon in a cloudless sky, will most certainly reveal him if he tried to cross the central plaza of the village.

This infuriated him more and did not want to take the long approach, the man in the window must die. The beast began looking at the lay of the plaza and what he could use as cover. His first move would be, to get to the overturned wagon with the dead horse, therein lies the gap between the wagon and the building. A window of opportunity shows itself when a small cloud passes in front of the moon. The beast sprints to the wagon but, a drowsy German sniper sees something moving. The sniper looks through the rifle scope, waiting for the cloud to pass and allow more light from the moon. The beast looks through the busted floorboards of the wagon and sees the weapon's barrel moving.

The beast must make a quick decision, the dimness of the moon is disappearing. The earth's lunar partner is glowing at full strength and the German's big cannon has just launched a projectile. The thunderous sound reverberated through the burned-out village. The beast sprang towards the building before the projectile could find its target. The sniper fired a round but missed his target, he doesn't know what's coming for him. The beast enters the lower part of the building's shell, only to come in contact with sniper at the top of the stairs. The sniper fires and makes a hit into the beast, the beast isn't slowing down. The sniper ejected a shell, pulling in another to take its place. The beast leaped up the staircase and was on the sniper before his finger found the trigger. The beast took away the weapon and shredded the sniper's body with his talon like claws, ripping away the flesh with his canine teeth. He ate of the sniper's headless body with tenacious anger until he had satisfied his hunger for vengeance. The beast looked from the window at the surrounding devastation, he also saw the placement of the big German cannon. He could see men with weapons placed around the big cannon like, soldier bees guarding the queen's hive.

As the big cannon spit projectiles from its mouth, the beast couldn't resist howling a long throaty "Ahrooooooo!" He looked towards the men and their weapon placements, to see if they heard and their reaction to his display. The men did not hear or react to his display, perhaps they are deafened by the belching of the big cannon. The beast has no desire to take on the men and their weapons, he would be approaching them in the open. The big cannon with surrounding weapons is on the crest of hill. The beast can hear the other big cannon placements down range from his view and to rear. The French are being pounded through the night and the Germans are also on the receiving end from the cannons of the French. A French shell exploded in the building; the staircase gave way as rumble fell on the beast. He dug his way clear of the brick and broken timbers, a bit stunned by the fall.

The beast shook it off and his body is giving him signs, signs that the morning approaches. He cautiously peers from the derelict building, sprinting from one hiding place to another. He is constantly keeping his head on a swivel, watching, listening and testing the air. The enemies on both fronts realize that the morning is coming and the shelling starts to increase. The sound of the big cannons is making the ears of the beast painful, he must make it across the plaza. The beast took the same route back, hiding behind the overturned wagon and sprinting to the collapsed building. He makes it back just in time for the worst of the pains to start, the change back to human form again. The shelling of the big cannons drowned out the painful yells of the beast, as the earth's lunar sister releases her grip. Judas is tired from the transformation and lies there on the dirt covered floor.

He looks up at the predawn sky, past the collapsed roof timbers, seeing distant stars begin to fade. I must hurry and get dressed because I can't stay here. As I put on the officer's uniform, I must think of a name for myself. I thought back to the nurse that was smitten with me. She made me think about Jean. The nurse had in my mind's eye, an almost angelic feature of purity about her. I'll use the last name Engel which is angel in German. Since I don't know the rank of this uniform, I'll wait until I am in contact with a regular soldier. The moment to put my plan into action is about to take place. Amid constant shelling from both fronts, my acute hearing caught the sound of someone running in my direction. I waited until the sound got closer an I stepped out from the shell of a building. The soldier was already carrying a weapon and shot me. I totally surprised him, and he shot by instinct. I fell to the ground; the projectile went through my chest.

The soldier realized that he had shot another German soldier and cautiously walked over to me. The soldier with his weapon still trained upon me, saw the severity of the predicament that we are both in. Before he could fire another shot, I said, "It is alright soldier, you won't be in trouble for shooting me. I should have announced myself before walking out. The problem is, I don't remember too much before the building collapsed upon me and some of my men. I couldn't tell you what my first name is, the only name that comes to mind is the word Engel." The soldier had put away is weapon and said," I could be shot for such an action You wear the uniform of a lieutenant and I am a corporal. My name is corporal Hitler and please forgive me for accidently shooting you." The corporal took a container from his pouch and sprinkled a white powder on the entry wound and the exit wound. I asked him, "What is that you put on my wound?" He said, "It is sulfur, it will stop the bleed as long as you remain still. I will bring help for you, stay still and help will come for you. I must get information to the main artillery group and I will be coming back this way. This is what I do! I am a carrier of information, a runner." The runner disappeared, as I leaned myself against the broken roof beam. I wasn't in pain, just thirsty for water. My body will repair itself in a day or so.

There won't be a third full moon tonight. Though I don't know what month or year it is, my body knows about such things. I'll stay here and wait to see if the corporal is true to his word. The change always takes a toll on my body and leaves me tired afterwards. I might as well take a nap and play the part of an injured lieutenant. I fell asleep, cutting off the sounds of the constant explosions brought about by the big cannons and rapid firing of the smaller weapons. I find myself seeing a different war, new and improved machines to kill man. The images flash before me as flying machines drop their payload of bombs on cities, lighting fires as people die in their sleep. Then I'm standing next to the dark master and he says," Look! Corporal Hitler is now a very powerful man. He is telling the people of Germany that they have control of their own future. He says the German people are the true blood of a superior race. I like the way this guy thinks. Intermingling of races wasn't part of the plan, just as it was the Jews that condemned your teacher to die. I looked down at myself and saw that I was wearing a German officer's uniform and staring out at the multitude of people listening to his speech. I was about to ask the dark master a question and I was awakened by the corporal and two soldiers. The corporal said," I told you that I would bring you some help lieutenant Engel."

The soldiers help me upon some carrying device, lifting me up and carrying me in the direction towards the big cannons. I caught the scent of the morning dew upon the ground but, it is overridden by the stench of rotting corpses and still smoldering ashes from the bombing. The corporal told the soldiers to take me the ridge. The corporal told me that he must get back to his unit and shook my hand. I thanked the corporal and said," Thank you, Corporal Hitler for getting me some help. Maybe I'll get to repay you someday."

I laid my head down on the portable bed as the two soldiers carried me. The sound of the big cannon increased as the men were carrying uphill. The men got to an area and entered a trench that went underground. The air smelled of wet soil and occasionally the trench would cross in the open, only to go into another trench like passageway. The walls and the ceiling of the passages were lined with timbers from the forest. The passage was only wide enough for two men side by side until, we reached a much wider passage that was wide enough for three or four men. The passage was lit with kerosene lanterns and I wasn't the only injured man there. A man with blood-stained clothes told the soldiers to place me on a cot next to the wall. I assumed that he's the physician, as he unbuttoned my jacket and saw the entry wound. He rolled me over on my side and saw the exit wound. He yelled for a nurse saying," We have an officer here! I need ether to put this officer to sleep. Not only did I catch the smell of wet earth but, the smell of death is heavy in this earthen cave. Men are slowly dying in their beds; the machines of war have taken its toll. It appears whoever has the most innovative way of killing has the upper hand. A nurse comes back with a glass jar and a white cloth, and she says to me," Count backwards from 100 as you inhale." She placed the rag over my nose and I smelled that familiar chemical odor again. I reached number seventy-five and I am asleep.

Lieutenant Engel (Judas) has left the confines of the underground hospital two weeks ago. This week, he has been trying to distance himself from the western fronts main line of fighting. He managed to rid himself of the uniform of a German officer and now wears the clothing of a Belgium commoner. Tomorrow night the full moon arises and the beast will kill again. All this constant moving and the fact that my body is getting for the change, I must find some food. The Germans have gutted the village I'm in and only a few of its survivors remain. Though there are a few German soldiers here, they are merely passing through on their way to the front. As I observe my surroundings, I see a man and boy trying to lift the back end of a wagon to replace the wheel. I go over to them and grab hold of the end of the piece of timber, that they are using for a lever. I pulled downward and told the man, to place the wheel on the axle. The man rolled the wheel up to the axle and slid it into place. He then secured the wheel with a large washer, a nail and bent the nail by hitting it with a hammer and chisel. The man thanked me and told me, he could offer me food for payment. I gladly took him up on the offer.

I followed the man and the boy into his home. I did not pry into asking if the man had a wife, I just needed the food. The man told me to have a seat at the table and his son will fetch the food. By the looks of the man and the young boy, their faces tell a story of loss and defeat. The man came to the table with a bottle of wine and two cups just as, the boy brought a block of cheese, a loaf of bread and a knife to slice with. The man said," Before I bless the food, where are you going?" I told him that I lost everything dear to me and I'm moving away from the war. The man simply said that he understood and blessed the food. The animal urge in me could've eaten everything on the table but, my feelings of sympathy as a man kept me in check. I ate and drank just enough to satisfy my hunger for the moment, thanking the man for his generosity and bid them goodbye. I really don't know where I'm going, I just know what is behind me. Tomorrow night begins the three phases of the full moon.

I can already feel some of the effects, sensitive hearing, smells and slight aches in the body. The beast doesn't care if he kills Germans or the common village person, the beast kills indiscriminately and without remorse. As I left the village, the scarring of the land by the Germans is evident. Once mighty forest are just stumps, devoid of greenery, a wasteland pock marked by shelling. I continued walking, stopping to rest, to conserve energy. My sensitive nose catches the scent of death,

I don't know if it is human or animal. My senses urge me forward, pushing me to investigate. I stand up and test the wind direction. The wind is blowing directly at me. I cross over a small hill and it is a dead cow. The cow was hit by a shell and left only the rear section intact. I gathered up some charred wood and built a small fire. I took a knife from my pocket and began removing the tough hide, revealing the flesh beneath. The maggots have already been feasting on the open end of the cow. I know the meat is tainted but, I am not worried about dying from it. I just need to cook it, to make it more palatable. I got a young sapling tree and made a skewer from it. I cut holes in the meat and slid the sapling through the holes. I sat there turning the meat and listening to sounds of the war many kilometers behind me. I think of the times that I've tried to distance myself from people but, I've found myself thrown back into humanity.

I made the dark master angry, and this is my punishment. My moment of solitude is broken by the sound of a familiar voice. "Do you think by cooking rotting meat it will taste better?" Said the dark master. "I'm hungry and there are no taverns to eat or drink from because, the Germans have obliterated them." The dark master said, "You shed the German officer's uniform for peasant clothing. You could be eating the best food and enjoying the best living condition. So, what the moon is full tomorrow night. You can eat some Germans and even get the opportunity to wear an even higher-ranking uniform. Why do you insist on making things more difficult for yourself? Use your brain. You are far more superior than any race of people walking this planet." I was about to deliver my reason for refusal and the dark master disappears. I looked at my meat on a stick and it was burned to a crisp. My mind began thinking of where I left the uniform but, that was weeks ago. There's no telling what lies between me and the uniform now. I just know that I'm still hungry and my body is crying out for fuel to burn.

I got up and turned towards the cow carcass, 30 or so meters away are a group of German soldiers approaching. They see the dead cow and with weapons drawn, they are running towards me. I place my hands up in the air signifying that I am surrendering to them. As they get closer, I could see their faces have sunken in and their clothing hangs upon their bones. They are starving to death. It is evident that they have left the fighting and scavenging, desperation has them. There are five of them and two of are of my same build. They tell me to get on the ground and I tell them," Nein!" One of the soldiers shot me in the leg. I smile at them and tell them that their mothers are dick sucking whores in German. They all fired shots into me, and I remained standing. I could see the fear in their faces as I plunged into them, knocking them to the ground. As they scrambled for their pistols and knives, I systematically killed them one by one. I snapped the neck of the first soldier, the owner of the uniform that I need. I didn't want it to be blood soaked.

The others, I took their weapons from them and used it on them. I hurriedly removed my clothes and wiped away any blood from my body. The wounds have already healed because, the healing rate is faster this close to a full moon. I put on the dead soldier's uniform, picked up a pistol, put it in the holster, grabbed a rifle and robbed them of their ammunition. I didn't need to stay here much longer, there's no telling who may have heard the shots being fired. My body is so hyped up from the action, I took advantage it and began running west in track of the sun and towards the German front. I ran for several kilometers until I ran out of steam. I'm extremely hungry now but, the sounds of cannons firing are getting closer. I had reached the remnants of a bombed-out village and my nose caught the aroma of something being cooked.

The smell had me spell bound, I followed it and it led me to a group of German soldiers and officers. As I walked up to the group, an officer asked me what division am I with?" The artillerie gruppe." I replied. The officer said," It is obvious that this is an artillery group. I asked you, what is your division?" "The best division." I replied. The other soldiers laughed at my answer and the officer did not think it too funny. The officer said," I have only enough food for my men in my division and you should find yourself back to your division." I said," Is this not a German uniform that I'm wearing or did I walk up on a group of boys pretending to be German men?" One of the German soldiers said," Let me teach him a lesson herr major." The Major said, "Your talk has insulted me and my men, let's see if you can back up such brash talk. If you can beat my best soldier in hand-to-hand battle, you can eat all you want. If you lose? You just limp on back to where you are supposed to be. Are we clear?"

I nodded and expected the major to send out the biggest German. Instead, he sent out a man the same build as I. I placed my rifle on the ground and released the pistol and ammo belt from my waist. I walked up to the German soldier, and he raised clinched fist in front of him. I could hear the major saying,"I must warn you. You are fighting one of Germany's best boxers." I let the German land a few hits and I returned harder hits into the German's head until he collapsed on his knees. I saw him grab a hand full of sand as he was getting up. I was ready for him to use it and when he did, I closed my eyes, stepped forward and back handed him. The blow sent him to the ground. As the soldier was regaining his footing, I said," We could stop now and call it a draw, or do you want me to continue, major?"

The major said," It is up to your opponent?" Germany's top shelf boxer said," Let's call it a draw but, I must ask you to apologize to the major and the men in my group for your comment." I held out my hand to the still dizzy boxer for him to shake. I then apologized to the men and helped the boxer over to a bench to sit down. The major said, "What is your name soldier?" "Hans Engel." I replied. The major said," Where did you learn to fight like that, Hans Engel?" I told him that I learned the tactics of street fighting as a kid growing up in a rough neighborhood." The major motioned for me to come and get something to eat. He walked up beside me and stopped. He had pulled out his pistol and said, "There are two things that I despise, one is insubordination and the other is flagrant arrogance." He shot me in the right side of my head. I fell to the ground, still fully aware of things, just my bearings were off from the bullet hole in my head. I lay there for a minute, a German soldier close to me told the major that I'm still breathing. I stood up and the other Germans had dropped their food and were backing away from this witnessed oddity. The major said, "This is against nature Hans Engel. You are dead. Why aren't you dead, Hans Engel?" I said, "I can tolerate ignorance but, I cannot tolerate stupidity.

You can't kill evil but, I can kill the stupid for trying." The major shot more rounds into me as the other German soldiers ran for their lives.

I just walked up to the major put my hands around his throat and squeezed until he breathed his last breath. I could hear the escaping Germans saying, "Teufel!Teufel!" (Devil!Devil!) I said," That's right, the devil will be coming for you tomorrow night and there's nothing you can do about it. I laughed at them as they ran to get as far away as they could from me. I took the major's uniform, put on his jacket and stuffed my shirt with food and headed northwest. I ran for several kilometers and got to an area that seemed almost untouched. I sat down by a tree in the shade and began removing the food from the shirt. I have cheese, bread, sausage and a full canteen to wash it all down. As I was eating, I looked around at my surroundings. Something isn't right about this; it looks untouched by the war. I hear a voice say," How do you like this oasis I created for you?" I turned to see the dark master walking up in a distinctive style of uniform. He said, "I am pleased that you are owning your gift as you should. You really put the fear of the devil into them, didn't you?" The dark master laughed and sat down on the ground across from me. The dark master snapped his fingers, a bottle of wine and two goblets appear on the ground. The dark master opened the bottle of wine; poured it into a goblet and handed it to me. He then poured himself a drink and saying," This calls for a toast." I held my goblet out and he said," To Hans Engel, the devil in disguise." We clinked the goblets together and drank wine. I said, "There's got to be a reason you're here other than observing what I've been doing." The dark master said, "Do you remember the soldier that helped you? The field runner Hitler?" I said, "I do remember him and you telling me that he'll be important man someday." The dark master said," This war will be over in three years and Germany will be vanquished. After the three phases of the moon is over, I'm going to advance you 17 years into the future. I will see you in four days."

He disappeared as quickly as he appeared. I'm sitting in the remnants of a burned down building with my canteen and the food I brought with me. The wine and the goblets left with the dark master. I continued eating and thinking to myself. The dark master is usually pissed off at me when he pushes me forward in time. It is evident that he has taken an interest in in the field runner …Hitler. I gobbled down my food and began to look for somewhere to sleep for the night. The sun is sinking lower in the sky, just a few more hours of daylight left. I could hear the shelling and sounds of the fight to my left, I'm several kilometers away. I decided to make clever use of the officer's uniform and headed towards the fight. I am still hungry and German officers don't sleep on the ground plus, they get better food.

CHAPTER 13

THE LAST NIGHTS IN 1915

I didn't have to go but a few kilometers to run into a group of German soldiers. They saluted me, and I asked them the whereabouts of their commanding officer. I went towards a tent as directed by the soldiers. The flap was closed on the tent, I stood in the front and said,"Guten abend,Major." (good evening). The major told me to enter the tent, I pushed the flap to the side and I walked in. The major seemed nervous and to ease his mind, I took the papers from inside my coat and gave it to him to read. The major handed me back the papers and said, "Have a seat Major Strum. What brings you to my division?" The words came forth out of nowhere, "I'm here to witness a new weapon upon Ypres." The major had a shocked look upon his face. "How do you know this?" Replied the major. "I am among but a select few that knows." I answered. The major told me that he knows that a 6 kilometer stretch of gas canisters are buried and are to be exploded tomorrow. I said," That should kill off a few French and English vermin."

The Major told me that he hoped that the new gas mask supplied to his men work and the wind doesn't change direction. I made direct eye contact with the major and said, "Get a spare cot for me to sleep and food, I'll be sleeping here tonight." The major went to the tent opening and called out for one of his underlings. I sat at the table and listened as the major tasked a sergeant with get the necessary provisions. The major came back to the table and asked me, did I bring any extra men with me? I told him that I had six soldiers to escort here, and I ordered them back to their original post. During this conversation, a soldier shows up and ask permission to enter. The soldier brought in a cot and a backpack. The soldier sat down the items and the major dismissed the soldier. I asked the major to join me in eating and he told me that he had previously eaten. I am starved, and I emptied the contents of the pack on the table. There's a small loaf of bread, cured sausage, cheese and a bottle of wine. I was expecting a canteen of water but, considering how quickly water can go stagnant, a bottle of wine is very welcome. I began eating but not at the pace I wanted to.

I feel like stuffing everything I can in my mouth at once, eating slowly and self-control are not my best traits. I finished eating and the major called for a subordinate to clear away the table. The major took two cigars from his jacket and asked me to join him. We smoked cigars and made small talk until dark and the major told me that he is going to turn in for the night. I told him that I too was ready to get some rest. The major extinguished the flame on the lantern as I lay down on the canvas cot. The cot has limited comforts but, it is better than sleeping on the ground. A loud shell explodes close by and I am awakened. I could hear men scrambling around the camp and I went back to sleep. The morning came early as I was awakened by the Major. "Major Strum. It's time to get up. We've got about 30 minutes before the experiment happens. We'll be in company of generals, do you need to borrow my razor?"

I felt of my face and it is feeling like a field of rough briars. I agreed with him that I needed to shave. I slid on my boots and knocked the dust from my uniform. I waited until the major finished shaving and he handed off to me a brush full of soap and the straight razor. I lathed up my face and looked in a mirror at a man that hasn't seen a mirror since the time spent with Jean D Arc. It is a sobering moment seeing a face that has been 38 years old since I walked with the teacher. I hurried and finished shaving, rinsed my face in a basin of water. The major handed me a cloth to dry with and said," "Let's get some coffee and some biscuit before we meet up with the Generals." I acknowledged his suggestion. My body is hungry and needs fuel because it knows in a matter of hours, the full moon will be in control. I followed the Major out of the tent and my senses were already picking up the smells and sounds of war. He led me towards a tent and I could see that high-ranking officers were entering it.

As we drew closer, I could hear the men talking inside. I watched the major enter first and mimicked his moves. He saluted superior officers and I did the same. One of the major's superiors asked the major, who I was. The major said, "This is Major Strum and he was sent here to witness the experiment." Before the superior officer could ask who sent me; I said," The laboratory will be anxious to find out how many rats will be exterminated today. The key factor being that the winds will be with us instead of against us." All doubts about my presence stopped after the superior officer laughed and said," Major Strum is absolutely right. Conditions are a precedent so, hurry up everyone. Get you something to eat and a coffee, the show will begin very soon and make sure you have your gas mask ready. I grabbed a cup, poured myself a coffee, picked up some bread and sausage. I shoved the bread and sausage in and chased it down with the hot coffee. As the officers were jockeying for attention with the Generals, I stuffed my pockets with food. I picked up a conversation from the other end of the tent. There are two high ranking officers talking about a rumor that he heard from the battle front. One officer said," A group of artillery soldiers witnessed something unnatural." The other officer asked him, what is he talking about? The officer began talking about a soldier named Hans Engel. I continued to eat and sip on my coffee and listen. I saw other officers were drawn in by the story.

I continued listening, waiting to hear if a certain name up… a Major Strum. The man whom I stole his identity from. A General overheard the tale and said," Did the French hire der teufel (the devil) to fight against us? He started laughing and said, "By the way, what was the major's name that Hans Engel killed? The officer telling the story said, "I think the major's last name is Strum. "I thought to myself, things are about to get messy. The General turned his eyes to me and asked," Isn't your last name Strum?" I said," Yes, General." The General asked for my papers and I calmly gave them to him. The General looked them over and gave them back to me. The General asked me did I hear any of the conversation about Hans Engel? I played dumb and told him no. The major that led me to the tent spoke in my defense saying, "General, Major Strum has prior knowledge of the experiment. I did no tell him of such." I looked at the officer that had spun the tale and said, "If I am indeed der teufel (the devil)? I cannot be killed, is that the story? Take out your Luger and shoot me in the heart. If I don't die, you all will die in this tent, in the case I do die, the General has grounds to have you shot." I then said," The accused has the right to know what the accuser's name is. What is it? Are you afraid of eternal damnation?" The accuser said, "My name is Major Von Stieger and I'm afraid of nothing." I said," It is evident that you are afraid of something by spreading such a rumor. You will have your own men afraid of their own shadow because of such talk."

The General chimed in and said," This sounds like ghost stories told around a campfire by children and we are grown men. This foolish talk ends inside this tent. Do I make myself clear to everyone here?" All of us subordinates complied by saying yes. The General told us to leave the tent and go to our appointed post and the rest is to follow him to the observation hill. The Major hat spoke in my defense is walking beside me and I said, "Major, you'll have to forgive my lapse of memory. What is your last name?" " krupp" He replied. I said," Aren't you worried, about what your contemporaries will be saying about you being friends with der teufel? Major Krupp laughed a subdued laugh because the General was close by. Major Krupp and I followed the group of Generals and other high-ranking officers to a hill, that housed a large caliber cannon. The sun is about to shine its rays upon the battlefield, the general picked up the phone, giving the order to light the candle. A series of explosions went off, stretching three maybe four kilometers in each direction. A fog is created by the explosion, and we wait. Major Krupp turned to me and said," Major Strum, that is waging war by science. Created by scientist in a lab as you know." Even though we are two the three kilometers away from the gas, my eyes began to tear up a little, I tolerated it. The yellow-greenish fog began hugging the ground and watched the reactions on the faces of the men with binoculars. They were smiling and pointing towards the battlefield. I got a turn to look through the binoculars and I saw men trying to get away from the gas by diving into the trenches, gasping for air, appearing to be drowning, then lifeless. I gave the binoculars to Major Krupp and said," The method certainly cut down the use of firing bullets and cannon projectiles."

A man that wasn't dressed in a uniform heard my comment and said," That is exactly what I said to the German high command when I proposed the concept." A General interjected by saying," I'm looking for a white flag to indicate a surrender Dr. Haber. How long must I wait until I see that flag waving?" The Dr. told the group that there will be air reconnaissance planes and zeppelins flying over the area filming and taking photos. A general made the remark," That sounds like a long time to find out the body count, after waiting for the film to be developed after the airships have returned to base. We need to know the results faster. How many men do we have that's equipped with proper gas mask? A major answered by saying, "An estimated guess General, would be about seventy-five to one hundred men on the front line have the mask." The general said," I want those mento advance forward and I want some men to return with some valid evidence. I can't wait for any damn film to be developed and someone to count the bodies on the film. Get me some answers!" The majors and their subordinates scattered from the observation hill. I followed Major Krupp back to his outfit on the way, I was thinking about a couple of things. The vision of a different kind of death etched in my mind watching men die slow horrific deaths. The full moon will be arriving.

Major Strum alias Hans Engel alias Judas Iscariot, manages to get some distance from Major Krupp's camp. The moon, the full moon is peeping at the horizon, Major Strum is beginning to feel the effects of lunar spectacle. It is not yet dark and Major Strum has found a burned out building to hide. The change began its course, changing man into an apex predator, a killing machine. Major Strum is no more, the beast is in control and he is hungry. Using the burned- out buildings to conceal his movements, not leaving himself out in the open. The sun is dipping lower in the sky as the moon continues moving upward to meet the night. The beast is constantly using his finely-honed senses to listen, to see and smell for potential prey to kill and devour. He has totally dismissed what happened with the encounter with the messenger. His primal instincts kicked into automatic, his only interest is to feed and nothing else matters. The sensitive nose of the beast catches the scent of smoke, it isn't a smoldering building, it is the smell of food cooking. The beast made his way towards the smell until, he had reached the end of his concealment of burned-out buildings. He can see where the Germans are but, the Germans are camped out in the open.

The beast must be patient and wait until it gets dark enough to make his move. His stomach yearns for nourishment but, he sees that the Germans that guard the perimeter, have automatic weapons and he remembers how the bullets feel as they rip through him. He waits and watches the German's movements around the camp. His animal mind asked the human mind of Judas for a plan. Judas advises to circle the camp once, after it gets dark enough to move and to look for the weakest area that is guarded. Judas then tells the beast to kill the guard silently and then kill the rest before they can use their weapons. The beast listened and took control of his mind, leaving Judas locked away until the beast relinquishes his control or until the rising of the rising sun comes. The beast waited until the sun's rays had given away to the night. He took the advice and began circling the camp, looking for a vulnerable spot to execute an attack. His movements were akin to a jungle cat, silently stalking its prey except, a jungle cat isn't at work here.

It is an apex predator with the mind to think and reason. The beast took an assessment of the number of Germans at the camp, he roughly estimated twenty plus men. He stopped and noticed a vulnerable gap to make his move. He catches a guard unaware as the guard is lighting his cigarette. The beast grabs the guard, snapping his neck and carries the German into the darkness. He carries the lifeless body effortlessly as if, the body was weightless. He takes his prize far enough away from the camp and begins devouring the soft tissue of the body. The heart, liver, and the lungs are his choice parts but, he must eat fast of what he can. The beast knows the absence of the German will be noticed and this one kill won't slake his hunger. The beast is facing the camp, as he swallows the last bit of German flesh, he stands up and starts moving towards the camp. He cautiously circles the camp, listening and watching the movement of his potential prey.

He stops and sees his next victim. Another guard that has his back to the darkness, the beast quickly makes his move. The guard turns around just as the beast is upon him. The guard manages to make a subdued whimper, as the beast slashes the head clean off the body with his clawed hand. The beast lifts the body and quickly carries it off into the darkness. He quickly begins tearing away at the headless body, gulping down chunks of flesh, while keeping an eye on the camp. His latest kill did not go unnoticed. A German soldier was sitting on the ground, eating from a bowl and saw movement from the corner of his eye. He saw the guard disappear but, couldn't reason in his mind of what he saw. The guard didn't just walk into the darkness, he was snatched away. The witness goes to his commander and tells him about the experience. The commander walks with him to where the guard should be and calls out the guard's name and waits for an answer. No answer came. The commander of the camp ordered a subordinate to check on the other placement of the guards at the perimeters of the camp. It didn't take long before the camp was stirring with movement. The beast moved away from his kill, still watching the camp and the report of a weapon being fired. The Germans had fired a phosphorous flair up into the night sky. The beast lies flat on the ground, motionless as the flair illuminated a large area around the camp. A soldier sees the body and head of the beast second victim.

A group of armed soldiers with torches are told to go out and investigate. They Find a gruesome sight and are overcome with fear. They have heard the rumor about Hans Engel, der teufel (the devil) and returned to the safety of numbers. A member of the investigating group tells his commander about the gruesome sight. The commander asked, did they see any animal tracks leading away from the body? Another member of the group says in a fearful voice," It is Hans Engel, der teufel has come to kill and eat us, commander. The commander quickly told the soldier to stop such talk and it must be an animal that is responsible. The beast still lies motionless and watching the camp. The flair has fallen to the ground and gone out; the darkness has returned. The beast stomach is full but, the urge to kill has not been satisfied. He also knows that he doesn't like the feeling of the sting, from the automatic weapons projectiles passing through his body. He decides to continue in the direction made by the messenger. His stomach is full and the body is fully energized. The beast decides to run, the urge to kill slips away as he focuses on his other senses.

The beast covered several kilometers upon reaching the remains of a skeleton of a building. He stops and listens before getting any closer to the war-torn structure. He hears off in the distance the rumblings of cannon fire but, that is behind him or now, he only hears the wind and with it, carrying the scent of long dead bodies and smoldering wood. He cautiously moves closer to the structure, gazing into the openings of the wall, listening for any signs of occupation. There are no sounds and he ventures inside. He is spent from the run and finds a place to lay down. He moves some broken timbers over the area to help conceal himself. He lays down and is at peace even though the change is hours away. Earlier that day on the western front, corporal Adolf has chance meeting with a man.

It happened as Adolf is doing his appointed task of running messages to and from German occupied positions on the perimeter of the front. As Adolf was running past a shattered brick wall that was once was a building, he hears a voice saying, "Hey soldier! Do you have a cigarette?" Adolf had looked at the other side of the wall as he passed it and saw no one. Now there is a man dressed in a German officer's uniform. Adolf stopped in his tracks and saluted the man of a higher rank. The German officer saluted back, told Adolf to relax and lend him a cigarette. Adolf took from his pocket, gave the officer a cigarette, took out his matches and lit it. The German officer took a long drag from the cigarette, as he leaned against the brick work. The officer said, "Have a smoke with me and what is your name corporal?" "I am corporal Adolf Hitler, herr Major" The German Major said," Corporal Hitler, I see that you are committed to your role in this conflict." "I am just a bearer of information and was appointed this task." Replied Adolf. The German Major said," I see greatness on the horizon for you corporal. I see that you carry the weight of what it means to be German. Are you aware, that there is a blight in Germany. This blight is what has, and will drag down the purity of the German race. Do you know what this blight is that I speak of?" Adolf with a look of puzzlement on his face said, "I don't know what you speak of herr Major. " Answered Adolf. The German Major told Adolf to look at the brick wall and at that moment, he saw a vision.

The vision is a replaying from the past, it is Jewish people of Israel condemning Jesus to be crucified. A frightened Adolf said," I must be asleep and dreaming this. This cannot be real!" The German Major said," You aren't asleep and you did see a replaying of history." Adolf stutters saying, "Who, who are you? Why, why are you showing this to me?" The German Major says, "I am a messenger so to speak. Today, we were predestined to meet, right here, right now. Did you understand the meaning behind the vision I just revealed to you. Let me give you a hint. It wasn't Pontius Pilot that sent the rabbi to his death." Adolf said, "The Jews of Israel sent him to his death. They chose not to recognize him as the Messiah and still don't." The German Major said, "Who owns the bank that you keep your money in? Who owns the jewelry stores where men by their potential wife, a wedding ring?" Adolf quickly answered, "Judean! (Jews). You are saying that the Jews are a blight and a risk for tainting the German bloodline?" "Yes! Replied the German Major. The Major told Adolf that, after the war, the Jews will put a great strain upon Germany. The Major said," There will be chaos during Germany's upheaval from the rubble. The German people will be on the verge of losing their heritage, their true birthright to be German; to become some mixed mongrel race." Adolf said, "You're telling me that Germany will fall in this war?

The Major said," Yes! The main reason behind it is that, your leaders were too quick to act and lacked proper planning. This war will bring Germany down to its knees. Now go, continue your job and make no mention of our meeting. You would be ridiculed and possibly placed behind bars." Adolf turned to leave and stopped to ask a question. The

German Major had disappeared into thin air. Adolf went on to the next German placement of artillery, handed the written report to a superior officer. Adolf waited until his superior had read the information and wrote down on paper that the message had been received. The superior officer gave Adolf the paper, corporal Adolf placed it in his field bag and headed back to his unit. The journey back is at least three kilometers. This gave him time to absorb the experience and even questioned his own mental state. He asked himself, did the encounter with the messenger happen or was the result of some tainted food that he had consumed? He knew no matter the information from the messenger, he would have to go on about his duty as a German .... win or lose. Adolf arrived back to the war, the trench network of forward German placements. He gave the note to his commander and was told to get some food and rest for his next assignment. The trenches are a different world versus the artillery placement, he had just left from. The trenches are a foul, smelling ditch that contained human excrement, urine and rotting corpses. All that lays between the German's and their enemy, is a place called, no mans land.

It is barren except for barbed wire, the rotting bodies of the dead from both sides that got caught in the crossfire. Adolf began to understand, the Germans nor the French were advancing. This trench warfare would eventually turn into a stalemate. neither side were gaining any ground. He got some bread, cured sausage, and found a place to rest. The sounds of constant shelling and automatic weapons firing from both sides, are an everyday and night occurrence. He sat there eating and thinking about his experience, shutting off the war even though, the shelling from the French side was so close, the dirt from the impact spot rained down on him. This isn't a new experience, it is everyday occurrence. One wonders when the time comes when your number gets pulled. Adolf continued to eat despite the dirt shower and pondered about what happened. The day is close to ending and Adolf Checks in with his commanding officer, to see if there is another run to be made. The commander tells Adolf to get some rest because, part of his unit is being repositioned. Adolf knew what that meant, it could mean that he will be in trench closer to the enemy. Adolf saluted his commanding officer and looked for a place to get some rest. A resting place sometimes came in the form of leaning against the upright timbers that lined the trenches, squatting down with your knees in your chest. There are no feather beds in the trenches, just men that wish they were at home. Adolf found a spot, put on his gas mask, and leaned against the rough timbers. The reason that spot was unoccupied is because, there are parts of what used to be human beings scattered around him.

A shell from the French had exploded in that area and he thinks to himself, maybe he'll get lucky a shell will put him out his misery. Before he closed his eyes, a thought sprang up, the messenger was speaking against God's chosen people of Israel. How could an agent of Heaven make such statements? Adolf's thoughts gave way to the body's urge to shut down for rest and the sounds of the war begins to fade as he drifts off to sleep. In a dream state, Adolf finds himself watching a man addressing a multitude of people. He is telling the populous that, the world has been put on notice. He says," The German people, the German race will not stand for nothing less than perfection, purging away anything that has corrupted the German lineage." The huge crowd of people cheer upon hearing the speaker's message. Adolf wonders, who is that man that has the crowd eating from his hands?

Adolf feels a touch upon his right shoulder, and it is the messenger. This time, the messenger wears the uniform of a German General. The messenger said, "That man is you, Adolf. In a few years, you will make the German people feel proud to be German again. I can make this vision possible if, you want to be that man?" Adolf said, "If you are a messenger from Heaven? How do you have this power to wield?" The messenger said," I originated from Heaven, and I am more than just a messenger." Adolf realizes the messenger's true identity and asked," Why did you choose me Lucifer, among all the other Germans to pick from?" Lucifer said," I saw your true potential and I am a sucker for a rags to riches story that, the world will never forget." Adolf backed away and said," What if I don't want this, then what happens?" Lucifer said, "You failed as an artist that wasted time in Vienna. Do you wish a French shell rips your body to pieces while you sleep or, do you want to be that man, the millions of Germans are cheering for and hailing your name? It is all about free will.

I cannot make your mind up for you." Adolf said, "Will I have to sign a contract in blood?" Lucifer laughed and said, "A hand shake is all that is needed. There is no need for such faustian reference, a tale about selling one's soul." Adolf said," The handshake means we'll be striking a deal, and I'm condemned to Hell for it, doesn't it?" Lucifer sternly said, "If the upper management loved you so much, would he just leave you in that trench, and be another member of the nameless dead that rots on the battlefield?" Adolf said," What about the statements in the Bible about eternal torment in hell?" Lucifer says, "The Bible was written by men to control man's built in impulses to sin. I can assure that I don't live in a place that fires never go out. To put your mind at ease, I promise that you will have a special place." A snap of Lucifer's fingers and they were in front of a lavish mansion. Lucifer told Adolf to open the door to his mansion. Adolf slowly opened the door and inside revealed a luxurious décor fit for royalty. There were scantily clad women inside the great room. Lucifer held out his hand and said, "All of this will be yours with a handshake." Adolf said," After the handshake, what happens? Lucifer said, "I will advise you every step of the way. You will look back at the days of being a lowly corporal and those that kept you beaten down; they will feel your boot heel upon them."

Adolf shook hands and was awakened by an exploding shell that, shook him from the log he sat on. The mask he was wearing, was dislodged from his head. The shell contained gas and Adolf was feeling the effects. He grabbed his mask and quickly scrambled his way out of the trench. The gas burns and he placed the gas mask on, trying to get clear of the gas cloud. He gets clear of the gas cloud, removes his mask and washes his face with water from his canteen. As he sat there on the ground, he hears a voice saying, "This is the first of near misses with death. You are under my protection; we have a deal remember?" Adolf looks up and sees a man in a general's uniform. Adolf said," I dreamed about the handshake. It didn't really happen, it wasn't real." Lucifer said," I assure you that it was real and to prove it, I am going to advance you in time. You will be in your last battle and will sustain an injury that will remove you from the battlefield." In an instant, Adolf was flung forward into time and in the thick of battle. Adolf was trying to get his bearings of where he is, and a bomb explodes. Adolf didn't have his gas mask and the gas blinded him and caused an injury to his inner thigh. He is taken to a hospital for the wounded. Adolf lies in the bed, his eyes still bandaged along with his leg injury, he hears a familiar voice besides his bed. The voice said," You almost lost your manhood from that bomb. You'll be healed up and your sight will return. Oh yes! I forgot to mention that the war is over, and Germany has signed an armistice." Adolf said," I cannot see! Who is that, that is speaking to me?" The voice said, "It is I, Dr. Faust. I came by to check on my only patient. You may remove your head bandages. Adolf began gently removing his head bandages. Layer by layer, the wrappings slowly let in the light. He pulled off the last layer and slowly opened his eyes. Adolf's vision was cloudy at first until, it was clear enough to see that he wasn't talking to Dr. Faust.

The beast finds himself far away from the battlefield. The beast feels the hunger in his stomach and the urge to kill draw him closer to his next hunting ground. He knows there is a high possibility of running into men with automatic weapons. His tactics of assaulting the quarry will need to be different than it was on the battlefield. His senses are overloaded with smells and sounds of a very populated area. He cautiously approached the edge of the forest and saw buildings that are alight for the night. The night sky is cloudless and he must make a mad dash towards the nearest building to conceal himself. He opts for climbing the brick wall and go for the roof top. Peering around the corner of the building could reveal his presence and a higher vantage point would be most advantageous. Using shear strength, clawing his way up the wall, he finally makes it to the top of the building. The building is large, and he walks over to the edge and peers down at the surroundings.

He sees people dressed in normal non-military clothing moving about the city streets. The street corners are gas lit lantern post casting a flicker dance of flame. There are also large trees that almost touch the building near his vantage point. He thinks that the tree could be a means for getting off the building or a means for escape to get back onto the building, if he needs a way out of a dire situation. He walks down to the far end of the building and looks at what is displayed from his roof top view. He sees armed German soldiers moving about the street. He quickly changes his mind and moves towards the other end of the building. As he moves across the building's rooftop, his acute hearing catches the sounds of people talking. He slows his movements and discovers the sounds are coming from the chimney that protrudes from the roof. He goes to the chimney and listens. There are people living above the store. His anxiousness for a kill grows stronger and having to cling to the masonry like a spider doesn't appeal to him. He peers over the side of the building, watching for the right opportunity to leap from the roof top. He sees a group of men entering the beerhall across the street, looks his left, then to the right and leaps from the building.

The moment he touches ground, he immediately goes to the front of the store, grabs the door knob and breaks the lock in one twist. He closes the door and hides behind the counter and listens. Through the dimly lit room, he sees a stairway to the second floor. He hears someone walking above him through the supporting rafters and floorboards. He makes his way towards the stairs and boards creak as he moves upward. He quickens his pace by bounding 3 to four steps ahead, the occupants may have heard the creaking of the stairs. He has reached the second floor and is at the door of the owner's home. He listens for movement on the other side of the door. On the other side of the door, a man has alerted his family of a possible intruder.

He has a pistol and tells his family to stay put as he opens the door to investigate. The man's pistol doesn't get a chance to fire. The beast grabs the man's hand holding the pistol and breaks it. The beast rips out the man's throat with a swipe of his talon like claws and goes into the living quarters of the dead man's family. The beast kills the wife and two children. He gorges himself until his hunger for human flesh is slaked. He remembers what his master has told him and that is to, pay homage to him. The beast scribes a five-pointed star on the victims. Being satisfied with his work, the beast goes downstairs, crouches down at the store front window and peers out. There are two German soldiers walking past the store front. The beast waits until they are at a sufficient distance away, he goes to the door and peers out. The beast hears a familiar voice behind him and he closes the door. The beast realizes that his master has returned. Satan says," I saw your handy work upstairs and that you have remembered the deal. I am impressed that you have chosen to appease me instead of making me angry. You have one more night, to do what you will with this town." The beast says in a gravelly voice, "Let me guess, the day after tomorrow night; I'll wake up in a different time? By the looks of your military type costume, I'll be involved in another war."

Satan chuckles and says, "How observant of you Judas? The answer is yes, a war that will surpass this current time. I will see you two days in the future. So, be thinking of a new German name besides Hans Engel. You've made the name Hans Engel infamous." The devil laughs and disappeared, leaving the beast alone for the moment. The night is still young and the beast lust for killing hasn't been satisfied. The beast seizes the opportunity to leave the scene of tonight's slaughter. He saw a light from the second story window as he sprints across the street. He grabbed the doorknob and powered through the door, the locking mechanism just gave way to brute strength. He enters and closes the door behind him, he hears something scampering down the stairs. The family dog approaches, then upon seeing the intruder, the dog crouches down on the floor in submission. The dog said," Please don't eat me or kill my family, konig eckzahn (king canine)." The beast says, "Give me good reason why I shouldn't." The dog told the beast that the German military has corrupted this once peaceful town and have crippled his owner to near destitute. The dog said," I smell the blood of the innocent on you. Please take out your wrath on the military. They occupy the buildings one street behind the building you came from. They deserve to die. I've seen them rape and kill their own people." The beast nodded yes, opened and closed the door behind him. The beast hears a faint "Kill them all!" by the dog, as he runs towards the darkness of the buildings shadow across the street, making his way to the next street.

The beast thought about his encounter with the dog and being called the king canine. He remembers his friends, King the leader of a wolf-pack and his son Star. He is accepted by his canine friends instantly and he wonders if it was their fear of him or was it because he was superior to them. His thoughts are redirected by movements being heard from behind the building. He slowly makes his way to the corner of the building and peeks around to see with one eye, being careful to risk exposure. He sees three German soldiers exit from a building near him. He also sees a barbed fenced enclosure across the street and knows he can't go that way as a means of escape from his next attack.

The German soldiers have their backs to the beast and the beast sprints into attack mode. He runs up behind them and with mighty outreached arms, he closes around the soldier's heads like a vise and decapitating them. The beast gazes up the street and sees that he has been noticed. He here's the sound of a police whistle being blown, as he heads back to darkness from whence, he came. The beast makes it to the back end of the building and goes towards the street he came from. He gets to the corner, peers out and there is a group of soldiers in front of the beerhall talking. He makes the decision to run for the forest, climbing onto the roof may leave him stranded when the sun comes up. The beast makes it back to the forest, a place he is more accustomed to. He goes deeper and reaches a point that he simply stops to taken in the smells and sounds of the forest. The beast catches the scent of water and follows his instinct. He continues forward as his nose guides him to a small stream that meanders through the forest.

The beast crouches down on his knees, cupping up water with his clawed hands. Cupping the water wasn't satisfactory enough for him. He placed his clawed hands in the stream, bracing himself to drink from the flowing water with his mouth. The beast feels the signs of the coming change. Lying next to the stream, the body of the beast is being ravaged by pain, due to the transformation back to its human form. The tattered clothes of a German Major Strum, alias Hans Engel, are bloodied and bear little resemblance of a uniform of prestige. He splashes water upon his face to remove the dried blood from the previous night's killings. He thinks to himself, "Do I just wait it out here in the forest until I change? Or do I risk going into town? The towns people have probably found the dead family of the store owner, and the German military are trying to figure out who killed a few of their own last night." His body desires food because the change robbed it needed energy. In the distance, he hears a motorized vehicle getting closer. He quickly gets up and runs towards the approaching vehicle. He lays down on the edge of the road and waits.

A scout vehicle stops and two German soldiers' approach, what seems to be an injured German soldier. As they got closer, Hans Engel here's one of the soldiers order the other to investigate. Hans springs up and snaps the man's neck like a twig. The other soldier wearing an officer's uniform shot three rounds into Hans. The bullets did nothing to slow Hans's advance. Hans wrestles the officer to ground and strangles him. Hans takes the bodies, threw them in the back of the vehicle and drove into the woods away from the road. Once in the woods, he takes the uniform off of the officer and puts it on. He takes the other body and hides it in thick underbrush. He finds the officers papers and now he has a new identity. He is Erik Von Stauffel and a German officer with a stolen vehicle that he just figured out how to operate. Erik drives the vehicle into the German city and parks it between two buildings. He proceeded into the city and found that it is heavy with activity. He catches conversations about last night's grisly murders as he passes by the mixture of military and civilian occupants. He is hungry and walks into a haufbrau with fellow German military.

The subordinates salute him as he enters and returns their salutes. He sits down at a table with his back against a wall and facing the front entrance. Hans Engel has placed his order of food and drink with a waiter. He looks around the room and sees a mixture of civilians and uniformed military. He begins to think that someone in this room could recognize the infamous Hans Engel, der tuefel (the devil) as the frightened men ran away screaming. He decides to change his seating position, putting his back to the crowd. The waiter brings a stein of beer and the food. He bows his head for a moment and breaks the bread. He picks up the stein takes a big gulp. He starts shoveling food in like a starving man, leaving no traces of food on the plate and gets the attention of the waiter. The waiter hurriedly makes her way to his table. "My goodness! Did you even taste the food? I just gave it to you." Said the waitress. "It was so good that I need more.

Can you bring me more food and another beer?" Asked Hans. "Ya!" Replied the waitress. Hans's body burns through the food and drink and needs more fuel. He dinks the last swallow of beer from the stein, and before he could sit it down on the table, a voice from the enter belts out," Achtung!" He hears chairs moving and he looks to his left and right as the uniforms stand to attention. An officer near him says to him, "Get up or you'll get into trouble!" Hans ignores the officer and remains seated. The officer yells at Hans saying, "You are going to get us all into trouble. Get up! Snell!" Hans hears boots storming in his direction and just waits. A captain walks up to the table and screams," Did you not hear my order? There's a General in the room and your respect is commanded. Now get up or I'll shoot you and make an example of you." "Tell the general to come sit at my table or I'll make an example out of you."

Hans calmly replies. The General quickly steps forward and tells the captain to step back and orders the rest of men to be seated. The General says, "Son! What is your name?" "I am lieutenant Nobody." Replied Hans. The General tells his subordinate to find a seat somewhere else. The General says, "Do you mind if I sit down at your table Lieutenant Nobody?" All of the random talking in the room became hushed tones of anxious fear of the unknown. Hans gestured the General to sit across from him at the table. The General sits down and asked, "Who is your commanding officer Lieutenant Nobody?" "It would cause much panic if I told you Herr General." Replied Hans. The General said, "Kaiser Wilhelm the second is my supreme commander. Why do resist telling me? Who is your commanding officer? Why would it cause a panic by telling me this?" Hans looked the General in the eyes, leans towards the General and in a low voice says, "Stand up General and tell the people in this room, their next beer is on you."

Without hesitation the General stood up and announced that everyone's next beer is on him. The room explodes with cheers to the General as he sat back down. Hans breaks eye contact and stands with a stein in his hand stating, "To the General!" The crowd follows suit and copies Hans. The General sits motionless, but in his mind, there is absolute terror. As the sounds reverberate throughout the room with scattered laughter and conversation. Hans stands up, salutes the General, reaches across the table to shake hands with the General. The nervous General grabs Hans's hand and as Hans shakes the General's hand he says," Pleased to meet you General, I'm Lieutenant Hans Engel." Just as the General was about to say," The Hans?" Hans stopped the General from saying anything else by saying," Yes! Just relax you have a tray of beers coming to this table sent by your men. Are you hungry, General? I can have food brought to you?" The supposed myth told about Hans Engel floods the General's mind and Hans Engel is sitting across from him. The General tells Hans that he is famished. Hans tells the General he knows what is going through his mind and tells the General," Many died that night, and many can be saved tonight. It is up to you General to stop it. The forest demon as men calls it, has followed me here.

It brought death last night. Did it not?" The General could only nod because he is in a state of nowhere to run. Hans motioned for the waitress to come to the table and at the same time the General was going for his side arm. Hans looked at him and said, Are you in good favor with the management upstairs? And I'm not talking about upstairs in this building." The General placed his hand back on the table and says," Where do we go from here? Lieutenant Engel?" Hans looks at the clock on the wall on the wall and says, "You need to pay the barkeeper now and get your food to go. Tell your subordinate that I'll be driving you to your next destination. Remember. Things can go terribly wrong really fast. All of this, is in your hands General." Scenes began flashing in the General's mind of the countless men he sent to their deaths as he sat safely in his confines. The waitress came to the table and the General asked for tally of his debt. The General paid the waitress and told her to prepare his food for travel. **BREAK** Hans had drunk many steins as the General sipped from his stein as if it could be his last. Within minutes, the waitress returns with the Generals food in a large paper bag.

Hans stands up and shouts, "Achtung!" (Attention!) The General rises from the table and makes his way to the exit. The General's subordinate walks up to the General and questions the General. The General tells his subordinate to stay here, and that the Lieutenant will be driving him. Hans follows the General to the General's staff car and gets in the driver's seat. He asked the General which way to get to the greatest distance from any civilian population. Hans starts the engine, and the General says, "How much time do we have before the forest demon comes?" "Could be an hour or could be two hours. Which way do we go General? Lives depend upon your decision." Remarked Hans. The General didn't respond right away. Hans explained to the General that if the general is planning something to double cross him. Hans said, "Like I said before, General things will not go well."

The General quickly gave Hans a direction by saying, "Take an immediate left after passing this next street." Hans took the left as instructed and saw that it was leading out of the city. As the two are heading down the road Hans says, "Is there anything you want to be forgiven for General?" "Are you a priest offering me to listen to my confession? The stories I heard about you paints a different picture than a holy person." exclaimed the General. Han's vision is much more advanced than the General's and sees a potential problem ahead." General, it is time for you to be honest. If you cannot? Then you are about to have your fate and the guards posted a kilometer from here." Said Hans. "You can see that far ahead?" Said the nervous General. "I can see them and you knew that they would be there." Replied Hans. "Don't worry. I am a General and they will wave us through." Answered the General. As the vehicle drew closer to the guarded outpost, Hans saw two armed soldiers standing in front of a barrier.

The vehicle came to a stop and the two soldiers saluted the ranking officers in the vehicle. One guard approached Hans and said," Can I see your papers herr Lieutenant?" As Hans reached into his uniform. The General yelled out, "I command you to shoot this man. He is Hans Engel! Der Tuefel (the devil)! The guards laugh loudly at the General's order. The guard near the General drew his side arm and asked the General for his papers. The General hands over his papers to the guard and the guard sees that the papers are legitimate articles, then hands them back to the General. Hans looks at the guard near him and says," This is only a test." The guard gives Hans his papers and says, "This is only a test." The other guard raises the barrier and waves them through. Hans puts the vehicle in gear and proceeds forward. The General becomes angry and says," Why did you single me out? You could have gone through the correct motions in the bar and simply walked out. I don't understand any of this." "Where does this road lead to general?" asked Hans. "It leads to a heavily guarded area controlled by my troops and beyond that lies a battlefield." Answered the General. "If you want God to forgive you of any sins that you've committed? You had better do it now.

The forest demon is coming, and I can't stop him." Stated Hans. Hans made the vehicle go as fast as it would go. The General kept looking around for something to rush the vehicle. The pains have already started to strike Hans and he yells at the General, "You better make your peace because it is too late for me." The General realizes what is happening and began asking God for forgiveness. Hans fights to keep control as long as he can until the pain makes it impossible. Hans violently jerks the steering wheel and causes the vehicle to tumble, ejecting both men from the wreckage. The General is stunned by the crash and tries to get up. His leg is broken, and one arm is also severely damaged. He looks for Hans and hears only the sounds of something crying out in agonizing pain. The sounds stop and the General calls out to Hans. A gravelly voice says, "Hans isn't here General." The General is frozen in horror as something steps out from behind the vehicle wreckage.

The General desperately tries to crawl away and the beast taunts the General. The same way a cat plays with the mouse before killing it. The General makes a last effort to draw his side arm. One round hit the beast and the General's struggle is over. The beast rips through the General's neck with his talon like claws and the beast began to feast upon the General's flesh. The beast ate enough to fuel his new body, but the desire to kill again raged on inside him. The beast made no markings of homage on the General's lifeless body. There are still remnants of the day before the sun goes down, and the beast remembers what the General said about troop placement, and the battlefield is beyond. A once silent inner voice spoke to the beast saying, "Remember, we both loved Jean before and after she changed." The beast stopped walking and said in an angry gravelly voice," Stop talking to me! Especially Jean! She is free now! It is me that isn't free and right now I am in control." The inner voice says," I know this and now you can take our revenge out on anyone or anything." The beast replies," The anything that you are referring to is our dark master?" "Yes! No more paying homage. Just killing those that are waging war. We will be in a new war in a new time period.

CHAPTER 14

A DIFFERENT KIND OF HELL

You heard what the dark master said. What is he going to do to us that he hasn't already done? What can he take from us that he hasn't already taken?" The beast thought about what his inner self was saying. He began a slow trot down this dirt road and thought about the moments he had with Jean, killing side by side and love they shared. He also remembered the men in the uniforms taking her away to be burned alive. As he thought about the uniforms, the rage began to fill him to a point that he is ready to just explode. The wind changed direction and is blowing in his face. The wind carries with it the smells of something unrecognizable. He began to run into the wind and as he ran, the wind became more intensive. The harder he pushed against the wind; it became physically impossible to hold his ground. The wind stopped abruptly, and the beast fell face first into the dirt. As the beast stood up, he wasn't alone. "You just can't do as I ask, can you? You gave the General salvation and thought you would just save a few lives in the German town. You were thinking you could try freelancing for yourself?" Said the angry dark master.

The beast said in a gravelly voice, "I don't know what freelancing is?" The dark master says, "I've been too lenient with you! I could let you experience Hell, but I have a better idea." The dark master snaps his finger and the next moment the beast is no longer the beast. He finds himself in a familiar place. He has the same clothing as the day he hung himself and he is in Jerusalem. He is going through the same motions, the day he betrayed Jesus. His mind tries to resist repeating what is to happen. His mind is trapped just as it is when the beast takes over. He can only watch as his former self goes through with his most regretted moment of his life. Everything is the same except, the devil isn't there to pull him from the grave. After he hangs himself, he just wakes up and repeats the same day. There is no death, no silence or waiting for something miraculous to happen. His mind stopped resisting trying to change the circumstance. Every day is the same. Nothing changes. He had long given up until one day the cycle stopped. He had placed the rope around his neck and was about to step off the pile of rocks he placed.

The dark master showed up and said," Judas! Do you want to keep doing this until whenever?" "What do you mean by whenever?" Asked Judas. The dark master laughed and said, "Whenever everything ends?" "I deserve this existence for what I did. Besides, I got to see the teacher every day." exclaimed Judas. "All of what you experienced. I took from your memories. I just expanded your biggest regret into a repeating scene." Replied the dark master. "So! What kind of twisted scene are you going to throw me in this time?" Asked Judas. The dark master snapped his fingers and instantly I am wearing a suit. Looking down at my clothes I said," What kind of identity will I have in this new time?" "You are already here." Replied the dark master.

The dark master now wearing an elaborate military uniform. He said," Have you been thinking of your new name?" "How about Hans Engel?" I replied. The dark master gave me an evil grin and said, "Hans Engel is just a myth now. A horror story told by the survivors of the great war, to frighten their children into being good little boys and girls, or Hans Engel or der teufel (the devil) will get them. You are about to be a prominent man in Berlin, herr Engel Stern." I said, "Engel Stern (Angel Star), how poetic the dark master chuckled and said, "I was once considered the morning star before the great revolt in Heaven." "There is nothing angelic about what you've done or what

I am." I replied. "Remember Adolf? The corporal that shot you? He is a prominent figure and only remembers the name you told him and that is Engel.

Besides, your light will continue to shine after Adolf plays out his part. He will be expecting you." The dark master disappears, and I make my way towards the city street in front of me. Engel Stern finds himself in the modern city scape of Berlin. He looks down upon himself and sees that he is wearing the suit of a businessman. He notices his skin tone is even lighter and continues walking forward, as his attention is averted toward me wearing military uniforms marched down the street. An automobile horn blows out a warning as Engel Stern is pulled onto the curb of a sidewalk. The man that pulled Engel from the street, he is dressed in a military officer's uniform, with all manners of medals upon his chest. The officer says, "You need to be mindful of your surroundings Herr Stern. You aren't walking around in the forest anymore. You are in the capital of Germany, this is Berlin." "I was wondering when you would show up?" Replied Engel. "Now! Is that the proper way to talk your benefactor?" answered the officer.

Engel feels the grip upon his arm grow tighter as the officer pulls him along the sidewalk. Engel tries to pull away from the officer, but the grip only tightens more to the point Engel feels his skin being penetrated by the officer's fingernails. The officer pulls Engel against a building's brick façade and says, "I can cast you in hell right now and be done with you. Is that what you want?" "I thought I was already in hell. What more torment can you do to me, that you haven't already done?" Replied Engel. The officer released his grip from Engel's arm and his demeanor changed. An evil grin shown upon the officer's face and he said, "Let's start this conversation over shall we, Herr Engel?" The officer snapped his fingers and time reversed itself. This time I didn't get pulled from the street, I was struck from behind by the automobile and I'm lying in the street hurt. I see the German officer looking at me from the sidewalk along with German civilians watching. I felt the massive injuries done to my body by the automobile. I picked up my head from the road and said," Okay! What do you want me to do?"

The officer snapped his fingers and I'm on the sidewalk again, like the accident didn't happen. The officer said, "You may address me as General Wolfstein. Don't you think that is a fitting name? The proverbial wolf in sheep's clothing so to speak. Let's walk to the end of the street, I have a car waiting for us. The officer was giddy with enthusiasm as we walked. He was telling me that we are going to meet someone important and this person has an ego almost as big as his. We approached the car and the driver was waiting and opened the door for the General, as I walked to the other side and got in. The driver got in, cranked the engine of the auto, and creeped forward. I said, "Can we speak openly in presence of the driver?" "Of course! We can speak openly now. The driver works for me." Answered the General. The driver looked into the rearview mirror and I saw his eyes change to solid black orbs then back to normal human eyes. The driver averted his attention to the road as the auto continued. I saw rampant etchings of the words, "Achtung! Juden!" scrawled upon storefront windows.

I asked the General about the meanings and he told me that, it is an indicator to the true German citizens of Berlin, the store is being operated by Jews. He also said that there is an ongoing boycott aimed at the Jewish owned businesses. He said, "This is just the beginning of my plan, I mean der Fuhrer's plan. I've already set up a meeting between you and der Fuhrer. I want you to follow my lead and do as I do, as we approach der Fuhrer. He thinks he knows your face and as soon as you shake his hand, the memory of him accidently shooting you will replay in his mind. He will feel ingratiated towards you. Don't mention anything about him shooting you, let him bring it up. As for me, I'm just a high ranking German General and that's all. Adolf and I had a meeting while, he was in the hospital towards the end of the first war. I appeared to him differently then versus my appearance now. You can have a life of leisure as long as you play your cards right. "I said," I assume that I'm meeting der Fuhrer about a job?" The General chuckled and said, "He will offer you a military officer's rank, but you make this suggestion. Tell him the German war machine can't operate without proper financing, and the takeover of Jewish operated banks by der Fuhrer would insure financing. He will like your way of thinking, because it plays right into der Fuhrer's game plan."

"You mean in your game plan. Don't you?" I replied. The General chuckled at my comment and said, "He will no doubt invite us for dinner tonight and finalize your job description after my suggestion. I said," What about my special condition that concerns every full moon?" The general said, "The full moon will occur in two weeks from now, but with your power of mind control over normal people, you could persuade a person to lock you up at night. The creature that was seen in Rhineland in 1915, has no purpose in the modern city of Berlin. The burden that you bear for the killing of the rabbi wasn't your fault. I saw the whole proceedings; Pilate asked the crowd in Jerusalem. Whom shall I set free? The thief Barabbas or Jesus, the king of the Jews? The crowd cried out to free Barabbas and denounced the rabbi. Your rabbi was betrayed by his own people and what race of people occupied Jerusalem. You once were a member of that race and now, you can right a wrong." I said, "The beast no longer must kill people and pay homage to you with their dead bodies?"

The general laughed sinister laughed and said, "The new German ideology will surpass the hundreds of people that the beast has killed or will ever kill. We will talk of this later we are at the chancellery." The automobile stops and the driver opens the door for the general and for me. We are at the front of a large building and armed soldiers salute the general, as we walk up the many steps leading into the building. There are more military uniforms scattered about and the subordinates salute the general and others of equal rank stretch out their arms saying," Heil Hitler!" The general returns their response by saying," Heil Hitler!" The general turned to me and said," Remember, follow my lead and do as I do." A ranking German officer came walking towards us and I followed suit by saying," Heil Hitler!" The German officer told us that he is head of security and asked for our papers. I didn't know if I had any papers on me and I reached inside my jacket. I felt something protrude from the jacket pocket, I pulled it out and it was a small book.

I handed it to the German officer, and he examined it. He gave it back to me saying, "Danke." (Thank you) "Bitte" (Your welcome.) I replied. I waited for the general to go through the same motions and the security officer led us to a door. He told us to wait for a moment and he would return. While waiting, the general was about to say something and I said, "I know, follow your lead." The door opens up to a large room and the security officer tells us that der Fuhrer waits for us. I could see a man being flanked by high-ranking military officers and they continued talking until we got about three to four meters from a large desk. The general stopped and reached out his arm and said," Seig Heil! Mein Fuhrer." I did the same as the man sitting at the desk stood and returned with the same greeting.

CHAPTER 15

1939 ENGEL STERN

The general clicked his heels and said, "This is the man I told you about mein Fuhrer. He remembers you from the battlefield in the first war. His name is Engel Stern. The Fuhrer told us to walk closer to the desk and we obliged ourselves to do so. I could tell by the look of the Fuhrer's face; he isn't sure of who I am. I reach out in gesture of a handshake, the Fuhrer grips my hand, and a smile shows up upon his face. The Fuhrer sits down behind the desk and starts chuckling. The officers that are around him are puzzled by this. I am relieved and the pressure is off. The Fuhrer says," Herr Engel, you haven't aged a bit since the day I helped you get medical care at the field hospital." The Fuhrer walks from behind the desk and places his hand on my shoulder. He says to the other officer's, "This man standing here is a true German patriot. He experienced the war first-hand like me. Herr Engel, those men standing behind my desk with the exception of Herr Goering, have never seen war.

Where have you been all of this time?" The general said," I met him in a haufbrau in Simbach Austria, mein Fuhrer." The Fuhrer's eyes lit up and said, " I was born in the town across the river from Simbach called Branau Am Inn. We must have a drink to this occasion. It is more than just fate that brings you Herr Stern." The Fuhrer barks out an order to someone to get us drinks. The officers behind the desk scramble to find the bottle of alcohol and glasses. An officer finds a tray placing the bottle and three glass upon it and hurriedly places the tray on the table before us. The Fuhrer takes the bottle and pours alcohol into the three glasses. We all pick up our glasses and the Fuhrer says, " A toast to the fatherland. Seig Heil!" We slog down the drink in one gulp and placed the empty glasses on the tray just as the Fuhrer did. We waited expectantly to see what happened next. It was as if time froze waiting for someone to speak or something to happen. The general said," Mein Fuhrer, I reserved a room for Herr Stern at the Kaiserhof."

"Wunderbar!" (wonderful) Exclaimed the Fuhrer. The Fuhrer then asked the general if he is staying in Berlin? The general said," Only by your will mein Fuhrer." The Fuhrer slapped his hand against his thigh and said, "I will send my staff car for you two and we'll have dinner together this evening." The general told the Fuhrer that we wouldn't hold up anymore of his time. I stuck out my hand and the Fuhrer shook it and I said, "auf wiedershen." (goodbye) the general and I gave him the seig heil salute, and we did an about face towards the exit. I had questions, but I knew this isn't the place to ask them. I followed the general to his awaiting auto and got in. The general told the driver to go down to the next building on the right and stop. I looked at the sign on the building and it read, Kaiserhof. I wasn't surprised at all at the circumstance. The general told his driver to fetch the baggage from the trunk as we walked towards the entrance. A uniformed doorman opened the door for us to pass and flashing a heil Hitler salute to the general as he entered. The general returned the salute without breaking a stride. We arrived at the hotel desk and the general said," You should have a reservation for General Wolfstein and Engel Stern."

The man at the desk looked at the hotel register and said, "Neine, Herr General Wolfstein." The agitated general asked for the register, the reluctant desk clerk handed over the register. The general placed his finger on the page and said," What do you make of these names?" The astonished clerk looked dumbfounded as he saw our names staring back at him. The clerk said, "I must get my eyes checked herr General. How many nights will you men being staying?" The general told the clerk that he would be staying the night, and I would be staying for three days. The general gave the clerk some money and the clerk looked surprised and said, "You've overpaid me herr General." "Consider that a prepayment for room service. " Replied the general. The clerk handed over the keys to us and told us that we would be on the second floor in rooms 205 and 206. "Danke." I replied to the clerk as we followed behind the general's driver, as he lugged our baggage effortlessly up the stairs. I've never experienced such opulence other than the dolphin's castle in France.

This is a whole new level of amenities as I unlocked the door of my room and looked inside. The general said," Powerful men have stayed here, but none wield the power that you have Herr Engel Stern. Oh! Don't leave your baggage in the hall. The driver is my valet, not yours. I'm going to lie down and take a short nap; I've had a busy couple of centuries. Relax or order yourself some food or drink from room service, I've already paid for it." "Danke." I said the general and he replied by saying, bitte as he shut the door. I watched his driver walk down the hallway until he disappeared. I closed the door to my room and placed the baggage on the bed. The baggage seemed light, I looked inside it, and it was empty. I opened what I assumed as a storage place and clothing is hanging neatly upon the wooden bar. I opened up the drawers of a piece of well-built furnishing to find a couple pairs of socks, under garments and a night shirt. I walked into the washroom and saw myself in the mirror. I saw a clean-shaven businessman.

I did not look like an Israelite. My eyes are even a distinct color, they're ice blue now. I thought to myself, the dark master is really taking a hands-on approach to this situation. I saw a device on the table by the bed. I walked over to investigate, and I picked up the object. It was attached by a chord and I heard a voice say,"Womit kann ich ihnen behilflich sein?" (How can I help you?) It took a second or two for my mind to comprehend what the person on the device said. "Zimmerservice?" (Room service?) I asked. The person on the device asked me if I was hungry. The voice on the device told me to look in the drawer of the table and a menu was inside. I opened the drawer, finding a piece of paper listing breakfast, lunch and dinner meals with beer or wine. I made a choice and the voice said," Someone will bring it to your room Herr Stern. Give us a few moments and a person from the kitchen will bring it right up." I replied by saying "Danke." "Bitte." they replied. I placed the device back down in its original location and I was marveled at man's latest innovation.

I went back to the bathroom and relieved myself in the porcelain basin. I saw the chain hanging down and, being curious I pulled it. I watched the waste swirl around until it went away as new water filled the bowl. I must admit, it is better than hanging my private part out of a window. That was the way I did it at the dauphin's castle in France, centuries ago. My heart still is an open wound from losing Jean. She knew me better than anyone. At least she is free of the dark master and I hope one day I'll see her again. I sat down on the bed and took off my shoes and stretched myself out on the bed. This is way better than lying on the ground and not having to deal with getting rained on. Considering what I've already been through, I know this won't last. My gut tells me that a large-scale war is looming on the horizon. I saw a lot of military types and men wearing suits with arm bands brandishing a strange marking. I saw the same symbol on the dark master's uniform as well as the leader they called der Fuhrer.

I lie there on the bed thinking about my situation and there's a knock at the door. I sprang up from the bed and opened the door. Standing at the door is a young man wearing a white jacket and a wheeled cart in front of him. He said," Herr Stern?" "Jawhol." (Yes.) I answered. I moved away from the door to allow him in, as he pushed the wheel cart into the room. There is a bottle of wine, a glass, and a silver dome covering. He lifted the covering revealing the food I had ordered. The young man asked me did I approve, and I told him that I did. He replaced the covering over the food and as I reached inside my pocket, the young man told me not to worry about the tip. It's taken care of he tells me and says he'll be back in an hour to retrieve the tray. He goes to the door and tells me to enjoy my stay at the Kaiserhof and walks out. I walk over to the cart and grab the handle of the cover. I quickly removed my hand because I felt searing pain like grabbing a hot fire poker. It wasn't the heat from the food, it is the silver that the dark master warned me about. I got the hand towel from the cart and used it to lift the cover. I saw that the fork and spoon are probably the same metal, and I didn't attempt to use them. I ate the food with my hands, it tasted good. I uncorked the bottle of wine, pouring it into a glass. I ate and drank my fill. I started thinking about the dinner invite by the Fuhrer, what if the eating utensils are silver? It went and washed my hands and face in the bathroom.

I sat down on the bed and put on my shoes, grabbed the room key, and placed it in my pocket. I opened the door to my room and the general was standing in the hallway. The general said," Going somewhere herr Stern?" "I was going to pay you a visit, but since you aren't in your room, can you step inside for a moment? I asked. "Jawohl." The general replied and he walked into my room. The general says," I see you've already made use of the room service. I hope the food was to your liking?" I told him that the food wasn't the problem, it was the silver container. Isaid, "What am I to do if the forks and spoons are silver plated tonight at the Fuhrer's dinner?" The general picked up a spoon from the dinner cart and held it out to me. He said," Take this. It isn't silver, it is only silver looking. The metal is stainless steel and the ornate food cover is only silver plated. I want you to take the knife, spoon, and fork, and roll them up in a napkin. Place them in your jacket pocket and when we set down to eat, wait until after the Fuhrer starts eating, take out your own eating utensils and using the napkin on the table, begin wiping down each one and placing them on the opposite side of the plate. Ignore the other utensils altogether and always after eating, wipe down the eating implements and wrap them up in your napkin. If anyone ask about the odd behavior? Just tell them that it is a compulsion picked during the great war. Say that you got extremely ill from eating from a dirty spoon in the battlefield.

The Fuhrer is a bit of an eccentric himself when it comes to race purity and the behavior will strengthen his bond to you. Since you were on your way to see me. I sense you have other questions besides your problem with silver." I told him that he needs to bring me up to speed of what is going on in this time period. I said," I see similarities between the German military and the Roman armies that took over

Jerusalem." The general said, "I'm glad that you have been observing and self-educating yourself on the world around you. Both races want conquest of territory. The Romans wanted land mass and to make slaves of the captives, the Germans want to surpass both objectives. Tonight, at dinner the Fuhrer will no doubt ask you this question. The question will probably go like this, do you think the German citizen should go on carrying the shame of losing the first war, because the German pure blood was tainted? Your answer will be, the Juden was responsible for killing Jesus and tainting the soil of Europe. After you say that, you will have all eyes on you, especially the Fuhrer. The Fuhrer will be offering any high-ranking military status that you could want but, make this statement. Say, mein Fuhrer. Who controls the banks in Berlin or Germany? I see the boycotts of Juden operated stores, mein Fuhrer needs money to fuel the military. I'm going to suggest appointing you the minister of finance. Do you think you can remember all of this, herr Stern?

The conversation may not be per verbatim. What I told you is an assumption." I told the general that I have learned how to be almost as good a liar as he is. The general laughed at the comment and said, "If the Fuhrer ask about your wife or girlfriend? Tell him that your wife died from the lung disease called tuberculosis. The Fuhrer will probably say the minister of Germany's finance will need a pure German woman as a wife to give the German citizens a pure appearance of security in their money." The general and I talked for a couple of hours until the general told me that he's going back to his room to freshen up and that I should do the same. The general said," Make use of the bathtub and be ready to go once the Fuhrer's staff car gets here." The general opened the door of my room and walked out. I locked the door and began taking off my clothes. I rolled up the eating utensils in the cloth napkin and placed it inside of my coat pocket. I placed the jacket on a hanger and continued undressing. I can't remember the last time I had a real bath, and I'm anxious to use man's latest improvement over bathing in a stream. I must admit, I do smell kind of gamey and need refreshing. I walked into the badezimmer (bathroom) and approached the tube.

I turned on the left knob and hot water came rushing out. I turned it off and turned on the other knob, icy water came rushing out. I placed the plug into the drain and turned the hot water knob, touching the water with my hand and adjusting the warmth as needed. I grabbed a washcloth and a towel, placing the towel near the tub. I got into the tub as it began to fill with water. I caught the scent of an object on the ledge of the tub. I picked it up and deduced it must be used for washing. I dipped it in the water and began gliding it over my left arm. A lather began to appear, and it was helping to rid my body of stains from the last time period plus, the stench. As the water got deeper, I was able to wash my hair with this lather. I finished washing and rinsed off the lather, pulled the plug and I could hear the water escaping. I stood up and let some of the water drain off my body, leaning beside the tub and grabbed the towel. I held onto the side of the tub and stepped out of the tub. I now know why there is a smaller towel hanging from the wall. I almost busted my ass on the wet tiled floor. If it wasn't for my quick reflexes, more than just my pride would've been injured. I finished drying off and walked back into the bedroom.

I picked up the baggage and placed it on the bed. I opened and it contained fresh clothing, undergarments, shirts and trousers, socks, and a small leather case. I opened it and it had a razor, a small cup, a brush, a comb, and a small aromatic bar. There's a piece of paper inside also. I took out the paper and read the note. The note said, "This is a shaving kit with soap. Place the soap bar into the cup, wet the brush and wipe the bar. This will create a lather to use on your face to shave. Take care using the razor, it is sharp. Lay the razor flat against your skin until you feel the blade removing your facial hair. I wrapped the towel around my waist, took the shaving kit to the badezimmer. Again, I used the water temperature at the sink and followed the instructions on the piece of paper. I nicked my face on the first try until I mastered the blade. I washed away the soap, wiped my face and looked in the mirror. The small nick had gone away, as the skin regenerated itself. My body is clean, but my conscious isn't. I looked down at my hands, many people have been slain by these hands. The remorse I feel isn't from the killings by my hands, but the killing set in motion by a gesture. I stopped dwelling on the past and focused on remembering what the dark master, I mean General Wolfstein had told me. I might as well enjoy this royal treatment while I can. There is always calm before the storm, especially when the general is involved.

I finished putting on fresh clothes, socks, and shoes. I looked at the note to see, if there is anything else left for me to complete. The note also spelled out directions for cleaning my teeth and to sparingly use the contents of a bottle labelled 4711 on the face after shaving. I picked up the bottle and opened it. The fragrance hit my nose before I could bring it closer to my face. I put a little in my hand and spread it across my shaved face. The liquid burned my face like the silver burned my hand, but only for a few seconds. I put the note back in the shaving kit, grabbing the toothbrush and paste headed back into the badezimmer (bathroom). I squeezed the product onto the brush bristles and started scrubbing my teeth. It was a strange experience, I looked at the labeling and saw that I was to spit out the paste after brushing. A mental note to myself is to read the directions first before using. I looked at my newly cleaned teeth and they sparkled like a shiny coin in the mirror. At once is when I noticed the pronounced pointed teeth on top and bottom.

I haven't paid much attention to other people's mouths as I speak to them, to notice if other people have the same display. I just need to be conscious not smiling such a toothy grin. I was wiping my mouth with a towel, and I heard a ringing noise. I went back to the bedroom and the sound was coming from the device on the table. I picked up the receiver and placed it to my ear, a voice on the device said, "The Fuhrer's driver is here to pick you up, the general has also been called herr Stern. Heil Hitler!" "Danke. Heil Hitler!" I answered and replaced the receiver. I put away my things and made sure that I had the eating utensils in my coat. I grabbed my room key, opened the door, and saw the general. I closed the door and locked it with the key. The general said, "I hope the note provide enough of instructions to help to prepare yourself?" "Danke." I replied to the general and told him that there is much for me to learn about this modern life. The general said that we mustn't keep the Fuhrer waiting and we headed for the elevator. I was reluctant to step inside the box and the general assured me that it is safe. The attendant closed the doors, and he pressed the button on the wall. I felt the floor drop gradually as I heard the whirring sound of an electric motor. The general said," First time in an elevator herr Stern?" "Ya, I took the stairs coming up. This machine could save wear and tear on a man's shoes." I said.

The general laughed at my comment and the elevator stopped as the attendant opened the doors. We stepped out and made our way past the front desk and out the main entrance. The Fuhrer's staff car and driver are at the edge of the street waiting for us. The driver opened the door for the general as a walked to the other side, opened the automobile door myself and got in. The driver got in, placed the car in gear and we were motoring down the streets of Berlin. I looked out from the auto's window at the layout of the modern German city. I saw more military type dressed people on the sidewalks versus the number of ordinary citizens. Again, I saw the boycott signs directed at the Jewish population. I looked over at the general and he gestured by pointing his finger forward. He told me to face forward without uttering a word and I complied. We arrived at the front of a restaurant and the driver turned off the engine and quickly opened my door and scurried around to open the door for the general. I walked over to the sidewalk and waited for the general to exit the auto.

The general placed his stately cap upon his head, and I walked beside him to the entrance to the restaurant. There is a heavy presence of military types here, but they wear a different colored uniform… black. As we got closer to the entrance, a black uniformed officer saluted the general and asked for his papers. The general said, "Here is both of our papers." The uniformed officer looked at the papers and gave them back to the general. Before we entered the building the general gave me the papers and told me to keep them always. I stuffed the papers into my coat pocket as the doorman opened the door for us to enter. The general removed his hat as we walked in. The smell of food and alcohol is in the air as well the smell of cigarette smoke. We walked up to a small podium and the man in a suit asked our names. The general told him our names and said, "Herr General Wolfstein and Herr Stern, the waiter will take you to the private dining room. The Fuhrer is waiting there for you." A young man came up to us and told us to follow him.

We followed the waiter to a small hallway and we see an armed guard at the room's entrance. The guard snaps to attention, saluting the general and the general said," Do you need to see my papers before gaining entry corporal?" The corporal said," May I asked herr general's name and the gentleman with you?" The general said," I'm General Wolfstein and this man here is Herr Engel Stern." The corporal opened the door for us, and I walked in behind the general.

There in the room sat the Fuhrer and six uniformed officers, generals no doubt. All eyes were upon us, and the Fuhrer stood up and said," Come and sit." The general raised his right arm saying," Heil Hitler!" I followed suit and repeated the greeting. The uniformed officers all stood up at the same time as the Fuhrer and repeated the same greeting. They remained standing until we reached our places at the table. I'm at the head of the table with the Fuhrer and general Wolfstein is across from me. The Fuhrer sat down, and we all sat down. The Fuhrer turned to me and said, "What does my friend herr Stern like to drink?" "Whatever mein Fuhrer is drinking?" I replied. The Fuhrer looked at General Wolfstein and said, "Have you been coaching him, herr general?" "Neine, mein Fuhrer." Replied the general. For a brief tense moment, one could hear a pin hit the floor and the Fuhrer laughed and said," Herr Stern, you will go far." It was like the other men at the table wanted to release a sigh of relief, the tension was off and it was okay to breathe again.

The Fuhrer placed his hand upon my shoulder and said," I cannot get over how you seem to not to have aged at all since that day on the battlefield." "Looks are deceiving mein Fuhrer. I'm not as young as I used to be. I try to take care of the equipment I was given." I replied. The Fuhrer said," I will send my personal doctor to give you an examination. You must have the healthiest body in Germany." As the Fuhrer was speaking, I got a mental message from the general and he said, "He's going to ask you how old you are? Tell him that you're thirty- eight years old and wait for the laugh and say that you are fifty years old." The Fuhrer said, "Herr Stern, exactly how old are you?" "Thirty-eight years old, mein Fuhrer." I replied. The Fuhrer hit the top of the table and laughed, the others at the table laughed at my commit and I told them that I'm fifty years old. The Fuhrer turned to the general and said," I'm glad you found Herr Stern and brought him. He has an honest sense of humor and not afraid to speak his mind." The general said," If I had a stein of beer, I wound toast you mein Fuhrer." The Fuhrer yells to an awaiting waiter to bring two more steins of beer and refills for everyone. The waiter scurries away but not before giving the Fuhrer a heil Hitler salute. There are menus laying in front of us, I look down at it and I am at a loss to what to order. I got a mental message from the general and he said, "Order the tafelspitz, it's veal and vegetables. It is an Austrian dish." The Fuhrer asked me what am I having? I asked him, "How is the tafelspitz in this place?" The Fuhrer said, "It better be good, or I'll have the chef shot." He started laughing and everyone followed suit. I got the impression that the Fuhrer is more full of himself than the general.

I understand the game, I play into whatever the Fuhrer wants to hear, and speak only when he speaks to me. I could feel that other generals and German officers were less tense because, the Fuhrer's attention is off of them and directed towards the general and I. The Fuhrer saw the waiter return to the room with a tray and said,"Wunderbar! Now, General Wolfstein can propose a proper toast after everyone's stein is refilled." The waiter precariously placed the steins in front of the general and I, refilled the Fuhrer's stein and the others from a large pitcher. General Wolfstein stood up, everyone followed the general's gesture and waited for the general's toast. The general said, "This is a toast to the newest star on the world's stage. A leader that will make every German proud to be German and his enemies will wish they were Germans. Heil Hitler!" The Fuhrer stood up and clinked the general's stein and mine also. We all turned up our steins and took a drink and waited until the Fuhrer sat down and everyone followed his lead. The waiter walked up to the Fuhrer and asked the Fuhrer, what did he wish to order from the menu. The Fuhrer looked at me and said, "I'll be having the tafelspitz with veal." The waiter turned to me and asked me the same question. I said, "I hope for the chef's sake that he has plenty of tafelspitz with veal." The Fuhrer hits the table with his fist and laughs at my comment.

I look at the general and he gives me an evil grin of approval. Needless to say, everyone at the table ordered tafelspitz whether they wanted it or not. The waiter took the orders and gave a heil Hitler salute to the Fuhrer before he left the room. The Fuhrer turned to me and said, "Only a true Austrian would order tafelspitz. Did you do that to make me homesick?" "Neine mein Fuhrer! My wife used to cook that for me." "Use to?" asked the Fuhrer. I told him that my wife had succumb to the lung disease, tuberculosis. I said," I told her that the cigarettes would be the death of her. I stopped smoking after the war and when I met her, she was sitting at a table in the beer garden. She was flipping the pages of a book with one hand, holding a cigarette in the other. I hand eighteen good years with her.

I think all the years of smoking made her barren, but I didn't mind that we didn't have children. I don't think I could've shared her even with our own children. It was like we were destined to be with each other. I'm sorry, I didn't mean to ramble on mein Fuhrer." The Fuhrer said, " I don't think you'll have any problem getting a new female companion. With this new position that I give you, a general's uniform draws the women like a magnet." I said," Danke, mein Fuhrer, but I think I could better serve mein Fuhrer with my skills with numbers." The Fuhrer turned to the general and asked what am I talking about. The general said, "Herr Stern was a banker in his town until his wife died and became a recluse. It was by chance that I met him at a haufbrau in Simbach. After I mentioned your name mein Fuhrer, herr Stern told me that you took him to a field hospital during the war. Herr Stern made an observation, coming to Berlin and I think best if he told you himself." The Fuhrer turned to me and said, "Please enlighten us with your observation."

I said," Mein Fuhrer needs funding for the military. How many banks are being operated by the Juden versus German operated banks? " The Fuhrer leaned back in his chair and said," General Wolfstein, you have brought me a valuable asset and speaking of assets herr Stern. Instead of turning you into a general, how does the minister of German finance sound. After the removal of the Juden from all businesses including banks, all of the banks will be German operated and will report to you. Yes, the military will need funding and I want you to find out the health of the banks by having them audited. You have really got me thinking in a broader sense herr Stern. You need to come to my office so that we can brainstorm on the subject." A man sitting at the table, wearing a black military type uniform said," Mein Fuhrer, may I ask her Stern a question?" The Fuhrer said," Ya! Herr Reichsfuhrer Himmler, ask what you may." Reichsfuhrer Himmler said," Herr Stern, do you believe in God?" I said," What you are really asking me is, am I a Jew pretending to be a German? The answer is no, I am not Juden."

As I was about to continue, I got a mental message from the general. I said, "A priest can listen to a confession and say that you are forgiven but, in reality only God has the final say. Reichsfuhrer Himmler are you Lutheran or Catholic?" The reichsfuhrer's face turned red, he adjusted his glasses and said, "For your sake, I hope the Gestapo doesn't find a menorah in your home." I looked Himmler in the eye and said," You better hope the gestapo hasn't been lining your pockets instead of going towards mein Fuhrer's military campaign." Himmler started back peddling and said," Mein Fuhrer, I am only trying to safeguard you from this outsider." Before the Fuhrer could utter a word, I said," Mein Fuhrer, I must decline the position as minister of finance because a house divided doesn't stand for long, and I do not want to be the one to cause such descension." The Fuhrer smashed his fist upon the table and pointed at the reichsfuhrer and said, "Heinrich! This was supposed to be a peaceful, relaxing dinner and not about posturing for my attention. If I hear one milligram of information about the gestapo even thinking about investigating herr Stern. You'll no longer be the head of the police; you'll be a policeman whose sole job will be directing traffic. Do I make myself clear?" "Ja wohl." replied reichsfuhrer Himmler. The Fuhrer turned to me and said," Herr Stern, was a field commander in the war. If Germany had won the war, this man would've have been a high ranking general already." The Fuhrer turns to me and said," Why do you think that Germany lost the war, herr Stern?" I said, "The blood of Germany has been tainted by the stain of the infiltration by the Juden. The Juden is responsible for killing Christ and staining all of Europe and possibly the world." The

Fuhrer hits the table with his fist and says," This man sees the whole picture and I'm not going to accept a resignation from a job that has not begun." The room became quiet as all eyes fell upon me. I stood up and reached out my hand, gesturing for a handshake to the Fuhrer. The Fuhrer stood up and those at the table followed suit. The Fuhrer grasp my hand and shook it and said, "Is this your way of telling me you'll accept my offer?" I said," I don't want to end up being shot like the chef for taking so long getting our food."

The Fuhrer smiled and General Wolfstein yelled out," Heil Hitler!" The men at the table followed suit as the Fuhrer told me to come to his office at the chancellery tomorrow. I gave the Fuhrer a nod and held up my stein and said, "To the fatherland!" The Fuhrer clinked his stein against mine and repeated what I said and sat down. A couple of waiters enter the room pushing carts laden with food. The waiters began laying food at the head of the table near the Fuhrer and Himmler told one of the waiters to taste the food before anyone took a bite. The nervous young man took a spoon and dipped it into the sauce, placing the spoon in his mouth. All eyes were upon him as he swallowed the sauce. The waiter stood there for a moment and said, "The tafelspitz taste excellent mein Fuhrer and I saw the chef tasting it as he was making it." General Wolfstein picked up his spoon and dipped it into the sauce and swallowed it. General Wolfstein said, "The tafelspitz is very tasty and then cut into the meat with a knife, picking it up with his fork, placing it in his mouth and started chewing, then swallowed.

The general gave a nod of approval and I didn't take a chance to touch the flatware on the table, I took the utensils wrapped in a cloth from my jacket and placed them on the table. The Fuhrer saw what I was doing and asked, "Herr Stern, the food is safe. Why are you going to such lengths?" I said, "Mein Fuhrer, I became extremely ill eating with dirty utensils in the battlefield. I guess the experience taught me to take precautions and I carry my own eating utensils with me always. My behavior embarrassed my wife in the beginning and gave up trying to change me. I suppose I may be a little eccentric when it comes to eating." The Fuhrer said, "I can remember, eating in the battlefield with limited access to water. I can see how your eccentricity could've evolved from that." The meal went on with casual conversations amongst the other officers at the table. After eating, the waiters came and cleared the table and asked did anyone would like to order a dessert. Everyone waited to see what the Fuhrer was going to do, and he said that he was stuffed.

The Fuhrer pushed away from the table, stood up as everyone followed his movements. The Fuhrer said, "I'm going to retire to room for the night, I expect my staff to meet me tomorrow in my office afternoon and Herr Stern I will send my staff car for you and general Wolfstein later tomorrow afternoon. Seig Heil!" The members at the table followed by yelling "Heil Hitler!" The Fuhrer exited the room as two armed soldiers went with him. The officers at the table began to make their way out except for one man at the end of the table. As I and the general were making our way to the door, the man said, Herr Stern are you staying here at the hotel?" I told him that I have a room upstairs. the general said, "What is the matter obersturmbanfuhrer Eichmann?" I saw the expression on Eichman's face, and it was of surprise.

Eichmann said," How is it that you know who I am, but I don't know who you are?" The general said, "You would be surprised of what I know. Let's have a meeting in Herr Stern's room, shall we?" I followed the men to the elevator, got in and pushed the button for the second floor. No one said a word as the elevator moved upward until it stopped, and the doors opened. The general told me to lead the way as we walked down the hallway, as I reached into my pocket for the room key. I stopped at the door to my room, stuck in the key and unlocked the door. I held the door open for the general and Eichmann, closing it and locked it. Eichmann said, "General Wolfstein, have you ever heard the story about Hans Engel?" The general said, "I've heard of this myth, a mere tale of fiction. Why do you ask?" Eichmann points at me and said, "This man isn't Engel Stern, he's Hans Engel. I saw this man get shot in the head, came back to life, and killed my commanding officer and took his clothes. After he killed my commanding officer he yelled out, "I'm der tuefel and I will kill all of you tonight." I got a lump in my throat after he said that and the general held out his hand, gesturing for a handshake saying, "Take my hand in friendship Herr Eichmann."

Eichmann said," What significance is that?" The general's voice changed tone, telling Eichmann that it wasn't a request but an order. Eichmann took the general's hand but the general didn't shake it, he tightened the grip upon Eichmann's hand. The general said, "Let me show you something." I don't know what the general was showing Eichmann, but by the looks on Eichmann's face was the face of fear. After a few moments, the general released his grip as Eichmann collapsed to his knees. The general said, "Stand up, herr Eichman." Eichmann found his footing and stood up. The general said, "Herr Eichmann, are you ready to make this deal or experience the future that I showed you if you don't?" Eichmann took a deep breath and said, "Since, I'm going to hell anyway, I might as well be in good standings with the dark lord himself. So, what am I supposed to do? Am I to forget about who you and Stern are really?" The general said, "Once, you walk out that door. You'll remember that Herr Stern is a close friend and nothing more. When you go to your home, I want you to type up your plans for the Juden solution, sign it and place it in an envelope. I want you to be the last remaining man in the room with the Fuhrer when you hand him the envelope.

He will ask you to stand by his desk until he finishes reading it. He will ask you if anyone else knows of this plan and you know the answer. The Fuhrer will study this plan won't give you the answer right away, but you will find great favor in the eyes of the Fuhrer. As Far as my true identity, you'll only remember meeting with me and Herr Stern and considering us as close colleagues and that is all. You may go Herr Eichmann." Eichmann goes the door and turns to us and says, "Heil Hitler!" He unlocks the door and closes the door as he leaves. I look at the general and said, "Another recruit acquired? " The general smiled an evil grin and said, "I'll be on my way. Himmler is about to have a visitor. I'll see you tomorrow. Order yourself a bottle of wine from room service, you've done well today, Herr Stern. You have become quite the student." "I've learned from the best." I replied and the general held up his hand saying," Heil Hitler!" He walked to the door and closed it as he exited. I sat down on the bed and removed my shoes; I began to wonder if the Fuhrer is a recruit also?

Engel Stern is now a high-ranking civilian in charge of the Reich's funding of the war effort being waged in Europe. Engel Stern's intended Maria Orsic, though of Austrian decent, and is highly favored by the secret Thule society. A group that used Maria's psychic ability to gain access to secret knowledge. Maria's first husband died in a freak accident. Some eyewitnesses say that he stepped out in front of truck and was killed instantly. Maria met Engel at a Thule meeting and was automatically drawn to him. It wasn't that she knew that Engel had money and an elite member of the Nazi party. She knew that something was special about Engel Stern. Engel didn't have to use any mind control on Maria as suggested by his dark master. Maria revealed that she picked up the duality within Engel.

She didn't realize the extents of the duality until, she had to lock him up for the first time. Maria did not believe the extent of what Engel had warned her about. The bank is empty except for Engel and Maria. A caged barrier is built in front of the main vault. Maria sees scratch marks left on the massive mechanical door, that has been made with the utmost precision. "Hurry! Lock the door with the key Maria! Do not open it! No matter what the creature says to you. Promise me! Tell me that you promise!" says a pain-stricken Engel Stern. "I promise! But I don't understand!" exclaimed Maria. "Don't stand too close to the cage!" Yelled Engel Stern. Maria watched in horror as the man she loves changes into something monstrous. She cries out. "Where did you go Engel? I want you to come back to me." In a guttural voice the creature says, "It is me! Engel Stern in a superior form. Open the cage and let me explain this to you." "I can hear you just fine, without opening the cage." Replied Maria.

The creature sprang from a crouched position to now gripping the caged bars, with deadly clawed fingers. The creature shakes the cage door violently and the lock holds steadfast. Maria has moved farther back away and sees a creature of evil intentions. Maria, still clutching the key in her hand, quickly stuffs the key into her purse. The creature sees this and becomes enraged. Shaking the door more violently. A horrified Maria opens the steel door leading back into the bank lobby and says, "I'll be back tomorrow morning to let my Engel out." exclaimed

Maria as she closed the heavy door behind her. After the anger passes from the realization that Maria wouldn't free him. The creature began to think about a particular phrase told to him by the dark one. The dark master told him to avoid psychics and now he's connected to one. There has to be some motive behind this. There is always something hidden until it's too late to do anything about it. To fight against his dark master would bring most certain retaliation. To be placed in a no-win situation again. The creature just realized something. If he wasn't caged up? He would be thinking about the urge...... killing, eating, and gorging himself on people. The creature isn't accustomed to just thinking. He looked around and saw the cold steel is unaffected by his claws. The creature laid down on the cool ceramic tiles and fell asleep. The morning came and the creature is awakened by the intense pain of changing back into a human form. Engel Stern is back and sat there waiting, listening for any activity on the outer door. He didn't have to wait too long. he hears the sound of a key sliding into a lock.

The lock clicks and Maria walks in. "Guten morgen." (good morning) Says Maria. "Morgen!" replied Engel. Maria hurriedly opens the cage with the key and gives Engel a change of clothes. The creature had made tatters of the clothing he now wears. "Do you know really know who I am Maria?" Asked Engel. "You're Hans Engel. The man that cannot die or has been said der teufel (the devil). But let's not talk about it here. You need to get changed and get ready to leave the bank. The manager will be here soon to open the bank." Fortunately for Engel Stern, he lives in an upstairs room above the bank. They only have a few minutes to be out of sight, before the mundane everyday existence of the normal working class begins. Maria and Engel got to the upstairs apartment just in time. While Engel is shaving. Maria said, "Engel. We've only known each other for a few weeks. I was drawn to you after meeting you. Last night was the most horrific event that I've ever witnessed. Is that thing you become? The reason you cannot die?" Engel places the razor down and turns to Maria. Engel said," Maria. Didn't General Wolfstein point you in my direction and did he say anything else, out of the ordinary to you?"

Maria's face changed to a look of fear. Maria started crying. Engel told Maria to take his hand and said," What do you feel now with your ability?" Maria said," I feel like I can trust everything that you say. You are trapped just like I am. I didn't have this much power until I shook hands with General Wolfstein. Before that chance encounter, I only received visions through a guide of sorts." Engel said, "Now you know who General Wolfstein really is don't you?" Maria said in a sorrowful shaky voice, "Yes! That is why I am so afraid." "Engel said, "Let me finish shaving and cleaning up. I'll get dressed and we'll go and have a nice quiet breakfast. Okay?" Maria said, "My body aches for you Engel. Don't put on your clothing just yet." Maria began undressing and Engel wiped the soap from his face. He removed his tattered clothes and made passionate love to Maria. In the frenzy of their love making, Engel was about to climax and withdrew from Maria. Maria said," Why did you do that my love?" "I do not want to make a person like myself. They would suffer the same fate." Maria said, "See! You are a good person inside Engel. You think of others before yourself. I am a barren woman and cannot have children according to the doctors.

Before my husband was killed, we tried many times. So please, I want you inside of me." After thrusting many times into Maria, both are satiated. Engel said, "Have you shaken hands with an agreement with General Wolfstein?" Maria said, "The general kissed my hand, and he told me that I have a gift. I felt a cold emptiness briefly. My long hair since I was a child has given me powers to contact others…. a different race of beings." Engel said, "The German's want some different technology and they are using you to get it." Maria nods yes. "The different race that you speak of. Where do they say they're from? " Asked Engel. "They are from another planet." Answered Maria. "Get dressed Maria. We will finish this conversation later tonight. Right now. We must continue as a normal couple. We can play along until you feel threatened. When you feel threatened you let me know who does this. I am already damned because of what I've done. I don't want you to be damned also. Just don't bargain with General Wolfstein. Promise Me!" Exclaimed Engel. "I promise!" Replied Maria. The two get dressed and proceed downstairs into the bank.

They are greeted by a group of SS soldiers and Heidrich Himmler.

"Guten Tag." Said Himmler. "Guten Tag Herr Reichsführer" Replied Engel. "Can we have breakfast together? It will be my treat." Said Himmler. "It is too early in the day for being shot for refusing a breakfast with the Reichsführer." Jokingly said Engel. "Don't be ridiculous. Mein Fuhrer would have me shot for doing so. My staff car is outside waiting for us." Replied Himmler. Maria took Engel's hand and squeezed it gently as they followed Himmler and his SS bodyguards out of the bank. The bodyguards filed themselves into a car behind us. Himmler says," I hope you are hungry? I haven't had breakfast myself. Only a cup of coffee today." "A good meal would be welcomed Herr Reichsfuhrer." Engel replied. Engel's body cries out for fuel. "Have you had any interesting visions lately my dear Maria?" asked Himmler. "I saw an unmanned device strike England, Herr Reichsfuhrer." Replied Maria. Himmler slapped his knee and said, "Again! You have amazed me, Maria. Such research and testing are happening now. The test so far hasn't been fruitful. Perhaps, your guides can give us an answer." "Perhaps, herr Reichsfuhrer." Replied Maria. The two autos stop at a haufbrau and the occupants go inside. Himmler's SS guards push their way through the doors and announce the entrance of the Reichsfuhrer. A nervous shop owner greets the entourage with a Heil Hitler salute and guides the party to a private dining area. Himmler's guards await outside the room and eyeing the movements of the wait staff. The wait staff quickly placed coffee cups, plates, and flatware on the table. As Himmler begins talking about Germany's rise from the ashes of the first war.

Engel feels his coat pocket and realizes, he doesn't have his own eating utensils with him. Maria notices Engel's movements and ask what is wrong. Himmler stops talking and ask Engel, "Is something wrong Herr Stern?" "I left my personal eating utensils in the apartment." Replied Engel. "If the wait staff has given you a dirty spoon? Somebody will get shot today!" exclaimed Himmler. Engel lays his hand on the handle of a butter knife, gripping and brings it up to face for close examination. He didn't feel a burning sensation, the knife wasn't silver. Engel went through the motions of wiping down the eating utensils with the cloth napkin. Repeating a ritual of a person that is obsessed with cleanliness. "Sorry to break your concentration Reichsfuhrer. It's one of my eccentricities I developed after the war." Replied Engel.

Himmler said, "I suffered from dysentery myself during war. Having access to clean water on the battlefield was scarce. No need to apologize." A waiter came in with a woman carrying a coffee decanter. She began pouring coffee into the party's waiting cups, as the waiter wrote down the orders placed by everyone. "The vision you spoke of Maria. Did you dream it or were you wide awake? I've seen you go into a trance like state during past meetings. I'm curious!" asked Himmler. Maria takes a sip of coffee and says," What I saw was a brief glimpse after just waking up from sleep, yesterday. You could say I was partially awake. When it happened." Replied Maria." "Perhaps. Your connection with Herr Stern, is increasing your enlightenment." Commented Himmler. Engel picked up his coffee cup and said," For the fatherland!" Himmler's bodyguards snapped to attention and shouted, "For the fatherland!" Himmler raised his cup and said," Of course. For the fatherland." Himmler took a sip from his cup and then said," Could you do a session with the Fuhrer, and a few select individuals, frau Orsic?"

Maria looked at Engel and replied," I'm positive the Fuhrer won't mind if Engel is there also. I can see that this will bring favor to you from the Fuhrer." Engel sees that the guards are waiting for him to do something. He looks at them and raises his coffee cup, "Heil Hilter!" He exclaims. The guards follow in unison. Himmler shouts, "Who do I need to shoot to get some breakfast around here?" Maria grips Engel's hand as Himmler sends one his guards to see what is holding up the service. "Since we're sitting here waiting for our damn food to arrive. Can you give me a reading Frau Orsic?" asked Himmler. "You need to calm yourself or I can't get through. Think of a time in your life when you were the most content. Close your eyes and see that moment." Replied Maria. "I was content until I thought about getting my breakfast sometime today." exclaimed Himmler. "Inhale slowly and exhale even slower and close your eyes as you do this. When I see you are relaxed? I prompt you to ask me a question. Said Maria in a calm voice. Just as Himmler exhaled for the third time; a waiter appeared at the doorway. Engel held up his hand to gesture stopping for a moment. The guard stood in front of the door and held his hand to his lips for quietness. "Ask your question Reichsfuhrer?" Replied Maria. "What do you see me doing in the next two years?" asked Himmler. Maria closed her eyes, placed her palms flat on the table and said, "I'm going to write an answer on a piece of paper because this is private." Replied Maria.

Engel took a pen from his pocket and she wrote the message on a piece of paper. She wrote, you will be a father again and it won't be with your wife. Maria folded it and asked Himmler to open his eyes. Maria gave the note to Engel, and he passed it to Himmler. Himmler didn't open the note right away. He looked at Maria and she said, "It's okay! I won't tell a soul." Himmler cautiously opened the piece of paper and read it. Himmler took the paper and stuck it in his pocket. He said, "Guard! Let the waiter in. We are starving." Himmler looked at Maria and said, "I'm going to hold you to that promise Maria." And he joyfully said," Anyone objecting to wine with our breakfast?" "I'm glad that it appears to be great news Reichsfuhrer. It is too early in the day to get shot for delivering unwelcome news." Said a relaxed Engel Stern. Himmler laughs at the comment and the tension in room has dissipated. Engel and Maria ate and made small talk with the Reichsfuhrer until breakfast concluded. The Reichsfuhrer takes Engel and Maria back to the front of the bank. As Maria exits the auto Himmler says, "You are a valuable asset. Remember our pact."

Himmler closes the door of the auto as Engel and Maria watch as the autos speed away. Maria kisses Engel and tells him that she must go to her apartment and do some laundry. "Do you want me to get my driver to take you home?" "No, my darling! I feel like walking. It isn't but a few blocks from here. Send your driver for me around five o'clock. I'll pick up something and cook us dinner. Love you!" "Love you too!" Replied Engel as he watched her walk down the sidewalk. Engel opened the door of the bank and thought to himself. Jean was the last person he could remember telling him such words. Engel's brief moment of reflection was stopped, by the man assigned to him to manage the bank. "Herr Finance Minister. Can I have a private word with you?" "Of course. Let's go into my office." Answered Engel. The two men go into Engel's office and Engel closes the door behind them.

"Please! Have a seat herr Burkhalter and tell me. What is troubling you?" Asked Engel. "It's my daughter, herr Minister Stern.

A gestapo agent raped my daughter because she neglected his advances. He then threatened to investigate my family's German lineage." Exclaimed the distressed bank manager. "When did this happen?" Asked Engel. "Two nights ago, after my daughter and her friends left from school. I figured all is lost until I saw Himmler take you and frau Maria with him this morning. The Reichsfuhrer sees favor in you. I know I am asking a lot here." Replied the manager. "I want a name of this agent. Get me the name of this bastard and I'll take care of the rest." Said an angered Engel Stern. "The gestapo is preying upon our own kind. I will get you the name. Thank you, Herr Stern." Replied the manager as he walked out the door. Engel was angered more than just about the manager's daughter. He didn't like to be used and didn't like to see people being used. He knows that he would have to deal with this without Himmler. The rest of the day was uneventful and the time came to close the bank for the day. Engel left his office and approached the manager before he left for the day. "Once you get the name. Don't call me on the phone tonight, to tell me.

The gestapo is so paranoid, the phones in the bank could be compromised." Said Engel. "What do you mean compromised herr Stern?" asked the bank manager. The gestapo is looking for enemies from within. They could be listening in on our phone conversations. By the way, how old is your daughter, herr Berkhalter?" Asked Engel. "She is seventeen and going to school. Why? Herr Stern." Replied the manager Berkhalter." Where was she? When she encountered the gestapo agent?" Asked Engel. "She was walking from school with other girls and was singled out by the agent. My wife told me this at the dinner table yesterday. My daughter wouldn't leave her room to eat with us. I banged on her room door to let me in. She unlocked the door and her room was darkened with lights on. I turned on the lights and she began crying and asked me to turn off the lights. She has a blackened eye, bruises on her arms and I asked a subjective question that as a father was heart wrenching.

I asked my daughter did the man enter her? She told me yes and told me that she was taken in an alley." The bank manager's tear-streaked face made Engel even more furious about the situation. Engel said in a calm voice. "Do you mind if Maria and I visit your home this evening. We won't trouble you for dinner. We will eat before coming over." The bank manager became nervous, and Engel placed his hand on the banker's shoulder, looked him in the eyes and said," Relax herr Berkhalter. No harm will happen to you or your family. Maria and I are seeking justice for what happened to your daughter. You trust me now, don't you?" The banker calmly answered, "Yes." Engel taps the banker on the shoulder and the banker blinks back into a new moment. Engel says," What time would be convenient for us to visit herr Berkhalter?" "Seven o'clock this evening would fine. My wife will be overjoyed to have my boss and Frau Orsic in our home." Replied a relieved man. "Go ahead and lock up on your way out as you normally do." Said Engel.

CHAPTER 16

ENGEL KILLS A RAPIST

Last night was the final full moon of the month. Otherwise, the streets of Berlin would run red with blood. Engel checked the lock on the door and made his way to his upstairs living quarters. Walking up the staircase, Engel began to replay things in his mind. Maria acknowledged him as Hans Engel, the man that cannot die. Is she holding back on what she really knows and is too afraid to say? She also revealed that she knows what General Wolfstein is from a handshake. Something doesn't add up. Engel goes into his abode, takes a bath and shaves. He readies himself for Maria's arrival. He looks at the clock on the wall and remembers to send his driver to pick up Maria at five o'clock. The clock registers at four forty-five, Engel goes to the phone and calls his driver instructing him to pick up Maria at five o'clock, at her address. Engel finishes getting ready and walks downstairs into the bank. He goes to the front entrance and waits for the driver to show up with Maria. Engel takes out a cigarette paper and rolls the tobacco into it. He knows deep down inside that something always happens.

He has either pissed off the dark master about something or the dark master just puts him in another situation on a whim. He knows he must think about his actions first, and not let his emotions control him. He would like nothing more than to strangle the gestapo agent for raping the young girl. For the moment, he only knows one side of the story from the father. Engel goes into his office and sits down, placing his cigarette in an ashtray. For the first time, Engel takes a real look at his surroundings. He had been walking in and out of the office like he normally does every day. Sitting at his desk and signing papers given to him by the staff and the manager. He hadn't noticed it before now, but there on the far wall is a shelf devoid of any books. Were there any books on the shelf to start with? The only artwork on the wall is a portrait of Adolf Hitler and there's a copy of MY Struggle by Adolf Hitler on his desk. Engel doesn't need to read what's in the book to know who really authored it. Things suddenly clicked in his mind. He is about to roll another cigarette when he hears a knock at the door. He gets up and goes to the door. He sees that his driver is standing at the door with Maria. Engel reaches into his pocket, gives the driver several marks and tells him to take his family out to dinner.

The driver looks confused and surprised by this and thanks Engel for the gesture. The driver says, "Your money is not needed herr minister. Will you need my services anymore tonight?" The driver hands the marks back to Engel, and Engel tells the driver to come back to the bank at a quarter til seven. "Tell me if you have other plans and if it will be okay to take a trolley. It's okay to tell me. We are friends, aren't we?" "My son has a piano recital at six thirty tonight, but he knows I am a driver for an important man." Said the driver. "If I didn't have an important meeting to go to? Maria and I would be at the recital to watch your son. So, go and enjoy this with your family. I insist upon it." Said Engel. "Danke, herr minister." Replied the driver. Maria gripped Engel's hand and smiled at him as the driver drove away. Engel opens the door for Maria, and she says," You've made the driver a happy man, my dear. There is a deeper goodness in you. Just don't let the wrong people see you do that to someone that works for you." "Since you said that. It might not be a clever idea for you to go with me to the bank manager's house tonight at seven." Replied Engel. "Something has happened to the manager's daughter?" Maria asked. "Your insights are on point.

The manager told me that his daughter was raped by a gestapo agent." Said Engel. "This could be potentially dangerous grounds to be walking on." Replied Maria." I see you've brought something with you to cook. I smell raw meat and bread. I'll help you do this, and we can talk about it in the process. I am starving." Exclaimed Engel. The two go upstairs to Engels living space, and they began preparing the food to cook. Engel says, "I've been walking on dangerous grounds for centuries." Maria looks at Engel and says, "I know you've been around for an exceedingly long time, but for centuries? There is something about you that I cannot unlock. It's as if I can only see you as Hans Engel. A German legend born on a battlefield of the great war. What am I missing Engel?" "Let's something to eat and I'll explain it all to you." Replied Engel. Maria said, "I don't know if I can wait that long." The two finished making dinner and sat down at the table. Maria takes Engel's hand and bows her head. Maria says a prayer over the food and closes the prayer by saying "In Jesus's name, amen." Maria's body became rigid as she squeezed Engel's hand harder.

In Maria's mind, images began to flash quickly in front of her. She is seeing all the people, places, and time periods that Engel Stern had been. She sees one last scene being played out. She relaxes her grip, raises her head, and opens her eyes. "I saw you with Jesus. I saw the real face of Jesus." exclaimed Maria. She becomes emotional and says," It wasn't your fault. I have proof that it isn't your fault. Do you have a Bible?" "I don't know what you are talking about." Replied Engel. "I am so overwhelmed right now. I don't know which question I should ask you first. There are so many. After we have dinner, we will go to my apartment. I have a Bible there. The one I have is a banned book. All works that relate to the original, have been indoctrinated to follow the Aryan propaganda machine." Engel sticks a piece of meat in his mouth, takes a couple of chews and swallows. He wipes his mouth with a cloth and says, "Every situation that I have been put in, has had a bad ending. Let's not hurry to speed things up."

Maria takes a piece of bread and says, "I'm having dinner with a man that was at the last supper with Jesus. Not just any man, but an apostle." "A cursed man that regrets every day because of what I did." Says Engel. Maria could hardly eat and ask Engel questions throughout the dinner. Each question always ended with a yes from Engel. "Please can we stop now? This is all very painful to me." Asked Engel? Maria kissed his hand and replied, "Yes." Maria's brain was spinning with questions that she wanted desperately to ask. They finish dinner and Engel helps Maria wash the dishes. As Engel places the dishes on the drying rack he says, "Are you talking about the Torah being the same as the Bible?" "I'm talking about a book that documents your fellow apostles as well as the same material extracted from the Hebrew Torah." Answered Maria. "With this latest information about me. Does this not question your faith? In these guides you are in contact with?" Asked Engel."

This evening's experience made me solid believer in the gospels and has forced me to rethink about what I'm doing." Replied Maria. "Do you mean what you are doing with me? Asked Engel. "No! I feel closer to you now than ever before. I am talking about how the regime is using me to further their cause. They want something that can kill on a massive scale and use it to gain power over nations." exclaimed Maria. "Every place in time that I've been. Man has been killing each other with every means of weaponry imaginable. Power is an addictive disease and there is only one cure." Said Engel. "What is the cure my darling?" Asked Maria. "The cure is when the great creator of everything brings everything to an end." Replied Engel. "The creator does bring it to an end according to the passages in Revelations contained in the Bible. We will go to my apartment, and I will show you. After we visit the bank manager's home, or have you forgotten?" Said Maria. Engel replies by saying, "No. I haven't forgotten. I will need you to sit with her parents while I get her to relive every moment. Don't worry. She won't remember how I pulled the information from her."

Maria says," You are using an extremely powerful hypnosis method. You had Himmler's guards under your command, and they didn't even know it. It's direct eye to eye contact, isn't it? "I don't know what hypnosis is. I am forcing my will upon the person or with eye contact." Replied Engel. "Amazing! Now, here's something for you to ponder. Why would the devil be walking around in the flesh, and have Judas Iscariot in Germany now?" asked Maria. Engel looked at his watch and said, "I'll try and put something in perspective when we get back." Engel locks the door of his upstairs apartment, and they proceed downstairs into the bank's operating floor. Engel unlocks the door, opens it, and sees a military staff car parked in front of the bank. As Maria exits the bank, Engels locks the door, and the driver of the staff gets out. Maria and Engel wait to see what happens. The driver of the staff car walks up to Engel and says, "Herr General wishes to see you Herr Minister." Engel approaches the staff car as the driver opens the door. Out steps General Wolfstein. "Can I offer you two a ride somewhere?" asked General Wolfstein.

"We appreciate the gesture Herr general. We are out just for walk. Maria made a large meal for us, and we are getting some exercise." Answered Engel. "Just get in the auto. I have something important to tell you both." Said General Wolfstein. The driver opens the door, and we get in the backseat with the general. The driver closes the door and gets back in the driver seat. "Shall I drive down the street herr General?" Asked the driver. "Just drive until I tell you to stop." Ordered the General. The auto pulled out into the street and the general said, "I just want to tell you both that Maria's apartment and phone has listening devices in it. The gestapo is a very paranoid organization. I'm telling you this because you'll need to be careful about what you talk about. Himmler had his eyes on Maria before you showed up herr Hans Engel, I mean Herr Stern." "Does Himmler work for you?" Asked Engel. "In a sense he does. He is jealous of you because you hold strong favor with Adolf. Himmler took offense to the parlor trick you pulled in the restaurant. I got a message from a little bird that Himmler wants to have you investigated.

I slammed the door on that action after having a talk with Adolf." Answered the general. "Do you have a question for me? Maria?" asked the general. A nervous Maria said, "You probably already know what I'm about to ask you. Don't you?" "The answer is yes! I am the prince of darkness, the first angel, Lucifer, but here I am General Wolfstein. You already know who the man is sitting next to you and his unusual predicament during certain moon phases. Speaking of that predicament, I've found you a safer place to be locked up than the bank. It wouldn't be good if your bank employee showed up early to find you in rare form. It would be to both your advantages if you were married. Of course, I wouldn't be able to attend a church wedding. To make it a solid event, one of you could ask Adolf, I mean the Fuhrer to officiate it. You are supposed to do a personal reading for him aren't you?" "Yes, but we don't know when this will occur." Answered Maria. The general said, "Driver, stop the car here. This is your employee's home, isn't it? "Yes." Answered Engel. "Let me embarrass Himmler instead of you. The gestapo agent will be taken care of. Let me handle it. Just tell the girl's father that the gestapo agent will disappear. That's all you need to tell him okay." Said the General.

The driver opens the door for Engel and Maria. "Danke general" Replied Maria. "Ja! Ja! "Answered the general. The driver closed the door, got into the driver's seat, and drove away. Maria and Engel were looking at each other in shock over what just happened. "Did the devil just do us a favor?" asked Maria. "It seems that his focus is on a larger scheme than us." Replied Engel. Engel took maria's hand and walked up to the door of the house. Engel was about to knock on the door, and the door opened by a joy filled face of Engel's employee. "Welcome to my home. Please. Come in." Exclaimed Klaus Burkhalter. Maria walked in first as Engel followed. Klaus's wife stepped forward and took Engel's hand and kissed it. Maria placed her hand on Klaus's wife shoulder and said," It is going to be fine, Ava." Mrs. Burkhalter wipes the tears from her eyes and joyfully says, "Of course! You would know my name. You're Maria Orsic. Please! Sit down while I get something for you to drink." "Don't go to the extra trouble for us. We just finished eating and drink a short while ago." Said Engel. "Please, just one drink. I'm the one that needs it. When I saw the auto in front of our home? I thought it was the gestapo coming in. Once I saw Minister Stern step out, my heart started beating again." exclaimed Klaus. Engel told Klaus and his wife to relax and sit down. Klaus and his wife complied with Engel's reply and sat down together on a couch facing Engel and Maria. "Is your daughter upstairs in her room?" Asked Engel. "Yes!" Answered Klaus. "Do you mind If I go up and talk to her?" Asked Engel. "Our daughter Elsa's character hasn't been the same since the incident. I pray that your visit can help her. Yes! by all means herr minister.

Her room is the first one on the right." Said an emotional Ava. "I'll only be a few moments with her, and I'll bring her with me." Said Engel. Engel walked up the stairs and his senses already knew where the daughter was. Engel gently knocks on the door and says, "Elsa, I am Engel Stern. May I come in for a moment?" A female voice answers by saying, "Yes! Herr Minister." Engel slowly opens the door and closes it behind him. He sees a young girl sitting on her bed facing the opposite wall. "Don't look at me! I'm hideous!" exclaimed Elsa. "I've seen hideous things and I promise that you won't scare me away. Can I sit with you? Asked Engel. "If you must?" She replied. Engel walked over and sat down beside Elsa. Elsa continued to face the wall and Engel reached out with his right hand saying, "Elsa, I am Engel Stern." The nervous teenager turns to face Engel and takes his hand. As she makes eye contact with Engel, Engel tells her to relax. He feels the tension released from the young girl. Engel sees the damage done by a fist strike and inside it makes him angry. "I want you to tell me if the gestapo agent had someone else with him?" Asked Engel. "There were two men. They have been watching us before I was raped. Watching my friends and I for at least a week." Replied Elsa.

Engel wants to erase the whole terrible incident from her memory, but an idea springs forth. "Elsa. When you go downstairs and shake hands with Maria. All of your bruises, the violations done to your body will be healed. All that you'll remember is we had a nice talk about you getting a job at the bank after school. You will tell your friends that you shook hands with Maria Orsic, and you were healed. Close your eyes, and when I tell you to open them. I want to see a smile on your beautiful face." Elsa closes her eyes and Engel says, "You may open your eyes, Elsa." Elsa opens her eyes and reveals an innocent smile to Engel. Engel says, "I want you to meet someone famous." He takes her by the hand and leads her downstairs. They get to the bottom of the stairs and Engel asked Maria to come over to meet Elsa. Maria stood up and walked over to them. "Shake hands with Maria Orsic or should I say my soon to be wife." Said Engel.

When Maria shook hands with Elsa, she felt something happen. Maria saw that Engel was still holding Elsa's left hand and saw the bruising leave the child's face. "I am glad to finally meet you, Elsa. Elsa, did you hear what I think I heard. Were you in on Engel's marriage proposal?" Said an excited Maria. Elsa's mother saw her child's face and immediately said, "Elsa! Look in the mirror. Go look!" Elsa ran to the nearest mirror and saw a face without any trace of violence inflicted. The child ran to Maria and began hugging her and thanking her. Elsa's parents were crying tears of joy. Maria kissed Engel and said "Normally, a person has an engagement ring in their pocket for such an occasion. Since tonight is a special night, I'll accept the proposal without a ring." Engel said," I'll take you shopping for a ring tomorrow." Engel takes Maria's hand and kisses it. The next moment, Engel turns his attention to the parents, and tells them that he will take care of the gestapo situation." Before we go. I told Elsa in our conversation, that I would ask her parent's permission to let her work part time at the bank part time. She would assist me in minor clerical work. This of course is all pending on Elsa returning to school tomorrow and following through about we discussed. No one at her school knows about the gestapo incident unless Elsa told her friends." Said Engel.

"I only told my parents, and I was ashamed to tell them. I made no mention to my friends about it, because it would bring shame onto my family and the fear of what the gestapo could do. I was in such a state of feeling of total despair. I thought of taking my life." Said a tearful Elsa as she lovingly hugged Engel and Maria. "Herr Minister Stern. Let me drive the two of you where-ever you wish. Let me get my identification, my keys and we'll be on our way." Remarked Klaus. Engel reached into his jacket, finding out that he left his identification at his apartment. Engel agreed with his employee's courteous suggestion. The bank manager quickly gathered his things and led the couple to his auto. On the way back into the city. Maria asked Klaus to stop at her apartment to retrieve some items. Klaus obliges her request and stops at her apartment. Engel waits patiently as Maria hurries into her apartment. Maria grabs some fresh clothes and a pair of shoes. She looks for the Holy book and it isn't there. She searches and looks at the overall appearance of her apartment, to see if anything has changed. She places her things in a leather bag, locks the door and heads back to the auto. Engel see a distraught look on her face and ask if everything okay? She nods her head and tells Klaus to drop them off at the bank.

The auto moves forward towards the center of the city and stops in front of the bank. Klaus expresses gratitude to both Maria and Engel for coming to his home for his daughter. Engel and Maria exit the auto and wave goodbye to Klaus. Engel unlocks the door as they go inside and locks the door behind them. Before Maria could open her mouth, Engel tells her the book isn't there." When the general showed up. He already knew something was happening. I believe what you've told me about what the book says. He just doesn't want me to see it in writing. He has an innate ability to show up out of nowhere. All I can say is that he's evil and a master at manipulating people. Let's go upstairs and have some wine and relax." Maria hugs Engel and says," I love you no matter what happens." They walk upstairs to Engel's apartment. They begin taking off their shoes and getting into a more relaxed state." Maria, free will got me in trouble a long time ago and I made a selfish mistake. I only thought of myself and when I realized my mistake, it was too late, and I took my life. My teacher came to me and told me to ask for forgiveness." Maria said," You were probably the first to witness his resurrection. What did you say to the Lord?" "I said how can you forgive me? When I cannot forgive myself. My teacher said it is never too late to ask, but you truly must mean it from the heart.

I know that it works because, it worked for Jean D' Arc." Said Engel. "You mean Joan of Arc? You knew Joan of Arc?" asked Maria. "I don't know of this Joan of Arc. I knew Jean D' Arc and I saw her being led to be burnt at the stake. I should've stayed away from her as the dark master asked me to. He knew I would not listen. She was a true messenger of God, and she became tainted with evil because of me." "You're telling me that she turned to witchcraft because of you?" Maria asked. "I don't know of this word witchcraft meaning, if it means she had a lust to consume blood of the living. Then she had witchcraft." Answered Engel. Maria says, "Can I fix you a drink? I need one." Engel tells her yes. Maria goes to the cabinet and pours two glasses of brandy and hands a glass to Engel. Maria sat down at the table across from Engel and said, "Jean wasn't a witch. She would be one of the first undocumented vampires in history. A vampire is supposedly a legend made famous by Bram Stoker in a novel called Dracula. A vampire is something that isn't living flesh and must drink the blood of the living to continue its existence. History painted her as a witch, or I should say that the church in France deemed her that distinction.

Did you love her Engel?" Engel reaches across the table and takes Maria's hand and says, "She was pregnant with our child the day she died. I loved her so much that I was able to help her get redemption before she was taken. She never felt the flames and her soul was washed clean." Maria said, "She asked for forgiveness and was redeemed? How do you know that she was forgiven?" Engel replied," I saw the change from a blood lust creature to the face of innocence. It was instant and it wasn't me that redeemed her. I don't have that kind of power." Maria began tearing up and said, "You kept her from going to Hell. I am sure that didn't please your boss. You told her how to get redeemed. I felt the power go through me when you healed the girl tonight. There is power of good in you. That is what the Lord Jesus saw in you. He saw something bigger than just the man." "I just know that wherever the dark master places me. Something always happens. Most of the time I do something that angers him, and he hurls me through time and drops me in the middle of a shit storm. If it wasn't for you. I'd just soon be let loose and kill the dark master's puppets, plus anyone else that got in the way. I believe that's the reason why the dark master wants me away from downtown Berlin. He doesn't want me to see something that would set me off." Maria could see the rage building in Engels demeanor and quickly changes the subject. "What time are you getting off from work tomorrow? My darling Engel." asked Maria. Engel gazes into Maria's eyes and he smiles. "Since you are staying the night with me of course.

The jewelry store won't be open until nine, the same time the bank opens for customers. You can make a grand entrance downstairs at nine thirty. You may even witness the bank manager shed tears of joy at just seeing you. You represent something more than a soothsayer. You are a healer now. Then I'll take the healer by the hand and we'll go to the jewelers." Said Engel. Maria walks over to Engel and takes him by the hand and leads him to the bedroom. Engel leans against the wall and takes off his socks. He watches as Maria undresses, and she ties up her long flowing hair. A vision of Maria with shorter hair flashed before his eyes. Engel rubs his eyes and Maria asked, "Does looking at me make your eyes hurt?" "I guess one of the things the dark master told me is happening. I haven't killed and eaten a human since I've met you. I will start to age and not look like a thirty- eight, year old man anymore. Will you still love me if I looked like a thousand-year-old man?" Exclaimed Engel. "You mean two thousand years old." Replied Maria. "No matter the number. I know a few people I would like to kill and enjoy doing it." Said Engel. "It could be the effects of the healing you did to young Elsa. I know what will get your mind off this useless worry." Said Maria. Maria pushed Engel back on the bed and began pulling off Engels trousers.

She climbed on top of Engel and began grinding her body against him. The lights are still on, and Engel watches Maria's beautiful breast bounce up and down, as he glides inside her. He can't help but wonder why he saw that vision and why now. Maria moans sounds of ecstasy as the thrust quickens until both are satiated. "That didn't feel like a two- thousand, year old man at all. How about a cigarette and some brandy before we go to sleep? It will help you relax and go to sleep." asked Maria. "Just a little brandy for me." Answered Engel. Maria walked to the kitchen, grabbed two small glasses, poured the brandy into them, and lit herself a cigarette, as she returned to the bedroom. Engel had gotten up and cleaned himself up and returned to bed. "Why did you wash yourself off for? What if I wanted you again before I go to sleep?" exclaimed Maria. "Even an immortal, needs rest my dear plus, there is always tomorrow morning." Replied Engel. Engel takes the glass of brandy and takes a sip instead of just gulping it down. He lets Maria enjoy her cigarette and watches her with patient eyes.

Their night comes to a close when Maria puts out her cigarette, swallowed down the brandy and sets the glass on the nightstand. Engel has gulped down his brandy and turned off the lamp near the bed. Maria kisses Engel and says," Will you love me any differently once we are married?" "What a silly question to ask? Of course not. How can it be any difference? Replied Engel. "I'm the mistress of the Minister of Finance for now. The intrigue will be gone. don't you think?" asked Maria. "My life is already complicated enough as it is. Intrigue as you call it. Means trouble down the road and I don't want us taking a shortcut to get there. Besides, you're the clairvoyant that is supposed to see it coming before it happens. Right? Asked Engel. "I see myself being the beautiful bride of the Minister of Finance, and we will be untouchable because of you, my darling." Said Maria. Engel kisses maria good night, settles his head in the pillow and closes his eyes. Engel drifts off to sleep as he listens to the calming sounds of Maria's breathing. Engel finds himself between two planes, he's not dreaming and not awake, and also not alone.

A long, forgotten voice says, "We saw how you healed that child without touching her." "I don't need to draw that kind of attention to myself. Was it you that sent me that vision, messenger?" Asked Engel. "Do you remember how Jean looked when you first met her? She had a natural beauty before she became corrupted by the evil one. Maria felt the power surge threw her as you healed the child." Said the messenger. "You're telling me that Maria has made a pact with the evil one?" Asked Engel. "She has not, but even the lamb was tempted. The vision you saw is perhaps a future scene in that which I am not permitted to reveal. There are things happening in Germany that have been hidden from you. Just remember who you are and where you came from. Now sleep and I'll be seeing you later." Said the messenger. Engel had many questions but did not get to ask. Engel had the most restful night's sleep that he could remember. Most of his dreams were filled with the horror of what he had done as the creature. He gets up before the alarm clock goes off, turns off the alarm, and quietly slips into the kitchen. Maria is still sleeping, and he decides to make breakfast.

On the other side of Berlin, a phone rings at the Fuhrer's residence. The housekeeper answers the phone." Guden tag. Can I help you?" "This is General Wolfstein. Is the Fuhrer awakened yet?" asked the General. "Nein. The Fuhrer is still sleeping. Can I take a message?" asked the house- keeper. "Tell the Fuhrer to call me at my hotel room after he has awakened. I have something important to discuss with him. Heil Hitler!" exclaimed the General and he hung up the phone. At the Burkhalter home, the family is still overwhelmed by the miracle from the night before. Elsa can't wait to get to school to tell her friends about Maria's visit to her house. Her father said that he would ask his boss if he could get off early to pick her up after school. Elsa made no qualms about it. She didn't want another incident with the gestapo.

Later that morning, General Wolfstein receives a phone call. "Good Morgan! Herr General. My housekeeper tells me you tried to call me this morning. How can I help my favorite General?" asked the Fuhrer. "Good morgan to you mein Fuhrer! I heard some disturbing news yesterday from the Minister of Finance. One of his employee's daughter was raped by a gestapo agent as she was going home from school. The gestapo's name is Erlich Weiss. I know his name because you know, I know things. If the girl had been Jewish? We wouldn't be having this conversation." Said the general. "I will make an inquiry with Himmler concerning this. I am outraged that this happened to one of our own people. Thank you general for bringing this to my attention." Replied the Fuhrer. "On a lighter note, mein Fuhrer, Engel Stern has asked Maria Orsic to marry him. They would be overjoyed if you would officiate the marriage. They haven't given me a date, but I am asking you as a favor." Replied the General. "I would be honored to do so." Replied the Fuhrer and told the general to let him know the date in order to make proper plans. "Danke, Mein Fuhrer and auf wiedersehen." Replied the general.

The Fuhrer quickly phoned Himmler and was furious about the incident and asked Himmler what he intends to do about. Himmler quickly told the Fuhrer that he would find the underlying cause of the incident and would have it taken care of. Before he could tell the Fuhrer goodbye, the phone went dead. Himmler calls the gestapo headquarters and begins asking questions." Who was with Erlich Weiss when the girl was raped? Asked Himmler. The head of the gestapo headquarters did not have an answer for Himmler and an angered Himmler wants answers today. Himmler hangs up on the gestapo. The gestapo sent an agent down to the bank. "Can someone direct me to the Minister of Finance?" asked the gestapo agent. The bank manager became nervous at this and took him to his boss's office. "I sorry to disturb you herr minister. But the gestapo insisted on seeing you." Said Burkhalter. "Engel replied by saying. "You may leave herr Burkhalter, I will handle this. Please close the door behind you."

The gestapo agent approached the minister's desk and demanded the name of his employee for interrogation. Engel stood up and said, it happened to my employee's daughter and that means she is my responsibility. My question to you is what you are going to do about it." The gestapo agent became angry and pounded Engels desk and saying, "Do you think you have more power than the gestapo?" In a quick movement, Engel grabbed the gestapo agent by the throat and began squeezing. "Who has the power now?" Asked Engel. The gestapo agent struggled to free himself and took out his pistol and fired a shot into Engel. The bullet went into Engels stomach and Engel threw the gestapo agent against the wall. Knocking the gun from the agent's hand. Engel picks up the gun and points it at the agent's head. Burkhalter rushed into the room to see what happened after hearing the gunshot.

Gestapo agents standing outside the bank came rushing in bearing their weapons. Engel told the gestapo agent to tell his men to drop their weapons or they will see their captain with a hole in his head. The gestapo dropped their guns at their side and Engel looked at the gestapo on the left and said," So you are the one that raped an innocent girl? A German citizen I might add." The gestapo agent raised his weapon at Engel and said," She refused me, and I took what I wanted. Just like I'm going to take your life." Before the gestapo's finger could squeeze the trigger, Engel shot the gestapo in the head. He held the rest at gunpoint. The frantic captain said, "There will be no more shooting, the investigation ends now." The gestapo captain tells the remaining guard to wait outside for him. Engel places the gun on his desk and the captain sits down in a chair. The captain says, "I can fix this but, first you must tell me, how did you know that Erlich would be with me?" Engel said, "I saw the smug look on Erlich's face and he gave himself away.

He didn't care if I shot you in the head and your other guard didn't go for his weapon. "How can you fix this captain?" Asked Engel. I'll say in the report that Erlich shot you and I'll threaten the guard with his sudden disappearance. I will forget about you trying to strangle me if you'll forgive me for shooting you?" "All is forgiven." Said Engel as he shakes the captain's hand and gave his gun back to him. The captain said, I'll take you to the hospital and have the body removed from the bank." The captain opens the office door and in rushes Maria and the bank manager. "You've been shot! Who shot you? asked a frantic Maria. "The dead rapist that's bleeding on my floor." Replied Engel. The captain told everyone to back away as he placed his arm around Engel and helped him to his auto outside. Engel Tells Maria to stay at the bank and he would be back to go to the jewelers. On the way to the hospital, the captain explains his guard's fate if he didn't comply with his wishes. Engel is taken into the hospital and a surgeon removes the bullet and stitches up the entry hole. Engels wakes up in a hospital bed with Maria sitting in a chair next to the bed.

Maria tells Engel that the surgeon said no vital organs were damaged and he suggested a day or two of bed rest. There's a knock on the door and in walks General Wolfstein. "Well, it seems that everything has been swept under the rug so to speak. How you were able to shoot the rapist with the captain's gun, I don't want to know. I do know that Himmler isn't the type to just forget about something like this." Says the General. Tell Himmler to come and see me and I'll put one in his head. Better yet, tell Himmler to come and visit me on a full moon. I haven't eaten a human in a while, and I am starting to age." Exclaimed Engel. "Keep your voice down. You never know whom will walk in. Look at me. I strolled in here and you had no idea that it is going to be me." exclaimed the General. "I had an idea. It would be you or Himmler. Lucky for Himmler it is you." Replied Engel. "What do you mean by that? Said an agitated General. "If Himmler had came in here making threats? What I am going to tell him, that will make him sleep with the lights on til his dying days." Replied Engel. "What? You are going to tell him who I really am? Said the General as he laughs at his comment. "No! Someone worse that Adolf Eichmann recognized. Hans Engel of course.

I saw the look in the gestapo captain's face when I didn't even flinch when he shot me. He was unnerved at how I didn't react to being shot. He is probably questioning himself about how it happened. I doubt the captain will bring up those particulars. You know what? I feel fine. I'll put on my clothing and walk out of here." Boasted Engel. "No, you won't You're still bleeding." Replied the General. Engel lifted his head and saw blood oozing through the sheet. The General pointed his finger at Engel and said, "Don't try me? You know I always get the last say. I will get the doctor and Maria; you need to make sure he stays here per the doctor's instruction." "Yes, General." Replied Maria. The General left the room and Maria went to the door to look outside before she said anything. Maria began crying and pleading with Engel in a subdued voice, not to anger the General. Engel assured Maria that he would comply with her wishes. Within minutes, a doctor and his nurse came into the room. The doctor removed the bandage on his stomach and rolled Engel over on his side, to look to see if the bandage was leaking at the exit wound. The doctor told the nurse to get a cart and said, "I need to get you back to the operating room to see what is causing this leakage. Herr Minister Stern." "Do what you must. You are the doctor." Replied Engel.

While the nurse was gone. The doctor checked Engel's pulse rate with his watch. He felt Engel's head for a fever. The nurse arrived with a cart and placed Engel on the cart and rolled him out into the hallway. Maria said," I'll be waiting for you Engel." Engel was rushed into the operating room and was given a sedative to put him to sleep. The doctor did a full exploration and found nothing that would explain the blood loss. The doctor stitched the wounds closed and the nurses bandaged the areas again. A couple of hours had passed, and Engel is back in his room. A groggy Engel opens his eyes and sees Maria smiling at him. Her smile widens and reveals she has fangs. A startled Engel said," No! Not again! Maria grabs Engel's hand and says," You were having a bad dream. The operation is over. Relax." Engel rubs his eyes and focuses on Maria and saw that she is normal. "What did you see darling?" asked Maria. "Perhaps a warning to me to what could happen.

I just hope that you haven't made a deal with a certain someone." Said Engel. "I told you, that I did nothing of a sort of thing like that!

I am cursed enough with this gift I was born with. Which I didn't ask for." exclaimed Maria. Engel squeezed her hand lovingly and said, "When I get out of here. We will go and get you that ring I promised." Maria leaned over and kissed him and told him to just rest. Engel told Maria to go to his apartment and get some rest for herself. He told her that he would be fine. "Are you sure? You won't get into any trouble while I'm gone, will you?" asked Maria. "I'll be fine. I promise I'll be good." Replied Engel. Maria left the room and Engel wanted to tell Maria something else that was on his mind. He wanted to tell Maria that they must find a way to get out of Germany. Yet, he stopped himself knowing that wherever he went to, the dark one would find him, and punish him or take it out upon Maria. Maria left the confines of the hospital and was standing on the sidewalk hailing a cab. She sees a cab coming toward her on her left. The auto is about fifty meters or so away, and before the cab could close the distance, a military staff pulls up. Maria's initial thought is, she is about to be assassinated by the SS or the gestapo.

The back door on the staff car opens and General Wolfstein gets out. The general says," Relax and get in the auto. No harm will come to you." Nervously Maria complies and says," Danke Herr General." Maria gets into the staff car and the general closes the door. The driver pulls away, as the general tells his driver to go to the bank. Maria tells the general that the bank isn't open now and she doesn't have a key. Then she quickly recants her statement by saying, "Forgive me General, for being shortsighted for a moment. You don't need a key, do you?" The general says," The gestapo captain's subordinate couldn't keep his mouth shut as he was told. We are changing the scene of the supposed crime, so to speak." The general takes from his coat pocket a P08 pistol, a spent shell casing and an envelope, tells Maria to place it in her purse.

The car arrives at the front of the bank and the general says, "Place your hand on the doorknob and walk into the bank. The alarm will be disabled, and you will place the pistol the envelope in Engels desk drawer, drop the shell casing on the floor and quickly return back to the auto. Now go before any vehicles show up." Maria opens the car door, grips the doorknob to the bank, turns it and the door opens. She quickly closes it and places the items as instructed by the general, then looks out of the bank window as the general motions continue. She closes the door, and she hears the locks engage. She quickly jumps into the staff car and the driver sped away. Maria takes a deep breath, and the general tells her to relax. He says," I'm going to visit Engel after we drop you off at your apartment. Don't worry about this. I'm the inventor of distraction." The staff car arrives at Maria's apartment. She thanks the general and bids him a good evening.

She goes into her apartment, locks the door, sits on her favorite chair, and starts crying. Maria is crying because she is in way over her head. She just did the devil's bidding for him. She's not only afraid for herself, but for Engel. At the hospital Engel has been visited. The general has spoken to Engel about the weapon in the desk drawer of Engel's office. "The gestapo captain's subordinate spoke about the incident to his girlfriend. The girlfriend couldn't keep her mouth shut and it got to Heinrich Muller. He is an underling of Himmler." Said the general. "So, I guess I'll be marched against a wall and shot by firing squad, and I disappear right?" Stated Engel. "If this happened to someone else other than you. The answer would be a definite yes. I happen to know that Muller and Himmler have been stealing money and stockpiling it and it isn't in the bank. I have in my pocket two separate documents from Muller and Himmler withdrawing considerable amounts of money from your bank. They have been skimming from the war effort. They didn't make the withdrawals themselves, but the sent subordinates to do it.

You will be out of the hospital tomorrow, and the following day that is when they will come to you. There is a photocopy of the two documents in an envelope in your desk. The envelope will be addressed to the Fuhrer Adolf Hitler and signed by you. Herr Burkhalter will be instructed to take the envelope to the Reichstad as soon as the Gestapo arrives. You'll need to instruct your driver to park on the other side of the street to take Burkhalter. Burkhalter will be told to wait for you or a phone call from you in 20 minutes after leaving the bank. If asked by the Fuhrer's staff, what is he waiting on? He tells them that he is waiting for you the Minister of German Finance to meet him there. If the phone to the central office of the Reichstad doesn't get through to

Herr Burkhalter? He delivers the documents to the hand of the Fuhrer and to only the Fuhrer."" So, you want me to make them sweat a little right? I look at my watch in front of them and after fifteen minutes or so I divulge the existence of the letter. Of course, they will try and send someone to head off the courier and they dare not tie up the phone line trying to call.

It all sounds feasible, but it is the what ifs happening. That can mess up such a delicate plan." Replied Engel. The general said, "You haven't outlived your usefulness to me yet. There won't be any what ifs. You only have to pay attention to your watch. I see what you see is all that matters. Get some rest and you'll be as strong as ever tomorrow." The general leaves Engel's room and Engel knows that the dark one isn't happy about having to clean up a mess that he created by shooting the gestapo rapist. He knows that this will be brought up as leverage at a later date. Deep down inside he only wishes that a firing squad could extinguish him from this existence. The next day, the doctor releases Engel that afternoon and he is taken to his apartment at the bank by his driver along with Maria. It is an hour before closing time at the bank when they arrive. A throng of employees welcome back their boss especially Herr Burkhalter, the bank manager.

CHAPTER 17

ENGEL BLACKMAILS HIMMLER

Engel is fully healed but must appear still recovering. Burkhalter asked to assist Engel up the stairs and Engel complies. Maria walked up ahead to open the door with Engel's key. Burkhalter said, "The gestapo has picked up my daughter. I should've kept my mouth shut and it wouldn't have gone this far. She could be dead for all I know. My wife is grief stricken and I tell her that she's alive to calm her. It is my fault that you got shot and now my daughter is missing." This infuriates Engel and he smashes a glass curio against the wall. He then remembers what is in his desk. He tells Burkhalter what to expect to happen to happen once the gestapo comes in. Engel says, "You daughter had better be alive and well for their sakes tomorrow or there will be more death." Herr Burkhalter burst into tears and begged that Engel didn't do anything else. Maria told Burkhalter to take her hand and she took Engel's hand. She closed her eyes and said," Everyone be calm and relax. I am looking for Elsa." Maria sees that Elsa is being held in a room and has been beaten up. Maria says that Elsa is alive but doesn't say anything about her condition. She releases their hands and Burkhalter wipes the tears from his face. Engel tells Burkhalter to keep the envelope safe. "More than the fate of Elsa rest in that piece of paper." Replied Engel.

Burkhalter said his goodbyes as he exited the room and went to Engel's office to retrieve the envelope from his desk. Burkhalter prepares for the bank's closing of the day. The vault is locked, all the days tallies have been accounted for. The employees began filing out the door as Burkhalter stands at the door to activate the alarm and lock the doors for the night. As the bank is shutting down, Engel asks Maria what did she really see? "I saw a battered and bruised and alive young girl. She isn't the only one kept there." Answered Maria. She then proceeded to tell Engel that she had been instructed to place the envelope and pistol in his desk. "I know. You don't have to explain.

He came to my room at the hospital. "Said Engel. "I'm scared!" exclaimed Maria as she started crying. "It is too late for me to be scared of anything. The day I took my life at the tree. I was ready to face the full brunt of hell because of the betrayal I brought upon my teacher. For all I know, I could be experiencing hell on earth." Exclaimed Engel. Maria wiped tears as a thought splashed into her mind. "My love. Do you remember what you felt or saw after your heart stopped beating?" asked Maria. "I cannot recall a feeling or a vision during that moment. Everything after that point in time is memories that are tainted with more dreadful things than good. If you weren't here to give me a purpose, to look forward to waking up every day? I guess I would be bigger thorn in the dark master's side." Replied Engel. As Engel was removing his daytime attire, he lifted the bandage on his chest. The surgeon's stitching has been reclaimed by his body's regeneration and is barely noticeable.

He knows that the cycle of change will occur in a couple of days. He asked Maria to remove the bandage from his back and she was astonished by this. Maria said," The doctor would be shocked if he saw this. He is expecting you to return to him for the removal of the stitching." "What do you think would happen, if I ripped my shirt open. To reveal no evidence of the shooting to Muller & Himmler during their visit?" Asked Engel. "They will be shocked if you did that after you gave them the withdrawal statements. Their minds would be awash with questions it cannot answer. They may even think I healed you, since I healed Burkhalter's daughter." Jokingly remarked Maria.

"I'll see how this plays out tomorrow, but for now I am starving." Said Engel. Maria is already getting some cured sausage and cheese from the cupboard. Engel retrieves bread, wine, and glasses. He places the items on the table. Maria finished off the table with plates and flatware. Maria reaches for Engel's hand and blesses the food. She takes a drink of wine and says," Do think after you've made Hitler's henchman shit in their pants. You'll have time to take me ring shopping?" Said a laughing Maria. "In another life. Hans Engel would kill both and walk out wearing Himmler's uniform. That would spark a war between the German army and Hans Engel. I do plan on making you my wife instead of my mistress. So, with that being said our plans will not be detoured." Replied Engel. The two ate dinner, cleaned up the kitchen and retired for the night.

The morning came and Engel awakens before the alarm clock rings. He turns off the alarm and quietly gets out of bed without disturbing Maria. Engels mind was busy before going to sleep and is still playing out different scenarios about what the day may bring. He quietly gets dressed, goes into the bathroom shaves, and puts on a clean shirt. Maria awakens and walks to the entrance to the kitchen. "You are up early. did you get any sleep last night?" asked Maria. "It took a while before I got to sleep. As usual, my mind kept showing me different scenarios of what could happen today with the leaders of the gestapo." Answered Engel. Maria put on her robe and sat down at the table. Maria said," I could do a reading for you, but there isn't a need for it. Your instincts will tell you. Trust your instincts. You operate on a level that the normal human cannot comprehend. You are only three days away from the first cycle. Your senses are super heightened right now. Me telling you to relax isn't going to help. Maybe put some brandy in your coffee to take the edge off, would be my suggestion." Engel stops for a moment, places both hands on the counter and says, "You are right! I'm not the one that needs to be worrying about this. What could they do? Shoot me again?"

Maria and Engel laugh at his comment. Maria built a magnificent breakfast, they ate and laughed about how insignificant of the gestapo powers compared to Engel. As time ticked by, Engel saw that it was nearing the time for the bank manager to show up. Engel kissed Maria and told her that he is looking forward to ring shopping. Maria said," Take the pistol from your desk, place on top of your desk after you've given herr Burkhalter the papers in the envelope and give him his instructions once the gestapo arrives. They will begin to question in their minds the validity of the story told to them. Plus, it will show that you are ready for them. You'll know exactly what to do when the time comes. I love you Judas." Engel was surprised to hear from Maria his true name. He winked and proceeded down the stairs. He walked to the bank entrance and saw the bank manager through the barred glass windows. Engel went to his office and waited for the manager to complete the opening of the bank procedure.

The tellers, the bank loan officer, and other works at the bank, have settled into their normal job duties. Engel goes to his doorway and motions for herr Burkhalter to enter his office. The bank manager Herr Burkhalter walks into his boss's office and sees a pistol lying on the desk. "Don't worry herr Burkhalter. The pistol is another insurance policy that may be needed. Take this envelope and put it in your pocket. The instant you see the gestapo enter my office. I want you to go to the Chancellery and go to the Fuhrer's office. Tell the office guard that you will be waiting on me, the Minister of Finance to show in next fifteen minutes. I won't be coming, but instead I will call the office and ask for you. If there isn't a call past sixteen minutes? You are to hand deliver the envelope to the Fuhrer's hand and his hand only. Is that understood?" "Ja! Herr Minister." Replied Burkhalter. "The clock starts as soon as the gestapo gets here. I'll be looking at my watch and you should also. Timing is everything.

My driver will be parked across the street to take you. Now, go back to work and I am calling my driver now." Stated Engel. The nervous bank manager goes back to his desk and ponders about this situation. Engel calls his driver and tells him to park the staff car across from the bank. The driver acknowledged his boss's request and says that he will be there in a matter of minutes. Engel fidgets with his papers and journals on his desk, preparing himself for the heads of the gestapo to show up. Engel takes a cigarette from his pocket a lights it. A half hour goes by and two gestapo guards leading Muller and Himmler storm into Engel's office. The guards see the P08 pistol on the desk and immediately point their automatics at Engel. Himmler says, "Put your weapons down guards. The minister isn't holding the pistol." The guards react to Himmler's order and stop pointing their weapons at Engel. Engel says," The gun is merely for show besides, what I have to tell you and Muller could result in someone facing a firing squad. That someone won't be me. Are you sure you want me to talk in front of your guard dogs? It is a very damaging conversation plus I have documentation in my desk. I also have documentation waiting to be placed in the Fuhrer's hand. The clock is ticking gentlemen." Said a confident Engel.

Himmler barked at the guards to stand outside the door and Burkhalter is on his way to the chancellery. Muller walks up to the desk and says," What is this damaging report that you have? I demand that you reveal this, or I'll shoot you myself?" Engel opens the desk drawer, unfolds the two bank withdrawal statements in view of Himmler and Muller. Himmler looks at the paper and says, the money wasn't withdrawn by me." Engel says," Look where the money is withdrawn from and isn't that your personal accountant that did this Herr Himmler? Are you keeping money from the military treasury for your own safe at your home or your mistresses house? You've got about eight minutes to stop this? Whatever you call this action by storming in here on me this morning?" "What do you mean eight minutes?" screamed Muller. "Now it is seven minutes before I call the Fuhrer's office and ask for my manager to come to the phone. After those minutes. My manager will hand deliver an envelope to the Chancellor of Germany." "Make the call!" Ordered Himmler. Engel picked up the phone and called the chancellery. Engel prompted the operator to put him through to the office of the Fuhrer, telling the operator who is calling.

The air in the office is thick with anticipation and the Fuhrer's secretary answers. "Can I help you herr Minister?" "Would you give my manager herr Burkhalter this message. Tell him to return to the office and I'll have to set up another time to see the Fuhrer. Heil Hitler." Stated Engel as he hung up the phone. "What would stop us from killing you or your manager, once he gets back with the envelope?" barked Himmler. Engel slowly stood up from behind his desk, unbuttoned his shirt and opened it for Himmler and Muller to see. He even turned around and showed them his back. The blood drained from Himmler's and Muller's faces as they saw no evidence of a gunshot wound or the surgeon's handy work. Muller said," You were in the hospital because you were shot. I sent an agent to the hospital to enquire about this fact. I see no entry or exit wound. What is going here?"

As he looked at Himmler. Himmler took out his gun and pointed at Engel. Engel said, "Before you pull the trigger, you need to talk to Adolph." "The Fuhrer?" asked Muller. "Nein! Adolph Eichmann!" Answered Engel. "Tuck your shirt in and get your jacket. We will take you see Eichmann." Said Himmler. Muller gets the documents from Engels desk and stuffs them in his pocket. They exit Engels office as Himmler barks an order to his henchmen, to escort Engel to the waiting staff car. The bank manager arrives back at the bank and his subordinates tell him about what has transpired. As Burkhalter gets to the bottom of the staircase that leads to Engels apartment. He sees Maria locking the door with a key. Burkhalter waits for her at the bottom of the stairs. Maria says, "They took him, didn't they?" "Ja!" Answered Burkhalter. "We can only wait." Maria goes into Engel's office and sits down.

She tells herself that Engel will know what to do. The two staff cars park in front of the S.S. headquarters. The two gestapo guards walk behind Engel with their weapons drawn, as they enter the S.S. headquarters. An S.S. officer asked," What is the meaning of this intrusion?" Himmler looks at Muller and Muller says, "Take us to see Obersturmbann Fuhrer Eichmann. Now!" The S.S. officer led them to an office and told them to wait. The S.S. officer walks into the room shutting the door behind him. The officer explains to the secretary seated at the desk about the visitors waiting outside the door. The secretary picks up her phone and dials. She hears a voice answer and tells her boss that the heads of the gestapo are here. Her boss tells her to tell them to enter. She thanks her boss, hangs up the phone and conveys the message to the S.S. officer. The officer opens the door and tells the guards they must remain outside as Himmler, Muller and Engel go into the office.

Eichmann sees Engel and a chill runs down his spine. Eichmann looked at Himmler looked at him and said," Why have you brought the Minister of Finance to my office?" Muller said," Have you not heard what happened at the bank?" "I heard that the gestapo was looking to justify the raping of an innocent German girl and the rapist got what was coming to him." Sneered Eichmann. Himmler said," There were two shootings. The guard and the minister. The minister raised his shirt to us and there isn't any sign of a shooting nor the surgeon's handy work. The minister has threatened to blackmail Muller and myself with a document, and told us that you know who the minister really is?" A furious Eichmann stands up behind his desk and says," Open up your shirt and show me where the bullet entered, herr minister." Engel slowly unbuttons his shirt, opens it to reveal his bare skin. "You've got no evidence of such a claim. I don't see any trace of the bullet. What do you think would happen if the Fuhrer knew about this made-up fantasy of yours?

This man was born across the river from where our Fuhrer originated." Eichmann looked at Engel and said," What is the documents that these men say that you would use against them?" Engel said," Muller has the documents in his pocket. Show him the documents herr Muller. An angry Mueller pulls from his pocket, unfolds the pages, and slams them on Eichmann's desk. Eichmann leans forward, looks at the papers and smiles. Muller looks closely at the papers and there just withdrawal bank notes with no numbers, dates of entry or names on the documents. Himmler is shocked to his being as well as Muller. Muller pulls his side arm and places it against Engel's head and says, "Who in the hell are you?" Engel smiles replies," Der teufel. (The devil). Eichmann says," I suggest you take herr minister back to the bank before I have you two committed for insanity and sent to one of Himmler's special camps. Now get the hell out of my office. Snell!" Himmler, Muller, and Engel exit Eichmann's office. In a chair in the hallway sits General Wolfstein. The general gets up as Himmler and Muller acknowledge him. Engel gives a greeting to the general as he straightens up his clothing. The general says, "Has the gestapo been leaning on you herr minister?" "Nein, herr general." Answered Engel. The general tells the gestapo guards to take Engel back to the bank. Muller protests and says, "They don't work for you!"

"They do today! Replied the general. He told Muller to sit and wait as he led Himmler into Eichmann's office. Muller could only watch as his guards walked in front of Engel, leading out of the building. It wasn't long before Himmler came out and his demeanor is a complete change from moments ago. Muller asked his superior, "What do we do now, mein superior?" "Today, never happened as far as the minister or the conversation with Eichmann. There won't be any blackmail and this conversation is over. If you talk about this to anyone. I mean anyone. Your life is over. Are we clear on this matter?" "Ja! Ja!" Answered Muller as he followed Himmler to his staff car. Engel is dropped off in front of the bank by the gestapo guards. Engel walks in and is met by a relieved bank manager.

Engel is about to open his door and there is his beloved Maria. "I knew that you would be back. Tell me what happened on the way to the jewelers." exclaimed Maria as she showered him with kisses. Engel called his driver and the driver picked up Maria and Engel. "I intercepted a call from the Fuhrer today. He asked to speak to you first, and herr Burkhalter told the Fuhrer that I was close by. The Fuhrer is sending his staff car to us this afternoon. He is giving us a house, but he didn't come out and say it. I saw a vision in my mind's eye. Let me guess? General Wolfstein showed up today at the S.S. headquarters?" "Ja!" Answered Engel as he steered her off the subject. Engel's driver was given to him by General Wolfstein and didn't want to talk in front of him.

Engel told the driver to drop them off at the jewelers. The driver did as he was commanded and dropped off the couple. Maria takes Engel's hand as they stop on the sidewalk. Engel said," Instead of an engagement ring pick out the wedding ring." Engel's thoughts aren't really on the wedding ring. The dark master knew that Himmler and Muller were not going to go away quietly with the blackmail scheme. He was betting that Engel would use Eichman as leverage and they took the bait. The jeweler walked up asked Engel could he of service. Engel appeared to be staring at a blue precious stone, but he was looking past it. He was looking much deeper. "Engel. Do you see something that you like?" asked Maria. "I'm sorry. The stones in the case remind me of the stars in the night sky. My dear, today is your day and I want you to choose. Just remember. I don't want to have to rob my own bank to pay for it." Replied Engel. The jeweler then realizes who is standing before him. "Please forgive me herr Minister and let me be the first to congratulate you.

Are you looking for an engagement or a wedding ring today?" Stated the jeweler. Maria spoke up and said, "We are getting married by the Fuhrer." The jeweler said," I have something to show you. I'll be right back." The jeweler leaves the counter and comes back with a narrow, elongated box. He places it on the counter and opens it for the couple to see the contents. The box contained precious cut stones. Maria thanked the jeweler for viewing and said that she wants to keep things simple and not gaudy. "How much for this ring in the corner of the display case?" asked Maria. The jeweler slid open the door to the case and picked up the ring pointed out by Maria. "Is this the ring?" asked the jeweler. Maria looked at Engel and said," Yes!" Engel reaches for his belongings in his coat pocket and realizes that the gestapo took them. Maria tried on the ring, and it was a bit large and the jeweler asked Engel his ring size.

Engel did not know so, the jeweler fitted Engel's ring finger. The jeweler said that he would have the rings ready in a week's time. Engel asked the jeweler the price for the rings, and he said eight hundred marks for both rings. Engel told the jeweler to call the bank when the rings are ready. He would have the payment dropped off and the rings picked up. The jeweler was pleased with the agreement. The couple left the jewelers and got into the waiting automobile. The driver took them back to the bank. The couple exits the auto and before walking in, Engel stops walking and turns to Maria. "Maria, you must be truthful with me now. How long do I have before all of this is taken away from me again? Said Engel. Maria pauses for a second and says," Things fall apart for Germany in 1945." "We have five and a half years from now until everything turns to shit in Germany? Who else knows this information besides you, and probably the dark master?" Asked Engel.

"No one!" Said an upset Maria. "What else have you kept from me? I have kept nothing from you. I have no one to confide with that I trust except you." Said Engel. Maria told Engel that she had more to tell him once they get to his apartment. Engel says," Let's not go in just yet." He leads her away from prying customers entering or exiting the bank. They stop in front of a blank wall of bricks, that make up the façade of some architecture. Maria says," Before I met you. An expedition was sent to Antarctica and a discovery was made. The beings that I have been in contact with are there. Certain articles of information were given to the expedition that are very advanced technology. The scientist and engineers of Hitler's regime have made weapons based upon this new knowledge. Because of my abilities, I have been used to getting more technology without physically going back to Antarctica. The Germans were told to never return there by the beings from another world." What is this place called Antarctica? If they were told not to return? Why are they still communicating with you? I do not understand. Does this being have a name? "Asked Engel."

"Antarctica is a very cold and uninhabitable place. A place where man isn't supposed to be. I only communicate with one being called Ziel and sometimes I think that Ziel isn't telling me everything." Answered Maria. Engel chuckles manically and says, "This is all a ruse. The dark master has out done himself this time. The beings you speak of are not just from another world. They are the fallen ones. The same beings you speak of built the massive structures in Egypt." "You mean the pyramids and the sphinx were not built by the ancient Egyptians?" asked Maria. "I do not know what the pyramids or this sphinx are that you speak of. The dark master showed me these things on my way to Cairo and told me that his followers built it." Replied Engel. "That explains that some of the fallen ones survived the flood and now live in Antarctica. They gave the early German expedition just enough of technology allowed, to the Germans and were told never to return." Said Maria. "I am unsure of this word technology you speak of. Is it a gift of some sort? "Asked Engel. Maria swiftly replied by saying it was an evil gift of new and horrible knowledge. "I must ask you this question again, and you must be truthful about it. Did you make an agreement with General Wolfstein?" Asked Engel. "I told you. I did not make any deal or agreement with him. He did try to entice me to make a bargain and I refused. My ability to see him as what he truly is stopped me from being swayed. Believe me! He showed me things and for a brief moment, I almost fell for it. Something deep inside my being stopped me." Said Maria.

Engel hears people getting near their location and decides to continue talking in the apartment. They enter the bank, and the manager Herr Burkhalter greets them both with a smile and says, "Herr Minister. An officer came by looking for you earlier and gave me this number to pass along to you. " Engel told Maria to follow him into his office. Engel sat down and called the number. It rang twice until a voice said," This is the central office of the Chancellery. To whom am I speaking?" "This is the Minister of Finance, and I was instructed to call this number. Do you have a message for me?" Replied Engel. "Yes! Herr Minister. The Fuhrer sent one of his officers to the bank to see you. The Fuhrer would like to see you and Frau Orsic. I am sending a staff car to pick you both up. Are you at the bank?" asked the voice on the phone. "Yes! We are both here at the bank." Answered Engel. "Excellent! I will notify the Fuhrer of your visit. Heil Hitler!" Engel answered back Heil Hitler and put down the phone.

He turns to Maria and tells her that the Fuhrer is sending over a staff car to retrieve them and take them to the chancellery. "I think we will be getting a gift from the Fuhrer." Said Maria. "The dark master made mention of a wedding gift from the Fuhrer. Maria opens her purse, removes her compact, and applies fresh lip stick to her lips. Maria finishes and says," I want to look good in case we are going to be shot." "I don't think this is a sentencing." Replied Engel. "I guess we'll have to pick up on our conversation once we get back?" Said Maria. "I am worried about what's coming down the road and I'm not talking about the Fuhrer's staff car either." Stated Engel. "Do not worry my darling. I was only joking about us being shot. We are valuable, and you know this. Don't you? Said Maria. "We are more valuable if we aren't in the public eye." Said Engel. Maria stops looking in her small mirror and looks at Engel. "You are brilliant my love. They do not want us to be available to the public. They want sole access to us or should I say to you." Said Engel. Before Maria could utter a word.

There is a knock-on Engel's office door. "Come in! Stated Engel. A German officer entered the room and said, "The staff car is ready Herr Minister. The Fuhrer is waiting in the auto." "Let's not keep the Fuhrer waiting." Stated Engel as he and Maria followed the officer to the awaiting staff car. As the group approached the car, the officer opened the rear door for Maria and Engel. As Maria enters the car, she sees a smiling Adolph Hitler. The Fuhrer held out his hand and aided Maria into the car. "We are honored to be in your presence mein Fuhrer." Said Maria. After Engel sits down, the officer shuts the door and gets in the front seat next to the driver. The officer barks an order to the driver and the auto moves forward. Engel and Maria wait for the Fuhrer to initiate the conversation out of reverence for the Fuhrer's Authority. The Fuhrer says, "General Wolfstein has told me that you two wish for me to officiate the wedding. Have you two decided on a date yet?" "The jeweler said that he would have our rings ready in a week. Mein Fuhrer." Answered Engel.

"Wunderbar! This will give me a week to put things in place for the Minister of Finance and the Reich's most valuable psychic's wedding day." Exclaimed the Fuhrer. "We are just honored that you will be performing the ceremony mein Fuhrer. We are under your service and the fatherland mein Fuhrer." Said Maria. "I know you were not born a German, but you speak as if Germanic blood flows through your veins. As far as the wedding, the Chancellery won't have the trappings of any cathedral. It will be the wedding fitted to the best that the Reich can offer. "Said, the Fuhrer. Maria knows what occurs in two weeks and she chooses her next words carefully. "I know what you are going to ask next mein Fuhrer.

You are going to ask if we plan on going anywhere for our honeymoon?" Said Maria. The Fuhrer slaps his leg and says, "I was thinking about Obersalzberg! Let me offer you two my mountain retreat for a few days. What do you say?" "To say no to the Fuhrer could mean a firing squad without a cigarette." Replied Engel. The Fuhrer chuckles and says," To anyone else that refused me? Yes! I understand that you were shot, and you killed the rapist. Which tells me that you do not fear death, and you put others needs before your own. I chose wisely to give you the appointment of Finance Minister." Just as the Fuhrer was going to say something. The officer in the front seat says, "Excuse me mein Fuhrer. We are here." The car turns into a driveway and stops. The driver gets out and opens the door for the Fuhrer and the officer does the same for Engel and Maria.

A modestly sized home is facing the group. "This is my wedding gift to you. No more living in an upstairs apartment in a bank. No more opening the bank in the mornings. Let's go inside and look at your new home." said a gleeful Fuhrer. The Fuhrer's personal guard opened the door with a key. Engel and Maria followed the Fuhrer into the home. The front room was almost devoid of furnishings. There was a table and a high back chair. The Fuhrer's aide told us that the previous owner was an enemy of the Reich, and that he and his family have been relocated. Maria walked over to the hearth mantle and touched it. Engel took a nervous breath and the Fuhrer asked Maria did she feel something? "Juden banker!" Replied Maria. "Amazing!" said the Fuhrer. The Fuhrer told his aide to take the couple through the house. The Fuhrer sat down in the chair in the front room and waited for them to return. The aide toured the couple through the house and finalized the tour by showing Engel and Maria an empty wine cellar. The aid said, "Herr Minister you can start your own wine collection." Engel and Maria followed the Fuhrer's aide back up the stairs from the cellar. Engel closed the heavy wooden door and continued back to the front room of the house. "What do you think of your new home herr Minister?" asked the Fuhrer.

Engel looked at his intended and turned his focus on the Fuhrer and said, "We are honored by such a gracious gift mein Fuhrer. We would've been just as pleased if you offered us a new set of plates to eat on as a fitting wedding gift." Replied Engel. The Fuhrer quickly stood up and Maria's grip increased upon Engel's hand. "If I didn't want you to have this? I would not have offered this. My Minister of Finance and his new bride needs a home besides living in a loft apartment where he works." Exclaimed the Fuhrer. The Fuhrer reaches out to Engel and speaks, "A handshake is all that is need my friend to seal the deal, and if Maria is up to the challenge? A reading of my future in your new home today?" A relieved Maria released Engel's hand and asked the Fuhrer if she could hug him. The Fuhrer obliged by opening his arms to her. A teary-eyed Maria gleefully hugged the Fuhrer and said, "I will gladly give you a reading mein Fuhrer.

Let's go into the kitchen where there are more chairs to sit." The Fuhrer said," Could we have a private session? Just you and I, Maria?" Engel said, "The Fuhrer's aid and me can go outside and smoke some cigarettes. Maria can let us know once she is finished. "Wunderbar!" Exclaimed the Fuhrer. As the Fuhrer's aide and Engel exit the house. The Fuhrer followed Maria to the kitchen, pulled out a chair for her to sit in and sat down across from her. "Do we need a candle to do this?" asked the Fuhrer. Maria said, "A candle is not needed. I just need to clear my mind and relax for a moment. This has been an exciting day for Engel and me. I'm going to close my eyes and when I open my hands to you, slowly lay the palms of your hands onto mine." Maria crossed her arms as if to hug herself and began slowly to inhale and exhale. An anxious Fuhrer to hear answers is forced to wait until the moment arises. Several minutes passed by until Maria lay her open hands upon the table.

The Fuhrer gingerly lay his hands onto the palms of Maria. The Fuhrer watched as Maria raised her lowered head, her eyes still closed and facing forward. "There will be multiple attempts upon your life, but none succeed." Says Maria. "Who are the traitors? Tell me!" asked the Fuhrer. "I can see the backs of their heads but not their faces. I can see that one is an injured man, possibly from the war. The group of men are of significant rank. Maria sees something that makes her body flinch. The Fuhrer asked what has startled her. "I see many ships with men going down into the sea." Says Maria. "Are they German ships?" asked the Fuhrer. "No! I see an English Flag." answered Maria. "That is wonderful news!" says an elated Fuhrer. "What else do you see?" asked the Fuhrer. "You are riding under the grand arch of Paris." Stated

Maria. The Fuhrer picked up his hands and clapped gleefully. "That's all I need to hear for now. Danke!" said the Fuhrer. Maria opens her eyes, and the Fuhrer says, "We must celebrate tonight. I will have my staff car retrieve you and the Minister. Let's go and tell Herr Engel." The Fuhrer opened the door for Maria as she walked out.

A jubilant Fuhrer tells his aide to plan for dinner tonight at the restaurant once they arrive back in the city. The aide answers back swiftly," Ja wohl, Mein Fuhrer!" as he opens the door of the auto for the Fuhrer and his guest. The aide hands Engel the keys to the house, gets into the auto and tells the driver to go back to the city. Maria and Engel sat and waited for the Fuhrer to initiate the conversation. "You are a lucky man, Herr Stern." said the Fuhrer." "We are lucky to have your favor, mein Fuhrer." Answered Engel. The Fuhrer said nothing else and the small talk ended. The Fuhrer only spoke to us as the auto dropped us off at the bank. He told us that his aide would be sending a staff car later today. The aide told us that he would call ahead to give us time to be ready. Maria and I gave the customary salute to the Fuhrer and the staff car drove away.

Maria gave out a heavy sigh as if she had just started breathing again. She clasped Engels hand as they entered the bank. The joyful bank manager Burhalter, jumps up from his desk and rushes to greet his boss and Maria. "My staff and I are glad to see you two come back to us. We didn't know what to think after seeing the SS officer lead you out. We can start breathing again." Exclaimed the manager. Engel thanked the manager for his kind concerns and Maria blurted out, "The Fuhrer is giving us a house for a wedding gift." The manager smiled and asked where is the house, so he'll know where to bring the housewarming gift? Engel told him the location and the manager's face changed to a look of fear. Maria spoke up and said, "It's okay! I know it is the former banker's home. He is Juden." The bank manager acknowledged Maria in saying "Ja! I must be getting back to work and congratulations." Engel glanced at Maria after her statement, and she followed him into his office. Engel closed the door behind him as Maria sat down in a chair.

Engel was about to speak and Maria pointed to the radio. Engel turned on the radio and the voice of the Nazi party is speaking. It is the voice of Joseph Goebbels. In a hushed tone Maria says, "This room could be monitored by the Gestapo. Remember I'm psychic and the Fuhrer said nothing about the house's former owners' line of work. At least, we'll have more room than the loft apartment." Engel said," I won't ask about the private session. I will leave it up to you if you want to tell me." In a low tone Maria answered that she would but not now. Engel began carrying on a normal toned conversation, talking about the dinner invitation with the Fuhrer and judging by the time piece on the wall, the day rapidly flying by.

Maria tells Engel that she is going to the apartment and start getting ready. Engel tells her that he has a few items to take care of on his desk and will join her. As Maria leaves the office, Engel turns the volume down on the radio and briefly listens to what is being said.

Goebbels is saying that Germany cannot be a strong Germany without true Germans living in the fatherland. The mixing of the races is an abomination, and the pure blood of the Aryan nation does not include the Juden. The Juden are a subhuman species that are a blight to Germany. Engel turned off the radio and sat in silence. The words sank deep into his consciousness. He is a seed of Abraham and back under the thumb of a new Roman empire, being run by the devil himself. The radio is poisoning the minds of people, and he is powerless for now. He will have to wait until tonight, after dinner with the Fuhrer to talk to his intended. Near the end of the day. Engel received a call from the Fuhrer's office. The person on the other end of the phone told Engel that a staff car will arrive at six o'clock to retrieve he and Maria. Engel gave the usual acknowledgement saying," Danke! Heil Hitler!" and hangs up the phone.

Engel bids the manager and the bank staff a good night and makes his way upstairs to his apartment. Engel unlocks the door and sees Mariais already dressed for the evenings occasion. "Go shave, wash up and put on some fresh clothes. You smell like an animal." Maria said jokingly. "Already cracking the whip and we aren't wed yet!" Engel replied jokingly. "That's impossible! Germans are the superior race!" Said Engel. Maria whispered. "You aren't German, but superior to everyone my love." Engel smiled and continued at the task of getting ready for the dinner with the Fuhrer.

The time came when the staff car arrived, and Engel set the alarm and locked the doors of the bank. As they approached the staff car, the driver opened the door for them to enter the back seat. General Wolfstein said, "Schnell! Schnell! You Know the Fuhrer is a stickler for promptness." Maria sat down next to the General and Engel got in as the driver quickly got to the driver's seat. The driver sped off towards the restaurant. The general spoke up and asked Maria, what did she think about her new home? "It is a very generous gift from the Fuhrer." Replied Maria.

"I am sure that the home will be more private than your current residence inside the bank. I will have the cellar door fixed. It was damaged during a raid on the previous owner. Your employee told you about the previous owner, didn't he?" Asked The General. "The banker was Juden according to what my employee told us." Answered Engel. Maria squeezed Engel's hand. Knowing that Engel was about to delve deeper into a subject she didn't want. The General sternly answered by saying, "The Juden banker was an enemy to the state and stealing from the Reich. Now. Let's talk about something more pleasant. You two will be husband and wife soon. And I might add that you'll be married by the Fuhrer himself. Many inside the Fuhrer's circle will be envious of such an occasion. Don't worry about any reprisals because they wouldn't go against the Fuhrer's wishes." He looked at Engel and said, "Be mindful of your manners concerning the Fuhrer because others will be watching." The auto stopped in front of the restaurant and the driver opened the doors to let everyone out. Maria and Engel followed behind the general into the restaurant.

The entrance was heavily guarded by the SS and Gestapo. We all had to show our papers, in order to go into the restaurant. The restaurant was nearly devoid of civilians other than the wait staff. The presumed owner of the restaurant took us to the Fuhrer's table and seated us. Maria was seated next to Ava Braun (the Fuhrer's mistress) and seated across from us Himmler, his wife and Joseph Goebbel's and his wife. They looked nervously at us and to break the tension of the moment. Engel grabbed his wine glass stood up and said, "I would like to propose a toast to our glorious leader, the Chancellor of Germany Adolph Hitler and to the fatherland." All at the table stood up and said "Heil Hitler and to the fatherland!"

A gleeful Fuhrer clapped his hands in joy and said," Everyone be seated and relax. Thank you for that toast herr Minister and we all want to welcome you and Maria to your dinner. I know this is more than you expected, but after the great news told to me today. I was compelled to bring about this occasion. Now, tell the waiters what you want to eat and drink since the finance minister is paying for it. I am kidding of course. So, thank you all for coming." The wait staff hurriedly made their way to the Fuhrer first and began taking everyone else's orders. The wives of Himmler and Goebbels were asking about the wedding date. Maria told them that we were waiting for the rings to be finished and then coordinating with the Fuhrer, since he is going to officiate the wedding. When Maria said that? All conversations stopped and the Fuhrer chimed in." She is correct. I am going to play the high priest at the wedding. Me. A priest." The Fuhrer laughed so hard and violently, he unintentionally knocked his wine glass over on to Himmler's wife's dress.

The Fuhrer apologized and yelled for a waiter to bring a towel. I found it hard to contain myself and I heard the dark master's voice in my head saying, "Don't even think about laughing. Not here! Not now!" I put my hand over my face because I was tearing up. I took some deep breaths to calm down. I was looking through my fingers at what was going on. Ava had taken her napkin and a glass of water to wipe the wine stain of Himmler's wife's dress. The Fuhrer began screaming "Who do I need to shoot to get some help in here?" I got up and said," I'll go and get things under control." When I said that? Himmler immediately sprang up and said, "No, Herr Minister allow me." The General tugged at my arm, and I obliged Himmler.

Himmler stormed into the kitchen, and we hear him screaming out that their families are going to be shot, if things aren't put to order right now. Himmler exits the kitchen and is followed by a stream of waiters carrying food and drinks. The air was thick with tension and I said to Joseph, "I heard you speak on the radio today. It was a compelling speech. Did you memorize the speech or were you reading it. It was so fluid. "Joseph looked at the Fuhrer and began speaking to Engel. He told Engel that he writes the speeches and practices on his wife first. Goebbel's wife chuckles at his comment and nods obediently to her husband's orations. The waiters began pouring more wine into our glasses and Engel is pretending to be interested in Joseph's conversation and all he hears is a jumble mix of meaningless words. By this time, the Fuhrer had calmed down and began speaking to Maria.

The Fuhrer said," I am about to make the first move on the world chess board. What are your thoughts on this soon to be bride of my finance minister?" Maria squeezed my hand, took a sip from her wine glass and said, "Mein Fuhrer. What I told you today would be your second conquest. The first conquest will be a total surprise to the defeated and an eye opener to the rest of the world." General Wolfstein stood up, held up his wine glass and said, "Heil Hitler and to the fatherland!" Everyone else stood and mimicked the general's gesture and sat back down. The jubilant Fuhrer kissed the hand of his mistress Ava as waiters began laying platters of food on the table. Engel noticed that no one blessed the food before eating. They just began stuffing their faces with food. Maria looked at her intended and gave a nod of assurance. Engel began scooping food into his mouth and listening to the conversations at the table. His mind is reeling with one solitary thought. How long will he have to sit there before he can leave with his intended.

He didn't like the feeling of being trapped between two evils at one table. The meal ended as the Fuhrer and Ava got up from the table and were led by the Fuhrer's S.S. armed to the teeth. Everyone stood up and gave the customary Heil Hitler. Everyone remained standing until the Fuhrer had left the room. General Wolfstein got up and congratulated Engel and Maria and said, "I have another matter to attend to. Herr Minister, the bill is taken care of. I'll be looking forward to the marriage ceremony. Heil Hitler!" The general put on his cap and left the room promptly. Engel turned to Maria and whispered, "It appears the general has an itch that needs to be scratched." "Apparently so!" replied Maria.

It wasn't long after that, the rest of the dinner guests began leaving. Maria and I made our way to the main desk at the restaurant. The attendant told us that everything has been taken care of. I asked the attendant if he could call us cab? The attendant said, "A car is waiting for you Herr Minister. Thank you for your patronage. Heil Hitler!" We returned the homage to the Fuhrer and exited the building. As we walked up to the edge of the sidewalk a car pulled up and the driver opened the door for us. The driver got back in the driver's seat and politely asked," Where shall I take you Herr Minister?" Engel told the driver to take him and Maria back to the bank. The driver put the car in gear and sped off down the street. After a couple of twist and turns the car arrived at the bank. The driver opened the door for us to exit the car.

Engel took money from his wallet and the driver refused. The driver said, "The Fuhrer instructed me to do this. Your money is no good. It was my duty. Have a good evening. Heil Hitler!" We returned the gesture, and we made our way to the door of the bank. Engel unlocked the door and quickly proceeded to turn off the alarm, before it sounded. He relocked the doors and rearmed the alarm. Maria was already on her way up the stairs to the apartment. There were many things running through Engel's mind. The one thing that sticks out the most is, in three days the change will come. Will he be locked up in the bank vault or in the basement of his new home? Will the basement door be strong enough to hold the beast he becomes? There are things he wishes to discuss with Maria, but fears that the bank could be filled with listening devices, placed there by the Gestapo. Engel makes his way up the stairs to the apartment and locks the door behind him.

He catches a whiff of Maria's perfume in the room. She isn't in the room. Engel could close his eyes and his nose would lead him to her. His senses are already beginning to be heightened. He hears her in the bathroom and he sits down and removes his shoes and socks. He feels the coolness of the wooden floor against his feet. For a moment, he thought about a time when he needed no shoes. Feel the earth beneath his feet as he lived by his senses in the forest. There was a feeling of peace and most of all freedom. Maria walked into the room in her robe and said, "You must've been in a deep thought? I stood in the doorway as you were blankly staring at the wall. What is troubling you? My love."

Engel motions Maria to come over and she sits in his lap. Engel whispered into her ear by saying," Do you remember telling me that this is not my fault according to the Bible? The Bible disappeared and there is not any evidence of what you told me." Maria whispered back, "He does not want you to see the truth. Bibles are now banned except for the ones that have been changed to suit the Aryan ideology. Every word that talked about the Jewish race has been erased from the Aryan Bible. They do not view Jesus as a Jewish man. To them he was placed here from somewhere else and was condemned to death by the Jews. Pontious Pilate asked the people of Judea? Who do want to be crucified Barrabas or Jesus of Nazareth? The people answered by screaming out to crucify the Nazarene and to free Barrabas. Pontious had washed his hands clean and let the people decide. You know the rest of what happened. If I could get my hands on a true Bible? I will show you. You must also know that the Jews still do not recognize Jesus as the true Messiah.

The Jews claim Jesus did not carry out the things a Messiah would do according to their doctrine The Torah. A book that the Jews solely based on the books of Moses. "Engel kissed Maria on the cheek and whispered, "Now I know why they are being targeted. They are God's chosen people even though they are wrong about Jesus." Engel began weeping. Maria spoke in a normal voice saying, "It isn't your fault. It was the devil that planted the thought, and he wasn't going to stop until someone pointed him out." She then whispered, "Jesus knew he had to die and be resurrected by God. You heard him say this. According to the Bible, you were there." Engel wiped his eyes and said, "Yes! I was there. I now feel helpless to what is happening. I do not know all of what is occurring, but it cannot be good." Maria said, "We cannot talk here, but I will find out all I can from Ziel. I do not trust any of the Fuhrer's henchmen. Now let's stop talking about things outside our apartment door.

Let me draw you a warm bath. I may get in with you." Maria kisses Engel and scurries into the bathroom. Engel loves Maria more than life itself. Yet, the information Maria told him about what is coming in 1945. He wonders what is beyond that. He knows an all-out war is coming and Hitler is ready to pull the trigger. "Your bath is ready darling." Maria exclaims. "On my way, my sweet." says Engel as he is slipping off his shirt and is walking to the bathroom. His beautiful Maria is standing there only in her under garments. She smiles a loving smile at Engel as he finishes undressing. He kisses Maria and tells her how lucky he is and test the water temperature with his finger.

He steps into the tub and before he sits down in the water, he insists on Maria getting undressed and joining him. Engel makes room for her as he lends a hand helping her into the tub. "Just don't wet my hair dear. I just washed it yesterday." says Maria. Engel tells her to turn around so that he can wash her back with a cloth and soap. She maneuvers herself and Engel began to gently rub her back with the soapy cloth. He is careful not to get her hair wet. Though she has bound her hair up, Engel is ever careful not to wet it. Then out of nowhere, Maria says," Did you and Joan, I mean Jean take a bath together?" Engel chuckles a says, "Her hand maid bathed me once and that was the only time I was clean. The French were not that hygienic then. This is a luxury that I am experiencing right now. Bathing in a tub with my intended bride to be. There is no other woman except for you. Right here and right now." Exclaims Engel.

Maria takes Engel's hand, kisses it and places it on her breast. She says," How foolish of me to say such a thing. Both of us had lives before we met. You are right! We have right here and right now! You turn around so that I can wash your back." Engel jokingly says," just don't wet my hair! Okay!" They both laugh as she lovingly smacks him with the wet washcloth. They finished bathing and Engel steps out of the tub. He grabs a towel and reaches out to assist Maria out of the tub. The bathroom floor is wet and slick. Engels doesn't want her to slip and fall. He handed her the towel and she began to dry herself off. She takes the towel and starts drying Engel with one hand and rubbing his man parts with the other.

Engel takes his hand and gingerly grasp Maria by the neck, pulling her face to his awaiting lips. As his other hand began to massage her lady parts. He is getting harder by the moment as he feels Maria's body tremble with excitement. She takes Engel by the hand and leads him to the bed. She climbs on top of him and glides his member into her. She sighs with relief and says," This is where you belong my darling. This is where you belong." She bounces upon Engel like a child jumps on the bed, moaning and sighing sounds of ecstasy until they both have an explosive climax. They hurriedly got up from the bed and got themselves cleaned up in the bathroom. They went back to the bed and collapsed together. Maria asked Engel, "did he want a cigarette? He declined and said," If you get pregnant? Do you think smoking or drinking will harm the baby?" "Our baby will be a superior baby. He or she could possess both of our powers.

You have never shown any kind of sickness since I've known you. You are immune to any kind of human disease. I get the sniffles and have had some stomach ailments, but you have not even shown signs of a runny nose. You are truly immortal and I am sure that our offspring will be also. I look forward to seeing my belly swell with a baby in it. You won't start cheating on me because of my swollen belly, would you?" Engel said," You are my chosen mate for as long as I can keep from making the General mad at me. I have experienced hell and it isn't pleasant." Maria sat up in the bed and said," You have been to hell? You are just now telling me this? What was it like?" "The first time I was there was because I mocked the dark master, and he placed me in darkness. I was chained up as the beast, taunted by the demons endlessly.

A darkness so heavy the beast could feel it. The dark master got tired of hearing me saying that I deserved to be there and shouting degrading things about him in front of his demons. He released me and gave me a warning. The second time there I was myself, reliving the same day over and over again. I was reliving the day that I gave up the rabbi to the Sanhedrin. I had no control of what I was doing. I couldn't change anything. The dark master used my personal guilt and turned it into a living hell." Maria started crying and said, "You have suffered so much and forgive me my love. My mind cannot possibly fathom what you have experienced. My mind was in shock the first time I saw you change. Any other person would have ran away in horror. I was drawn to you like a moth to the flame. So, please promise me that you'll do nothing to make the general angry. Our future will be over." Engel says, "I promise! It will be hard to contain myself especially around Hitler's henchmen. They remind me of the demons in hell. The only difference is they want to taunt me and don't. Whereas the demons weren't afraid to taunt me and did it endlessly." Let's get some sleep and leave the horrors of today's conversation behind." said Maria. Maria gently kissed Engel and laid her head on his shoulder. Engel turned off the lamp next to the bed with his free hand, hugged his betrothed and told her good night.

He eventually went to sleep and for the first time in a long time, his dreams were peaceful and not filled with torment. The next day came and both arose to meet it. Maria gave Engel a kiss before she started getting dressed. Engel said," I guess we need to start packing our belongings today and get ready for the move." "I have a feeling that our new furniture will be there in our new house today. " Said Maria. "I have a feeling that you are right. For some reason, I don't think I will be holding this bank position much longer either." Stated Engel. "War is coming, and the German war machine will take control over everyone's accounts." Answered Maria. "If I try and warn people, that this is coming. We will become a target, won't we?" Asked Engel.

Maria said," Right now! We are in an elite circle, and we have to go along until the right time reveals itself." "The dark master told me once, that I cannot take on the whole Roman army by myself. He said to leave Rome to him. So, this is a repeat of what I surmised as Rome fell. I just wasn't there to see it." Said Engel. "Rome has a new Caesar named Mussolini. The Fuhrer idolizes Mussolini and will ask Mussolini to join his cause. There's nothing you or I can do except to watch. My darling. I must ask you to do something for me and promise that you'll do it." Stated Maria. "You want me to control my hate towards them. Is this what you are asking?" Replied Engel.

"I saw how Himmler looks at you. He's afraid of you and I don't know if he's in league with the dark master or not. Himmler hates the fact that the Fuhrer has been catering to you. us and he isn't in getting the special treatment. Make friends with Himmler. Even if you are just pretending. Invite him to dinner or take him to lunch and get a beer. I know I am asking a lot. You know how you pretended to take interest in Goebbels radio speech. You have got a brain in that head of yours. You were chosen as an apostle. The Lord saw you as someone special. Be that someone special. Not just for me, but for us." Said Maria as tears ran down her face. Engel Kissed Maria and gave her a strong embrace. "I need to make us something to eat while you get dressed for work." Stated Maria. Engel nodded in compliance and went to shave. A lot of things were going through Engel's mind as he looked at himself in the mirror.

The different lives and identities he had to use, but behind the eyes of the man in the mirror is still Judas Iscariot. He finishes shaving, getting dressed in his work clothes and helps Maria in the kitchen. They have a quick meal in time for Engel to go downstairs to work. Engel walks to the door of the bank as his manager appears through the window. Engel opens the door and quickly disarms the alarm to the bank The bank manager smiles at Engel and gives him a proper greeting. "Good morning! Mein herr." stated the bank manager. Engel replied by saying," Good morning Herr manager. How is your family?" The manager's face lit up because he saw Engel's humility shining through. "My family is doing well because of you and frau Maria." said a gleeful manager.

The other workers were filing in and bidding Engel and the manager a good morning. Engel acknowledged them as he turned to go into his own office. He closed the door and sat down at his desk. He remembered what Maria told him. So, he picks up the phone and gets the operator to connect him with Himmler's office. Himmler's secretary answers the phone and tells Engel that the Reichs Fuhrer hasn't arrived yet. Engel informs the secretary that the moment that the Reichs Fuhrer arrives to call him. He then closes the conversation by saying Heil Hitler and hangs up the phone. A kind gesture would be to ask permission of Himmler to send Himmler's wife flowers. If Himmler asked why? Engel would say that it is from he and Maria for attending the party last night. Engel couldn't say because Hitler had spilled his drink on her. That would probably embarrass and infuriate Himmler. So, Engel began to look over some paperwork on his desk and his phone rang a few moments later. He answered the phone, and it was Himmler. "Good morning ReichsFuhrer and heil Hitler! I am glad that you returned my call.

The reason I called your office is would it be okay if I sent your wife some flowers from Maria and I. I intend to send Mrs. Goebbel's and Frau Braun flowers as well for attending the occasion last night?" There was a pause and then Himmler said, "That would be very nice of you and Frau Orsic. It would make my wife very happy." "Wunderbar!" Exclaimed Engel and he told Himmler that maybe next week they could have lunch. Himmler seemed to be very cordial about the conversation and the invitation. He told Engel that He would take him to lunch. After conversation ended with a heil Hitler and the phones are placed in the receiver. Engel immediately got the operator to ring the florist and he ordered flowers to be delivered to the Himmler's, the Goebbel's and to Ava Braun's location. He tells the florist to bill him and says heil Hitler and hangs up.

Today, Engel's body experiences the usual signs days before the change. A heightened sense of hearing, smells, the tautness of the muscles and even his mental sharpness all come into play. His nose picks up the other women's perfume, the musky smell of unbathed men and the smell of the exhaust from vehicles that past down the street, as the opening and closing of the bank door brings in the odors from outside. As he looks over the paperwork on his desk, the telephone rings. Engel picks up the telephone and says," Der Minister of Finance, can I help you?" He hears a familiar voice say," This is General Wolfstein. I am calling to tell you that the furniture will be delivered today. I also have changed the cellar door to a steel door. To the outsider, it will appear to be wooden. I can assure you that you will not escape from the cellar. I can't allow the beast to ruin my plans. Do you want to say goodbye to Maria forever?"

Engel quickly answered by saying" Nein, mein General" "Wunderbar, herr Stern! I know the change will be coming soon and Germany will be steam rolling over Poland soon. There won't be a need for you to go to the bank every day either. You will still hold your title, but the German military will control the banks of Germany. Don't worry about the gestapo listening to anything. They cannot hear our conversation; they couldn't hear anything unusual at all. All they hear is normal pro nazi conversation. Even when you and maria are talking intimately to each other about your past. They hear nothing but pro nazi conversation. I made it that way. I know it was very kind of me, but they cannot know who you really are, or who I really am. Now, the furniture movers will be there at your new home at two o'clock today. Can you be there to unlock the door for them?" Asked the General. Engel quickly replied," Ja wohl, Mein General! I can be there at two o'clock sharp." Heil Hitler!" said the general and the phone clicks to a dial tone.

Engel hangs up the phone. He remembers what Maria said last night. Things are progressing and not in a positive sense. He worries about the common people, the people that have families and he wonders about what has happened to the Jewish people that were in Berlin. He starts thinking that Maria is shielding him from something. He looks at the clock and the hands tell him that it is almost nine in the morning. He wonders how long before he'll be cut off from the bank's inner workings, the military moving in to control the working-class family's finances. He knows better than to ask the General such questions about what has happened to the Jewish population. That would only anger him and jeopardize him and Maria's future. No matter how long or short it is. He is trapped to an existence that he has no control over.

It is better than hell, he admits, but what if this is a different kind of hell. He has witnessed wars, the killing and spilling of blood by men and the beast. A phrase comes to his mind that was told to him by his dark master. The dark master said at the time in his past, that they are standing on a mass graveyard. Many wars, battles won and lost. Yet the bones lie covered by time. Engel takes a cigarette from his pocket and lights it. We watched the smoke rise to the ceiling and it reminds him of the distance fires from the past. Seeing the smoke from burning buildings, homes and even bodies. He finishes his cigarette, and his thoughts are on his people in the bank. What about them? They go to work and have families to feed. They didn't bring this war about, that is about to start. He also knows he can't just tell them to draw all their money out either. That would cause an immediate panic. Plus, unwanted attention towards him. If he can't help the whole family, at least their children. He thought about the rapist he shot, and the welfare of Elsa, the girl that was brutalized.

Engel gets up and goes to the manager's desk. As he approaches the manager, the manager sees Engel walking towards him and he starts to smile. as Engel drew closer, the manager stood up and gave the nazi salute, and said," heil Hitler!" Engel returned the gesture and asked the manager to walk with him to the office. Engel sat down at his desk and asked the manager to close the door and have a seat. The manager's face changed from happy to one of concern. Engel saw his face and told the manager to relax. He asked the manager. When was his last increase of income? The banker said, "Am I in trouble, herr Minister?" "Nein!" Replied Engel. "How many employees here have children besides yourself, herr Burkhalter?" Asked Engel. The manager paused for a moment as he was gathering his thoughts and said, "Everyone has a child except for one of the tellers.

Most of the women's husbands have been recruited into the wermacht. I have passed the age of recruitment, herr minister. "Replied the manager. "I will be leaving early starting tomorrow for the next three days. I want you to bring me the amount of every employee's wage in a month. Create the list of employees with their monthly wage on the handwritten list. I want it within the next hour. Can you give me a definitive answer in this time frame? Let me ask you a question. Are you loyal to the Fuhrer or loyal to me? I killed the person that raped your daughter, and I didn't face a firing squad for doing it. Is it because of my relationship with Maria or do I possess some secret knowledge about someone in power? Maybe both. What I am saying determines the lives of Elsa and your wife, plus the other employees here.

Now where does your loyalty lie, her Burkhalter?" Asked Engel. A bead of sweat popped out on the manager's forehead as he stood up from his chair. The manager said," Herr minister, Hitler didn't kill my Elsa's rapist you did. Hitler didn't heal the marks upon my daughter's body, your intended Maria did. You are an honest man and I trust my whole family's life in your hands. Does this answer your question, herr minister?" Engel stuck out his hand for the manager to shake. The manager obliged the gesture and told Engel that he would have an answer within the hour. The manager opened the door and gently closed it behind him, hurriedly made it back to his desk. Engel has a plan. A plan that won't cause a rift in the establishment. Engel signs some documents on his desk and continues working on other things.

The hour is nearly up as Engel hears a knock at his door. Engel tells the person at the door to enter. It is a nervous bank manager with a piece of paper. The manager closes the door, gives Engel the paper and sit down in a chair. Engel looks at the list of names with their monthly wages. Engel looked at the list once more before looking at the manager. Engel said, "At the end of this week, before you issue out checks to the employees. Everyone will receive compensation, let's call it a gift from Maria and myself. The money for the checks will be taken from high-ranking officer's accounts with no trace of extraction in any ledger. That means my account also is subject to this. The checks are to be cashed only at this bank only. The employees are not to buy us wedding gifts, this is a gift to my loyal employees.

The bank manager had tears rolling down his cheeks as Engel was telling him this. The bank manager understands that hard times are approaching and that his boss is God sent. The choked-up manager gathers his composure and says, "Herr minister, what about the missing money?" Engel laughed and said, "What missing money?" Don't worry about it. I've got a feeling they won't miss it." The manager told Engel Danke and gently closed the door behind him. Engel's heart was filled with joy about doing this gesture. He only wished he could do more. Lunch time came and Engel had lunch with Maria and told her that he would need to be at the new house around two o'clock today for the furniture movers. He told her that he received a call from General Wolfstein and asked her did she wanted to go with him to the house.

Maria told him of course she wanted to go. He told Maria he would finish some things and be back upstairs later to the apartment He kissed her and said nothing about what he is going to do for the employees. The time came for Engel to get his driver to take him and Maria to their new home. The moving truck and men were already there at the location. Engel quickly left the vehicle and unlocked the door for the men. Maria got busy telling the men where to set the furniture as

Engel watched her in her element. Engel even offered to help the men, but they wouldn't hear of it. Engel got out their way as they unloaded and placed the furnishings in the home as Maria pointed out where the furnishings went. Time began clicking on by as Engel watched until everything had its place and Maria is ecstatic about their new home. Engel gave Maria the house keys and told her that the driver would be taking her to the bank. He would ride back to the city with the movers. The movers obliged Engel and was humbled by Engel's presence with them. Engel just needed to get back to work and he knew Maria, would be busy.

The end of the day came employees were making sure everything balanced out at the end of the day. The head teller gave the manager the day's total intake. The manager thanked the teller and told her that he would see her and the other employees tomorrow. The employees gathered their belongings and headed out the door. The manager brought Engel the total for the close of business. Engel told the manager to not to mention the wage increase. He said, "I want this to be a total surprise. Can you keep this a secret just between us?" The manager nodded and smiled and told Engel he would see him tomorrow. As the manager was about to leave, in walks Maria. "I hope I am not interrupting anything important, gentlemen?' stated Maria. The bank manager asked Maria if he could see her hand. Maria held up her hand and the bank manager kissed her hand.

Maria said, "What did I do to deserve such a noble gesture?" The manager said, "Your husband is a saint, and I don't think it would be proper if I kissed his hand." Chuckled a joyful man. Engel said, "Good night! Herr Burkhalter." The manager told Engel and maria goodbye as he closed the door behind him. Maria walked over to Engel and sat in his lap and kissed him. "A saint! If he only knew. So! What did I miss? My darling." asked Maria. "Let me lock up the bank and I'll meet you upstairs darling." Said Engel. Maria said, "Did you do something spectacular and didn't tell me about it? Engel wrapped his arms around Maria, squeezed her gently, released her and said," The general said Germany is going to roll over Poland, the war is about to begin.

I am giving the employees of the bank a pay raise. They will see it on their check at the end of the week. I informed herr Burkhalter of the increase. I told him that this was a secret. The money will be skimmed from the high-ranking military elites and not logged as such. The money will be taken, it just won't be shown that it is taken." Maria said jokingly, "Not only is my husband a saint, he is Robin Hood. Taking from the rich and giving to the poor." "I don't know who this robin hood character you speak of.' says Engel. Maria chuckles and said, "Lock up the bank, set the alarm and I'll be upstairs naked, and waiting for you." Maria takes her purse and hurriedly goes upstairs, unlocks the apartment and begins taking off her clothes. Engel locks up the bank doors and arms the alarm system. He knows for the next three nights; he won't be sleeping with Maria. The beast will be locked in the cellar instead of the bank vault. Engel walks up the stairs, opens the door and locks it behind him. His nose catches a whiff of Maria's perfume, as he enters the front room.

His senses are already heightened. He closes his eyes for a moment and takes a deep slow breath. His mind erases the image of the day and refocuses. Engel walks into the bedroom, and he sees Maria covered only by a sheet of bedding with just her exposed. maria chuckles and says, I have something waiting on you, my love. Do you wish to see it?" she quickly flashes Engel a glimpse of her naked body and quickly covers herself back up. "Are you trying to tease me? You temptress!" Says Engel as he continues to get undressed. "You've e never called me a temptress before. Wherever that came from I like it and yes, I am teasing my mate. Do you not like what you saw?" asked Maria.

Engel has taken off his undergarments and he is almost erect. "Do you see what you are doing to me, my temptress?" replies Engel. Maria says, "Yes, bring it over her so that I may hold it." Maria lovingly said. Engel pulls back the sheet and lays down beside Maria. Maria leans in to kiss Engel as she gently grabs his manhood in her hand. She whispers that she has been wanting him all day. Engel gingerly caresses Maria's vagina as she moans with delight. He feels her wetness and now his member is engorged with blood, throbbing and waiting to enter her. Maria climbs on top of Engel as she slides him into her pleasure hole.

She begins to slowly grind against Engel as he fondles her breast and kisses her. She quickens her movement only to be slowed down by Engel.

He grabs her waist to push into her and whispers, "Slow down, we have plenty of time." Maria began to slowly move up and down his shaft as he felt her body tingle with delight. She gets to a point of no return and hastens her bounce until they both climax. Maria collapses on top of Engel as she nudges, her last plunges against Engel. Engel removes a pillowcase from the pillow and gives it to Maria, to case the spent fluid as she moves off Engel. Maria asked Engel where did he learn the pillowcase trick? Engel replied saying that he didn't want to lay in the wet spot and the pillowcase came to mind. Maria laughed and said, "This is the last night we'll be sleeping in this bed. for that matter, this is the last night we'll be sleeping in this place. I'm sure you didn't mind laying in Joan of arc's love juice, did you?"

Engel said," You are with me now. Stop fretting over something that happened centuries ago. I am to be your husband. I'll be legally bound to you." Maria kissed Engel and said, "I am just jealous that's all that I couldn't have been your one and only. I am acting like a silly girl. Forgive me my love. Now let's get washed up and we'll go and eat at a restaurant. No cooking here tonight. Things are packed up anyway." They go to the bathroom and get cleaned up. Engel washes his face and gets ready to shave. Maria goes into the bedroom and puts on her clothes, sits in front of her vanity and begins fixing her hair and makeup. As Engel shaves, he thinks about the places where there was no such thing as a bathroom. No indoor plumbing and bathing in a stream or even in the Nile River. No soft beds to lie down on, only the hard ground of the unforgiving earth beneath him. Tomorrow night the change comes, and his body is already showing signs.

His muscles all over his body is taunt and defined. He will have to leave work early every day for the next three, maybe four days. Depending on the moon cycle. Engel puts on clean clothing and a voice in his head said," What has happened to the Jewish people?" Engel stops and looks around the room. He sees no one else. He walks towards Maria and said, "Something strange just happened. I heard a voice in my head say, what has happened to the Jewish people?" Maria stopped putting her lip stick and turned to Engel. "They have been taken to Dachau, a work camp. Who did the voice sound like?" Asked Maria. Engel stated that he doesn't recognize the voice and ask Maria more about this place called Dachau. "It is a place where Jews, homosexuals, gypsies and others that don't fit in this new German society.

Engel please don't talk about this except between us. This is a very dangerous subject, and things are good for us now." exclaimed Maria. Engel sat down on the bed, put on his socks and shoes. "You told me we have until 1945 to get out of Germany before things turn bad." says Engel. Maria tells Engel that Germany loses another war. She then tells Engel that they won't be in Germany, when things go sour. She takes Engels hand and kisses it saying, "My love, do you love me and trust me with all your heart?" "With every ounce of my being." Replied Engel. "Ziel, gave me a glimpse of our future. We just need to follow our course that we are on now. We will be husband wife and I will be carrying your child. So, please I beg of you. Don't make the dark master mad with you.

He's focused on Hitler and not you. Do you think it was Hitler's idea to give us a house outside the city? The idea was planted by the dark one. He knows things are changing in Germany and he wants us out of the bank. Believe me! We do not want to be a part of this. Yes, the German's are using my gift, but I am not telling them everything I receive form Ziel. So, let's continue getting dressed. You really zapped my strength from the lovemaking, and I am starving." Stated Maria. Engel straightened his shirt and put on a dinner jacket. He got his identification papers, stuck them in his jacket and waited for Maria to get her belongings together. He opened the door for her as she walked down the stairs. Engel locked the door and followed her.

Engel said, "I won't bother my driver. He's with his family. We'll get a taxi to take us to dinner." Maria took Engel's hand and held it to her face and said, "You were chosen by Jesus because he could see into your heart. The mind can be corrupted, but the heart cannot." Engel could only nod in acknowledgement of her comment and went to disarm the bank alarm. He unlocks the door and tells Maria to step outside as he sets the alarm, closes the door behind him and locks it. The walk to the edge of the sidewalk and a taxi pulls up. Engel opens the car door for Maria as she steps in, and Engel gives the driver instructions of where to take them.

The driver nods his head as the car pulls away from the curb and into the somewhat busy street. The taxi didn't have to travel far before reaching its destination. Engel pays the driver a few marks, opens the door and gives Maria his hand to help her exit the cab. He closes the door, and they walk into the restaurant. The waiter greets them and takes them to a table. Another waiter comes to the table hands off two menus and asked what they would be drinking tonight? Engel asked the waiter to get a bottle of wine while they decided what to eat. The waiter obliged the request and left the couple to get the bottle of wine. Engel took at glance at his surroundings and saw a familiar face across the room. General Wolfstein made eye contact with Engel and smiled. The general was not alone. He had a beautiful female sitting across from him. Engel only nodded back at the general to acknowledge him. "Let me guess. The general is here, and he has a lady friend." Said Maria. Engel chuckled and said, "You saw them before you sat down, didn't you? I was too busy thinking about putting something in my stomach." Maria having her back to the general's table told Engel that the general will probably show off his lady friend before he leaves the restaurant. The waiter arrives with a bottle of wine and two wine glasses and asked if they had decided on their meals yet. Engel asked the waiter if he could bring some bread and cheese until they decide. The waiter nodded his head and whisked away to the kitchen. Engel asked Maria what she wanted to eat. Maria suggests the sauerbraten as Engel reads what it is. He jokingly said, "Do I get a whole roast for myself? Maria said, "neine! that would draw too much attention, you can fill up on bread and cheese." The waiter brings the couple bread and cheese as they make small talk.

Engel flexes his neck and rubs it with his hand. Maria asked him what is the matter? Engel tells her that it is early signs of the real pain to come. Maria takes Engel's hand and kisses it. "I love you Engel Stern." said Maria. Engel smiles at Maria and says, "I love you, Maria Orsic." Engel says, "A toast to the woman who is to be my bride." He raises his wine glass and clinks it against Maria's wine glass. Engel sliced the bread up and offered it up to Maria. They ate cheese and bread, sipped their wine as the presumed restaurant owner walked out to the middle of the floor. He says," Can I have everyone's attention for a moment. It seems our glorious leader will be adding Poland as another conquered territory. Long live the fatherland! Heil Hitler!" Everyone in the restaurant repeated the homage to Hitler and the man returned to the kitchen. Engel looked at Maria and then turned around to look at general Wolfstein. The general held up his wine glass to Engel and Engel returned the gesture. Engel said in a low tone, "I wasn't expecting it this quick. Maria told Engel that the Reich had taken Austria and Czechoslovakia without firing a shot. "I guess the Poles didn't want a peaceful agreement." Stated Maria. By this time the main course was brought out by the waiter. Place the dishes in front of the couple. Engel was about to bless the food and Maria stopped him before he did it. She said in a low tone, "Not here darling." Engel held Maria's hand closed his eyes for a moment and released her hand.

CHAPTER 18

LENA VONN
(THE DEVIL'S BITCH)

They began eating the main course. Engel fought hard against his instinct to just start shoveling food in his mouth. His body craved it already. He had drunk his wine in a gulp and poured more wine into his glass. He then noticed that the sounds of people talking had toned down. The room changed after the announcement made by the man. Engel continued to eat until he felt a presence that he knew near him. He then felt a hand on his shoulder. Engel turns his head to see the general and his female companion standing to the right of his table. "Let me introduce this vision of loveliness to you. This is Lena Vonn. Lena, these two friends of mine are the minister of finance herr Engel Stern and his soon bride to be is the Maria Orsic." said General Wolfstein. Lena says, "I hope you will give me a reading sometime Maria and have you two set a date yet?" We are waiting for our rings to be finished from the jeweler and the Fuhrer will declare us man and wife at the wedding. I am sure that the general will bring you because I just invited you." said Maria. The general said, "We will be there to celebrate such a day. Now we bid you both a good evening. Heil Hitler!"

The general and his voluptuous partner made their way to the exit and left the building. Maria gave him a look and Engel said," I know what you are about to say. She really had a tight dress on, didn't she?" "The buttons on her blouse are barely holding those things in place." Said Maria with a smirk on her face. Maria grabbed her breast and said," Are you happy with these Engel?' Engel almost choked on his food from that comment and said, "You are real to me and of course I love every part of you. You are my intended. Lena may just be another of his creations." I saw how she looked at you. She was verfuchting (fucking) you with her eyes." exclaimed Maria. Engel grabbed Maria's hand and said, "The only one that is verfluchting me is you. Whatever that word means." Maria laughs and said, "Verflucting means to make love to someone. This is the first time you've heard such a word?" Engel blurted out, "We are going to do verfluchting in our new house."

The man with his wife at the next table dropped his silverware on the floor after hearing Engel's comment. Maria laughs nervously and says, "Try not to blurt out that word so loudly next time in public okay, my dearest!" There was giggling at other tables. Was it because of Engel's blurt? Engel's senses are on full tilt. Lena's breast did excite him but so did this food and the wine. Engel takes in some deep breaths to calm himself, refocus on who is in front of him. Maria is the cornerstone of his foundation. He drinks all his wine in one gulp. Maria sees that he stressed and she lays her hand on his and tells him to relax. Engel fills his glass with wine, he was hoping that the wine would soothe him, and it isn't working. He starts just shoveling food into his mouth, swallowing it without tasting it. Maria motions for the waiter to come to the table. Maria asks the waiter to place the remaining food in a bag.

The waiter asks if there is a problem. Maria just tells him that her husband isn't feeling well and could she have the bill. The waiter says that the general had already paid for everything. Engel reaches in his coat and gives the waiter a few franks and thank the waiter. The waiter gets a paper bag and places the bread cheese and the bottle of wine in the bag. There was nothing in Engel's plate and Maria told the waiter everything was good. She takes Engel's hand, and they head to the exit. They get to the sidewalk and a taxi pulls up to the curb. Engel opens the car door for Maria and tells the driver to take them to the bank.

Engel turns to Maria and tells her this will be the last night in the apartment. "Our own house my love." says Maria. Engel kisses Maria hand and holds it against his face. Maria says, "You feel extra warm are you okay?" Engel says that he is fine and is still hungry. Maria tells him that it is a good thing they brought food with them.

Maria knows what is wrong with her intended. It is his body preparing itself for tomorrow night's change that will last 3 maybe 4 nights, depending on the phases of the full moon. The car arrives at the bank and Engel pays the taxi driver. Engel assist Maria as she grabs the bag of food. Engel reached into his pocket and unlocked the bank door, rushing inside to disable the alarm. The alarm is disabled, and Engel relocks the door of the bank and rearms the alarm system. Maria had already gotten halfway up the stairs as Engel hurried to catch up to her, to unlock the apartment door and takes the bag of food from Maria. Maria says that she wants to get out of shoes and put on something comfortable. Engel said, "Since our wine glasses are already packed away, an ordinary glass will just have to work."

Engel poured wine into the glasses for Maria and himself. Engel takes of his shoes and shirt and sits down at the table waiting for Maria. Maria walks back into the room wearing a bra and her undergarments. Engel smiles at her as she sits down next to him. She leans into him and gives him a kiss and says, "I am the luckiest woman alive right now!" Engel tells her that he feels that he is the luckiest man to have her and kisses her. He picks up the glass and says, "To the luckiest people in all of Germany!" They clink their glasses together. Engel reaches into the bag and begins placing the food onto the table. Maria gets up and grabs one plate from the dish rack and says, "We'll share a plate okay! I'm still kind of full of dinner." Engel gets a knife, slices up the cheese and the bread. He bows and says grace of the food. he starts stuffing cheese and bread into his mouth and his thoughts go back to what the restaurant manager said about Germany going into Poland.

Engel has seen firsthand what war means. It means death for many on both sides. The devil is getting laid tonight and is happy with his plans of death and destruction that is to come. Maria says," Stop worrying my dear. I 'll tell you when it's time to start worrying.

Just focus on the here and now with me." Engel nods and continues stuffing food into his mouth. Maria nibbles at a piece of cheese and drinks wine. She takes her free hand and gently runs her hand on top Engels maleness and begins rubbing him. Engel swallows his food and says, "Is this what leads to this verflucting word you told me about?" Maria says," Yes, my darling. I want you inside of me. Can you stop eating and take off your clothes for me?"

Engel took a sip of wine and immediately took off his clothes. Maria led him by the hand to the bedroom. Maria slipped off her under garments and lays down on the bed. Engel is almost erect as he looks at his beautiful mate's nakedness. He caresses her legs as he lays down beside her, moving his hand to his favorite place to touch. He slowly rubs her fleshy mound as she releases a relaxed moan. Maria takes Engel's throbbing member in her hand, gently squeezing and stroking him. She is getting wet inside as Engel kisses her breast and then Maria's mouth. Maria pushes Engel onto his back and straddles him.

Gliding him into her wetness as she grinds her body against his. She quickens her movement and Engel slows her down. He does not want to spew into her yet. He wants his mate to climax first, he waits until he feels her fluid flow against him. He quickens his thrust until he can no longer hold it back until the release happens.

Something different than anytime he has made love to his Maria, feels different. Is it because he is one day away from the change. He feels like the pressures of this world have been released at this moment. He grabs his mate and gives her a passionate kiss and tells her that he loves her. Maria raises up and catches the juices flowing out of her in her hand. She wipes it on the end of the bed spread. She tells Engel that this is the last night sleeping on this bed anyway. "Tomorrow is a new day for us my love. We never have to stay in this apartment again. We will have our own home. It will be ours. Just as you belong to me, and I belong to you, my love. We don't need the Fuhrer to tell us we are husband and wife. Do we darling?" says Maria as she gets up and moves towards the bathroom. Engel follows her and says, "I know it is merely a ritual, but normally done by a holy man, not a mad man intent on conquering. We are just going through this motion, aren't we?"

Engel stands in the tub with his intended and washes her off as she washes him off. They are clean now. He steps out of the tub and gives Maria a towel to dry herself. He helps her out of the tub to prevent her from falling. She takes the towel and dries Engel off and even dries his feet. Engel stops her and tells her that it isn't necessary. Maria looks up and says, "These feet have carried a man that was chosen by Christ himself. You'll be an apostle right up to the day you meet your teacher again." "Why would you say that darling? "Asked Engel. "He will release you of your burden. Just as you released Jean D Arc. It was you that made her clean again. Or should I say you showed her how."

Maria started crying and Engel held her. "What will become of me? Will you help me to be redeemed when its time my love?" asked Maria. We will both have to ask for forgiveness when it comes." said Engel. He wipes the tears from Maria's face and tells her that she will be with him. They put on their undergarments and retire in each other's arms for the night. Maria goes to sleep with head on Engels chest and Engel's mind turns loose of the day's action and slips into a peaceful sleep. The next came and Engel tries to slip out of bed without waking Maria. "Where are you going darling. It isn't time for you to get up yet. Lie back down with me, baby." says Maria. Engel rubs his jaw and says, "My jaws are aching. I must get up and look in the mirror. It is too soon for this to be happening." Maria turns on the bedside lamp and tells Engel to come to her, so that she can look into his mouth.

Engel complies and sits on the edge of the bed and opens his mouth. Maria looks at his teeth and she doesn't see anything abnormal like really pronounced canine incisors. "I don't see anything out of the ordinary darling. You may have been clinching in your sleep. Did you have a disturbing dream to wake you up?" asked Maria. "I only remember a part of the dream. I was fighting Saladin's army by myself, and Jerusalem still fell. I must have killed hundreds of men and Jerusalem still fell into Saladin's hands." "It wasn't your fault that Jerusalem fell, my darling. It was Jerusalem's faith that caused it to fall. Even today, the Jewish people don't regard Jesus as the true Messiah. They only view him as a prophet.

You know that he was more than a prophet. You were with him.

He chose you. So, I say again. Jerusalem fell because they continued to cling to the books of Abraham and disregarded what Jesus did for them. He took the sins of the world with him to the cross and set us free with his blood. The cross killed his physical body, but it didn't kill his undying spirit. He appeared to you; you told me of this. So please put your mind at ease. You were chosen by the son of God. That means no matter whatever the devil throws at you. The heavenly host will always have your back. We have each other to walk through this now. I feel there's a grand plan behind all of this. So, until it is revealed. Let me fix us some breakfast, I think there's enough food here so we can do this. This will be our last breakfast here. I am so excited to get out of here. I'll be needing the key to our new home. I must go to the market and get us some food today." said Maria.

Engel got his wallet and took out some money and placed it on the table. He told her that if she needed more, he would get more. She kissed him and told him to go and shave while she fixed breakfast. Engel goes into the bath and turns on the light and looks at his teeth and jaw line. He doesn't see the signs, but he feels the signs. The full moon rises today, and he must leave the bank early today. It wouldn't be good to change in downtown Berlin. Engel cleans up and puts on his clothing for the day. He smells the aroma of food from the kitchen. He goes and helps Maria with the meal. She tells him to sit at the table and drink some coffee. Maria looks at Engel, smiles and says," I love you Judas, I mean Engel." Engel tells her that he loves her and says to be careful about what she says. Maria acknowledges this and finishes cooking the eggs.

Maria jokingly says, "We would have some bread and cheese to eat this morning if someone hadn't eaten it last night." Engel chuckles at her comment as she sets the plates with eggs on the table. Engel says grace over the food, and they eat their scaled down breakfast. Engel doesn't mind. He'll send one of the workers to get him something else to eat once the bank opens. They have small talk, and they are both glad to be rid of the cramped living quarters that they have endured. time clicked until was time for Engel to go downstairs. He gives Maria the key to their new home, gives her a hug and kiss, and locks the apartment door as he leaves. As he walks down the stairs, he can see movement at the bank entrance. He continues his way to the main entrance and sees that it's the manger Herr Burkhalter unlocking the main doors. Engel goes and disarms the alarm system and waits for the manager to enter the bank.

The manager sees his boss and smiles and gives Engel a warm greeting. "Today is a good day for you herr Minister. You and your intended will be moving to much better environs. Once you get settled in. will it be okay if my family brings you and Maria a housewarming gift." asked the manager. The manager saw the puzzled look in Engel's face and said, "A nice bottle of wine with bread and cheese. For you and Maria." Engel told the manager that it wouldn't be necessary to bring anything. "Just let me know when you are visiting, and you and your wife can have dinner with us. If you want to bring a bottle of wine? That will be okay also. Maria and I would be glad to have your family over." said Engel. The other employees were filing in and giving their greetings to Engel and the manager as they went to their workstations for the day.

As Engel opens his office door a hunger pain hits him. The small breakfast only kick started the need for more food. His body needs fuel for what is to come. He turns around and goes to the manager. He asks the manager could he send someone out to the bakery and get some strudel for everyone. Engel says, "Have the bakery bill me for the strudel." "What kind of strudel do you want, herr Minister "asked the manager. Engel said, "All kinds of strudel from whatever fruit that is in season now. Maria and I didn't have much of breakfast this morning because of the moving, and today I feel like treating everyone to some strudel, and do we have enough coffee cups and coffee for every one of the employees? "We can't have strudel without coffee now, can we?" asked Engel. The manager smiled at Engel and told him that he would get right on it. An employee overheard the conversation and began walking around telling the other employees what was about to happen. Engel had gone into his office and shut the door behind him. His senses are very acute today, the ticking of the clock on wall sounds like he is holding the clock to his ear. He starts thinking he may have to leave the bank sooner than he expected.

The spell of the full moon feels extra stronger than usual. He looks behind him at the calendar on the wall. Today is a new month and a full moon. His body knows the moon is coming but does not care about the day or the month. His body craves fuel he could probably eat every piece of pastry from the bakery and still not be full. He puts his mind into his work, refocuses off the hunger. He also thinks about the new house and the basement where he'll be locked up for at least 3 nights. He examined the steel door yesterday that the general had installed for him. He is concerned for his intended's safety. The house isn't close to anyone else, it's secluded. He knows that the beast has no boundaries and can travel tirelessly looking for a kill.

He hears someone at his door and light knocking happens. "Eintreten!" (enter) says Engel. the door opens and it is Maria. She closes the door and walks over and kisses Engel. Engel tells her that he sent an employee out to the bakery to get strudel and coffee for everyone. "Are you hungry my darling?" asked Maria. "Hungry is an understatement, my body is starving for something to eat." says Engel. Maria takes Engels' hand and says, "We can have a strudel and coffee with the employees and leave to get a huge breakfast at the nearest restaurant. They will be expecting you to say something once the pastries get here. Have you thought of something to say?" asked Maria.

Engel paused and said," Today is appreciation day for all the employees of this bank. This is my way of saying thank you all. as I hold up my cup of coffee in a salute to them." Maria then said, "You may also throw in a heil Hitler in the end. To cap it off dear." "You are right my dear. I am so glad you walked in to keep me on the path. Did I tell you that I loved you today? "Said Engel. "You don't have to say it. I know it!" exclaims Maria. Engel hears activity outside his door and tells Maria that he thinks the food is here. Engel gets up from his chair, opens the door as Maria follows him. An employee also brought in someone from the bakery, they were carrying in the containers of goods from the bakery. The bakery employee dressed in white attire placed his packages on the table. He carries with him a piece of paper and approaches Engel. He stops in front of Engel and does a heil Hitler homage and tells Engel this is the bill from his boss. Engel takes the bill and tells the baker to wait a moment. He goes to a teller and asks her to issue a cashier's check to the baker and he would sign it. She asked Engel from which account she should withdraw the funds? Engel tells her to use his account.

The cashier smiles at Engel and makes a notation in the bank ledger, creates the cashier's check and hands it to Engel to sign. She smiles at Engel and tells him thanks for his generosity. Engel gave the baker the check and the baker did his homage to Hitler and left the building. As people were making their way to the food and coffee cups. Engel waited until everyone had food and coffee and stepped into the middle of the bank floor and said, "If I can have everyone's attention for a moment? There's something I would like to say. Today is this bank's employee's appreciation day. This is my way of saying thank you to everyone for your diligent hard work that you put in every day. Heil Hitler! Now enjoy your strudel and coffee plus have a good day." Maria walks up and in a low tone to Engel," You would make a great statesman my dear. Let's get a coffee and strudel." Engel took her hand and went towards the table holding the strudel and cups of coffee.

The smell of the apple strudel is almost spell binding to Engel's senses. There are only three in the box, he only grabs one and must contain himself from just stuffing it all in his mouth and downing the cup of coffee in one gulp. He takes a bite, and the flavors explode in his mouth. Maria takes one of the strudels and follows Engel with her coffee. Engel takes three more bites, and the strudel is gone. He licks his fingers and gulps down the hot coffee without any hesitation. Maria is still blowing across her cup to cool the coffee down before drinking it. Engel felt the heat of the coffee but was impervious to pain. There was no pain. He only tasted the coffee as he gulped it down like a glass of water. Maria and Engel walked around in the bank for a moment and Engel told the manager that he would return in a moment. The manager held out his hand gesturing a friendly handshake.

Engel returned the gesture by gripping the manager's hand and giving him a firm shake. The manager told Engel to take Maria for a proper breakfast. Engel agreed to the manager's suggestion and left with Maria to get breakfast. Engel and Maria Walk out on to the sidewalk. The streets in Berlin are busy with people, ordinary citizens and military alike. To Engel's perception, the invasion of Poland appears to have no effect upon Germany's citizens. He thought that their actions would be withdrawn to war. Before Engel had a chance to say a word. Maria says, "Looks like the invasion of Poland has brought about a change hasn't it. Germany's economy is about to take off." "Where will the money come from?" asked Engel.

Just as Maria was about to answer, a taxi pulled up and retrieved Engel and Maria. Engel directed the driver to take them to the nearest restaurant. They discuss their conversation in front of the taxi driver. They changed the conversation to something more mundane kin to normal German lifestyles. They arrive at the restaurant; Engel pays the taxi driver, and they enter the establishment. They are greeted and taken to a table; the restaurant is fairly busy with customers. To Engel, the smell of food has taken over his mind and his body craves it. The waiter asked them would they like some coffee while they looked over the breakfast menu. Engel nodded and told the waiter to get two coffees. Maria saw how intense Engel was gazing over the menu. She jokingly said in a subdued tone, "Please don't order everything on the menu. I know you're hungry. I'm going to suggest a large potato and ham omelet and they will be bringing us bread anyway." Engel smiled and said, "How about just half the menu?" They both laughed at his comment. The waiter came back with two coffees on a tray and issued out the items to the couple, took their orders and disappeared back into the kitchen. Engel then said, "Since we are on the subject of food. We are going to need provisions for the house. I still have the driver; he can assist you this morning." "We have an auto now. I can drive." answered Maria. Engel paused for a moment to take a sip of his coffee. "I will teach you to drive my love." said Maria. Engel almost spit out his coffee at such a suggestion. The moment of levity quickly passes as Engel notices that a group of Gestapo officers enter the establishment.

Maria's back is to the entrance, and she notices his facial expression change from happiness to contempt. The waiter takes the four gestapo officers to a table seated to the right of he and Maria's table. Maria placed her hand on to top of Engel's hand after she saw the men being seated. One of the gestapo officers recognized Engel and says to the others at his table, "We have a killer in our midst." Engel turns his head and looks at the man who said it. Engel says, "Maybe I should suggest to Himmler to move the gestapo to Poland so that they can harass them instead of the citizens of Berlin." One of the subordinates says to his superior, "He should be shot in the street for what he done to one our own."

"Does the gun and the uniform make any of you a man or are you a man without it?" asked Engel. The commanding officer said, "How dare you make such a provocation? Do you know we could shoot you and your woman right here and nothing would be done about it.?" "Yes! And all of you would still be cowards in a gestapo uniform with a gun." Replied Engel. The gestapo aggressor pulls his side arm to point at Engel. Engel with his honed quickness grabs the aggressor's gun hand and points it at the gestapo commander's head. The restaurant falls silent at that moment and Engel says, "No one must die today, do they commander?" asked Engel. The commander said," I could have you shot for this, but how could a dead man make such a demand. Do you think this is over after to release my subordinate's hand?" Engel now positioned himself behind the aggressor and placed his free arm around the aggressor's neck. Engel told all the men to put their guns on the table. Engel tells a nearby waiter to pick up all the guns and place them on another table. The hesitant waiter complies and does what Engel tells him. Engel then forcefully removed the gun from the aggressor's hand released his grip upon the aggressor. Engel now has a gun in his hand and says, "The Fuhrer is going to officially consecrate my marriage to my new wife and I'm not going to let you stop it, because of your stupidity." Engel shouts, "Shop keeper! Lock the front door and alert me if any gestapo or military personnel tries to come in. Is that understood?" A nervous shop keeper complies, and Maria says," Take them out back and shoot them.

That is what they would do to any of us." "Now you see commander! You've even corrupted my wife into wanting to kill all of you. Is this really what you want? Yes! I could kill all four of you in the back alley, but then there would be inquiry. The shop keeper and everyone in here would be suspects. Now we could forget about all this of course I keep all your guns." At that moment a familiar figure appears at the front door. The door unlocks and General Wolfstein walks in. Everything seems to stop in the room except for the general's movements and that of Engel's. General Wolfstein walks up to Engel and takes the gun from Engel's hand. All the guns on the table are now back in their original location. "I can change the situation in the room, but I cannot change you. You cannot take on the whole German Reich by yourself. Do you remember about what I said about Rome?" asked the General. "You said that Rome would take care of itself. So, you are saying that Germany is going to take care of itself.

Maria and I only came in for breakfast and this happened." stated Engel. The general snapped his fingers and things started moving again. The gestapo men continued their conversations and the general sat down at Engel's table. "I have been preoccupied with the inner workings of the Reich and I sensed something bad was about to happen. I know what is going to happen in the next three nights, and today of all days you were about to set things into motion, that there would be no returning from. You two are in a very good position right now. Many will be clamoring for your attention in the days to come. As a matter of fact, I need a small insignificant favor. Lena wants to open her own beauty parlor. I told her that I could finance it, but she insisted upon standing upon her on two feet. That's why I like her. She's so independent. She'll be coming by the bank in the morning. So do you have any questions for me while I'm here?" "Is the steel door going to be strong enough?" asked Maria. "Yes! The steel door is more than adequate to do the job. Any more questions?" asked the general. "Will I be targeted like I was today again." asked Engel.

"Only by me, if you try to undermine the grand plans I have for Germany." replied the general. A waiter came by the table and asked the general did he wanted anything. The general told the waiter that he was only stopping by. As the general stood up. He said, "The jewelers will have your rings today and I'll be seeing the Fuhrer today, so next week would be good time for the wedding. Heil Hitler!" The general looked at the table with Gestapo personnel and said,"Heil Hitler!" This time the gestapo all jumped up and gave their salute to the Fuhrer. The general left the restaurant, Engel and Maria breathed a sigh of relief. The waiter brought the food to the table and Engel took the hand of Maria, bowed his head for a moment. He looked back up and began eating. He wanted to scoop the food in, but he contained himself. Maria said in a low voice, "Let's hurry and finish our food and get out of here." Engel nodded in agreement and thought to himself, that the dark master has taken a deeper interest Germany. So deep an interest that he doesn't want Engel Stern to complicate the situation.

Engel had already plan in his head if those men had tried anything, but he didn't get to execute it. He continued to eat and tried play out a scene that didn't happen. Maria placed her hand on his arm because she could sense that his mind was awash with violence. She must get him calm and get him out of the restaurant before something else triggers something that could get way out of control. She hurriedly puts food in her mouth and gives her intended the look of calmness and love. Today is not a good day for any kind of confrontation. Maria also sensed the general's immediate appearance as a sign, that the devil's hand is directing the course of Germany as he did with the fall of the Roman empire. She stopped sipping her coffee and began drinking it down.

She got the waiter's attention, and he quickly came over to the table. She asked the waiter to bring some water for her and Engel. Coffee is the last thing that Engel needs to crank up his already heightened senses. Engel had drunk his coffee and was shoving food in his mouth without anything to drink. He was already taking his bread and dragging the plate clean of any of the juice contents. The waiter brought the glasses of water and Engel down the water like a man dying of thirst. Maria had taken a few drinks out of her water glass and sat it down on the table. Engel took the last morsel of meat from Maria's plate and drank her glass of water. Luckily the gestapo was too busy talking to notice Engel's eating habit. The waiter came to the table and asked if he could be of service. Engel asked the waiter for the bill so that he could pay for it. The waiter told Engel that their bill had been taken care of by the general that was here.

Engel takes out his wallet and gives the waiter a few marks. "Heil Hitler!" stated Engel. As he and Maria make their way out of the restaurant. They didn't have to wait long for a taxi to pull up. Engel opens the door as Maria enters the backseat. Engel gives the driver the destination and the driver pulls out into the busy street of Berlin. The couple doesn't speak in the cab, they only wait until the ride has made it to its destination. The cab stops in front of the bank and Engel and Maria exits the cab. Engel pays the cab driver, and the cab moves back into the flow of the day's traffic. They didn't go into the bank. Engel kissed his betrothed and told her that he would see her at the house around lunch time, if not sooner. She tells Engel that she is going to the market and asked Engel to summon the driver. Maria says, "You have the auto, get to the house as quickly as you can. Things are different now and time is an enemy.

"Engel knows to well about the ticking of the clock. He tells her that he will see her soon, gives her a kiss and enters the bank. Engel only gets a few steps into the bank lobby after closing the door, the bank manager approaches him and tells him that he has a visitor waiting in his office. Engel thanks the manager and opens the door to his office to find that he does indeed have a guest. "Good morning frau Vonn! What do I owe the pleasure of meeting such beauty this morning." said Engel. Lena uncrosses her legs and stands and offers her hand to Engel. Engel kissed her on her hand and sat back down. Engel fights the temptation of looking at the bulging mounds of her breast as the buttons strain to hold back the proverbial dam from busting. He instead looks into her piercing blue eyes and gives her a smile as he sits down behind his desk.

"Before we get started, I need to call my driver." says Engel. He picks up the phone calls his driver. He tells the driver to pick up Maria in front of the bank. The driver acknowledges the command and Engel hangs up the phone. Lena says, "Lucian told me that you would loan me the marks for the business. He insisted that I talk to you since I refused his offer. I have found a location and I just need some start-up money to get things going." "Did Lucian, I mean general Wolfstein help you arrive at a specific number of reichsmarks you would need? How many employees are you planning to hire? Are you going to rent the building or buy it?" Lena leans forward showing Engel her pronounced cleavage and says, "The previous owners were Juden and now I own the building. She leans back into her chair, opens her purse and produces a document and hands it to Engel. Engel glances at the document and sees that the building ownership is now being held by Lena Vonn.

Engel looks at the clock on the wall and it shows that it is nine thirty-five in the morning. Engel says, "Normally, my manager handles small business loans. Since the general steered you to me. The building will be used as collateral for the loan. Have you thought of an amount that you would need to get going with today, frau Vonn?" "Can I borrow a pen and paper herr minister?' asked Lena. Engel complies by handing Lena a pen and paper as he watches her lean over on his desk to write down a figure. She places the pen and paper down on Engel's desk at sits back down in her chair. Engel picks up the paper and reads the amount to himself. The amount is five thousand reichsmarks. He quickly attributed the amount to what he would make in six months on his current salary. He also knows that regardless of the amount, he would have to comply with her wishes or face the consequences.

Engel leaned back from his desk and said," According to the document the building at its location would be more valuable than five thousand reichsmarks. I don't know what the current condition of the building is, I can only speculate that it would require some renovation to get presentable for business. What if I float you a loan and your first payment isn't until three months from now. Since this is a business loan. What do you plan on calling this new business? "Lena bounced with excitement as she clapped her hands together gleefully. "It will be called Lena's Laden Haus (boutique house)." stated Lena. As Lena was talking about the paint color of the walls and the store front. Engel was writing down some instructions for his manager to handle. Engel had only one thing on his mind and that was to get out of the city of Berlin before it was too late today.

Lena is a very voluptuous woman and her dress looked like it was painted on her. He also knows that the woman in his office belongs to the dark master, and she needs to be gone from his office and quickly. Engel stands up and hands Lena a piece of paper and tells her to take it to the manager. "The manager will have everything typed up by his secretary and you can come by here in an hour to sign the documents for a business loan and you can have the money. I will give the manager the property deed to add to the paperwork. I mentioned earlier that the property is more valuable than the five thousand reichsmarks so if you need more money in six to twelve months from now, we can renegotiate the loan terms. This will give you some leverage for your new business to grow." Engel stuck out his hand for Lena to shake, but instead Lena kissed his hand." Danke! Herr Minister! Frau Orsic is a lucky woman, and I will tell Lucian that you were very accommodating in this transaction." Said a very happy Lena as she opens the door of Engel's office and gently closes it behind her. Engel let out a sigh of relief that the encounter was over.

Engel found out two very important things today. One thing he already knew was that the dark master is always aware especially when it concerns his pet project which is him, and Engel learned what the dark master's name is other than General Wolfstein, it is Lucian Wolfstein. Engel isn't even worried about the loan, even though he'll be signing the business contract. It isn't his money; it is the German war machines money. Other things started to come to his mind. How he had to use mind control on the bank manager to lock him up and free him from the old vault room. Meeting his betrothed and she took over the locking and unlocking of the old vault room. Now the situation has changed. He will have to be home before the change starts. Changes in every aspect of his life happen very quickly.

He didn't want to think what his old life was like. He only knows that he doesn't want to go back to that old life. Today, he is at war with time. He told Lena to come back in an hour to sign the papers and get her money. Engel got up from his chair and went to the manager's office and asked about the status of the loan application. The manager informed Engel that his secretary should be finished with the hour. Engel told the manager that he would be leaving early and needed the transaction completed before he left today. The manager says," Today was a first for this bank. You are a good man herr Stern and today you showed your goodness to your employees. My previous boss was a task master and Juden. The employees will really be surprised at the end of the week due to their pay increase. I am grateful for my increase as well." "I did this show of gratitude this morning because I wanted to. I am signing my name on this loan because I must. "Said Engel. Engel opens the manager's door, closes it behind him and walks across the bank's floor space and leaves his door open. Engel's thoughts are now on how to get home in time.

He has a vehicle and has never driven an auto in his life. He looks at the clock on the wall and it says ten in the morning. Engel's personal driver is assisting Maria today. He has watched other people drive but attempted it himself. Today, he has no choice but to accept the challenge. He walks into his office and sits down behind his desk. He thinks about all the things that he has endured from be shot, stabbed and even hung. In his mind, he would rather deal with an angry group of gestapo agents than try to master a machine. Today he would welcome violence because he is already like a wound-up spring ready to uncoil all this pent-up energy. Perhaps a cigarette to calm his nerves. He reaches into his coat pocket and finds nothing. He opens his desk drawer and finds a lighter but no cigarettes. Maybe someone in the bank has a cigarette. He opens the door and there standing in front of him is Lena Vonn. "My apologies Frau Vonn. Please come in.," said Engel. Engel steps aside as she enters the office and sits down in a chair.

Engel calmly sat down behind his desk and says, "You wouldn't happen to have a spare cigarette I could borrow?" asked Engel. Lena smiled and says," Yes! I have them in my purse." replied Lena. Lena opens her purse, takes out a cigarette from her cigarette case, places the cigarette on her lips and lights it. She takes the cigarette and hands it to Engel. "Do I make you nervous herr minister?" asked Lena. "It is not you that makes me nervous. I'm kind of perplexed about something right now, but it is nothing that you should be worried about." as Engel takes a long drag from the cigarette and exhales the smoke. Lena notices the calmness of Engel's demeanor change as he exhaled the smoke. Engel smiles at Lena and looks at her as if he is looking at her soul. She adjusted her body to the chair and feels a tingle between her thighs. Her lips become pursed, and her pulse quickens. Engel takes a deep breath and breaks eye contact with her. Lena opens her purse and takes out a cigarette and lights it.

She had become sexually aroused by Engel's gaze and now she feels elation. "Is it warm in here is it just me?" Ask Lena. Engel knows what is going on and tells her to relax as he picks up the phone to call the manager. The manager answers by telling Engel that he will bring the documents into his office. Engel thanks the manager and hangs up the phone. Engel tells Lena that the manager will be on his way with the documentation. Lena squirms nervously in her chair and puffs on her cigarettes like a locomotive puffing steam. Engel is trying his best to turn off this switch he has turned on. He starts talking to Lena and getting her redirected on her new business. "So, Lena! When do you think you'll be in operation of this new business of yours?" asked Engel. Lena takes a puff from her cigarette and tells Engel that she plans on getting the business open as early as next week. There's a knock at the door and Engel says,"Einkommen!"The manager walks into the room and places the documents on top of Engels desk. "Danke herr Burkhalter." says Engel and the manager closes the door behind him.

Engel looks at the documents, signs his name in the appropriate location and places the pen on the paper and slides the papers towards Lena. Lena stands up and leans to sign the documents. Lena's breast is almost about to bust the button her blouse and she says in a low voice, "Wouldn't you like to slide something in me herr minister?" Engel almost dropped his cigarette and pretended he didn't hear what she said. "Take the top document to the teller and she will give you the reichmarks you need for the business. Thank you for your patronage and choosing our bank. Heil Hitler!" Exclaimed Engel. "Danke herr minister and heil Hitler!" replied Lena as she opened the door and closed it behind her. Engel did not stand when he said heil Hitler because he had a throbbing erection. Engel is glad that Maria isn't there to witness what happened.

In Engel's mind, Lena represented a test of his will sent by the dark master. Today Engel didn't fail the test. The smell of Lena's perfume still present in the room left an indelible mark in the room. The effect of the moon is strong today and as soon as his erection subsides. He will get up and leave the bank regardless of if he knows how to drive the auto or not. So, Engel sits there and waits, he relaxes by finishing the cigarette and puts it out in an ashtray. He opens his drawer, puts the lighter in it and closes it. He stands up adjusted his trousers and made sure that the bulge was gone. He checks his pocket for the keys and leaves his office. He goes to the manager's office and tells him that he's leaving for the day. Engel walks out onto the sidewalk and takes in a deep breath of air.

The auto is parked on the corner, and he opens the door and gets in. He sticks the key in the ignition and before turning it, he looks over the situation and goes through all the moves in his mind, that he remembers seeing other drivers do. He steps on the clutch, releases the brake, turns the key and the engine starts. He places the gear shift into gear and slowly releases the clutch. The auto moves forward as Engel presses the accelerator pedal. He presses the clutch and grinds a gear into second and into third. The auto is moving and now maneuver through the busy streets without hitting someone or something. He is confident and weary at the same time. He must down shift to keep from colliding with other vehicles in the street. Engel is gripping the steering wheel tightly and mindfully drives the auto through the twists and turns of the streets of Berlin. He makes the last turn that he needs to get home. As he turns on the street, he sees that the traffic is stopped up ahead.

He sits there for a moment and listens to hear what the cause may be. He hears a person yell out," The man is pinned, and I cannot free him!" Engel turns off the ignition, takes the key and heads towards a gathering crowd. Engel continues to listen to what is going on and he pushes himself forward into the crowd of people. He finally sees what has transpired. A man is pinned underneath a vehicle. The man was trying to change out a tire when another auto struck the trapped man's auto. The auto that delivered the strike, its bumper is jammed under the pinned man's auto. Men are feverishly trying to jack up the autos and the jacks aren't working.

The man's leg is pinned underneath, and Engel quickly tells two men to help him lift the car up. The men tell Engel that they have tried it, and it didn't work. Engel gets close to man and assures him that he is going to free him. Engel leans against the auto, puts both hands under the fender, makes a firm grip and slowly lifted the auto enough so that another man could pull the trapped man free. Once the man was free, Engel dropped the vehicle, and the other vehicle became free as well. A man witnessing this recognized Engel and yelled out, "Herr minister Stern! The strongest banker in all of Germany has saved this man. Sieg heil! Sieg Heil!" Engel went over to the man to look at the damage caused to the man's leg. He could see that it has been crushed and the man still moaning from the pain, held out his hand to Engel.

Engel grabbed hand and shook it as the man said, "Bless you sir!" Engel could still hear the mutterings of the crowd saying. "That man lifted two autos by himself!" as he quickly made his way to his auto. The crowded street moved to one side to allow Engel auto to pass. Engel's heart swelled with joy as he moved through the gears of the auto, as he headed for his new home. While Engel was lifting the auto, he could feel the signs of the coming change. The tightening of the jaw muscles in his face as well as the muscles in the rest of his body. He lifted the vehicles effortlessly and now he must get home in time. He pushes the auto to its limits until he sees a familiar path. He is on the driveway to his new home. Home. A word that has eluded him in his many guises throughout time. He pulls up to the house and sees his driver waving goodbye to Maria standing at the door. Engel rushed up to the driver's car and bid him graciously thanks for his help for the day.

Maria could see the urgency unfolding in front of her. Engel wanted to run into the doorway but couldn't risk the driver glancing back to see from his mirror. Engel hurriedly made it into the house, kissed Maria and quickly headed to the wine cellar. He hears the key activate the locks in the steel door. "I love you and I'll see you in the morning." said Maria. Engel standing on the other side of the steel door tells his intended that he loves her and as the pain started, he tells Maria that he saved a man today. Maria keeps him talking and listens until the pain becomes unbearable. She presses her head against the steel door and listens to her intended moan and yell out tortured rage. She continued to listen until there was no sound. She pushed herself from the door and waited.

She watched the doorknob twist and then came the banging on the door. The banging stopped and the beast said, "Let me out Maria! I won't harm you! I promise!" Maria answers back, "I won't let you out until my husband returns!" "Damn you! I am your husband! Now let me out!" Yells the angered beast. "There is food in the cellar for you! Go eat your food!" Yells Maria. The beast stopped pulling on the doorknob. He heard one word that triggered something in his animal like brain. That word was food. He sprang from the top steps, down to the cellar floor and into the next room. There in the corner of the room was a bucket of water and a whole cured pork ham. The beast began shredding the meat from the salted ham and stuffing it in his mouth. The salt slowed the beast but only momentarily, he continued eating until just the bones were left.

The beast now thirsts for water and he all but emptied the bucket of water, wiped his mouth and placed the bucket on the floor. He listened to the foot falls of Maria as she walked around the house above him. He could hear everything. He heard her moving stuff around and he made his way back to the cellar stairwell and sat at the top step. Maria is still putting the house in order by placing the plates in the cabinet and flatware in the drawer. She stops for a moment, and she listens. knock, knock, knock went the beast knuckles on the steel door. The beast listens to Maria's foot falls as she makes her way to the cellar door. Maria sits down at the door and says," We can talk if you promise to be nice. Can you promise?"

In a gravelly voice the beast utters, "I promise." "Do you want to tell me how you saved a man today?" asked Maria. "The men were weak and couldn't release the trapped man. Engel used my strength to release the trapped man." said the beast. "How did the man get trapped?" asked Maria. "The man was changing tire on auto and another auto crashed in man's auto. Causing auto to trap and break man's leg under auto. Many men tried to free the man, other auto pushing down on trapped man's leg. Engel lifted two autos to free the man. People saw this." said the beast. "Do you think the people were afraid of Engel when they saw this?" asked Maria. "They saw a miracle happen today. They paid tribute to Engel." said the beast.

"Engel came very close to being out of control today, didn't he?" asked Maria. "Yes! In more ways than one. The dark masters whore came to the bank today. She got her money and tried to tempt Engel. Engel is stronger than me. I would have fucked her." "I bet you would." replied Maria. "Engel listens with his heart. I listen with my instincts. No more talking. I would rather kill than to think about things. " said the beast as he walked back down the steps, finds the pork bone to chew on until he went to sleep. Maria went to the kitchen and brewed a cup of tea and thought about what the beast told her. It was things that she already knew especially with the likes of the general's woman Lena Vonn. Maria knows exactly where the general got Lena from. Lena is branching out from her old haunts at the kitty salon in Berlin. The elite bordello of the Reichs upper crust.

Maria wonders if Lena really knows who her boyfriend is. Lena sees the uniform of a high ranking general and with that comes power and prestige. Maria has concluded that the general is simply posing as the general otherwise she wouldn't need a loan from the bank. Lena is playing a high stakes game, and she doesn't know that the dealer of the cards is the king of lies. Maria sits at the table and listens to hear if the beast is tearing up the empty shelves in the wine cellar. She doesn't hear anything from her chair, and she places her head against the floor and listens. She hears her own breath bouncing off the floor. It appears that the beast has had his fill of the pork and has gone to sleep.

Maria stands back up takes a sip from her teacup and fixes herself a light meal to eat. She is tired from moving and arranging things in the new home. She takes off her shoes and drops them in the bedroom and returns to the kitchen. She is relishing the feelings of having a real home even though it will be a burned-out pile of rubble in 1945. This is what her guide Ziel told her. Everything that Ziel has told her so far has come to fruition. It had been a while since she contacted Ziel. The last contact was when she did a reading for the Fuhrer. The Fuhrer was very happy to hear that he would be riding under the Le grande arch in Paris. That reading was the first reading in the new house. She eats her small meal and drinks her tea and takes a cigarette from Engels coat pocket, strikes a match and takes a few puffs to get the cigarette going. She gets an ashtray and sits it on the table. She must relax to open her mind to communicate with Ziel. She must shut down all her feelings of anxiousness and fear.

She takes a puff from the cigarette and exhales the smoke, places the cigarette in the ash tray and places her hands on the table. She takes a slow breath and exhales it at a slow speed. She does this several times until she feels completely calm and serene. Her breathing is slow and rhythmic and now she sends out a telepathic message asking, "Ziel! Are you there? Can you hear me?" She waits for a few moments and then an answer comes in a whisper to her mind. "Yes Maria! I am here. I've been waiting for you." says the voice. Maria pauses and is about to ask Ziel a question, but instead Ziel tells Maria to listen, and he says, "I want you to know that Hitler possesses the spear of Longines. Longines was the Roman centurion that pierced the side of the Christ on the cross. The spear is a holy relic and Hitler thinks he is invincible by having it.

He also thinks that he can use it against the one he made the deal with. It doesn't work that way." "So, you are aware of the dark one that now walks among us?" asked Maria. "Yes! He is the reason why I am here." Replied Ziel. "I don't understand Ziel. I thought you were on a distant planet and sending me messages by thought." stated Maria. "We were exiled here because of him." said Ziel. Maria hesitated as her mind was reeling from Ziel's statement. "You mean...the fallen ones?" asked Maria. "Yes, but we have separated ourselves from him or I should say most of us. The dark one as you call him doesn't know that it is me that you are in contact with. He has his own agenda, and we have ours. Yes, we have been giving you and the Germans ways of making warfare.

This warfare goes on after the defeat of Germany. We also know who your betrothed is, and he has been getting our help and just doesn't know it. He has not been fighting this war by himself. You cannot tell him because the dark one will know. If the Germans continue to get outside help from beyond, the dark one doesn't care as it doesn't interfere with his agenda. You must never give into him no matter what he promises. I am going to plant an image in your mind, and I want you to draw it after we have talked. You can title the drawing wunderwaffen (wonder weapon) and give that drawing to the Fuhrer at your wedding. Tell him you saw this in a vision. Now you must rest. We are finished."

Maria opens her eyes and gets up from the table, finds a piece of paper and begins drawing the object on the paper. She drew a cylinder with a pointed end and drew fins on it much akin to a fish and a flame from the bottom and labelled the drawing wunderwaffen and she folded the paper and placed it in a book for safe keeping. She tiptoed back into the kitchen, crouched down on the floor and placed her ear to the floor and listened. She heard nothing but her own breath against the floor. The beast is asleep, and she felt assured that she could go into the bedroom and go to sleep. She still locked the door behind her it would be her last line of defense, but she feels safer after hearing what Ziel told her. She undressed herself and put on her night gown and laid down in her new bed. Her mind began to think about what was written in the holy book concerning the war in Heaven. A third of the angels in Heaven were cast out with Lucifer and now she knows where some of them are.... in Antarctica.

She drifts off to sleep, and she finds herself witnessing the war in Heaven. It wasn't like the angels she had seen in paintings. She saw beings of pure energy having a battle and the exiled angels were a different color than those that remained in Heaven. The color was a dull amber versus the ultra-white color so intense she could not look directly at them. She saw some of the figures with their heads down and could only guess that they were mourning the loss of their kind. A large bright figure approached her and told her that she seen but a glimpse of what is beyond the sunlight that warms the earth, and he touches her forehead, and she wakes up. She sits up in the bed and hears something. She looks at her door and it is still closed. She gets out of the bed and slowly walks to the door and unlocks it. She opens it and listens. The beast is twisting the knob on the steel door, trying to get out and isn't having any success. Maria walks to the door and knocks on the door. The beast stops moving the knob and Maria says, "Engel would you kill me if you got out?" In a gravely growling voice, the beast says" Not Engel! I am albtraum (nightmare) and I wouldn't kill you. You belong to Engel." "Who would you kill if you could get loose?" asked Maria. The beast hits the steel door with his fist and growls out, "The men in uniforms, I would kill as many as I could in three nights, rip out their hearts and liver and eat from them." "General Wolfstein wears a uniform would you kill him?" asked Maria. There was a pause before Maria got an answer.

In a subdued gravelly voice the beast says," Don't want to go back to that evil place. I want to stay here." "I don't want you to go to that evil place either. Will you lay down and rest for me? When Engel wakes up in the morning? I will fix him a large breakfast for him to eat. Do you think he will like that?" asked Maria. "I am still hungry!" growls out the beast. "The sun will be up in a few more hours. That hole in the bottom of the door, stick your finger out and let me see it." The beast stuck his talon pointed finger through the hole. Maria said," When I see the finger of Engel, I will unlock the door. Now, go and rest and I will fix Engel a large breakfast in the morning." says Maria. Maria stands at the door and listens to the beast's footfalls on the steps as he goes down. She walked past the clock in the hallway, and it had four fifteen.

She went back to the bedroom and locked the door behind her, laid back down and finally drifted off to sleep. The beast found a spot on the cool dirt floor of the basement and closed his eyes. He drifted off to sleep and he was back with Jean. They were a force to be reckoned with, they both loved killing. It was like an addiction that they couldn't stop. The beast dreams were filled with the bloodlust of carnage. The beast dreams ended by the pains of the change from beast to man. His body racked with pain as his very being was taking form back to that of a man again. The pain took a toll on him, and he laid back down and went to sleep. The sun has risen, and Maria awakens to see the time on the clock. It is seven a.m., and she quickly gets up and goes to the steel door that leads to the basement. She kneels at the face of the door and wraps upon the steel door with her knuckles and waits. She listens and hears nothing, so she taps on the door again with her knuckles and calls out," Engel! Are you ready for some breakfast my love?"

Engel wakes up and looks at his hands. He's back to being Engel again and he hears Maria talking. He gets up from the dirt floor, runs up the stairs and sticks his finger out of the hole in the door. Maria unlocks the door and Maria greets Engel with a hug. "You need to go wash up before you sit at the table darling. Go take a bath while I fix us a breakfast." Says Maria. Engels heads off to the bath as Maria heads to the kitchen. She is still taking things out of crates from the old apartment like pots, pans and eating utensils. She fills the coffee pot with water and places it on the stove and lights the burner. She put oil in a pan, cracked some eggs and put them in the pan. She lit the burner, and the cast iron heats up until the eggs begin to sizzle in the oil. She turns down the flame and flips the eggs over, to finish cooking on the opposite side. Maria missed the coffee she had in Vienna and now with the strict regulations imposed by the Reich, only decaffeinated coffee is available due to the strict Aryan code prohibiting the use of real coffee.

None the less, she trudges forward with the morning breakfast and her mind pieces together a preconceived conversation that she is about to have with her beloved about what she can and cannot tell Engel about Ziel's conversation. She does feel good about the fact that Ziel and his followers are looking out for her and Engel. The possibility of being free from the Reich and even the devil himself makes her smile the smile of confidence. She removes the now cooked eggs from the pan and cooks sausages in the oil. She slices up the bread as Engel walks into the kitchen, and he is buttoning up his shirt, raking his fingers through his still wet hair. He approaches Maria and says," You'll make someone a very good wife one day. He'll be a very lucky man to have you." Maria gives him a kiss and tells Engel to sit at the table. "Her new husband had better hurry home today or they'll be carnage in Berlin." says Maria.

"I hope no one says anything about me picking up that truck to free the trapped man yesterday." says Engel. "If anything is said darling, you'll be hailed as a hero. I wouldn't be surprised if you are being paid a visit this morning by the man's relatives at the bank." replied Maria. "I was really cutting it close to getting here yesterday. Stopping to save that man could've been a grave mistake." said Engel. "It wasn't a mistake darling. You were supposed to be there at that moment at that time. There is a deep goodness in you that you cannot deny. The teacher chose you because he saw it in you. Here is a fresh cup of coffee my darling and today be ready for a little bit of hero worshipping going on." says Maria. "You are going a little too far aren't you darling. Hero worship?" Engel jokingly replied. Maria placed her arms around him, hugging him and said, "Yes! Hero worship! My betrothed is a hero. Now, let's have some breakfast and be thankful for everything." says Maria.

Maria and Engel even talked about how soon they would be wed. The jeweler may already have their wedding rings completed. Maria is ready to be Engel's new wife and yet, she isn't pushing the effort to make things happen quickly. Things are already moving quickly, and she knows it. Her mind is awash with the information given to her by Ziel. She has no choice but to internalize much of the information and she also must be Engel's rock of foundation. She even asked Engel did he recall any of the conversation that she had with the beast last night. Engel wasn't surprised and had little to no memory of such a conversation. Engel finished eating and told Maria that he must get ready to go to work. He started removing the plates from the table and Maria told him to leave it for her, because she would be cleaning up and needed to finish putting things in their rightful places.

Engel takes one last sip of coffee, hurries off to the bathroom to void himself before leaving to go to work. He grabs his jacket and his keys and borrows a cigarette from Maria, gives her a kiss and is almost out the door. Maria says," I love you darling and be humble. Someone will have no choice but to pay you an important visit today." Engel says, "You already know who it is don't you?" Maria makes a gesture with her hand to lock her mouth with a key and throw it away. Engel tells her that he loves her, locks the door and closes it. He gets into the auto, places the key in the switch and presses the starter button. The engine sputters to life and Engel goes through the motion of shifting gears to get the auto aimed towards Berlin. As Engel makes his way to the city of Berlin, Joseph Goebbels receives a very intriguing phone call. The caller tells Goebbels that the minister of finance came to the aid of a person in dire distress. The caller tells Joseph that the finance minister did a miraculous thing by saving a man's leg from being cut off.

Joseph asked the caller who was this man that the finance minister had rescued. The caller said," The man is a merchant named Walther Kreuger. My uncle Ernst Heydrich was there and witnessed this. He said that Herr Kreuger was trying to change a flat tire when another vehicle struck the vehicle being worked on. This caused the auto to trap the man's leg and men tried to free this man and were not able to. The minister of finance pushed through the crowd of people, lifted the auto high enough so others could pull the trapped man free. This would be a great opportunity to show German's that indeed they have a super Aryan in their midst. Germany's banker is more than just a banker. I'm sure that your newspaper editor could create some brilliantly crafted words and a photo of him shaking hands with the Walther Kreuger. Don't you think herr Goebbels?"

Jospeh said, "I think you are after my job, aren't you?" Goebbels laughs jokingly. "I will send someone to corroborate this story and have a photographer to frame this piece of collaborated news from a reliable source. Of course, you'll be mentioned in the article as an eyewitness herr Heydrich." "Danke! Heil Hitler! Herr Goebbels. and the caller ends the conversation. Goebbels quickly starts dialing his phone and calling the Berlin Press. Goebbels relays the information to the editor and the editor assured Goebbels that the work will appear in the newspaper tomorrow. In another part of the city, Engel has made his way into his office and is busy looking over some important documentation that requires his approval. Engel's body is burning through his breakfast and still needs more fuel.

Engel goes out to the where the coffee is brewing to see if there is any food. he saw an empty plate that had strudel in it. He can smell it. He stops by the manager's desk and says that he will be back if someone asks about him. Just as he is about to exit the manager's officer, Engel hears a man's voice and the voice say, "There he is! Germany's strongest banker. I saw what you did yesterday, and I came here to shake your hand. I'm James Krueger and the man you rescued is my brother. You did a miraculous thing yesterday. I would like to do something for you." Engel felt a lot of eyes upon him and the gentleman. Engel said, "My wife's breakfast didn't quite feel me up this morning. Let's go get a coffee and something to eat and it is my treat okay." Engel walked the man out of the bank as the customers and bank employees are curious to what just happened. Engel and the man walked down the sidewalk and heading to the nearest coffee shop. An auto moving across the street from them pulled up to the sidewalk. A voice said," Herr minister! Herr Minister can you stop for a moment." The man speaking gets out and is followed by a photographer.

Engel and Herr Kreuger are both taken by surprise by this. They didn't know whether to be frightened or excited by this. The man says that he is a reporter for the Berlin Press and would like to interview Engel. Herr Kreuger says," I was there! This man saved my brothers leg from being amputated." Engel quickly says, "Can we carry on this conversation in the coffee shop?" The last thing that Engel wants is to give the gestapo any reason to hassle him or anyone for that matter. Herr Kreuger places his hand on Engel's shoulder and says in a low voice," Herr minister, you are more than Germany's strongest banker. You have something that is greater within you, and I cannot find the right word for it in my mind." Engel smiled and said," A man's will is stronger than anything that man can create."

The newspaper man heard Engel and wrote on his pad as he followed them into the coffee shop. The coffee shop was full with the smell of different flavored strudel and the strong aroma of coffee. Engel sat at a table and the other men sat with him. The newspaper man started in on Engel. Herr Kreuger told the newspaper man, "Can herr minister at least get something to eat and drink before you start interrogating him?" The newspaper man quickly says," You must have me confused with the gestapo!" The men chuckle at the comment as the waiter came to the table and took everyone's order. Engel's senses are on full alert. His nose alerts his hungry body that there is food nearby and his body craves the fuel that his body is screaming for. The smells in the shop are intoxicating. The newspaper man looks at herr Kreuger and asked him to give an account of what led up to his brother's rescue yesterday?

Herr Kreuger says," My brother Walther was removing a flat tire from the auto. He was getting ready to put the replacement tire on, when another auto accidently hit the auto off the lifting jack and trapping my brother's leg under the weight of two autos. The front bumper of rear auto was stuck on the rear bumper of Walther's auto. Other men and I tried lifting the auto and we only made matters worse. That man, herr minister placed his hand under the fender of Walther's auto and picked up the auto so we could free my brother. My brother is in the hospital now with a broken leg and the doctor said, if herr minister had not freed my brother when he did. The doctor would have had to amputate the leg because the weight of the truck was blocking blood flow to the rest of my brother's leg."

By this time the waiter had dropped off the coffee cups and placed a platter of strudel on the table. Engel wanted to take handfuls of strudel and start stuffing in his mouth. He took two strudel and placed them on a plate. He takes a sip of the hot coffee and starts eating the strudel. His stomach is telling his mouth to eat faster and get two more strudel. Engel takes slow deep breaths to calm himself. The apple strudel with cinnamon and sweet sugary goodness is sending him into a sensory overload. He finishes the first and bites into the second one, it is pear laced with cinnamon and oozing with sugar. He downs the hot coffee without slowing down. The photographer says," Looks like herr minister skipped breakfast this morning." and he tells the waiter to bring more strudel. By this time more people had entered the coffee shop and Engel saw that these people were wearing uniforms. A man with the uniformed men points out Engel and they came towards the table.

The table fell quiet as the uniformed men gathered near. Engel recognized the man in the officer's uniform. He had seen him at the Fuhrer's office. Engel wiped his hand with a napkin and stuck out his hand to greet the officer after he had given the Heil Hitler salute. The officer said, "I'm Reinhard Heydrich and this is my uncle Ernst. He tells me that you are Germany's strongest banker." Engel tells the men to sit down, and the coffee and the strudel is on him. Reinhard says," We are here to pay homage to you, and you are not paying for anything. My uncle Ernst says you did something miraculous yesterday." James Kreuger spoke up and says," He did! He saved my brother's leg from being amputated by the doctor. He would be here now if he wasn't in the hospital with a broken leg." One of the three men with Heydrich's was a large muscular German soldier of lower rank. Engel knows why he's there. He knows what is coming. It is a test.

Reinhard says, "My uncle told me that herr minister lifted two autos to free herr Kreuger. Perhaps we can persuade the newspaper man to photograph you lifting two autos." The men at Heydrich's table chuckle. Herr Kreuger says, "Five marks that your muscle-bound sergeant can't beat herr minister arm wrestling. We can get the photographer to take a picture of the winner for the paper." Engel was already nervous and now this. Engel saw Reinhard's face change from happiness to a face of disdain. Reinhard said, "Let's make this interesting. How about 20 marks?" Engel took out his wallet and placed twenty marks on the table and says, "Here's your twenty marks and we just forget about this whole story? You'll be twenty marks richer compliments of the minister of Germany." Reinhard said, "Are you going to give up that easily? Are you afraid to show your weakness herr minister?" Engel says," What if your muscle-bound boy can't beat me? Are you going to put a bullet in my head and then explain to the Fuhrer why you shot his minister of finance?"

Ernst Heydrich quickly spoke up and said, "There will be no shooting today!" He pointed at his nephew and said, "You are turning something that is good into something that is bad. Let's go!" Reinhard became enraged and said," You are a civilian! We go when I say we go!" Reinhard looked at the muscle-bound sergeant. The muscle-bound sergeant knocked the sugar bowl off the table he was sitting at and told Engel to sit across from him. Engel took a sip from his coffee and wiped his mouth with a napkin. He walks over and sits down at the corner of the table across from the sergeant. Before Engel puts his elbow on the table he says," Reinhard are you doing this because I killed one of your little girl rapers in the ss?" Ernst says," What is he talking about Reinhard?" "Shut up uncle!"

The newspaper man was scribbling on his note pad and Reinhard saw him doing it. He told the newspaper man that his family would be shot if he printed any of what the minister just said. He answered

Engels question by saying," No this isn't about the rapist. This is a fact gathering enquiry only. Now arm wrestle the sergeant!" Engel opens his hand as the muscle-bound sergeant locks hand with Engel and squeezes Engels hand. Engel tenses his muscles in his arm and squeezes the sergeant's hand more. He feels the sergeants arm tense up as if to quickly try and slam Engels arm down. Engel slowly pours power into his arm and the sergeant's arm is shaking, the sergeant has sweat popping on his forehead.

Reinhard screams at the sergeant to put Engel down. The sergeant is struggling, his muscles are at their peak and Engel is just holding him. The muscle-bound sergeant tries a last-ditch effort to snatch Engel down, but Engel poured more strength into his arm to the point of breaking the sergeant's wrist. Engel felt the sergeants' wrist bones give in to his strength and the sergeant had no choice but to yield and he was in great pain. Reinhard threw his money on the table and said," I guess you are the strongest banker in Germany herr Minister of Finance." He left taking his uncle and the injured sergeant with him. Everyone in the coffee shop started breathing a sigh of relief that the tense situation had ended. Engel said, "Gentlemen, I must get back to work. I have things on my desk that require my attention.

The newspaper man said, "Herr Minister, do you mind if I take you and herr Kreugers picture in the bank for the paper? Don't worry! I won't put anything about arm wrestling in the paper. I would be in more trouble than you. You know the people I work for. Now. Let's go take your picture jack the giant killer." "What do you mean jack the giant killer?" asked Engel. "You've never heard the heard the story of jack and the beanstalk?" asked the newspaper man. Engel looked at the newspaper man and said," I haven't heard such a story. Maybe one day you can buy me a cup of coffee and you can tell me about Jack the giant killer.

The newspaper man put his hand on Engel's shoulder and said," When I'm through writing this story about you today and it will be printed tomorrow. People will feel a warm sensation in their soul about someone, a total stranger from the upper class helping the working man, when he is in a dire state, in extreme need of someone to be there for him. Those people that will read about you will see that there are some things that are truly good about this world. Damn I'm making myself teary eyed." The newspaper man, the photographer and her Kreuger followed behind Engel as he went down the sidewalk and into the bank entrance. The newspaper man told Engel and Herr Kreuger to stand by the wall and shake each other's hand and smile for the camera.

So, Engel and herr Kreuger posed for the picture as the photographer took a couple pictures at different angles. Then the newspaper man and his photographer were gone. Herr Kreuger held out his hand and Engel took his hand shook it and told herr Kreuger that he will have candy and flowers delivered to his brother in the hospital. Herr Kreuger told Engel that his brother is going to be mad at him. Engel was puzzled by the comment. Herr Kreuger said, "Ill tell him about the will of a man being stronger than the man." Engel chuckled at his comment and told him to be careful working on cars near the street. Engel walked into his office sat in his chair and lit a cigarette. He thought about what Maria had told him about hero worship. He also thought about how wrong things could have gone if Reinhard's uncle hadn't been there. It wasn't long before there's a knock upon his office door.

Engel tells the person to enter, and it is the manager, her Burhalter. "Herr minister, one of my tellers told me about an amazing event yesterday. Seeing you and the gentleman getting their picture taken by the press. This makes her amazing story come true. Do you mind telling me about it herr minister?" asked herr Burkhalter. Engel placed his cigarette in the ashtray and began telling herr Burhalter what had happened yesterday. After Engel finished telling herr burkhalter the account of yesterday's events. Herr Burkhalter stood up and held out his hand for Engel to shake. Engel stood up and shook his hand. Engel asked," Why did you shake my hand herr Burkhalter?" "It is too often that a man can shake hands with greatness herr minister. When people read about you in the paper? You will give the people of Germany something that they really need now is hope. Danke herr minister!" Herr Burkhalter opens the door and closes it behind him.

Engel recalls what Maria said about hero worship. The rest of his day was normal until he left the bank to go to lunch. Engel exits the bank and is met at the curb by a military staff car. The driver gets out and opens the door for Engel. Engel peers into the car and Joseph Goebbels tells Engel to enter the car. Engel gets into the auto and the driver closes the door. Engel asks Goebbels what does he owes for such esteemed company? Goebbels tells Engel that he is taking Engel for lunch. "I heard about what happened in the coffee shop this morning from my newspaper reporter. Don't worry, it's not going in the paper. I only wished I could've witnessed it myself firsthand. So, you really broke the sergeant wrist?" asked Goebbels. Engel nodded yes. Goebbels slapped his leg with glee and tells the driver to take them to a particular restaurant.

The auto pulls out into the street into traffic and Goebbels continues talking to Engel about the incident that happened yesterday and the incident in the coffee shop. Engel tells Goebbels that he was only trying to get home and that the traffic had prevented him from moving. Engel tells Goebbels his curiosity drove him to the accident scene. Engel says that desperation propelled him to help the trapped man. The auto stops and the driver opens the door for Goebbels and Engel to exit. Engel sees that there are men with cameras on the sidewalk in front of the restaurant. Goebbel's stand besides Engel as men take picture with their cameras and reporters begin asking questions. Goebbels being the showman that he is takes over the scene.

Telling the newspaper reporters that he is taking the minister of finance to lunch, for gratitude of his heroic service to Germany's citizens. Engel could only smile and wave to the reporters and camera flash as Goebbels finished his oration and pulled Engel into the restaurant. The waiter quickly takes Goebbels and Engel to a table. The people in the restaurant are trying to figure out what is happening. Goebbels sits down and Engel follows by sitting down at the table. Goebbels ask Engel has He and Maria decided on a wedding date yet. Engel tells Joseph that he has gotten the rings from the jeweler yet and suspects that they should be completed by now. As far as an actual date, he and Maria have not decided on a date yet.

Engel says, "Things seemed to be going faster than he can control." "i know what you mean herr minister. My wife and I have six children and it seem we've been married forever. Do you and Maria plan on children?" asked Goebbels. "We have touched on the subject herr Goebbels and pondered the possibility." said Engel. Children are our legacy her minister, and you need to think about stories you can pass down to them. Just like what is happening today. This is a momentous occasion." stated Goebbels. A waiter came to the table, and we placed our orders and the waiter left. Another waiter came by with wine glasses and a bottle of wine. Engel was wishing that Maria was there with him, but he already knew that she is. She foretold this to him.

Engel only wants to eat. The smell of food in the restaurant is intoxicating to his senses. His body craves food, it demands fuel to burn. Tonight is another full moon, and his senses are on full alert. Engel feels slightly hot and excuses himself from the table and goes to the bathroom to urinate. He goes to the sink, washes his hands and looks in the mirror. He opens his mouth, and his teeth still look normal. He dries his hands and walks out of the bathroom. Up exiting the bathroom, he sees a group of gestapo are standing near Goebbels. Engel gives the gestapo a heil Hitler salute and sits down at the table. Engel looks at Goebbels and at the gestapo and waits for something to happen.

Goebbels tells Engel that the gestapo wanted to know why the newspaper men were in front of the restaurant. Goebbels being the consummate orator, took control of the scene. Goebbels even asked them where were they when a fellow German citizen needed them. Engel was getting nervous and Goebbels was relentless on the gestapo. He said," If any of you can read, you'll find out what a real German is in the papers." The gestapo officer scoffed at Goebbels and left with his men. By this time two waiters appeared with plates of food. Engels stomach and his body was screaming for the food. Engel had to calm himself. Joseph Goebbels was talking about how he diffused a bad situation with the gestapo and how they are such mindless dogs and need to be controlled. All Engel could think about was the food. As Joseph was putting food in his mouth. Engel put a piece of bread in his mouth, swallowed it without chewing it. Then he said, "I shot one of them for raping a young girl." Joseph choked on his food a little. He took a drink of wine and asked Engel what was he talking about? Engel had scooped two loads of food in his mouth and swallowed it whole. "Those men in the gestapo uniform. I thought they were coming for me." said Engel. "

No! They are inquisitive and would investigate anyone. They saw the reporters from the street." Joseph lowered his voice to a whisper and said," You killed one of them because he raped a girl, and they didn't come after you?" "They tried, but let's say that a higher power prevailed." stated Engel. Joseph stopped eating and asked Engel again. Engel stopped eating and said," What if the girl was your daughter?" Goebbels wiped his mouth with a napkin and said," It was justified Engel, wasn't it?" "The young German girl was as innocent as rain." said Engel. Goebbels cleared his throat and said, "I came to find out you myself and found someone with real integrity. What the reporter said to me about you is real. What I do is paint a picture with words and create a scene for the German mind to see that scene. My reporter will paint a scene with words depicting a divine act by a man helping another man in dire distress. I hope if I'm ever in dire distress that someone like you will come to my aid herr minister."

Engel had all but wiped out all his food while listening to Goebbels. Engel picked up his wine glass and said, "To intervention!" Goebbels clanked his glass with Engel. Goebbels noticed that Engel had totally cleaned his plate while he was talking. "I guess you were hungry her minister and I really enjoyed meeting you. I feel like I was in the presence of greatness today. Goebbels stood up and gave the heil Hitler salute and told Engel that he would take care of the lunch. Goebbels shook Engels hand, paid the waiter and left the restaurant. Engel finished his glass of wine, wiped his mouth and left the restaurant and headed towards the bank. As he was walking down the sidewalk, he thought to himself this is what Maria told him about. The story doesn't come out in the paper until tomorrow. He also has to leave work early today because there's another full moon tonight. Engel makes his way back into the bank and into his office.

He sits down behind his desk, takes a cigarette from his coat and lights it. He thinks about what had transpired in his past and what he had endured to reach this point. He also realized that something always happens to mess things up. He had angered the dark master in the past to cause things to be taken away from him. What he fears most is losing Maria. As the smoke rises from the cigarette, there is a knock on his door. He tells the person to enter. A familiar man enters Engels office. It is the jeweler." I hope I am not disturbing you herr minister. I have your rings ready, and I brought them with me." The man takes a small box from his pocket and places it on Engels desk. Engel asked the jeweler how much is the final payment for the rings? "One hundred marks herr minister." Engel tells the jeweler to wait for a moment as he creates a withdrawal ticket to give to a teller.

Engel fills out a withdrawal ticket and leaves his office to go to the nearest teller. Engel Approaches the teller and hand her the ticket for withdrawal of funds. The teller greeted the minister and quickly made the transaction. She handed Engel the money and Engel went back into his office and closed the door. The jeweler stood up as Engel entered the room and Engel placed the money in the jeweler's hand. The jeweler said," Now you have the rings. Have you and your wife to be set a date yet?" Engel told the jeweler that the date would probably be soon now that the rings are in his hand. "My intended will be surprised this afternoon. Thank you for bringing this to me. You could've called and I would have brought the money to you." Said Engel. "I heard about what happened yesterday. My business is one street over from herr Kreuger's store.

My niece was on the sidewalk and saw what you did. She had bought goods from Kreuger's store. She said that what you did was nothing short of a miracle. I had to bring these rings to you myself and shake your hand. I hope that if I am in dire need someday, that someone like you will step in and rescue me." Engel shook the jewelers' hand and thanked him for bringing him the rings. The jeweler bid Engel a good day and walked out of the office, closing the door behind him. Engel sat down and opened the small box. He saw Maria's ring with the glistening blue sapphire setting. He looked at his ring and something is different about it. He sees some symbols etched on the side of the ring.

They weren't there when he picked out the rings with Maria. He placed the lid back on the box and placed it in his pocket. Engel decided that he was going to leave a little earlier than usual and go by the florist shop to get Maria some flowers because today is a special occasion. Engel gets his jacket, closes his office door, locks it and stops to tell the manager that he got the rings today and is leaving early to celebrate. The bank manager bids Engel a good day as Engel leaves the bank. He heads to the street to where his auto is parked and gets in, cranks the motor and moves into traffic. Engel isn't sure, where a florist is so he gets to the end of the street and asked a man on the corner where the nearest florist is. The man gives Engel directions and Engel knows where he's going. He was on that street yesterday as he was going home. There's a florist across the street from Kreuger's store. The place he rescued the man the day before.

Engel makes his way down the street and parks his auto at the curb and walks into the florist. A young woman was busy creating a flower arrangement and sees Engel as he walks into the store. The woman politely tells Engel to wait one moment as she disappears into a back room. She is followed by an older man. The older man smiles and said, "Herr minister, we sent the flowers that you ordered for herr Kreuger that is in the hospital. What can we do for you herr minister?" Engel asked the man; how did he know who he was?" The man says," I've known the Kreuger brothers for a very long time and I left my daughter to watch the store to try and help the trapped man yesterday.

A group of men and myself tried to free herr Kreuger and we couldn't pick up the autos to free him. You pushed your way through the crowd of people like an angel of mercy picked up the autos and freed herr Kreuger. Here you are in my store. I didn't know that you were the minister until someone in the crowd recognized you. What can I do for you herr minister?" Engel told the florist the reason for his visit and the florist said," My daughter just created this arrangement, and we would be honored if you give this to your new wife." "I am willing to pay for such a beautiful arrangement. Your daughter worked very hard on such a masterpiece." Replied Engel.

The florist quickly said," Your money is no good here herr minister. Please take the arrangement and all I ask is that you use us for your wedding." Engel held out his hand and shook the florist's hand and told him that he had the job for the wedding. Engel told the florist that a day isn't set but he would let him know. Engel gets to his auto cranks the motor and is moving into the flow of traffic. He made it out of the city scape and out into outskirts of Berlin. He pulls into the drive of his home, parks the auto, unlocks the door to the house and is greeted by Maria. She was waiting for him. He has a flower arrangement behind his back and he gives it to her. She gives him a very passionate kiss and says," Let me guess? You got the rings today and that explains the flowers." Engel says," I can't surprise you when you already know when it's coming can I? Today was a very interesting day. Have you put me some food in the cellar darling?"

Maria quickly answers yes and asked Engel if he is starting to feel achy yet? Engel grabs his jaw and rubs it and says it might be a good idea if he gets locked up already. Engel removes his coat and gives it to Maria, and he makes his way to the door of the cellar. Maria kisses him and tells him that she loves him. She takes the key and locks the door of the cellar and sits down on the floor to continue the conversation with Engel. Engel tells her to look in his coat pocket and look in the box. He tells her that there is a symbol engraved on the outside of his ring. Maria tells him that is the symbol for the Vril society and now he can go to their meetings." So, did you experience some hero worship today darling?" asked Maria." Reinhard Heydrich's uncle witnessed what I did and told Reinhard. Reinhard brought a muscle-bound sergeant to test my strength and I broke the sergeants wrist arm wrestling in a coffee shop.

Reinhard's uncle wasn't very pleased with Reinhard for doing it. A newspaper reporter was there to see that but was threatened to publish it. Then I was on my way to lunch and was picked up by Joseph Goebbels. His newspaper reporter told him about the coffee shop incident and Goebbels interviewed me himself. Things got scary for a moment went the gestapo showed up and Goebbels diffused the situation. I told Goebbels' that I thought the gestapo was after me about shooting one of them. Goebbels said he had heard about it, but not the details. I asked Goebbels how many children he had and if he had any daughters? I asked him what would he do if someone raped his daughter? Goebbels said that I was justified in doing so and he was there more or less to test my allegiance."

The pains start to hit Engel and he tells Maria that she will have to finish the conversation with the beast. Engel crawls down the steps and collapses on the floor and his body goes through the agonizing change from man to beast. Maria places her ear to the door and listens. She hears her love going through the metamorphosis as he yells out in agonizing pain. Within a few moments, the change is complete. Maria hears hurried footsteps running up the stairs and sits back from the door. The beast tries desperately to open the door and the doorknob stops shaking. In a stern gravelly voice the beast says, "Maria! Are you listening?" "Yes! I'm right here with you. I left you more food. Go! Eat and come back to talk to me." Said Maria. She hears the beast running down the stairs. Maria had placed two pork shoulders on the floor. The one from the previous night wasn't enough. While the beast is shredding the meat from the bone, maria took this chance to get herself something to eat in the kitchen. She had prepared food earlier because she knew that she would be eating alone again. She had brewed some tea, poured her a cup and ate some sausages, cheese and bread.

CHAPTER 20

CONVERSATION FROM
THE CELLAR

A few moments go by while she is eating, and she hears a knocking sound on the cellar door. She takes her teacup with her and goes to the cellar door. "I'm here! You can stop knocking now." Said Maria. The beast stops knocking and says in a gravelly voice, "I know you have questions. Ask me?" "Engel told me about what happened about breaking the man's wrist today. They wanted to test Engel's strength." And before Maria could say another word the beast said," Engel held back and didn't use all his strength. He only used what was necessary. I would've torn the man's arm off." "I know you would have." Replied Maria. "I don't really want to talk about what happened today. I knew what was going to happen to Engel and tomorrow more people will seek him out after he is in the newspaper. I want to ask you, what can you tell me about the teacher?" There was a long pause before the beast answered by saying," Are you trying to cause me pain by making me remember what I did?" "No! I'm trying to find out about the man that chose you. What was he like? You knew him and you followed him." asked Maria. The beast says, "This is very difficult for me, and I would rather slaughter a thousand men and feel nothing, than to describe to you a man that was more than a man.

I saw him do impossible things and he made it an absolute possibility." The beast slammed his hand against the steel door and said," No more questions about the teacher. I know something that you don't know about Engel. Do you want me to tell what it is?" "Yes! Tell me!" replied Maria." Have you noticed how animals especially dogs react around Engel, or have you even noticed it?" asked the beast. There was a pause in Maria's response. She was trying to trace through her mind any incident and she couldn't find one. So, she says," I haven't noticed anything strange. What happens when Engel is around any animals or dogs?" "Animals such as horses are afraid of Engel unless Engel tells them that they have nothing to fear. Dogs can speak to Engel and me. To you, you hear a bark or a yelp. But to us, they are telling us something.

The gestapo has dogs watch, what happens if they get near Engel. If Engel sees the dog before the dog sees Engel. Engel will try to avoid contact with the dog, because the dog would act differently towards Engel, and it would look unnatural to the people that witness it. The dogs will be completely obedient to him. Engel could make the gestapo dogs attack the gestapo and they wouldn't be able to stop them except to shoot them. Engel wouldn't do that to the dogs because of that outcome." An intrigued Maria then asked the beast when he first encountered this particular trait. "I was in Egypt when it first happened to me. I was a man; not like I am now. I heard this voice, and I looked down beside me. A dog asked me if I had come to Egypt to kill and eat him? I thought I had been walking in the sun for too long and I kept walking and ignored the dog. I thought the dark master had sent something to torment me. The dog was persistent, and I had no choice but to talk to him."

The beast heard Maria chuckling on the other side of the door and asked her why she is chuckling. "I am laughing because if someone saw you having a conversation with a dog? Those people would think that you had lost your mind." jokingly said Maria. The beast said, "That is exactly what the dog said to me. The dog told me that if I did that people would see me as a harmless imbecile. But in reality, I was a killer that had killed some assassins the day before and took their possessions. I had never raised my hand in anger towards anyone until that day. The assassins thrust their swords into me and tried to kill me. An ordinary man would've died from such wounds. I took one of their swords and slaughtered those men. I never held a sword in my hand until that day and I wielded it like a seasoned swordsman. It was like I already knew what to do." The beast told Maria many things about his exploits until Maria could no longer keep her eyes open.

She told the beast that she would see Engel in the morning and told the beast to get some rest. As maria turned to go towards the bedroom the beast says, "The teacher came to me in the desert and told me that it doesn't have to be this way. I told him that I couldn't ask for forgiveness because I cannot forgive myself." Maria stopped and said," We all will have to ask for atonement before the end. I hope I have time to do that before my last breath." She then heard the beast walking down the steps of the cellar. Maria goes to the bedroom, puts on her nightclothes and turns off the lights in the house except the table lamp by the bed. Before she lay down, she said a prayer, turned off the lamp and laid down. The next morning, Maria went to the door and asked Engel to stick his finger out of the hole in the door. Engel obliges and shows Maria that he has a normal human finger again and she unlocks the steel door. She hugs and kisses Engel. She tells Engel to get cleaned up and ready for breakfast.

She says, "The bank will be extra busy today after people see your picture in the paper." "I hope the attention doesn't attract the wrong kind of people." Replied Engel. Engel Goes to the bathroom, cleans himself up from the previous night and puts on clean clothes. He sees the ring box on the table and says," How did the jeweler know to put the vril symbol on my ring?" "The jeweler is a member also. Speaking of rings. Do we need to ask the Fuhrer if his schedule is freed up for us, since we have our rings now?" replied Maria. The two sat down and had breakfast. Maria asked Engel if he remembered the conversation she had with the beast. Engel again tells her that he doesn't remember any conversation, he only remembers seeing the two large chunks of meat before the beast shredded it.

Maria looks at the clock on the wall and says," Do you think that you have time to satisfy me this morning before you go to work my love?" "I think you already had this planned since you are only wearing your robe my darling" Answered Engel. Engel gets up from the table, walks over to Maria and slides his hand inside her robe and gently caresses her breast. Maria unzips Engel's trousers and began fondling him. The two move from the kitchen to the bedroom. Engel slides his pants down, lays down on the bed as Maria glides his erection into her pleasure hole. She bounces on Engel with great ferocity until both have an explosive orgasm. They go and wash up in the bathroom. Engel gets redressed and offers to help clear the breakfast table. Maria tells him that he has got to get going and get ready to meet his destiny today.

He kisses Maria and tells her that he loves her, grabs his coat and keys and heads for the door. He locks the door and gets into his auto. He fires up the engine and it roars to life. Engel leaves the countryside and moves into the busy streets of Berlin. He arrives at the bank, parks the auto and goes into the bank. The employees give him a greeting as he goes into his office and closes the door. The morning was uneventful until about eleven o'clock. A bank customer enters the bank with a newspaper and goes to the teller's window and enquires about the minister. The teller asks the man what can she help him with. The bank customer then shows the teller the picture on the front page of the newspaper. "That's herr minister Stern, my boss. Why is he in the paper?" asked the teller. The bank customer hands her the newspaper and she read why her boss is in the paper.

Other tellers close to her, rush over to see the newspaper. The bank manager herr Burkhalter happened to see what was happening and decided to investigate. He saw the photo and asked the man could he have the newspaper for a moment. Herr Burkhalter goes to the entrance of Engel's office, knocks on the door and he hears Engel's voice tell him to enter. "Excuse me herr minister, but I have something I would like to show you." Said herr Burkhalter. Engel looks at the front page and sees himself shaking hands with herr Kreuger. The brother of the man whom Engel had rescued. "Herr minister, you have helped my family, and the family of the employees here. You can't hide from greatness. My heart swells with pride just knowing you herr minister." exclaimed the bank manager. Engel said, "You would've done the same for me if I was that trapped man. I am glad that the man didn't lose his leg because of it. Thank you for showing me the paper and your gratitude. I just hope today doesn't get too crazy because of this newspaper article." Said Engel.

The bank manager takes the newspaper, closes the door to Engel's office and gives the paper back to its original owner. The bank customer wanted to see Engel for himself, and the bank manager told the customer that Engel is on an important phone call and couldn't be disturbed. The bank manager thanked the bank customer for his patronage and watched the customer exit the bank. The lead teller asks the manager could she go and purchase some newspapers for the employees. The manager agreed and gave her money to do so. He wanted a copy for himself and told her to buy one for the minister. It was long after that that, that indeed an important phone call came for Engel. Engel is smoking a cigarette when his phone rings. He answers the phone, and the operator tells him he is about to be connected to the Fuhrer.

Engel tells the operator to proceed and he says," Guten tag mein Fuhrer! What do I owe this pleasure mein Fuhrer?" The voice on the phone says, "Guten tag Herr minister! I just saw you on the front page of the newspaper. I want to commend you on your gallant heroism, and can you meet me at the hospital in an hour? I've called Goebbels and a photographer is going to meet us at the hospital. You and I will be visiting herr Kreuger, the man you rescued. I'll have my staff car pick up and I'll see you there." "Yes, mein Fuhrer" answered Engel. The Fuhrer hangs up and ends the conversation. Engel looks at the clock and in one hour it will be twelve o'clock. Engel knows what is happening. Goebbels is the reason that phone call was made to him.

Tonight, is the last night of the full moon phase for a few weeks. Engel can only hope that he can get home in time. He reaches for his cigarette box and there isn't any more. His senses are already on edge. The third day before his last change is always the strongest. Having sex this morning helped release some of his pent-up energy, but he is still a wound-up spring and has no way to unwind. Just sitting in this room watching the clock move doesn't sit well with Engel. He puts on his coat and opens the door of his office. He sees there is a considerable amount of people in the lobby of the bank. He also sees gestapo agents mixed in with the group of people. Someone in the group says," There's the minister!" The group converges on Engel and he is surrounded by well-wishers and people with their cameras wanting their picture taken with him. Engel just wants to run away from this. He takes a couple of deep breaths to calm himself and smiles.

He does a salute and says, "Heil Hitler! Long live Deutschland!" The group claps their hands in approval of Engels display of reverence to Hitler and Germany. People clamor to shake Engels hand and take their picture with him. Engel works his way towards the bank main entrance only to be greeted by general Wolfstein with Lena Vonn on one side and another voluptuous woman on the other side of him. "Where are you going herr minister? We came to get our picture taken with one of Germany's own native son." said general Wolfstein. "I don't have any more cigarettes and I was going out to buy more, herr General." Said Engel. General Wolfstein reached into his coat and took out a cigarette case. "Take this as a small token of my appreciation." Says the general just as a photographer's flash bulb flashes. "What do I owe the pleasure herr general, with these two lovely ladies that you have with you?" said Engel. "We came by to make the first payment on Lena's loan and pay homage to you." Replied the general. "One of my tellers can take care of the transaction with no problems herr general." stated Engel. "Maybe we should go into your office her minister." insisted the general. Engel led the way to his office door and opened it for them. Engel closed the door, and he heard the door lock.

Engel sat down behind his desk and took a cigarette from his newly acquired cigarette case. The general sat down as the two women remained standing. The general reached into his coat and took out a stack of marks and laid them on Engel's desk. Engel took the marks and counted them and said," This amount will take care of two months payment her general. I will write a receipt of payment for you." Engel opened the desk drawer to get his lighter and the other woman stepped forward and lit Engel's cigarette with her lighter. "She's beautiful isn't she Engel? Meet Lena's mother Inga. Lena did something thinking I wouldn't find out about it.

She fucked somebody other than me and that's why I brought her pretty mother Inga here. Lena is going to watch her mother suck your cock." Inga said," I'm going to do what?" Lena was begging the general for forgiveness. Engel is already a bundle of nerves and the general pointed at Inga. Inga moved forcibly by an invisible force towards Engel. Engel said," You don't have to do this. Maria will know about this and what am I say?" "Maria will know nothing unless you tell her. The only people that know about this. Are the people in this room. Now unzip your pants or Inga will do it for you. Lena get over there and watch your mother suck the minister of finance's cock." Inga got down on her knees and started stroking Engel's cock until it became erect and then she started sucking on it. Engel could do nothing but to try and enjoy this in front of an audience.

"Are you enjoying this Engel? You need to pick up the pace Inga I want Engel to cum already." exclaimed the general. Inga quickened the up and down movement and Engel grabbed her head and exploded in her mouth. Inga wiped her mouth and got up. Lena was crying and her mother had tears running down her face. "Wow! That was great! Can I have a cigarette Engel?" asked the general. Engel opens up the cigarette case and holds it out for the general to take one. The general takes out a cigarette and says," Light me up Inga!" Inga nervously lights the general's cigarette, and the general takes a long drag off the cigarette and then says, "Lena if you disappoint me again? I'll get you baby sister to suck Himmler's cock. Thank you for cooperation Engel.

Hitler's staff car is at the curb waiting for you." Engel hears the door unlock as the general gets up and the two women follow behind him. Engel is still in shock about what happened, but he does feel like he got to release that pent up energy. The crowd had thinned down in the bank and Engel goes out of the exit to see a staff car waiting at the curb. As he gets closer to the vehicle the driver opens the door for Engel and Engels gets in, the driver closes the door, gets in the driver's seat and speeds away into the traffic. It is evident to Engel that Lena doesn't know that she is really fucking the devil. Engel knows what Hell looks like and Lena experienced a different kind of hell. The staff car went down a couple of streets until it reached its destination. The staff car is parked behind another staff car and the driver gets out and opens the door for Engel.

Engel gets out and waits on the sidewalk. The driver of the other staff car opens the door and out steps the Fuhrer and his bodyguard. Engel gives the Fuhrer a salute and holds out his hand to shake the hand of the Fuhrer. The Fuhrer shakes Engel's hand and says, "Let's go and visit herr Kreuger." Engel leads the men into the hospital and there are two men waiting for us inside. A reporter and a photographer are waiting to get the proceedings documented. Engel asked a nurse to take them to herr Kreuger's room. The hospital staff saluted the Fuhrer as he went down the hallway until we arrived at the patient's room. Herr Kreuger has his leg suspended in plaster cast held by ropes from the bed framing. Herr Kreuger was shocked to see the Fuhrer in his room and a smile came to his face when he saw Engel walked in.

Engel waited for the Fuhrer to shake herr Kreuger's hand so that the photographer could take a picture. The Fuhrer told Engel to get on the other side of the bed so the photographer could take another picture. Once the picture was taken, the Fuhrer and his entourage began leaving the room. Engel said," Mein Fuhrer! Can I have a moment of your time before you go?" The Fuhrer stopped walking and said," Of course herr minister!" Engel then told the Fuhrer that he had gotten the wedding rings the day before. He then proceeded to ask the Fuhrer would he be able to perform the wedding next week. The elated Fuhrer clapped his hands together and said," Yes! I told you before I would do this and now, I'll have my secretary arrange everything for next week. Can Ava be your wife's bridesmaid?" asked the Fuhrer. Engel then said "Of course mein Fuhrer! Maria and Ava are already friends.

I just need to know which day next week so I can tell Maria." The Fuhrer told Engel that his secretary would call him a few days in advance and his entourage followed him out of the hospital. Engel went back into the room, stayed a moment and spoke to herr Kreuger briefly and told him if he needed anything to just call him. Herr Kreuger got a little emotional and said he wished his wife was there to see this. Engel asked herr Kreuger the where abouts of his wife and he told Engel that she had died of tuberculosis a year ago. "She is free of all of the hurt that this world can give her. You just get well and be careful working on autos." Engel bid herr Kreuger goodbye and headed for the hospital exit.

Engel looked at his watch and it is almost one o'clock. He doesn't have time to get back to the back and get his auto and then drive home. He goes to staff car driver and ask the driver to take him to home. He told the driver he left his medication at home and needed it urgently. The driver cranked up the staff car and quickly took Engel through the streets of Berlin and to Engel's home. By the time the staff car gets to Engel's driveway, Engel begins feeling the first signs of change is coming. He felt pain in his jaws and the staff car had stopped and Engel thanked the driver and hurriedly made his way to the house. Just as Engel reached for his key to unlock the door, Maria opened the door and knew timing was imperative.

Engel pulled off his jacket and his trousers, dropping them in the floor as he hurriedly went towards the cellar door. He opened the door and closed it. Maria quickly locked the door and waited by the door. "Im sure you have a great explanation why you weren't in your auto darling. We didn't have any more meat, so I got a farmer to bring us a goat." said Maria. Engel sitting on the top step on the other side of the steel door began thanking her for being so brilliant to think about getting a live animal. He talked until the pain became so intense that he could no longer control it. His body rolled down the stairs and hit the floor of the cellar. His body riddled with unbearable pain as the change from man to beast takes place. Maria waits patiently at the door and listens. The beast has found the goat and Maria hears the goat bleating out in horror as the beast quickly kills the animal. Maria gets up and goes to the kitchen and pours herself a cup of tea, lights a cigarette and sits at the table. She looks at the clock on the wall and sees that it is two thirty in the afternoon and thought to herself that Engel barely made it back to the house in time today. Things could've gone very bad today but it didn't happen. Maria isn't too hungry right now thinking about what has transpired in the cellar.

Maria takes a drag from her cigarette and decides to turn on the radio. She doesn't turn the volume up because she knows there will be a banging on the steel door after the beast finishes eating the goat. She listens to some orchestrated music that is strictly sanctioned by the ruling party. She then gathers up the clothing that Engel had pulled off on his way to the cellar and puts them away. All the while she continues to listen for anything outside the ordinary. She has taken off her shoes and walking in her bare feet to lessen the noise of her shoes against the wooden floorboards. She is glad that this is the last night for a couple of weeks before the cycle starts over again. She'll have her husband back in the morning and hopefully the beast will be more satiated with a live kill.

She goes back to the kitchen and pours herself some more tea and lights another cigarette. She knows that Engel had a very busy day due to the newspaper article. She'll have to wait to see if the beast will shed some light on what happened today. From her conversation last night, the beast is only interested in talking about his killing exploits and definitely doesn't want to talk about the teacher. The subject brings him much mental anguish, he has deep rooted regrets that he wears like prisoner wears a ball and chain. Maria kept waiting and a couple hours went by and no noise. She fixed herself a light meal, cleaned up the kitchen and took a tub bath. She left the bathroom, put on her night gown, softly walked to the cellar door and listened for any sound. She crouched down, listened and waited. She couldn't hear any movement. She slowly walked to the bedroom, closed the door and locked it. She eased herself down into the comfortable bed. Maria could only surmise that the beast had gorged himself on the goat and went to sleep. Maria took a few puffs off a Cigarette, put it out in the ashtray, turn off the lamp and settle down in a pillow.

She finally went to sleep. It was a quiet night until one a.m. in the morning. Maria was awakened by the beast banging on the steel door and the beast was calling her," Maria! Maria! Can you hear me, Maria!" Maria grabbed her robe, unlocked the door and yelled back,"

I hear you! I'm on my way! Just Relax!" Maria gets to the door and sits down on the floor in front of the door. "I'm here! Are you okay?" says Maria. In a soft gravelly voice the beast says," I had a very bad dream about being trapped in a box. I couldn't move, and there was no one around to hear me call out. I think the dream has a meaning about guilt, and how guilt can make you feel trapped. The dark master made Engel do something today. He may retaliate if I tell you. Engel didn't have a choice and maybe I should just keep my mouth shut. I've said too much. "I'm here for you and you are not alone. If you think that the general will retaliate? Then don't tell me. I don't want anything to happen to you or Engel.

I thought you would like a fresh kill, but I won't do that again okay!" said Maria. "No more goat." said the beast. "Thats' right I won't get you any more goat. Nothing but pork from here on out. Okay! Just get some sleep. The sun will be up soon and Ill fix Engel a big breakfast." exclaimed Maria. "He won't be hungry." replied the beast. The beast went back down the cellar steps and laid down on the floor and went to sleep. Maria went back to the bedroom, locked the door and wondered about what had happened. She couldn't see in her mind's eye what occurred. It was like her vision was cut off from what happened. She laid down and went to sleep. The morning came and she unlocked the cellar door for Engel. Engel did the usual thing. He got himself cleaned up and thanked Maria for the fresh kill. He apologized for the mess and told her that he would clean up the mess when he got home today. He explained to her about the staff car and the meeting with the Fuhrer.

Maria was excited to hear about the Fuhrer's compliance to move forward to the wedding next week. She began cooking something in the kitchen and Engel told her that he wasn't hungry. He told her to just fix something for her and he only wanted some coffee. As he was shaving in the bathroom, Maria came to the door and asked him did anything else unusual happen today? Engel told her that the general Wolfstein came to the bank and paid two months in advance for Lena's business. "I'll have to call the driver to come and pick me up since I left the car parked in front of the bank." Said Engel." You almost didn't make it in time yesterday. Did you dear?" replied Maria. Engel finished shaving and said," I didn't have time to go and get the auto at the bank. I told the staff car driver to get me home quickly because I needed my medication for my heart. Yesterday was a real close call." Maria didn't ask Engel about what the dark master did. She remembered what Ziel told her. The conversation went to the possibility of the wedding next week and Maria asked Engel, whom would he choose to be his best man. Engel thought for a moment and said, "There will be a photographer at the wedding right! Then maybe I should choose General Wolfstein, so that someone in the future will see what the devil actually looks like." They both laugh at Engels comment as Engel continued to get dressed to go to work.

CHAPTER 21

THE PHOTOGRAPH

The photograph and the article about Engel in the newspaper gets scattered throughout Berlin and neighboring cities. A man that lives near Berlin had gotten the paper and was looking at the photo of the men shaking hands. He read the article and took another glance at the men shaking hands. There is something familiar about one of the men in the photograph. He thought to himself, where had I seen that face before? He then decided to go through a box of photographs that he had taken when he was a field photographer in the great war. He found the box of photos that was stashed away in a closet. He feverishly combed through the hundreds of war time photos until he found the photo he was looking for. I got the photo and took it in the kitchen and placed the photo next to the image in the newspaper. The wartime photographer had to sit down because what he saw struck fear deep into his very soul. He had taken a photograph of a man fighting with Germany's best boxer. Germany's best boxer was beaten by the man in the photo.

That man was Hans Engel. The same Hans Engel that he witnessed get shot in the head by the commanding officer. The wartime photographer and other men witnessed Hans Engel get shot in the head. They also saw Hans Engel come to life and killed the commanding officer that shot him. That was twenty-four years ago and the man in the newspaper hasn't aged a day. The frightened men in the company could do nothing but watch as Hans Engel took the clothes off the dead officer. One of the witnesses yelled out, "Its der teufeL (the devil), It's derteufel!" The photographer remembers what Hans Engel said in response. Hans Engel said I am der Teufel and I'm going to kill all of you tonight. The photographer ran away with some of the soldiers and returned the next day to find out that the forest demon that always followed Hans Engel had slaughtered and even consumed some of the men's flesh.

The wartime photographer is either looking at someone that favors Hans Engel or he is looking at der Teufel himself Hans Engel. The war veteran photographer got his wife in the kitchen and showed her the two photographs. He asked his wife does she see the similarities in the photos. His wife pointed out that Engel Stern had a striking resemblance to the man fighting with another man in the old photo. She said, "Why are you showing me this my husband?" Her husband said, "Have you ever heard the story about Hans Engel?" "Of course! Yes! I've heard that story and other ghost stories around the campfire told by my parents. To keep us inside at night or Hans Engel the forest demon would rip us to shreds and eat us. But that is just a ghost story."

The photographer said," He saw Hans Engel get up after being shot dead, point blank in the brain. Hans Engel killed the officer with his bare hands and took his clothes after he killed them. I saw it happen. I was there and now the nightmare is in Berlin." "Do you know what will happen to you and me if you start talking to people about this? You are saying that Engel Stern which is Germany's Minister of Finance, a hero for rescuing a man from being crushed, to being Hans Engel the man that cannot die, the bringer of the forest demon. If the people you talk to think you are crazy? They aren't the ones that I'm worried about. I'm worried about the ones that can ship us off to Dachau.

Do you know what Dachau is? That is where the enemies of the Reich are sent. The minister of finance is one of Germany's elites plus a local hero and you want to smear that guy's name. Please don't do this. We have a good life. You have a good job and who will take care of our children if we are sent away to Dachau? Not only would you be sealing our fate to be damned but that of our children as well. Please put the photograph back in the box, put the box in the closet and forget about this. Nothing good could come of this." The man listened to his wife. He placed the old photograph in the box along with the newspaper, picked up the box and placed it in the closet. The man finished his breakfast and left to go to work. On his way to his work, he couldn't shake the image of what he saw that day.

He went into work and all day, he tried to think of any man that was in his unit that witnessed it. If he could only find another man that was there. He could show the two photographs and get some kind of resolution from this. He knew what he saw that day and it was unnatural. How can someone get shot in the head, awaken from the dead and kill the man that shot him. The man finished his shift at work and didn't speak about it at work in fear of being ridiculed or worse. He simply returned home to his family and kept everything as a normal everyday occurrence in a typical home setting. The man had conversations with his children, had dinner with his family and everyone went to bed that night. The man joins his wife in bed and his wife says," I hope you didn't mention the photograph to anyone at work, did you? ""No! I didn't say anything about it.

Like you said. They would either think me crazy or report me as a dissident to the Reich. After I saw the photograph, I still can't get that image out of my head. At least I haven't heard of any unexplained murders in or around berlin so, the forest demon must be gone." The husband kisses his wife good night and turns out the light. Across many kilometers away and days later, a meeting is taking place with the Vril society. A group of German socialites along with Maria Orsic and her intended Engel Stern attends a special meeting. This meeting would discuss the messages that Maria had been receiving from her guide. She told the people there that there will be a great leap in technology because of her connection to off world allies. She told them that she has been sharing this knowledge with Reich scientists and engineers. Some of the vril members did not want the Reich to gain such power.

They see the Reich becoming too powerful and their influence upon society is going in the wrong direction.

Maria quells the group's fears and tells them that the Reich could shut down the group and label them as dissidents. As the meeting progresses, Maria gets the group to calm and hold hands. She says," Tonight, I feel there could be breakthrough of some kind. I am not sure if it will be a message or a sign of some sort. I want everyone to relax, close your eyes and look up with your eyes as if your trying to look through your forehead. If it is uncomfortable then don't try it, just keep your eyes closed. A few moments go by and there was a loud bang in the room. Like someone had slammed a door. We opened our eyes and the main entrance door and the other two doors in the room were wide open. They were closed before the session. Maria asked, "Is there something you want to tell us or show us?"

One of the female members collapsed on the floor and began convulsing. Engel quickly got up and went to her. She started choking. Like she was strangling something and began coughing up blood. Another man in the group said the woman suffers from tuberculosis. Engel took the woman's hand and whispered into the woman's ear, "If you want to live? Ask to be forgiven." The woman said in a subdued voice asking for forgiveness. Engel sat the woman up and told her to breath slowly. The woman held Engel's hand even tighter as she began to breathe air into her lunges. Engel sat there holding her up until the woman turned to Engel and in a soft voice," I can breathe again without pain. You've healed me." Engel told the woman that it wasn't him that healed her. Engel helped the woman to her feet and sat her back into the chair she fell from. Before Engel could step away, the woman grabbed Engel's coat and said in a low voice, "You are the messenger. Bless you."

Engel sat down next to Maria. And Maria told the people at the table she had received a message, and the message was that all of Europe will be bleeding. The meeting ended abruptly, but not without reverence. The woman that had collapsed on the floor, got up from her chair and walked over to Engel and Maria. The woman is the wife of a wealthy industrialist in Germany. She held out her hand to Engel and she took Engel's hand and kissed it. The woman said in a quiet voice," Don't worry! Your secret is safe with me messenger." She smiled at Engel and told Maria that she would see her at the next meeting in a month. Maria only nodded yes and told her that she'd be delighted to see her again. Maria waited for the crowd of people to thin out because she had a question for Engel, that she didn't want anyone else to hear. Engel waited by Maria until it was time to go. They left the building, got into the auto and onto the roadway. Maria turned to Engel and said, "You healed her, didn't you? You knew she was dying." "I gave her hope that someone was listening. She will die but not from tuberculosis." said Engel. "She called you the messenger. Why would she do that?

That is the second time I've witnessed you heal someone. Maybe she is right and I see yet I'm blind. I love you so much Judas, I mean Engel. I can't wait to be your bride." Maybe in a few days we'll hear from the Fuhrer's secretary about the wedding date. The day came when Engel received the call from The Fuhrer's secretary and the wedding arrangements were made. In three days, the wedding would take place in the chancellery. A wedding announcement was placed in the newspaper. Many well-wishers were sending Engel and Maria gifts and congratulations. The veteran photographer also saw the announcement. The photograph had been chewing at his soul since he saw Engel's face in the newspaper. In his mind Hans Engel is getting married to a renowned psychic and the photographer is still just a regular nobody special.

The photographer began to play out scenarios in his head and it consumed him to a point of complete obsession. The wedding cake, the flowers and the photographer had all been arranged for the wedding day by Engel and Maria's hand. The day of the wedding came with a list of high-ranking German officer's and their wives, and a veritable who's who among Germany's elite were there. General Wolfstein is Engel's best man and Maria's bridesmaids are Ava Braun and Lena Vonn. The Fuhrer dressed in all white military uniform officiated the ceremony. As the Fuhrer said," I now pronounce you man and wife." The veteran photographer stepped out from the crowd pointed his gun at the back of Engel stern's head and shouted, "Look at me Hans Engel and as Engel Turned his head the shot rang out.

One of the Fuhrer's armed guards shoots the gunman dead. General Wolfstein told Engel to lie still and don't move. Maria cries in anguish as her husband lies there with a gunshot to the head. A furious Hitler began screaming, "Get this man to the hospital. Now!" Maria Takes Engel's hand and Engel squeezes her hand. Maria feels a little relieved but still unsure about what's to come. A group of officers pick up Engel and carry him to a staff car. Maria gets in the staff car and places Engel's blood-soaked head in her lap. She screams at the driver, "Please take him to the hospital and hurry!" The driver said," We are not going to a hospital. We are going to the airfield to get on a plane and then we are getting on a U boat. You need to put this on your husband's hand first." The driver handed Maria a small golden box. She opens the box, and it is a ring with three different colored stones. She takes the ring out of the box and slides it onto Engel's hand. The driver said," Ziel sent me and now your husband is wearing King Soloman's ring and the dark one cannot touch him or us again.

On the other side of the world. A man walks into a bar, sits down and told the bar tender to pour him a draft. His attention is drawn to a large screen monitor on the wall. A television reporter closing the end of the news broadcast says, "The Associated Press just released a report that a group of scientists made a discovery. They found a completely intact Nazi u boat number U-455 was discovered encased in ice in the south pole by the team just days ago. I'm Marcy Cannon and my news team here at channel six Chicago, goodnight and a happy new year on this first day of 2036.

ABOUT THE AUTHOR

Being a child of the seventies. I was drawn to comic books like today's youth is drawn to video games. I didn't collect comics like Spiderman or Batman like my childhood friends. I was collecting comics called, House of Secrets, Jonah Hex, Weird War, Vampirella and other horror / macabre materials. This book talks about how all of us can be tempted and none of us are immune to the evils of the world. I reside in small town near Macon georgia with my wife Lenora.

www.ingramcontent.com/pod-product-compliance
Lightning Source LLC
Chambersburg PA
CBHW032112310726
48972CB00001B/197